Other titles by D.

The Lost Pharaoh
An old journal dat
on an adventure th
the pharaohs. The 1   ....   1ales of Egypt series.
Illustrated with vintage photographs and sketches.

Return of the Pharaoh
Book Two in the Tales of Egypt series. Return to the story of the lost pharaoh Neferhotep and the men obsessed with discovering the secret of his final resting place in a mysterious and deadly desert canyon.

Lair of the Jackal
Archaeologists Catherine and Steven Gordon track down the lost tomb of the heretic pharaoh, Akenaten, while discovering mystery, murder, and more in this exciting adventure thriller set in modern Egypt.

The Final Oracle
Catherine and Steven Gordon dig up another archaeological mystery as they race from the ancient sewers of Rome to the mountaintop shrine of the Greek god, Apollo, chased by a ruthless killer whose destiny may have been foretold by the gods themselves!

The Ones
The story of a young boy who vanished without a trace 15 years ago is revealed by the man who tried to save him from the fate he seemed destined to meet. Includes historical documents and photographs from the author's archives.

Hello, My Dearest One!
A hilarious collection of ridiculous exchanges between the author and a parade of clueless internet scammers.

Deluxe trade paperback editions available at
www.lulu.com/spotlight/molitor

eBook editions available at
www.amazon.com and *www.barnesandnoble.com*

Copyright © 2021 by Daniel Molitor

ALL RIGHTS RESERVED

No part of this book may be reproduced in any form
whether mechanical or electronic
with the exception of brief selections
for inclusion in positive reviews
or if such reproduction is a precursor
to the author receiving a major award,
lucrative contract, television or movie deal,
or a large cash prize.

While based on a true story,
most of the names in this book
have been changed, not because
anyone did anything wrong,
but just because it makes
the lawyers sleep better.

ISBN 978-1-7948-3107-0

Dynasty XVIII
www.lulu.com/spotlight/molitor

FIRST EDITION

BURYING CHENG

a mostly true story

DYNASTY™
XVIII
PUBLISHING EMPIRE

BURYING CHENG

Daniel Molitor

1

HOW MANY MEMORIES DO YOU NEED TO ACCURATELY REASSEMBLE A DEAD MAN'S LIFE?

CAN YOU FIT TOGETHER A FEW FRAGMENTS OF HIS PAST WITH ANY LEVEL OF CONFIDENCE THAT YOU'RE EVEN CLOSE TO UNDER-STANDING THE ENTIRETY OF WHO HE WAS?

WHAT MADE MY FATHER TICK? WHAT DID HE BELIEVE OR NOT BELIEVE? WHAT SET HIM OFF, MADE HIM HAPPY OR SAD? WHAT MADE HIM ANGRY?

WHAT MADE HIM SCARED?

SHANGHAI, CHINA
好吃的食物
THIS ISN'T THE STORY OF A WAR, BUT WHAT A WAR LEFT BEHIND AND THE EFFECT IT ULTIMATELY HAD ON SOMEONE WHO WASN'T EVEN THERE.
SOMEONE WHO WOULDN'T BE BORN UNTIL ALMOST A DECADE AFTER IT WAS OVER.
DING! DING!
IF IT WAS EVER REALLY OVER.
DING! DING!

VRRRRRRRRR!

I SUPPOSE IT'S ALSO A STORY OF SELF-DISCOVERY, INCLUDING THE USUAL AMOUNTS OF DOPEY NAVEL-GAZING, DENIAL, ACCEPTANCE, AND ATTEMPTS TO OVER-SIMPLIFY THE COMPLICATED MESS THAT IS A LIFE.

AND, IF I'M REALLY HONEST, IT'S ABOUT A KID WHO WANTED TO DO RIGHT BY HIS DAD, EVEN THOUGH HIS DAD DIDN'T ALWAYS DO RIGHT BY HIM...

...OR TURNED OUT TO BE SOMEONE DIFFERENT FROM THE MAN THAT KID THOUGHT HE KNEW.

呼嚕

IT'S A STORY WITH CHARACTERS I DIDN'T REALLY KNOW...
...AND LIKELY NEVER WOULD KNOW WITH ANY REAL FAMILIARITY.
THERE WEREN'T ANY HEROES.
BUT I DESPERATELY DIDN'T WANT THERE TO BE ANY VILLAINS, EITHER.

ESPECIALLY IF ONE OF THEM TURNED OUT TO BE THE MAN WHO WOULD BECOME MY FATHER.

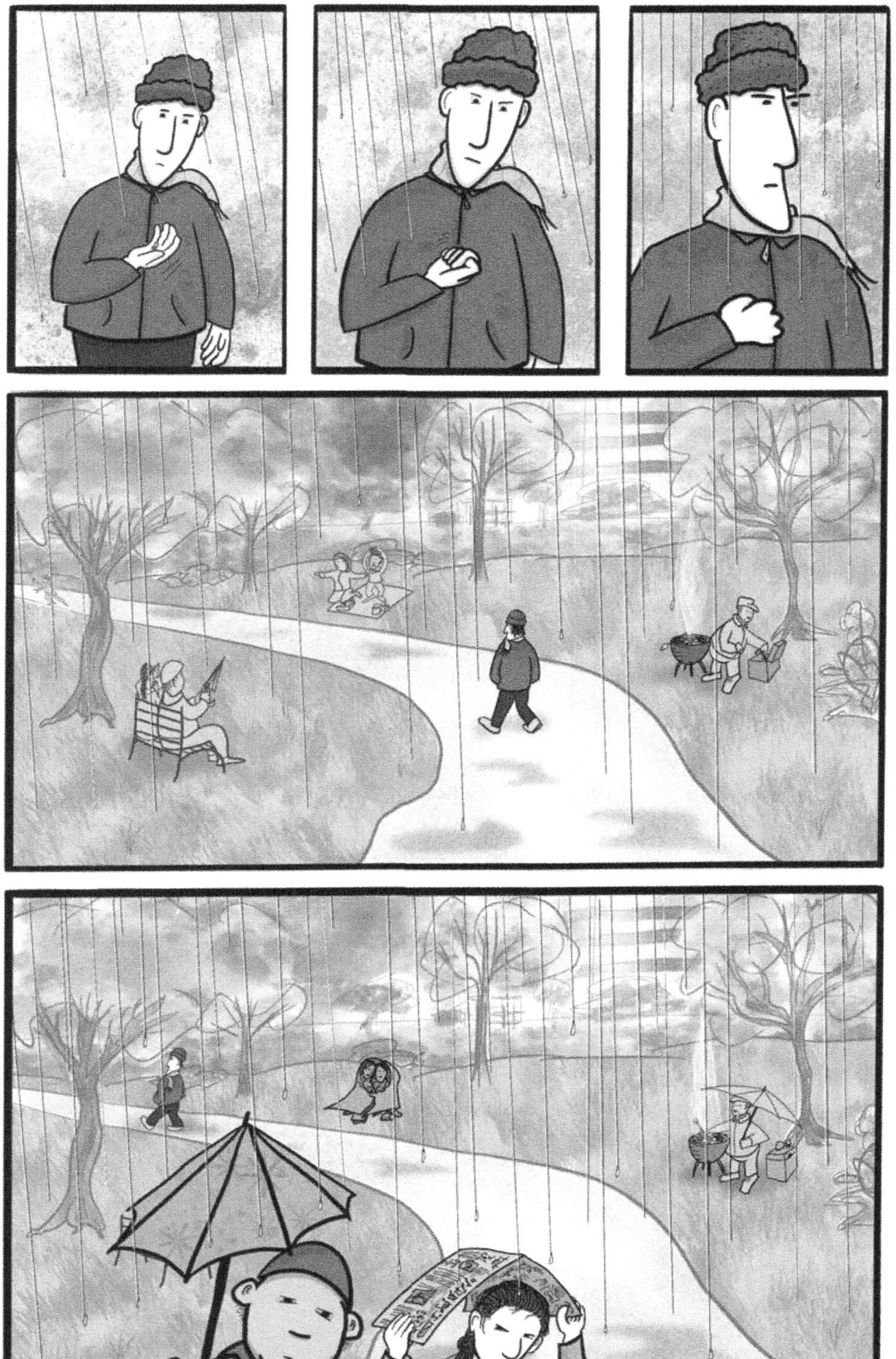

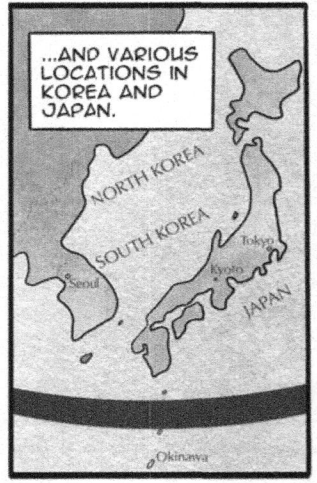

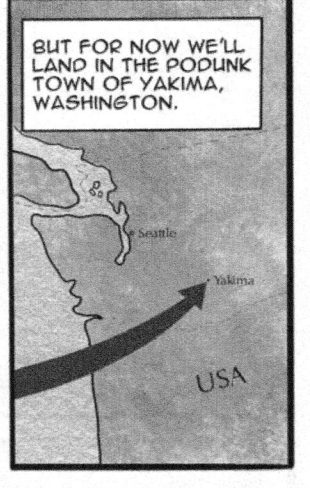

IT'S NOT A LINEAR STORY. THERE'S A CONSIDERABLE AMOUNT OF JUMPING ABOUT THROUGH TIME AND SPACE AHEAD. FIRST, WE HAVE TO LEAVE THE PRESENT BEHIND AND HEAD BACK ABOUT SIX MONTHS AND SIX THOUSAND MILES OR SO.

WE'LL COME BACK TO SHANGHAI EVENTUALLY...

...AND VARIOUS LOCATIONS IN KOREA AND JAPAN.

BUT FOR NOW WE'LL LAND IN THE PODUNK TOWN OF YAKIMA, WASHINGTON.

YOU'VE NEVER HEARD OF IT, BUT THIS IS WHERE VARIOUS LINES OF HISTORY CONVERGE.

IT'S WHERE WE'LL PICK UP A FEW OF THOSE FRAGMENTS, THE ONES THAT WEREN'T STASHED AWAY OUT OF VIEW...
...BUT HIDDEN IN PLAIN SIGHT, OBVIOUS, MAYBE TO THE ONE WHO PLACED THEM THERE, BUT MUTE ENIGMAS TO EVERYONE ELSE.
I ♥ Yakima

MY FATHER LIVED OUT THE MAJORITY OF HIS ADULT LIFE HERE, STAYING LONG AFTER HIS FAMILY HAD GONE.
GETTING HIM TO LEAVE YAKIMA, EVEN BRIEFLY, WAS LIKE ASKING A TORTOISE TO LEAVE ITS SHELL.

SKWEEZ!
KNOCK! KNOCK!
READY TO GO?
I RETURNED TO YAKIMA EVERY SO OFTEN TO SEE HOW HE WAS DOING.
I'VE **BEEN** READY.
USUALLY, THIS WAS AN EXERCISE IN FRUSTRATION.

SOMETHING WRONG?
NO.
NO, OR YOU DON'T WANT TO TELL ME WHAT IT IS?
I SAID THERE'S NOTHING WRONG!
OKAY THEN, LET'S GO.
SURE, WHY NOT? IT'S A NICE DAY FOR A DRIVE.
CREEEEEEEK!

IT WOULD HAVE BEEN FASTER IF YOU'D JUST LET ME PICK UP WHAT YOU NEEDED.
SO *NOW* YOU'RE IN A HURRY? WHAT'S THE MATTER, ANXIOUS TO GET AWAY?
NO, BUT IT'S A LONG DRIVE TO LOS ANGELES.
RIGHT. BACK TO THE LAND OF FRUITS AND NUTS.
NEVER COULD FIGURE OUT WHAT YOU SAW IN THAT PLACE.
APART FROM THE OBVIOUS.
SED CARS
SALE
SALE
GAS
JEEZUS, IT'S A JOKE.
HA.

SAVE U MAWF
I'LL GO IN BY MYSELF.
ERMPHH!
SLOUCH!
HUFF! HUFF! HUFF!
FLU SHOT

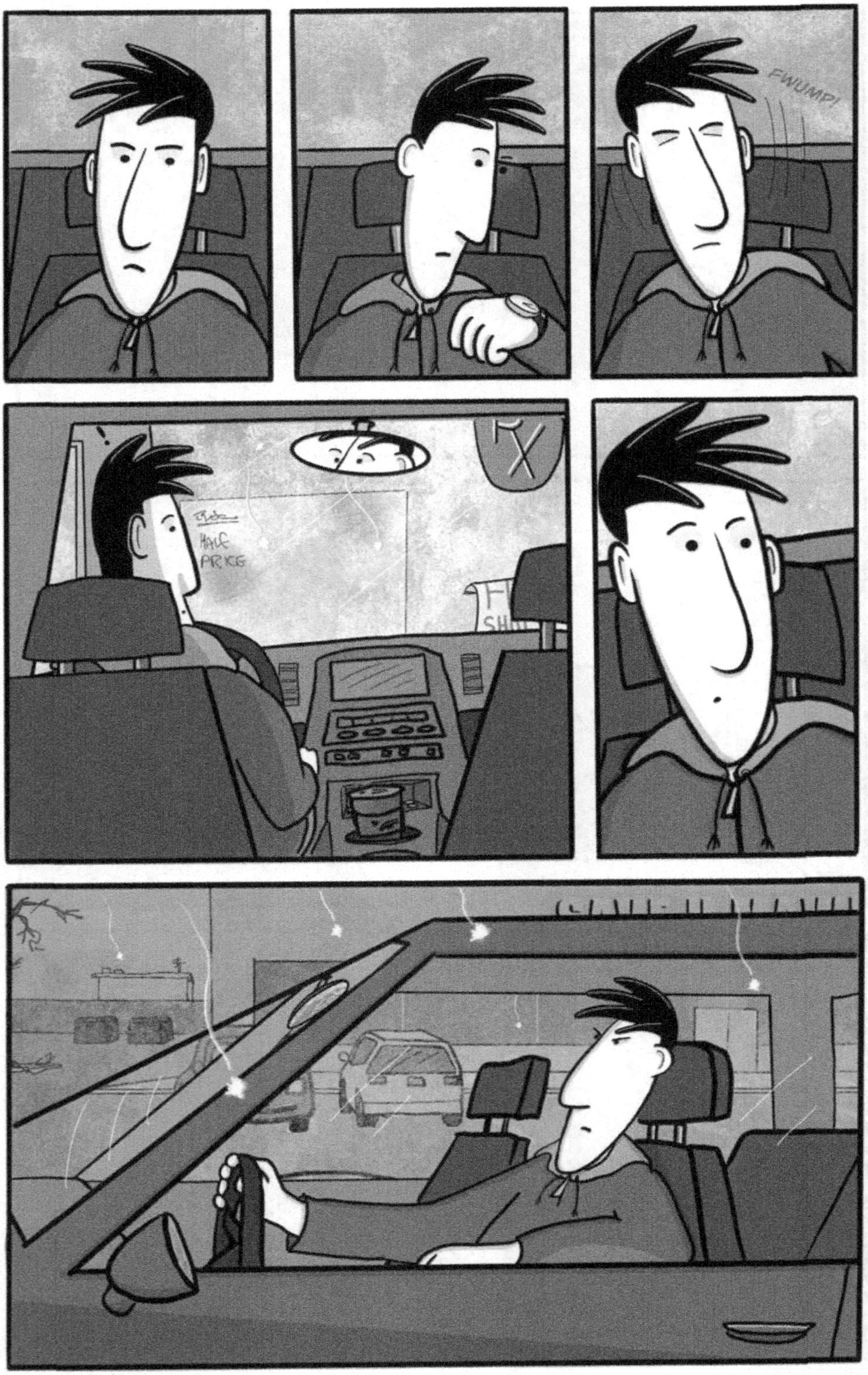
FWUMP!

TWIDDLE
TWIDDLE
HONK! HONNNK!!
FWISK
AUTOMATIC DOOR
HOOF!
HUFF!

HUFF!
HUFF!
HOOF!
KLIK!
COOL
FAN
HEAT
FWOOSH!
NEED HELP?
DO I LOOK LIKE I NEED HELP?
IT'S COLD OUT. CLOSE THE DOOR.

I KNOW! I KNOW! YOU'RE IN A GODDAM HURRY!
I COULD HAVE GONE IN FOR YOU. IT'S NOT LIKE I DIDN'T KNOW WHAT YOU NEEDED.
Dependo™ Safe-T PANTS
CRUMPLE!
SLAM!
KLIK! VRRRROOOM!

IS IT WARM ENOUGH?
I SAID, IS IT WARM ENOUGH?
...
HOT!
SCHLUMPF!
!
THU-WHUMP!

AND THAT WAS THAT.

BEEEEEEEEEEEEE...

...EEEEEEEEEEEEEEEEEEEEE!

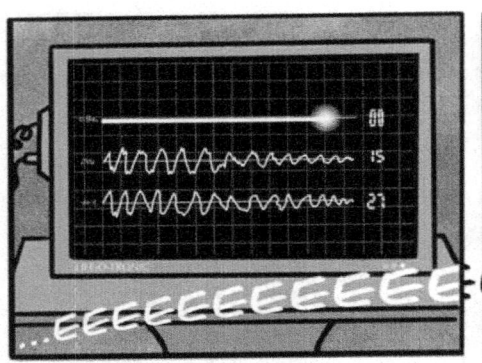

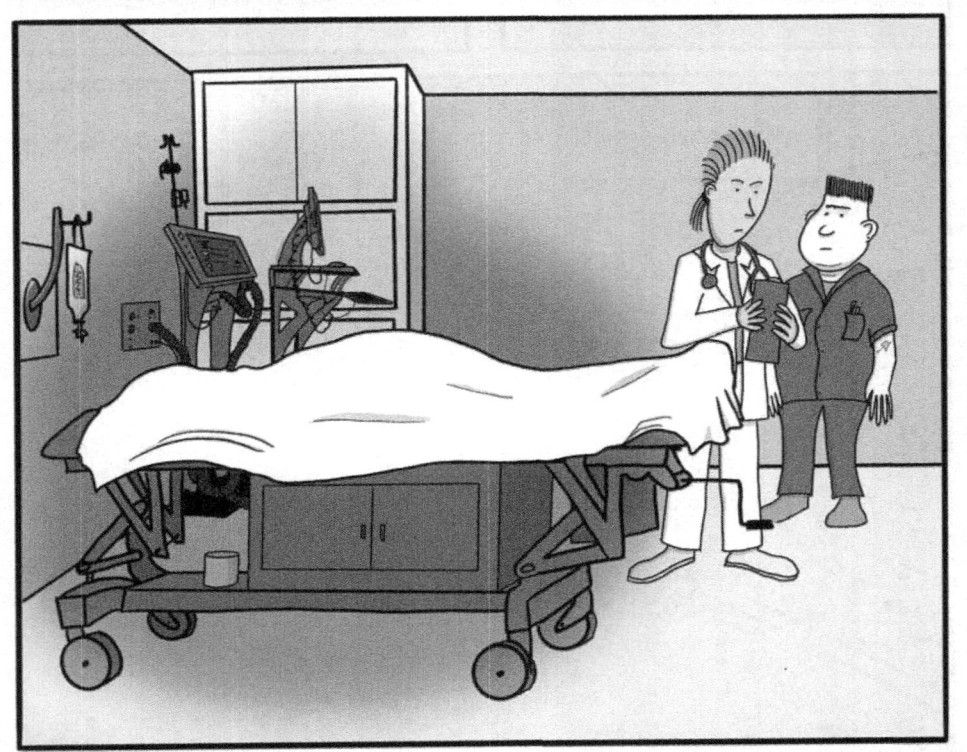

ER
ER
MR. MOLITOR?
TWILIGHT
ZONE
I'M SORRY, BUT THERE ARE FORMS TO FILL OUT.
YOU'LL HAVE TO MAKE ARRANGEMENTS...
...FOR THE BODY.
HERE ARE YOUR FATHER'S PERSONAL ITEMS.
BLAH BLAH BLAH BLAH
BLAH BLAH BLAH BLAH BLAH BLAH BLAH
BLAH BLAH BLAH BLAH

TICK
TICK
TICKA
TICK!
BWEEP!
SLURRP!
I have no idea how much longer I'll have to stay here. .V.
POIK!
Stay as long as you need. <3

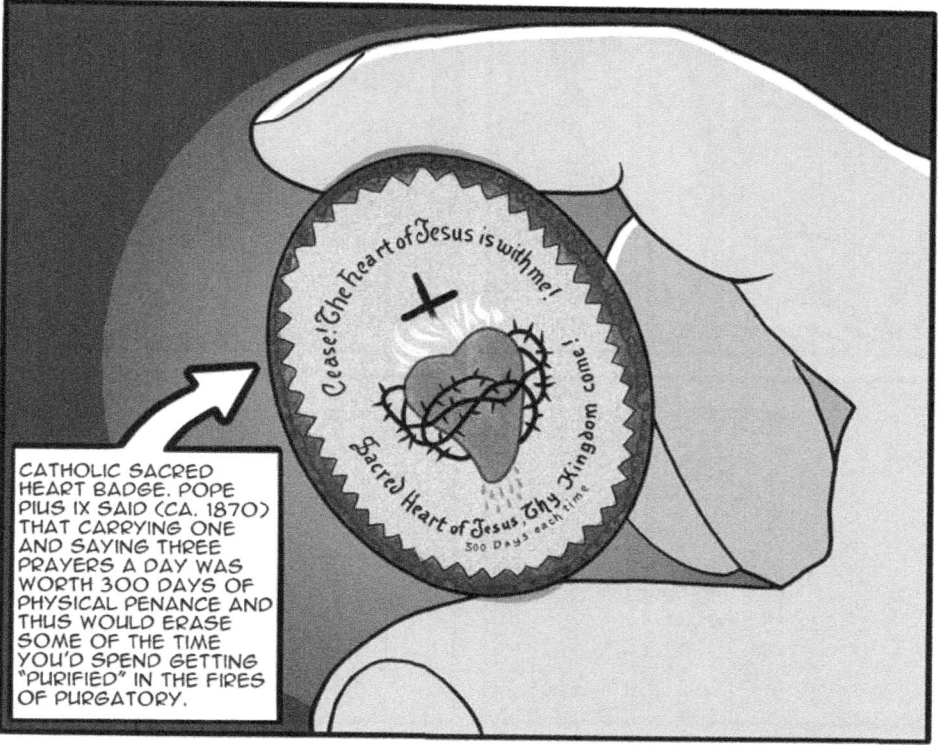

CATHOLIC SACRED HEART BADGE. POPE PIUS IX SAID (CA. 1870) THAT CARRYING ONE AND SAYING THREE PRAYERS A DAY WAS WORTH 300 DAYS OF PHYSICAL PENANCE AND THUS WOULD ERASE SOME OF THE TIME YOU'D SPEND GETTING "PURIFIED" IN THE FIRES OF PURGATORY.

AT THAT MOMENT, AND MORE THAN EVER BEFORE, I JUST WANTED TO GO HOME.
MY HOME.
CLICK
SHLOOF!
THIS PLACE HADN'T BEEN HOME IN A LONG TIME.

I GREW UP IN THIS HOUSE, BUT IT WAS ODDLY DEVOID OF SENTIMENT. IN THE YEARS SINCE I'D LEFT, IT HAD BEEN SWEPT CLEAN OF ALL BUT A FEW TRACES OF MY LIFE, MOST OF THEM REPLACED BY A SELECTION OF CAREFULLY FILTERED MEMENTOS OF MY FATHER'S OWN PAST.

THAT WAS OKAY. AFTER ALL, OUR LIVES HAD DIVERGED A LONG TIME AGO.

STILL, I WONDERED ABOUT SOME OF THE THINGS HE CHOSE TO SURROUND HIMSELF WITH. FOR EXAMPLE, A SMALL BRASS BUDDHA FROM JAPAN. IT WAS A SOUVENIR FROM THE KOREAN WAR AND THE ONLY REFERENCE TO DAD'S MILITARY SERVICE THAT I REMEMBERED SEEING AS A KID.

DAD NEVER TALKED ABOUT THE LITTLE STATUE — OR THE WAR — AND IN MY MEMORY IT WAS ALWAYS JUST "THE FAT GUY."

HAD THE FAT GUY GAINED SOME NEW SIGNIFICANCE? HE'D JOINED A HANDFUL OF PHOTOS AND THE ART FROM AN OLD CATHOLIC CALENDAR AS THE SOLE DECORATION IN HIS ROOM.

THE PHOTOGRAPHS TOLD OF A STRICT RELIGIOUS UPBRINGING: LITTLE DICK THE ALTAR BOY DRESSED UP FOR SUNDAY MASS, ENTERING 1ST GRADE AT ST. JOHN'S ACADEMY IN SEATTLE, AND AT HOME ALL WELL-SCRUBBED AND STRAIGHT-LACED.

RELIGION PLAYS A BIG PART IN DAD'S STORY, AS WE'LL SEE. ODDLY, THOUGH, IT WASN'T SOMETHING HE EVER TALKED ABOUT MUCH, ESPECIALLY AFTER MY OWN TEENAGE YEARS.

BY THEN I'D LONG REJECTED HIS BLACK AND WHITE CATHOLICISM FOR THE INFINITE RAINBOW OF THE WORLD AS I EXPERIENCED IT.

PERHAPS IN HIS OLD AGE, MY FATHER RETURNED TO THE SIMPLE TRUTHS OF HIS CHILDHOOD.

THE ANGEL ON THE WALL, ONCE RESPONSIBLE FOR PROTECTING THE YOUNG BOY IN THE PHOTOS, NOW WAS EXPECTED TO LOOK OUT FOR THE OLD MAN THAT HE'D BECOME.

WAS THAT ALSO WHY DAD CARRIED THE LITTLE PRAYER BADGE IN HIS POCKET, THE SCHOOLBOY EQUIVALENT OF A GET OUT OF JAIL FREE CARD?

BUT IF THAT WERE THE CASE, WHY DID THE FAT GUY REMAIN SO PROMINENTLY DISPLAYED IN DAD'S ROOM? THE BUDDHA HARDLY HAD MUCH STANDING IN CATHOLIC TRADITION.

PHHHEBLLT!

MAYBE THE ONCE-LITTLE BOY HAD ISSUES THAT COULDN'T BE SOLVED BY ANGELS AND SAINTS ALONE.

OR MAYBE HE THOUGHT THAT THEY'D DESERTED HIM...

...OR BEEN DRIVEN AWAY.

WHATEVER THE REASON, I DOUBT IT WAS QUITE SO MELODRAMATIC.

MY TENDENCY TO EMBRACE IMAGINARY DRAMA WAS INFLUENCING MY WHOLE REACTION TO DAD'S DEATH.

SURE, IT WAS A BIT OF A SHOCK (MORE TO HIM THAN TO ME), BUT DID I REALLY HAVE ANY REASON TO BELIEVE HE DIED IN FEAR OF SOME SCHOOLBOY VIEW OF THE AFTERLIFE?

SO HE KEPT A MEMENTO OF HIS PAST IN HIS POCKET. HE PROBABLY THOUGHT IT WAS AN IRONIC JOKE. SAME WITH THE FAT GUY. HA. PROBABLY BEST JUST TO FORGET IT.

29

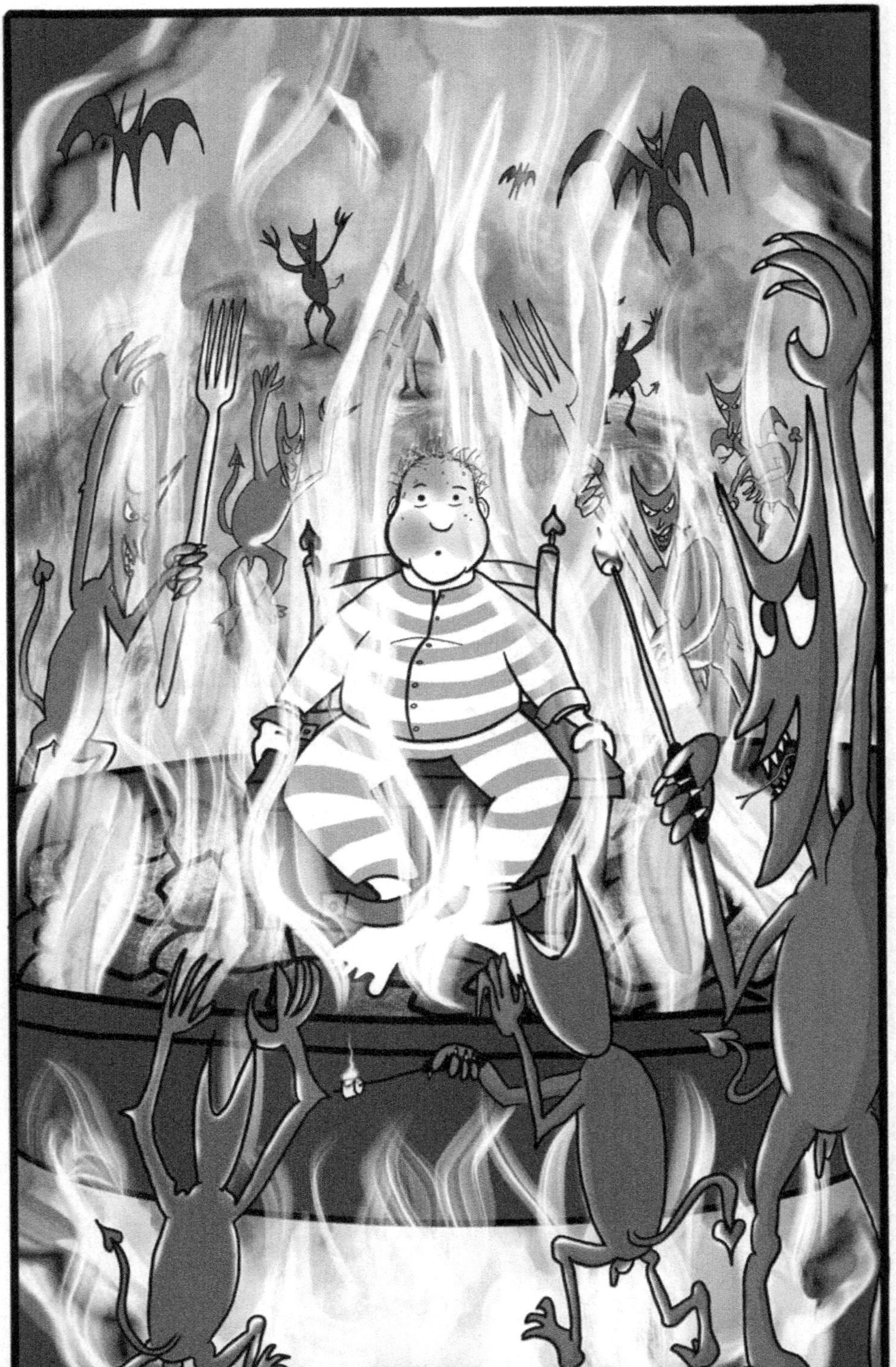

VRRRRROOM!

IS IT WARM ENOUGH?

GAAAAAAA

HOT!!

AAAAAAAAHH!!
FORGETTING WAS EASIER SAID THAN DONE.
BEFORE I COULD LET GO OF HIM, HE HAD TO LET GO OF ME.

2

EVEN THOUGH WE HADN'T BEEN THAT CLOSE, MY FATHER'S PASSING TRIGGERED THE USUAL FEELINGS OF LOSS AND REGRET...AND THEN SOME.

YEARS AGO, AS SOON AS I WAS OLD ENOUGH, I'D MOVED AS FAR AWAY FROM HIS BELOVED - AND MY DESPISED - YAKIMA, WASHINGTON AS I COULD GET. SINCE HE WOULDN'T TRAVEL ANYWHERE ELSE, WE SAW EACH OTHER ONLY ON THE RARE OCCASIONS I'D DRIVE UP FROM LOS ANGELES TO SEE HOW HE WAS DOING.

ADDED TO THAT FOUNDATION OF FILIAL GUILT WAS THE GUT FEELING THAT I WAS AT LEAST PARTLY RESPONSIBLE FOR HIS DEATH. I COULDN'T STAND YAKIMA AND HAD WANTED THIS LATEST VISIT TO BE OVER AS QUICKLY AS POSSIBLE. I RUSHED HIM, AND POSSIBLY TRIGGERED THE STROKE THAT DID HIM IN.

EVEN WORSE, IN HIS FINAL MOMENT OF CONSCIOUSNESS I THINK I BROUGHT TO THE SURFACE A LONG-SIMMERING BELIEF THAT HE WAS ON THE WAY TO AN ETERNITY IN HELL OR, IF HE WERE LUCKY AND HAD SAID ENOUGH PRAYERS, A TEMPORARY STAY IN PURGATORY.

I WASN'T SURE OF ANY OF THIS, OF COURSE, JUST LIKE I WASN'T SURE OF ANYTHING ASSOCIATED WITH DAD.

FOR ONE THING, DAD SEEMED TOO BORING TO MERIT SUCH A MELODRAMATIC END.

HE HAD ALL THE USUAL ISSUES, OF COURSE, MADE WORSE, I SUSPECT, BY SOMETHING HE'D EXPERIENCED DURING THE KOREAN WAR.

HE WASN'T THE GREATEST FATHER, BUT MY COMPLAINTS WOULD HARDLY EARN HIM AN ETERNITY IN HELL OR EVEN A BRIEF STAY IN SOME PURGATORIAL TIME SHARE.

YET I WAS CONVINCED THAT'S WHAT HE THOUGHT LAY IN STORE FOR HIM.

FLIP! FLIP!

PLEASE WAIT TO BE JUDGED

Le Pearly Gates

FAST PASS HOLDERS ONLY →

The SINS of Richard Edward Moliter

Recommendation for Redemption: PURGATORIO 5 Million Years

HMMPH

PLEASE WAIT TO BE JUDGED
BZZZZZZZ!
FWISSSSS...
...SSSSS!
LEVELS
DING! DING!
UP
DOWN

DAD'S CATHOLICISM WAS BORN IN AN AGE OF DRAMATIC CHANGE FOR THE CHURCH. THE TURMOIL IN EUROPE THAT LED UP TO THE SECOND WORLD WAR FORCED CATHOLIC LEADERS TO DISMISS THE IDEA OF HOLDING ON TO TEMPORAL POWER AGAINST THE RISE OF SECULAR TOTALITARIANISM — FASCIST, STALINIST, OR EVEN DEMOCRATIC — AND REFOCUS ON A LESS STATELY DOMAIN: THE SANCTIFIED FAMILY.

THE CHURCH DEFINED FAMILY AS A MALE-DOMINATED INSTITUTION BASED ON PROCREATION. GET THEM WHILE THEY'RE YOUNG, IN THEIR HOMES, AND RUTTING LIKE RABBITS, THE REASONING WENT, AND THE CHILDREN THEY BRED WOULD GROW UP TO BE ADULTS WHO WOULD NATURALLY SUPPORT CATHOLIC SOCIAL AND POLITICAL GOALS.

FROM WHAT I COULD DISCOVER OF DAD'S SPECIFIC RELIGIOUS INSTRUCTION, THIS LED TO A VERY SIMPLISTIC DIGEST-VERSION OF WHAT, BY THE 20TH CENTURY, HAD BECOME A LABYRINTH OF COMPLEX THEOLOGY. I DIDN'T WANT TO REDUCE MY FATHER'S BELIEFS TO GROSSLY SIMPLIFIED CARTOONS LIKE SOME COLLEGE KID FRESH FROM HIS FIRST PHILOSOPHY COURSE, BUT I COULDN'T HELP BUT THINK IT REMAINED TO HIS DYING DAY A FAIRLY WATERED-DOWN, DARE I SAY IT, CHILDISH VIEW OF AN EXTREMELY COMPLICATED SUBJECT.

DING! **WASH**

IN DAD'S LITERAL CATHOLICISM, PURGATORY WAS WHERE YOU WENT TO GET SPIFFIED UP BEFORE MOVING ON TO MEET GOD.

DRY

IT WAS A LENGTHY AND UNPLEASANT ORDEAL, THOUGH DETAILS WERE SKETCHY...

...AND FAR FROM AGREED UPON. WAS IT AN ACTUAL PLACE OR A PROCESS? AT LEAST ONE POPE SUGGESTED PURGATORY WAS THE JUDGING GAZE OF JESUS HIMSELF, WHICH FRIED THE EVIL FROM SINFUL FLESH LIKE A SUPERCHARGED X-RAY MACHINE.

MORE POPULAR NOTIONS SAW IT AS A SORT OF TEMPORARY HELL, SITUATED NEAR THE REAL THING TO TAKE ADVANTAGE OF THE PROXIMATE FIRES AND SLOWLY TOAST OUT NON-MORTAL SIN.

DING! DING!

FOR WHICH VERSION DAD THOUGHT HE HAD A CONFIRMED RESERVATION I COULDN'T BE SURE.

THE SCHOOLBOY IN HIM PROBABLY THOUGHT HE'D BE SPENDING A LONG TIME IN A VERY LARGE AND VERY HOT CONVECTION OVEN.

PAF!
DING!
DING!
Incoming Call
MOM
Phoenix, AZ
DING!
MY MOTHER DOESN'T FIGURE MUCH IN THIS STORY, NOT BECAUSE SHE WASN'T A PART OF IT. FAR FROM IT. SHE HAD A HUGE INFLUENCE ON MY LIFE.
SHE JUST HAD HER OWN WAY OF DEALING WITH DAD'S ISSUES, INCLUDING, EVENTUALLY, GETTING AWAY FROM THEM ENTIRELY.
HI, MOM.
WHERE ARE YOU?
ROBBIE SAID YOU'D GONE NORTH.
I'M IN YAKIMA.
OH. LUCKY YOU.
LISTEN, MOM, I'VE GOT SOME BAD NEWS.
————.
MOM?

WAS HE ALONE?
WHAT?
WAS HE BY HIMSELF... WHEN IT HAPPENED?
I WAS WITH HIM.
THAT'S GOOD. I DIDN'T WANT HIM TO BE ALONE AT THE END.
BUT...HOW...?
AFTER 60 YEARS YOU JUST KNOW THINGS, EVEN IF YOU ARE APART.
ARE *YOU* OKAY?
I'M FINE, I GUESS. WE'LL HAVE TO FIGURE OUT WHAT TO DO WITH THE HOUSE.
I'M NOT GOING BACK THERE. YOU KNOW THAT.
YEAH, I KNOW.
YOU SHOULD GET OUT, TOO, AS QUICKLY AS YOU CAN.
MOVE TOWARD THE FUTURE, NOT THE PAST.
ESPECIALLY WHEN IT'S YOUR FATHER'S PAST.

THERE'S MORE THERE THAN YOU WANT TO KNOW ABOUT.
YOU KNOW SOME THINGS.
YOU'RE TALKING ABOUT THE SPOOKY SPY STUFF, RIGHT? I KNOW ALL ABOUT THAT.
BY ANY CHANCE, DID DICK HAPPEN TO TELL YOU ANYTHING OR ASK ANY STRANGE QUESTIONS WHILE YOU WERE VISITING?
NOTHING STRANGER THAN USUAL. WHY?
THERE WAS SOMETHING HE WANTED...NO, SOMETHING HE NEEDED TO SAY TO YOU.
THAT I'M AN ANNOYING FRUITCAKE?
MOM
YOU'RE NOT ANNOYING.
THANKS... I THINK.
BUT NO, HE DIDN'T TELL ME ANYTHING. YOU KNOW DAD WHEN IT CAME TO SHARING.
THAT'S DISAPPOINTING. I THOUGHT FOR SURE HE WAS FINALLY GOING TO TALK TO YOU.
ABOUT WHAT?
MOM
I WISH I KNEW. HE NEVER TOLD ME. BUT THERE WAS SOMETHING THERE. I'VE ALWAYS FELT IT. SOME HEAVY WEIGHT HE NEEDED TO GET OFF HIS CHEST.

SAY, SINCE YOU'VE BEEN WORKING ON YOUR PROJECTS IN CHINA, HAVE YOU EVER LEARNED ANY OF THE LOCAL LINGO?
MOM
NOT REALLY. A FEW WORDS, MOSTLY HAVING TO DO WITH FINDING THE NEAREST RESTROOM.
WAS DAD PLANNING ON BECOMING A CHINESE LINGUIST?
MOM
PLEASE! I COULDN'T EVEN GET HIM TO TRY CHINESE FOOD.
SO, YOU THINK HE WANTED TO TELL ME SOMETHING IN CHINESE? OR IS THIS MORE SPY BUSINESS?
I DON'T THINK ANY OF DAD'S SPOOK WORK INVOLVED CHINA.
IT DIDN'T. FORGET IT. IN FACT, FORGET THE WHOLE BUSINESS. I'M SORRY I BROUGHT IT UP.
IF HE NEEDED TO TALK ABOUT SOMETHING, OBVIOUSLY HE DIDN'T FEEL COMFORTABLE GETTING INTO IT WITH YOU.
THAT'S...UH... NICE TO KNOW.
OH, DON'T BE SO SENSITIVE! I DIDN'T MEAN IT LIKE THAT!
LOOK, IT'S PROBABLY NOTHING. DON'T TURN IT INTO THE NEXT BROADWAY PRODUCTION.
LEAVE IT ALONE AND GO HOME AS SOON AS YOU CAN.

TAKE CARE OF YOURSELF.
BWOOP!
MOM WAS RIGHT, OF COURSE. WHAT WAS THE POINT?
HOW DO YOU EVEN BEGIN TO UNDERSTAND BEHAVIOR THAT MUST BE ROOTED IN A PAST SO LONG GONE EVEN MY FATHER HIMSELF PROBABLY DIDN'T REMEMBER WHY OR WHEN IT GOT ITS START?
AND WHAT DID I HAVE TO WHINE ABOUT ANYWAY? SURE, WE DIDN'T EXACTLY GET ALONG, AND HADN'T FOR A LONG TIME, BUT IT'S NOT LIKE THERE WAS PHYSICAL ABUSE OR SOMETHING. I NEVER STARVED. WE ATE A LOT OF PEANUT BUTTER SANDWICHES AND MACARONI WITH FAKE CHEESE, BUT I NEVER SAT DOWN TO AN EMPTY PLATE.
THE EMPTINESS WAS ELSEWHERE, SITTING AT THE END OF THE TABLE.

SCOOT! SCOOT!
KOREA
I KNEW MY FATHER WAS MESSED UP SOMEHOW IN THE WAR, BUT I DIDN'T KNOW WHY OR HOW, OR HOW MUCH IT PLAYED A PART IN WHO HE BECAME LATER ON.
NOW THAT HE WAS GONE, I'D PROBABLY NEVER LEARN THE TRUTH.
IF SUCH A THING EVEN EXISTED.

MOVE AHEAD ONE MONTH AND SOUTH 1000 MILES.

GATE 12
KA 538 SHANGHAI

LOS ANGELES, CALIFORNIA

FOR THE PAST FEW YEARS, MY JOB HAD BEEN TAKING ME TO CHINA AND KOREA. BUSINESS TRAVEL CAN BE INTERESTING, BUT MORE OFTEN THAN NOT IT'S TIRING, DISRUPTIVE, AND NOT A LOT OF FUN. ADDITIONAL STRESS IS NOT WELCOME.

TAPPA TAPPA BWIP!

MESSAGE FROM
Robbie

Welcome home! How was the flight?

BWOOP!

Long. I'm beat. :(

BWOOP!
MESSAGE FROM
Robbie
BTW, you had two more calls from the realtor. More trouble with the house.
?!
SHAKE!
SHAKE!

(MENTAL BLOCK)
BWOOP!
MESSAGE FROM
Sally
The studio called to ask when they'll get the production sked.
Correct answer:
>>>>ASAP!<<<<
-S
TAPPA TAPPA TAPPA!
MESSAGE TO
Sally
Working on it.
TAP!
BWIP!
MARCH
DEADLINE
BWOOP!

MESSAGE FROM
Robbie
The realtor from Yakima called again, complaining about all your dad's stuff.
She said she can't show the house.
BWOOP!
MESSAGE FROM
Robbie
You have to go up there and clear it out.
TAPPA TAPPA TAPPA!
MESSAGE TO
Robbie
#*!@#%&~!!!
BWIP!
BWOOP!
MESSAGE FROM
Robbie
I'm just the messenger, sweetheart.
You can't keep putting it off.
THUNK!
BWOOP!
MESSAGE FROM
Robbie
Maybe you should talk to Dr. Levine about it.
SIGH!!!

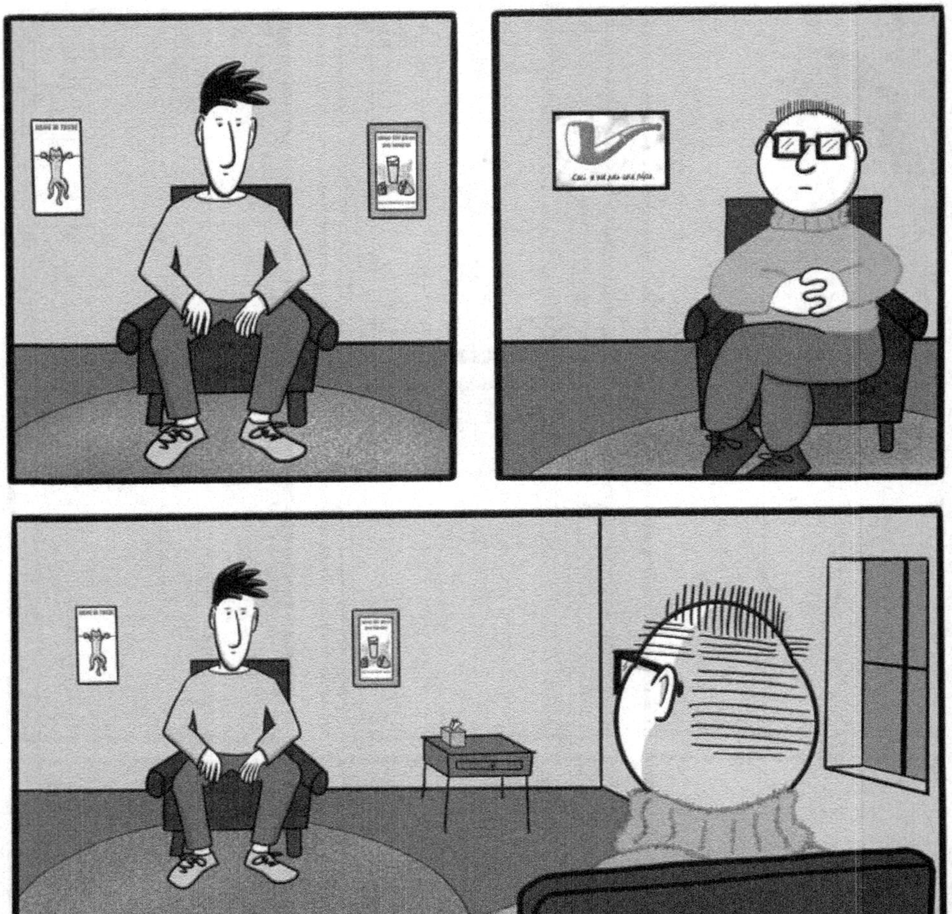
PUSH!

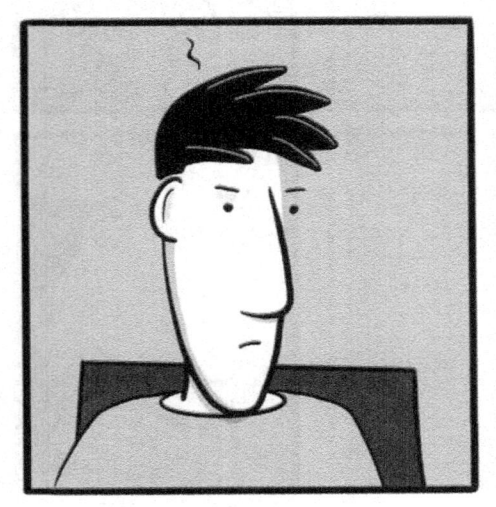

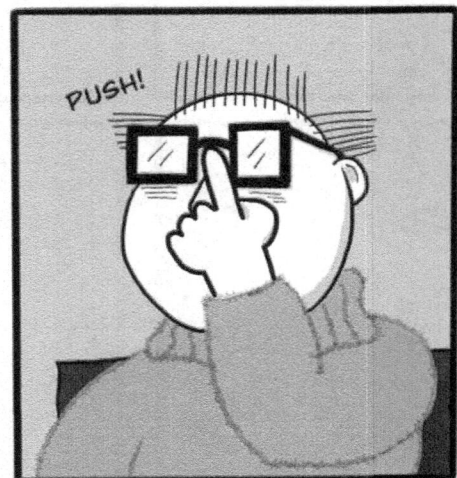

YOU THINK I SHOULD GO.
WHAT MATTERS IS WHAT YOU THINK.
AND WHAT YOU DO.
I HATE THAT PLACE.
DID YOU HATE YOUR FATHER?
OF COURSE NOT!

BUT YOU DIDN'T LIKE BEING AROUND HIM.
IT WAS KIND OF MUTUAL.
AND YOU'VE NEVER ASKED YOURSELF WHY?
DAD WASN'T EXACTLY ONE TO OPEN UP ABOUT THAT SORT OF THING.
HE DIDN'T ANSWER MY QUESTIONS WHEN HE WAS ALIVE.
I DOUBT HE'LL BE MORE FORTHCOMING NOW THAT HE'S DEAD.
SOMETIMES THE DEAD SAY MORE THAN THE LIVING.
?
BUT THE LIVING FEEL TOO GUILTY TO LISTEN.

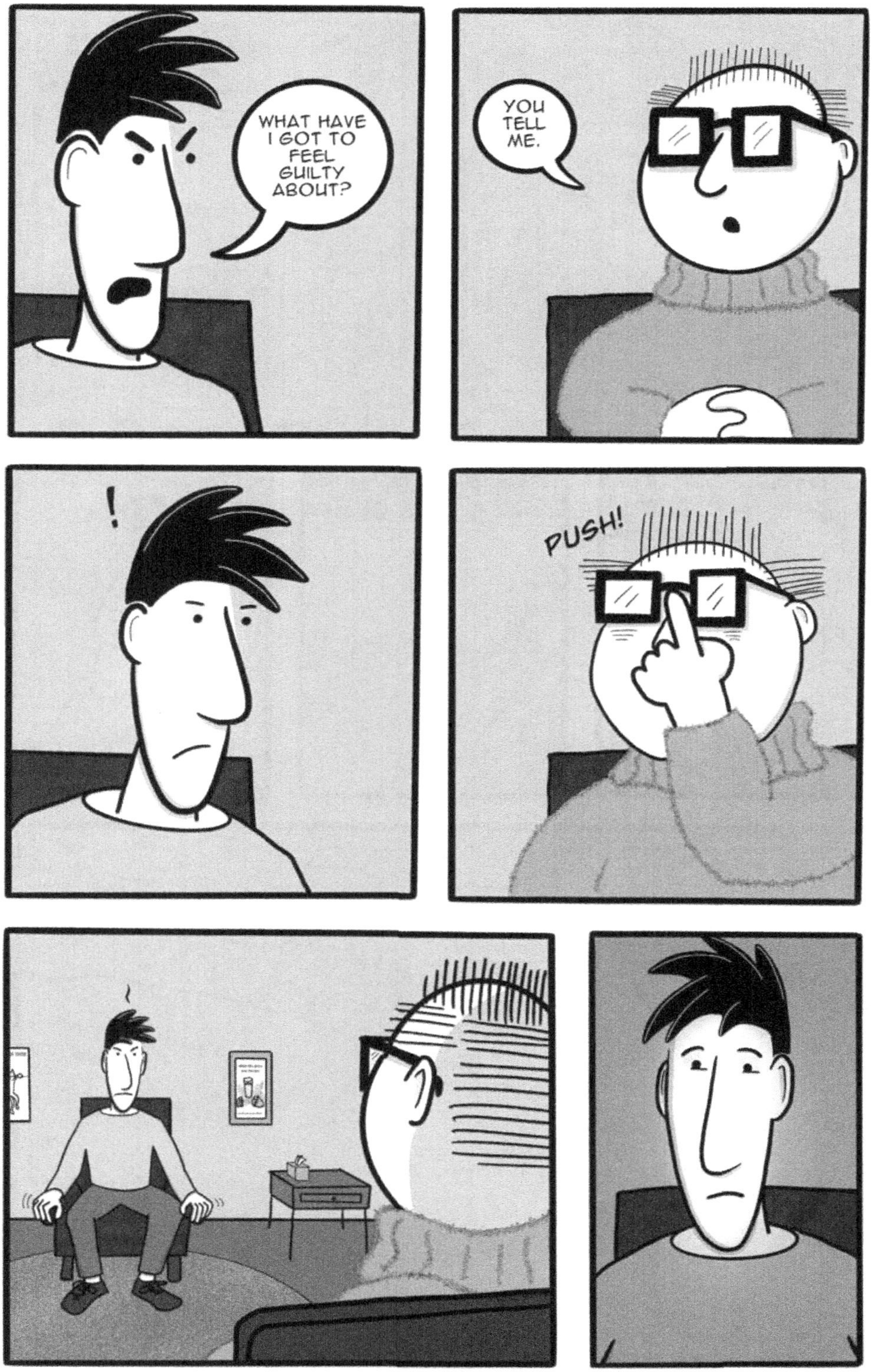
WHAT HAVE I GOT TO FEEL GUILTY ABOUT?
YOU TELL ME.
!
PUSH!

SLAM!
NOW THINGS WERE ABOUT TO GET INTERESTING.
MONTEREY
NORTHERN SPRAWL
Pathetic Ocean
CALIFORNIA
Valley of Trepidation
SANTA BARBARA
Dreamscape of Denial
5
NORTH
SOUTHERN SPRAWL
BAKERSFIELD
FRESNO
Forgetful Forest
Emotional Desert
N

WHINE
COUNTRY
!#*!!@#*!
Just blame
your old man.
If it seems
messed up...
Enjoy it while
you can.
Life is short...

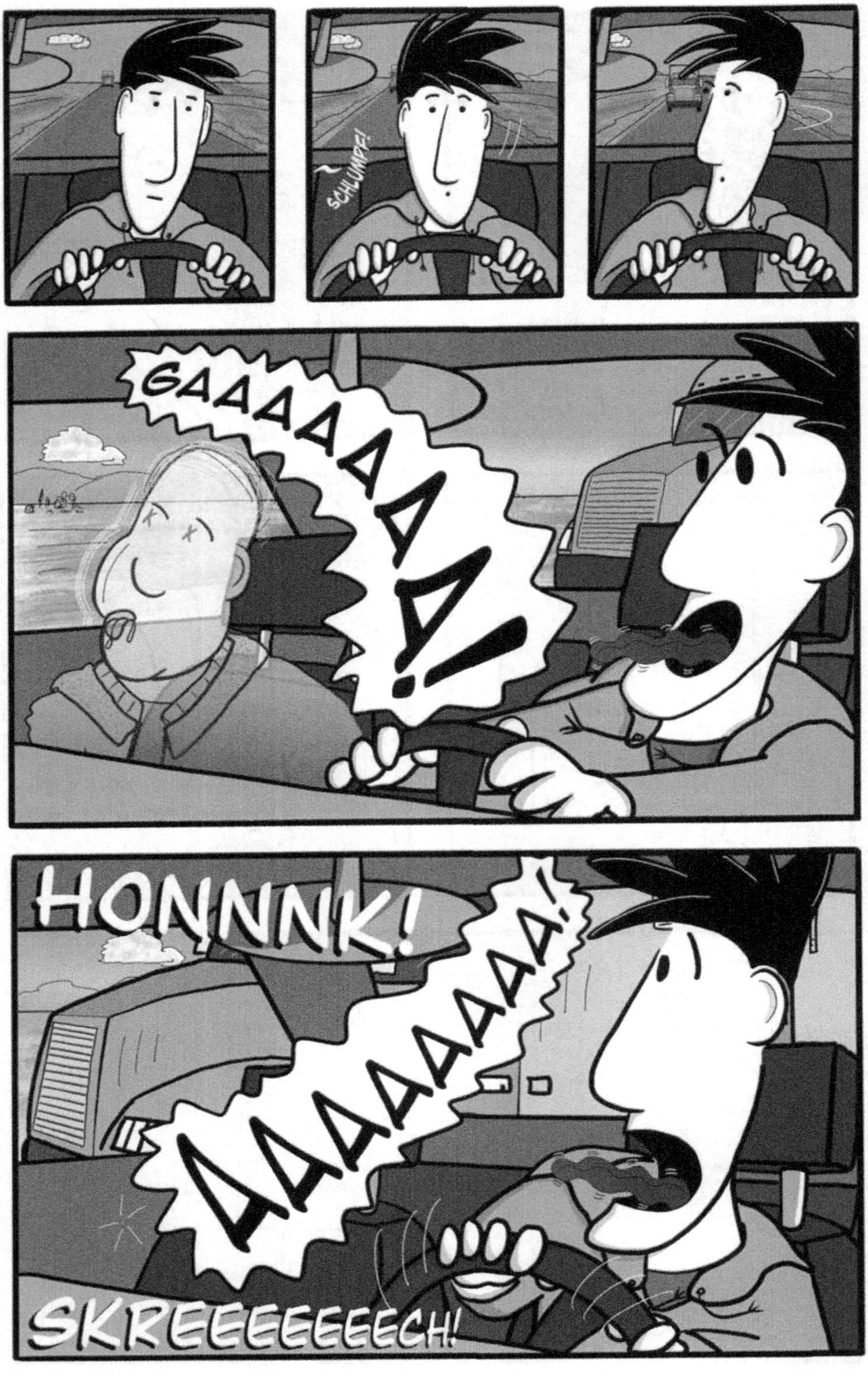
SCHLUMPF!
GAAAAAAAA!
HONNNK!
AAAAAAAAA!
SKREEEEEEEECH!

ॐ

California
Oregon
Mountains of Guilt
Ommmmmmmmmm...
Ommmmmmmmmmm...

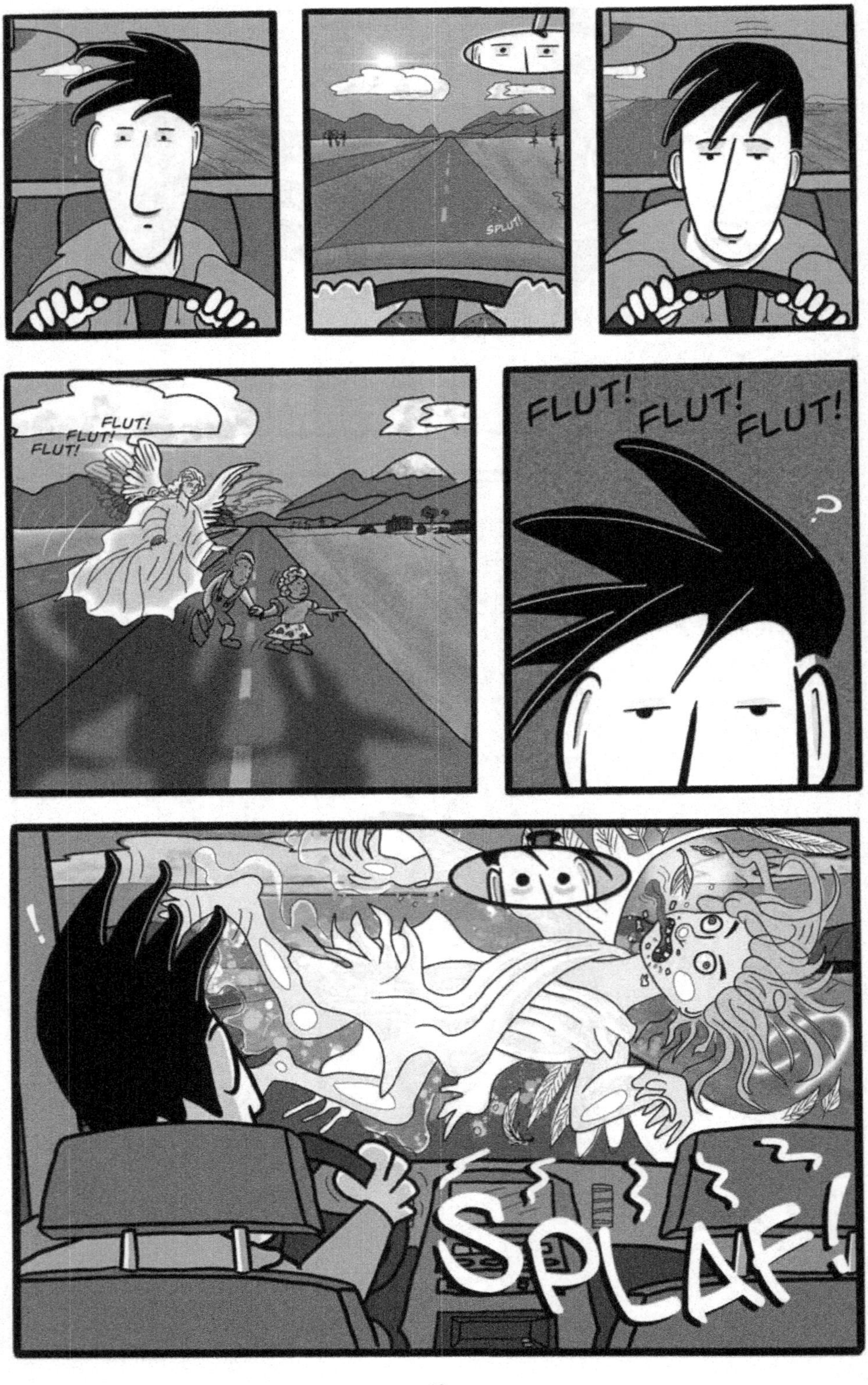
SPLUT!
FLUT!
FLUT!
FLUT!
FLUT!
FLUT!
FLUT!
?
!
SPLAF!

AAAAAAA!
PORTLAND
ZONE OF WEIRDNESS
COLUMBIA RIVER
WASHINGTON
OREGON
SHANIKO
PLAINS OF PASSIVE AGGRESSION

ACTUAL SIGN
Welcome to Yakima!
THE PALM SPRINGS OF WASHINGTON
EXIT
EVERY TIME I CAME BACK, I COULDN'T HELP BUT DREDGE UP OLD MEMORIES. SOME WERE GOOD. MOST WERE NOT. MY PSHRINK SAID I HAD BORDERLINE MARTYR SYNDROME. I ASKED HIM IF HE'D EVER BEEN TO YAKIMA. OF COURSE, HE HADN'T.
WE DROPPED THE SUBJECT.
ONE OF THE REASONS DAD LIKED THIS PLACE MUST HAVE BEEN ITS REACTIONARY AVERSION TO CHANGE.

MAYBE IT WAS THE JOLT OF HIS FATHER'S DEATH AND THE SUDDEN END OF HIS OWN CHILDHOOD - AS HE DEFINED IT - THAT SET THE STAGE FOR THAT, OR PERHAPS THE IMPLIED UNCERTAINTY INHERENT IN CHANGE ITSELF WAS ENOUGH TO THREATEN A WORLD VIEW WRIT IN STONE.

ONE THING I KNEW, THOUGH...SOME OF WHAT NEVER CHANGED IN YAKIMA WAS SO FAR OFF DAD'S RADAR IT COULD HAVE BEEN ON ANOTHER PLANET. LIFE IS ALWAYS MORE COMPLEX THAN YOU THINK IT IS, EVEN IN A LITTLE TOWN IN THE MIDDLE OF NOWHERE.

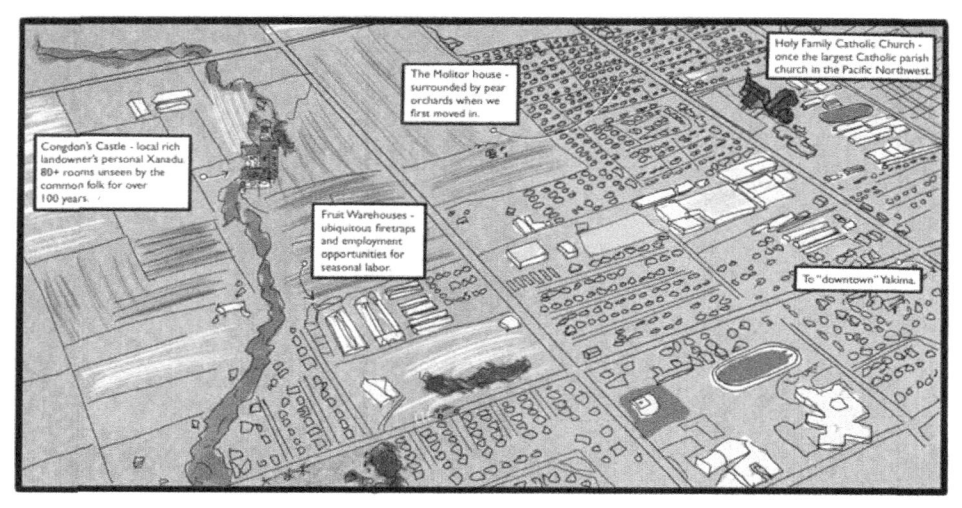

Holy Family Catholic Church - once the largest Catholic parish church in the Pacific Northwest.

The Molitor house - surrounded by pear orchards when we first moved in.

Congdon's Castle - local rich landowner's personal Xanadu. 80+ rooms unseen by the common folk for over 100 years.

Fruit Warehouses - ubiquitous firetraps and employment opportunities for seasonal labor.

To "downtown" Yakima.

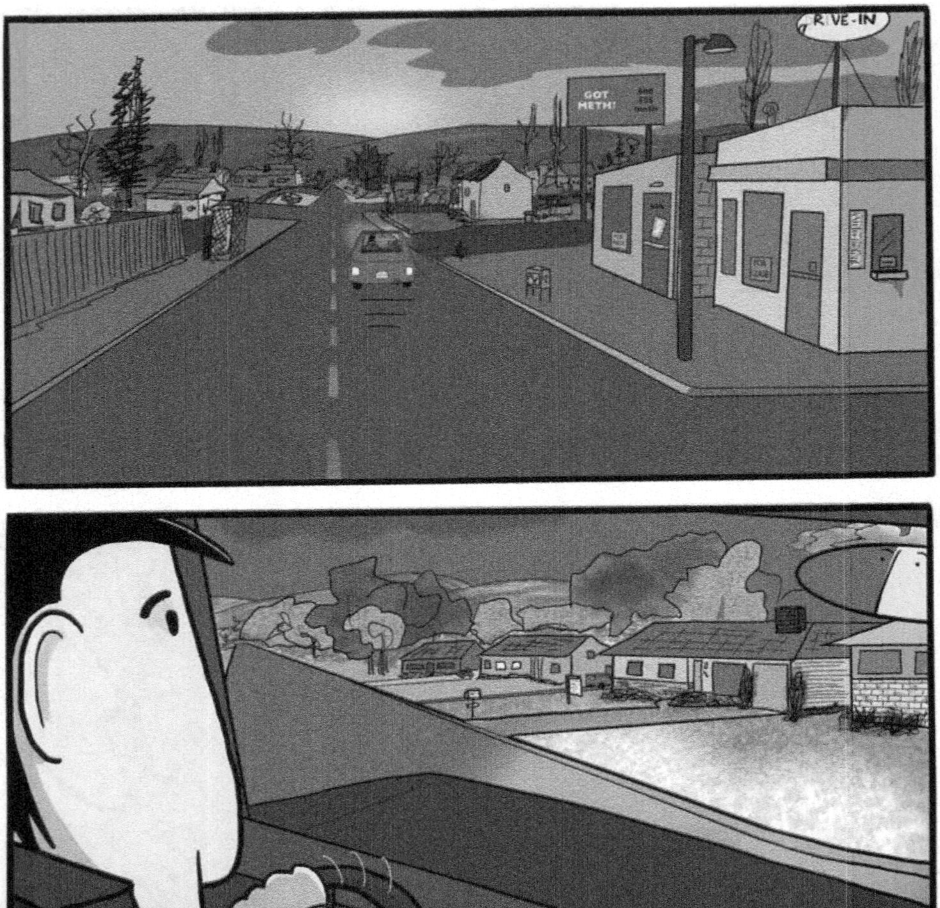
RIVE-IN
GOT METH!

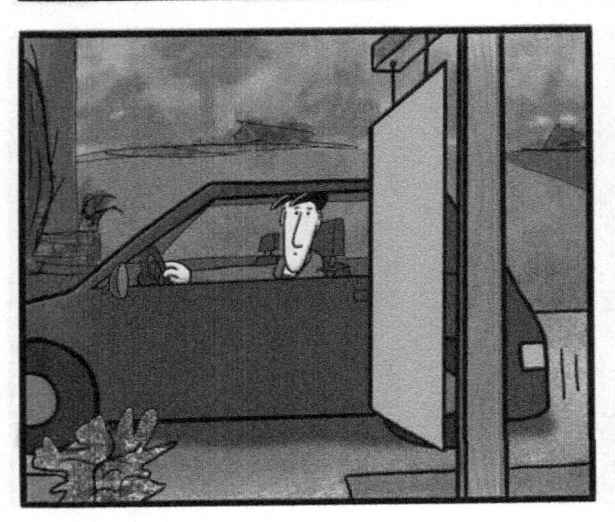

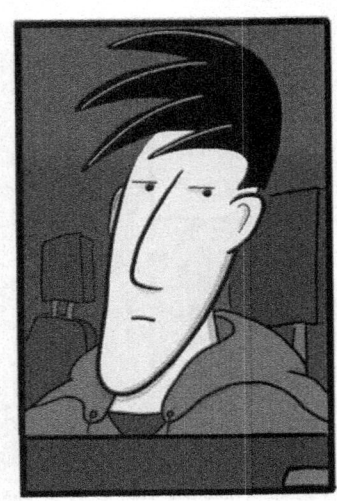

65

WHEN HOWARD CARTER OPENED THE TOMB OF EGYPT'S BOY KING, TUTANKHAMUN, IN 1922, HE GAZED UPON A STASH OF GOLDEN BURIAL GOODIES THE LIKES OF WHICH THE WORLD HAD NOT KNOWN FOR OVER THREE THOUSAND YEARS. "CAN YOU SEE ANYTHING?" HE WAS ASKED. "YES," HE REPLIED. "WONDROUS THINGS."

I COULDN'T HELP BUT IMAGINE WHAT HIS REACTION MIGHT HAVE BEEN IF, INSTEAD OF COLORFULLY PAINTED WALLS, SOLID GOLD STATUES AND COFFINS, AND PRICELESS WORKS OF ART, HE'D PEERED IN AT A SCENE OF PLAIN PAINTED PLASTER AND OLD CARDBOARD BOXES STUFFED WITH WHO-KNOWS-WHAT?

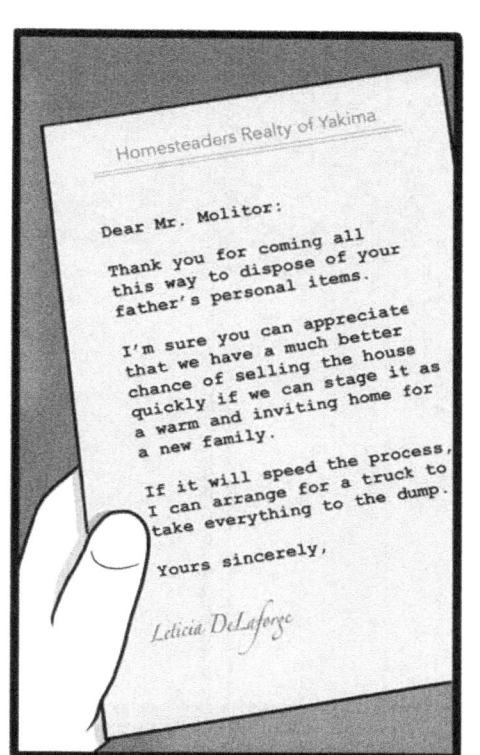

Homesteaders Realty of Yakima

Dear Mr. Molitor:

Thank you for coming all this way to dispose of your father's personal items.

I'm sure you can appreciate that we have a much better chance of selling the house quickly if we can stage it as a warm and inviting home for a new family.

If it will speed the process, I can arrange for a truck to take everything to the dump.

Yours sincerely,

Leticia DeLaforge

THE IDEA OF THIS OLD HOUSE BECOMING A WARM AND INVITING HOME TO A BIG, HAPPY FAMILY WAS ODDLY APPEALING, IF A LITTLE DIFFICULT TO IMAGINE.

BUT GETTING TO THAT POINT WAS MORE COMPLICATED THAN JUST TOSSING DAD'S POSSESSIONS INTO THE TRASH.

FOR SALE

COZY MID-CENTURY RANCH

PERFEC...

MOTIVA...

I COULD HAVE JUST THROWN IT ALL AWAY, I SUPPOSE, BUT LOOKING AT DAD'S STUFF PILED UP ON THE FLOOR MADE ME WANT TO DIG THROUGH IT ALL AND SEE WHAT THERE WAS TO SEE.

SURPRISINGLY, I FOUND MYSELF WISHING HE COULD HAVE BEEN THERE TO SHARE IT WITH ME HIMSELF, BUT IT WAS TOO LATE FOR THAT.

IT HAD BEEN TOO LATE FOR AS LONG AS I COULD REMEMBER.

3

IT SEEMED STRANGE TO THINK ABOUT MY FATHER IN THE PAST TENSE. HIS DEATH UNDERSCORED JUST HOW LITTLE I ACTUALLY KNEW ABOUT HIM.

WE WERE NOT A TALKATIVE FAMILY KEEN ON SHARING SECRETS. ABOUT MY PARENTS' EARLIER LIVES I LEARNED ONLY THE BASICS – WHO, WHAT, WHERE, DEFINITELY NOT WHY – FROM STRAY BITS OF CONVERSATION AND THE OCCASIONAL RELUCTANT RESPONSE TO DIRECT INQUIRY.

IN OUR HOUSE THE PAST TENDED TO STAY IN THE PAST...

POP! FWIZZ!

...EXCEPT WHEN IT CAME BACK TO HAUNT THE PRESENT.

I WAS SURPRISED AT HOW MUCH OF HIS PAST HE HELD ONTO.

EXCEPT FOR A FEW GLIMPSES NOW AND THEN, MOST OF THIS STUFF I'D NEVER SEEN BEFORE.

JUST THEN I PROBABLY WAS LOOKING AT MORE OF MY FATHER'S LIFE THAN HE'D EVER SHARED WHILE HE WAS ALIVE.

"SOMETIMES THE DEAD SAY MORE THAN THE LIVING."
BUT THE LIVING FEEL TOO GUILTY TO LISTEN.
WHAT *DID* I HAVE TO FEEL GUILTY ABOUT? MY FATHER DIED OF A STROKE BROUGHT ON BY HEART FAILURE THAT WAS A DECADE IN THE MAKING.
OKAY, SO I TURNED UP THE HEATER A LITTLE HIGH! HOW WAS I TO KNOW THAT WOULD RESURRECT HIS OLD CATHOLIC FEARS?
PIZZA BOY-O-BOY! PIZZA BOY-O-BOY!
WAS IT MY FAULT THAT AN 84 YEAR-OLD SCHOOL BOY HAD CONVINCED HIMSELF HE WAS GOING TO BAKE LIKE A POT ROAST IN THE LORD'S ALL-YOU-CAN-SUFFER DINER?

1930

MIND YOU, I COULD SEE WHY THE RELIGIOUS STUFF HAD STAYED WITH HIM, EVEN AFTER HIS OWN FAMILY FAILED TO EMBRACE IT.

CATHOLIC DOCTRINE HAD BEEN SLATHERED ON PRETTY THICK FROM A YOUNG AGE.

1940

I'M SURE THE FEAR OF PUNISHMENT WAS A BIG PART OF HIS CHILDHOOD GROWING UP IN THE LARGELY IMMIGRANT PHINNEY RIDGE NEIGHBORHOOD OF SEATTLE.

BUT PUNISHMENT FOR WHAT?

DAD WAS MANY THINGS, BUT A *BAD* PERSON DESERVING A LENGTHY VACAY IN PURGATORY... OR A PERMANENT RELO TO HELL?

FWIP!

76

MOM'S WARNING CAME TO MIND. I DIDN'T COME UP HERE TO GET STUCK IN THE PAST. BUT I ALSO COULDN'T OVERLOOK A CHANCE TO LEARN MORE ABOUT MY FATHER, IF FOR NO OTHER REASON SO I COULD ONCE AND FOR ALL SAY GOODBYE.

RUMMAGE RUMMAGE

I ONCE HEARD MOM SAY THAT MY GRANDMOTHER HAD WANTED DAD TO BECOME A PRIEST.

FROM PAROCHIAL KINDERGARTEN THROUGH HIGH SCHOOL, THAT WAS THE PATH SHE'D CHOSEN FOR HIM.

BUT THEN HIS FATHER DIED.

DAD WAS 16.

NO LONGER A SPOILED FIRST SON, SOON HE WOULD HAVE TO FIND WORK TO HELP SUPPORT HIS FIVE SISTERS AND ONE LITTLE BROTHER.

HE'D HAD A PAPER ROUTE WHEN HE WAS 12, JUST LONG ENOUGH TO SAVE UP $7 FOR A BIKE.

THIS WAS DIFFERENT. AFTER HIS FATHER'S MEAGER PENSION RAN OUT, THE OLDEST MOLITOR BOY HAD TO HELP PUT FOOD ON THE TABLE.

AS LUCK WOULD HAVE IT, LESS THAN A MILE FROM O'DEA HIGH SCHOOL WAS THE DOWNTOWN LOCATION OF A SWANKY SUPPER CLUB THAT WAS LOOKING FOR A YOUNG BELLHOP. WITHOUT ASKING PERMISSION FROM HIS MOTHER, HE INTERVIEWED FOR THE JOB AND WAS HIRED.

FOR THE NEXT COUPLE OF YEARS HE'D WALK TO THE CLUB AFTER SCHOOL, WORK A FULL SHIFT, THEN TAKE A LATE NIGHT BUS BACK HOME.

NEVER A BRILLIANT STUDENT IN THE BEST OF TIMES, HIS GRADES REALLY WENT DOWN AFTER HE STARTED WORKING.

I COULD ONLY IMAGINE HOW "THE BROTHERS" AT O'DEA REACTED, LET ALONE HIS MOTHER, WHO MUST HAVE WORRIED ABOUT HIS PRIESTLY PROSPECTS.

78

IF HE HAD AMBITIONS OF HIS OWN, HE HID THEM WELL BEHIND A FACADE OF JOKEY INDIFFERENCE.

GLUK!

RICHARD EDWARD MOLITOR - St. John's; Chimes 4; Pep Club 2; Stamp Club 2; Propagation of the Faith 3; Glee Club 1, 2; *Nickname:* "Dick"; *Favorite Pastime:* Anything connected with loafing, such as sleeping; *Ambition:* To build a rest home for the Brothers.

I WONDERED IF HE REALLY DIDN'T HAVE ANY PLANS FOR THE FUTURE OR IF HE'D JUST BECOME RESIGNED TO A FATE CHOSEN BY OTHERS.

THE ANONYMOUS AND TYPICALLY SOPHOMORIC CLASS PROPHECY FROM HIS GRADUATION YEARBOOK OFFERED LITTLE IN THE WAY OF ENCOURAGEMENT, ALTHOUGH ITS GLUM PREDICTION FOR 1967 AT LEAST PRESENTED A CAREER *HE* HAD CHOSEN, NOT HIS MOTHER OR THE CHURCH.

29

I glanced at the neon sign above my head: Northern Lights Motel, modern rooms 25¢ and up.
I decided to go in and have a look around and get a cup of coffee. DICK MOLITOR, the head bellhop, showed me the way to the cafeteria.

WHAT WITH SCHOOL AND THE JOB AT THE KLONDIKE KLUB, MAYBE HE JUST DIDN'T HAVE TIME FOR DREAMS.

AFTER HIGH SCHOOL, DAD MANAGED TO ENROLL IN COLLEGE. OF COURSE, IT WAS A JESUIT-RUN SCHOOL NOT FAR — PHYSICALLY AND THEOLOGICALLY — FROM O'DEA. THE BUS RIDES BECAME A BIT LONGER, BUT HE STILL MANAGED TO WORK FULL TIME AT THE CLUB WHILE BEGINNING HIS STUDIES IN INTERNATIONAL TRADE.

POP! FWIZZ!

GLUK!

A COPY OF HIS GRADES FROM THE FIRST YEAR AT SEATTLE U SUGGESTED HIS ATTITUDE TOWARD STUDYING HADN'T CHANGED MUCH SINCE HIGH SCHOOL.

THAT DIDN'T SURPRISE ME, AS I NEVER SAW DAD AS THE STUDIOUS SORT. HE'D ALWAYS BEEN QUICK TO RIDICULE ANYTHING THAT SMACKED OF INTELLECTUALISM.

I OFTEN THOUGHT THIS WAS A DEFENSE MECHANISM AND NOT-SO-SUBTLE HINT OF AN INFERIORITY COMPLEX, POSSIBLY THE RESULT OF WAITING ON CONDESCENDING HIGH SOCIETY FOLKS AT THE KLONDIKE KLUB.

WHAT DID STRIKE ME AS ODD ABOUT HIS TRANSCRIPT, HOWEVER, WAS THE COMPLETE ABSENCE OF RELIGIOUS SUBJECTS THAT FIRST YEAR.

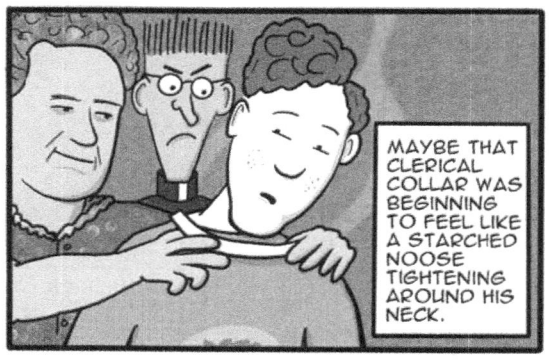

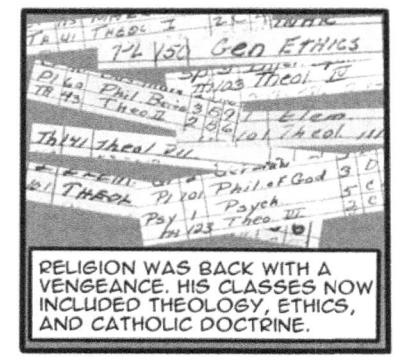

HAD HE HAD ENOUGH OF THE CHURCH? WAS IT AN OPEN ACT OF REBELLION AGAINST HIS MOTHER AND THE BROTHERS AT O'DEA?

MAYBE THAT CLERICAL COLLAR WAS BEGINNING TO FEEL LIKE A STARCHED NOOSE TIGHTENING AROUND HIS NECK.

AND YET...

FWIP!

...AFTER THE THREE YEAR HIATUS OF THE WAR, WHEN HE WAS BACK AT SEATTLE U ON THE G.I. BILL, HIS CURRICULUM DID EVOLVE SOMEWHAT.

RELIGION WAS BACK WITH A VENGEANCE. HIS CLASSES NOW INCLUDED THEOLOGY, ETHICS, AND CATHOLIC DOCTRINE.

DID THIS REFLECT THE LATEST ROUND OF PUSHING AND PRODDING FROM HIS MOTHER AS SHE RECLAIMED HER ROLE AS THE OFFICIAL PLANNER OF HIS FUTURE? OR HAD THERE BEEN A CHANGE, SOMETHING WROUGHT IN KOREA, PERHAPS?

OR, AS SEEMS MOST LIKELY, WAS IT JUST A CONCESSION, A TEMPORARY APPEASEMENT TO BUY TIME SO MAYBE FOR ONCE HE MIGHT CHART HIS OWN COURSE? IF THE YOUNG MAN SHARED THE TEMPERAMENT OF THE OLDER VERSION I GREW UP WITH, I COULD ONLY IMAGINE THE CONFLICTS BOTTLED UP INSIDE HIS HEAD.

IT'S TOUGH FIGURING OUT THE PLOT WHEN YOU DON'T EVEN KNOW ALL THE CHARACTERS.

HERE AND THERE I FOUND A FEW CAST BIOS...

...ALTHOUGH I DIDN'T KNOW FOR SURE THE ROLES THEY PLAYED.

O'Dea Staff
Brother Michael O'Flynn
History, Theology

*Dick,
Beware the guides who would lead you along a shadowed path.
Br. OF*

FWIP!

MOSTLY, I JUST FOUND NAMES AND FACES OF PEOPLE I'D NEVER KNOW.

SEATTLE STAR NEWS

Phinney Ridge Boys Sail for Korea

Robert Moreland, Frank Duquesne, Jack Valentino, and Dick Molitor are among nearly 5,000 soldiers departing for the Republic of Korea on board the U.S. Army transport ship, Daniel L. Sultan.

AND YET MORE MYSTERIES.

WHAT WAS THE DEAL WITH THE INKED-OUT FACE? HAD THERE BEEN A FALLING OUT AMONG THE "PHINNEY RIDGE BOYS?" IF SO, WHEN?

AND *WHY?*

TWO OF THE OTHER "BOYS" IN THE NEWSPAPER PHOTO WERE GRADUATING SENIORS FEATURED IN DAD'S O'DEA YEARBOOK. LIKE MANY OF THE OTHER STUDENT PORTRAITS, THEY WERE MARKED WITH AN *X* AND A DATE.

I GUESS HE'D BEEN KEEPING TRACK OF HIS CLASSMATES' MORTALITY.

SO ONE OF DAD'S BUDDIES HAD DIED IN KOREA.

I WONDERED IF HE'D BEEN THERE AND SEEN IT HAPPEN?

ONCE AGAIN, I REALIZED HOW LITTLE I KNEW ABOUT MY FATHER.

I DIDN'T EVEN KNOW WHY HE JOINED THE ARMY IN THE FIRST PLACE. AFTER A YEAR IN COLLEGE, WERE HIS MEDIOCRE GRADES TO BLAME? DID HE THINK A MILITARY CAREER WOULD BE LESS CHALLENGING?

ENOUGH QUESTIONS FOR ANOTHER SLEEPLESS NIGHT...

KA-CHOK!

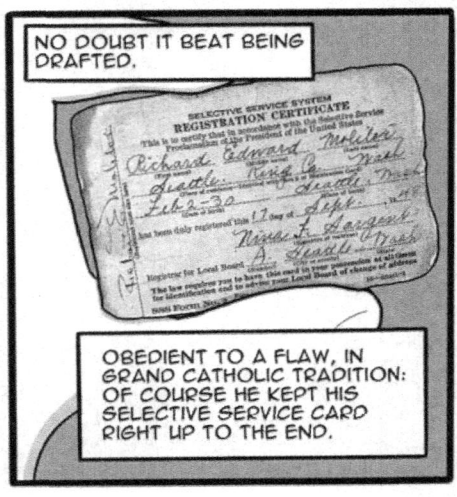

NOODGE NOODGE

MAYBE THE ANSWER TO WHY DAD ENLISTED IN THE ARMY WAS RIGHT IN FRONT OF ME.

NO DOUBT IT BEAT BEING DRAFTED.

OBEDIENT TO A FLAW, IN GRAND CATHOLIC TRADITION: OF COURSE HE KEPT HIS SELECTIVE SERVICE CARD RIGHT UP TO THE END.

REGARDLESS OF HOW OR WHY IT STARTED, I TOOK IT FOR GRANTED THAT MY FATHER'S SHORT MILITARY CAREER HAD A HUGE IMPACT ON THE ENTIRE LIFE THAT FOLLOWED.
G.I. JOE, G.I. JOE!
FIGHTING MAN FROM HEAD TO TOE!
ON THE LAND
ON THE SEA
IN THE AIR!
ARMY
HE REFUSED TO TALK ABOUT HIS EXPERIENCES, BUT MILITARY "HEROES" WERE BUILT INTO MY CHILDHOOD.

ONE THING I DID LEARN HAD TO DO WITH HIS ROLE AS A "RADIO MAN."
I REMEMBER MAKING A COMMENT ABOUT LUCKY RADIO GUYS STAYING OUT OF THE REAL FIGHTING.
CLEARLY IRRITATED, DAD CORRECTED ME. HE HAD BEEN IN THE THICK OF THINGS, HE SAID, BUT OFFERED NO MORE DETAILS.
RADIO CONTROLLED KILLBOT ACTIVATED
KILL! KILL! KILL!
SUBSEQUENTLY, I MADE UP AN ALTERNATE VIEW OF HIS EXPLOITS DURING THE WAR.
KILL! KILL! KILL!
*
*Confusion about the enemy was common in the '60s.
HINTS OF A DARKER REALITY CREPT IN VIA THE OCCASIONAL CONVERSATIONAL NON-SEQUITUR.
ALWAYS KEEP YOUR RIFLE LOADED! THAT WAY YOU CAN BLAST IT FREE IF YOUR BAYONET GETS STUCK IN A CHINK'S GUTS!
G.I. Joe and G.I. Joe theme song © Hasbro

IT WASN'T JUST COMBAT SHAPING DAD'S VIEWS. QUITE OBVIOUSLY THERE WERE OTHER ASPECTS OF ARMY LIFE THAT AFFECTED HIS ATTITUDES...

I STOOD IN ENOUGH LINES IN THE ARMY. WE DON'T NEED TO SEE SOME FISH MOVIE!

...AS WELL AS HIS EXPECTATIONS FOR WHERE MY LIFE WOULD LEAD.

I CAN'T WAIT UNTIL YOU'RE IN THE ARMY!

MAYBE THEN YOU'LL LEARN TO DO AS YOU'RE TOLD!

IF THERE WERE ONE PRINCIPLE THAT GUIDED MY FATHER'S PARENTING, IT WAS THE RULE THAT YOU DID WHAT YOU WERE TOLD, NOT BECAUSE IT WAS RIGHT – THOUGH IT MIGHT BE – BUT BECAUSE SOMEONE WHO WAS HIGHER UP KNEW BETTER THAN YOU.

A MILITARY OFFICER, A PRIEST OR A NUN, A GOVERNMENT BUREAUCRAT OR A PARENT, THE NATURE OF THEIR POSITION GAVE THEM A BIG STICK – METAPHORICAL OR REAL – AND THE AUTHORITY TO DICTATE.

YOU DISOBEYED AT YOUR OWN PERIL.

NO QUESTIONS.
NO DOUBT.
NO NON-BELIEF.

IN SPITE OF DAD'S RELUCTANCE TO SPEAK OF HIS OWN MILITARY DAYS, HE LEFT LITTLE DOUBT ABOUT HIS VIEWS ON THE SUBJECT IN GENERAL. I WAS RAISED IN AN ERA OF UNABASHED MARTIAL PLAY.
GO GET 'EM BOYS!
EXPLODING ARMY HAND GRENADE only $1.00!
TV
FIGHT! FIGHT! FIGHT!
DESPITE ALL THAT, I NEVER QUITE GOT THE HANG OF IT.
UT-UT-UT-UT-UT!
YOUR GUN SOUNDS LIKE A GIRL'S FART!
NEIGHBORHOOD BULLY
THIS IS HOW IT'S S'POSED TO SOUND!
KHKHKHKHKH KHKHKHKHKH KHKHKH!
MAYBE THAT'S WHY THAT LITTLE BOY PRETTY QUICKLY OUTGREW THE ACTION FIGURES AND PLASTIC GUNS, AND BEGAN TO SEE THE WHOLE ENTERPRISE IN LESS THAN HEROIC TERMS.
TV image based on "The Terror of War" by Nick Ut, © The Associated Press
WHICH LAID THE FOUNDATION FOR THE USUAL VOLLEYS ACROSS THE GENERATION GAP.
McGOVERN
EAGLETON
Shriver

OF COURSE IT WAS MORE COMPLICATED THAN THAT. SOONER OR LATER, EVERY BOY MUST BECOME HIS OWN MAN...
...AND DECIDE FOR HIMSELF WHAT'S RIGHT AND WRONG.
YAP! YAP!
!#%!*#@!!
DIG! DIG!
DIG! DIG!
?
POP!
YIPE!
GASP!
YIPE! YIPE! YIPE!
I FOUND MYSELF WONDERING, FOR HOW MANY YEARS WAS HE RECITING THAT PURGATORY PRAYER?

CLEARLY, DAD HAD ISSUES. ANGER MANAGEMENT WAS ONE, INTOLERANCE OF NONCONFORMITY ANOTHER.
WITH THAT COMBINATION, IT WAS ONLY A MATTER OF TIME BEFORE WE CLASHED.
AND YET, SURPRISINGLY, IT TOOK HIM A LONG TIME TO FIGURE OUT I WASN'T THE TYPE TO FOLLOW EAGERLY IN ANYONE'S FOOTSTEPS.
1979
Daniel Steven Molitor
I WAS WELL INTO ADOLESCENCE BEFORE HE NOTICED HIS INNOCENT LITTLE BOY WASN'T QUITE SO INNOCENT.
UNLIKE HIM, I'D VERY QUICKLY DISCOVERED THAT THE PEOPLE IN CHARGE DIDN'T ALWAYS HAVE THE ANSWERS I WAS LOOKING FOR.
KLIK!
AND I DIDN'T HESITATE TO LOOK FOR ALTERNATIVE SOURCES OF INFORMATION.

DISCOVERING WHO YOU ARE, FOR REAL, ON THE INSIDE, AND FULLY BECOMING THAT PERSON, AS OPPOSED TO TRYING TO PRETEND YOU'RE SOMEONE THAT SOMEBODY ELSE THINKS YOU ARE, IS EXHILARATING.

I DON'T KNOW THAT MY FATHER EVER EXPERIENCED THAT THRILL. I SUSPECT HE NEVER REALLY KNEW HIMSELF, ONLY THE BOY AND LATER THE MAN OTHER PEOPLE WANTED HIM TO BE.

LOOKING BACK, THOSE STOLEN NIGHTS WERE SOME OF THE FEW BRIGHT SPOTS IN AN OTHERWISE RATHER DARK ADOLESCENCE.

TWEEEEEEEEEEE....!

I DON'T KNOW HOW EITHER MOM OR DAD MISSED IT. EVEN WHEN I WAS A LITTLE KID IT SHOULD HAVE BEEN OBVIOUS I WASN'T TAKING THOSE MACHO ARMY MAN ROLE MODELS TO HEART.

WHEN I WAS IN THE FIRST OR SECOND GRADE, DAD TOOK ME TO A COUPLE OF FOOTBALL GAMES AT THE LOCAL CATHOLIC HIGH SCHOOL, MOSTLY, I SUSPECTED AT THE TIME, BECAUSE THEY WERE FREE AND HE DIDN'T HAVE MUCH MONEY...

...BUT NOW I REALIZE HE MIGHT HAVE BEEN TRYING TO DO SOMETHING HE NEVER GOT TO DO WHEN *HE* WAS A KID.

HE TRIED TO EXPLAIN THE GAME TO ME AND GET ME INTERESTED IN THE COMPETIVE ANGLE OF IT ALL.

I DID MY BEST.

YAY TEAM! KICK A HOME RUN!

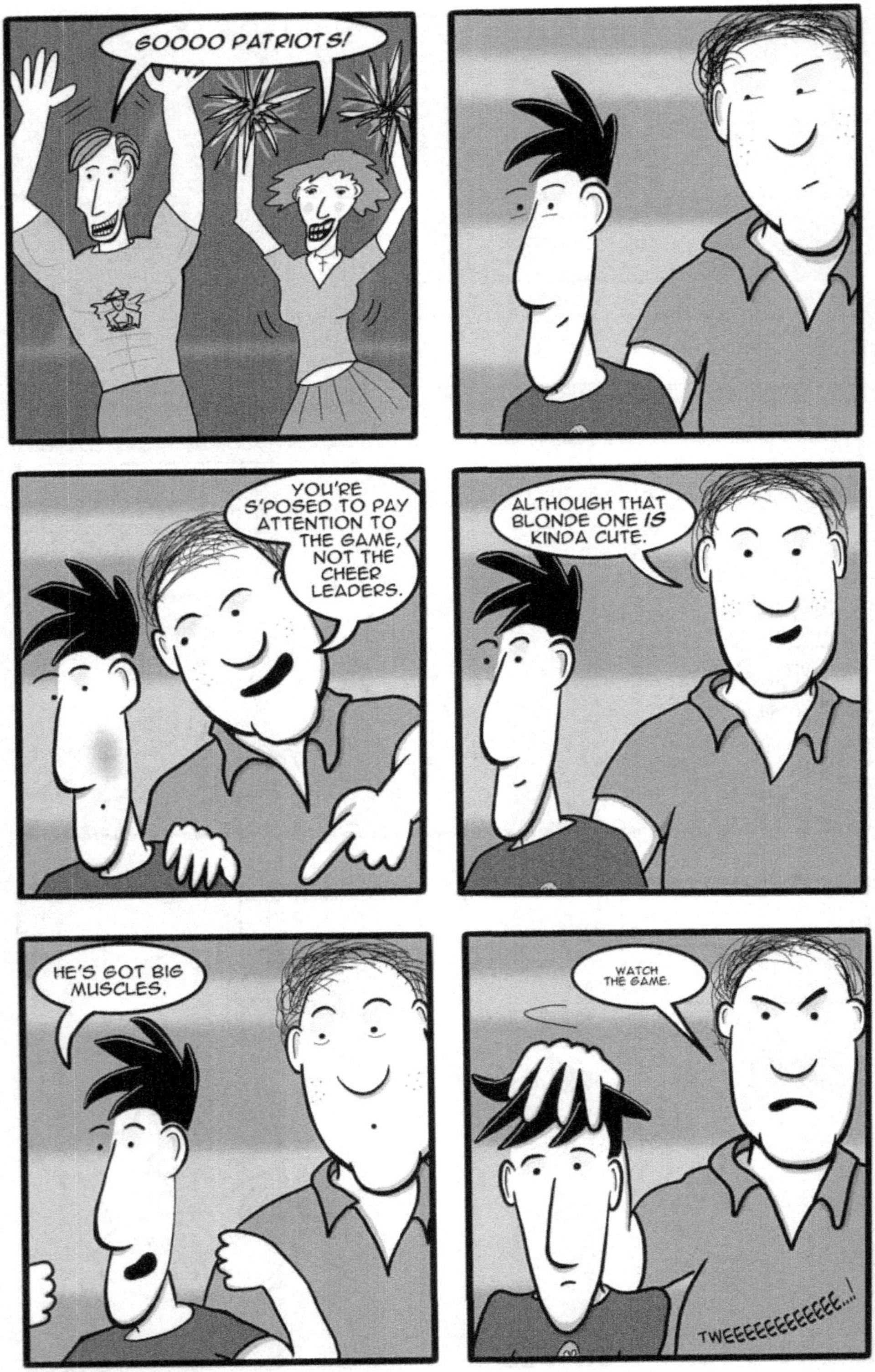
GOOOO PATRIOTS!
YOU'RE S'POSED TO PAY ATTENTION TO THE GAME, NOT THE CHEER LEADERS.
ALTHOUGH THAT BLONDE ONE *IS* KINDA CUTE.
HE'S GOT BIG MUSCLES.
WATCH THE GAME.
TWEEEEEEEEEEEEE...!

AN EX-THERAPIST OF MINE ONCE RESPONDED TO ONE OF MY COMPLAINTS ABOUT DAD BY EARNESTLY PROCLAIMING, "HE WAS A MONSTER!"
THE COMMENT SHOCKED ME.
"NO, HE WASN'T!" I SAID, SURPRISED AT HOW ANGRY I'D BECOME. "HE TRIED HIS BEST BUT HE JUST WASN'T VERY GOOD AT BEING A PARENT."
FOR SALE
I THINK THAT WAS THE FIRST TIME I EVER ACKNOWLEDGED MY FATHER'S FRAILTY.
...EEEEEEEEEEE!
SLLRRP!
MANY YEARS AGO, BEFORE WHATEVER IT WAS EATING AWAY AT HIS SOUL HAD DONE ITS WORST, DAD HAD BEEN MY HERO.
ONE TIME, BACK WHEN I WAS IN GRADE SCHOOL...

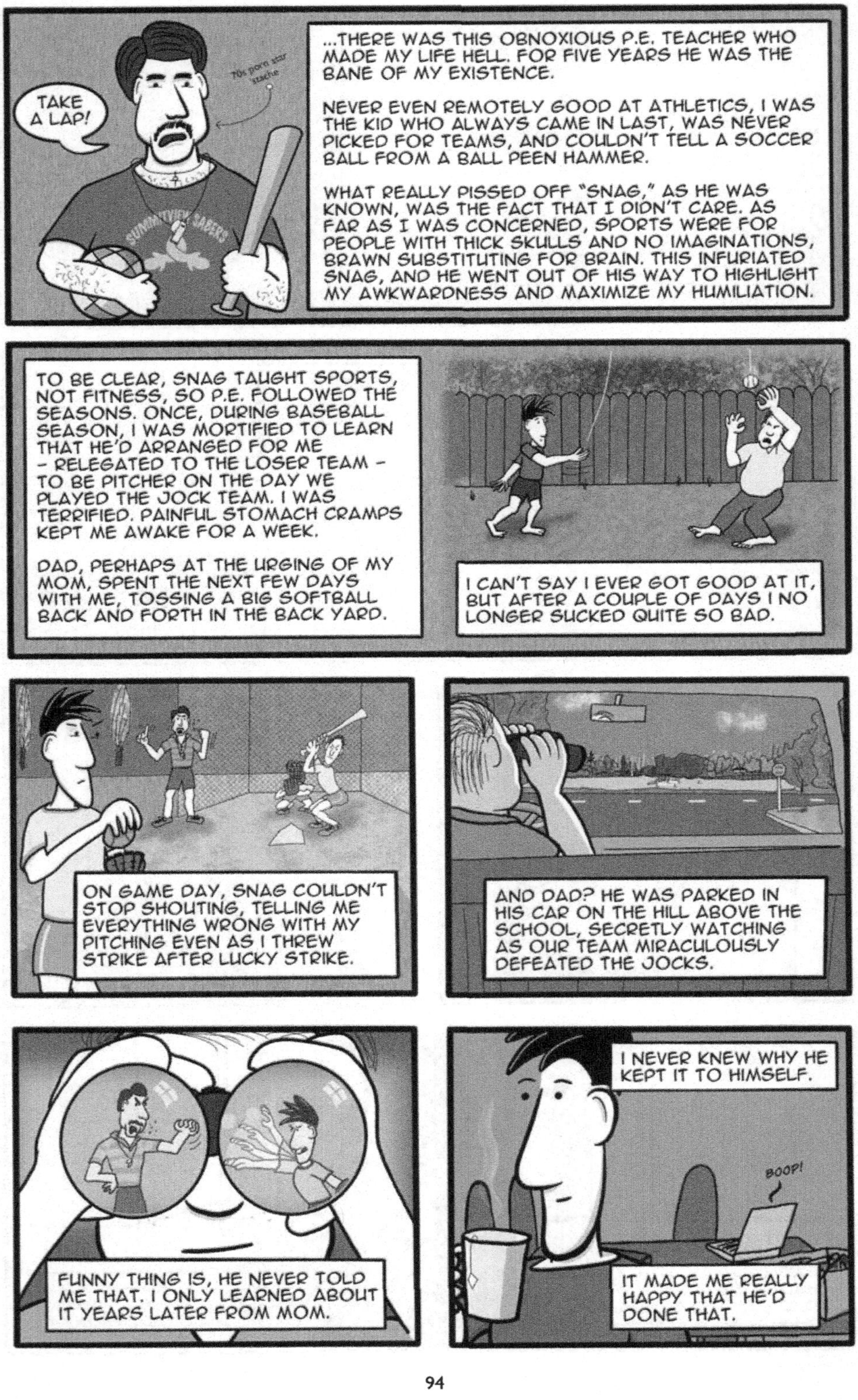
TAKE A LAP!
70s porn star 'stache
SUMMITVIEW SABERS
...THERE WAS THIS OBNOXIOUS P.E. TEACHER WHO MADE MY LIFE HELL. FOR FIVE YEARS HE WAS THE BANE OF MY EXISTENCE.
NEVER EVEN REMOTELY GOOD AT ATHLETICS, I WAS THE KID WHO ALWAYS CAME IN LAST, WAS NEVER PICKED FOR TEAMS, AND COULDN'T TELL A SOCCER BALL FROM A BALL PEEN HAMMER.
WHAT REALLY PISSED OFF "SNAG," AS HE WAS KNOWN, WAS THE FACT THAT I DIDN'T CARE. AS FAR AS I WAS CONCERNED, SPORTS WERE FOR PEOPLE WITH THICK SKULLS AND NO IMAGINATIONS, BRAWN SUBSTITUTING FOR BRAIN. THIS INFURIATED SNAG, AND HE WENT OUT OF HIS WAY TO HIGHLIGHT MY AWKWARDNESS AND MAXIMIZE MY HUMILIATION.
TO BE CLEAR, SNAG TAUGHT SPORTS, NOT FITNESS, SO P.E. FOLLOWED THE SEASONS. ONCE, DURING BASEBALL SEASON, I WAS MORTIFIED TO LEARN THAT HE'D ARRANGED FOR ME - RELEGATED TO THE LOSER TEAM - TO BE PITCHER ON THE DAY WE PLAYED THE JOCK TEAM. I WAS TERRIFIED. PAINFUL STOMACH CRAMPS KEPT ME AWAKE FOR A WEEK.
DAD, PERHAPS AT THE URGING OF MY MOM, SPENT THE NEXT FEW DAYS WITH ME, TOSSING A BIG SOFTBALL BACK AND FORTH IN THE BACK YARD.
I CAN'T SAY I EVER GOT GOOD AT IT, BUT AFTER A COUPLE OF DAYS I NO LONGER SUCKED QUITE SO BAD.
ON GAME DAY, SNAG COULDN'T STOP SHOUTING, TELLING ME EVERYTHING WRONG WITH MY PITCHING EVEN AS I THREW STRIKE AFTER LUCKY STRIKE.
AND DAD? HE WAS PARKED IN HIS CAR ON THE HILL ABOVE THE SCHOOL, SECRETLY WATCHING AS OUR TEAM MIRACULOUSLY DEFEATED THE JOCKS.
FUNNY THING IS, HE NEVER TOLD ME THAT. I ONLY LEARNED ABOUT IT YEARS LATER FROM MOM.
I NEVER KNEW WHY HE KEPT IT TO HIMSELF.
BOOP!
IT MADE ME REALLY HAPPY THAT HE'D DONE THAT.

HI.
HEY, SUNSHINE! DON'T YOU LOOK JOYFUL! DISCOVERING GOOD THINGS ABOUT DEAR OLD DAD?
HARDLY. ALL I HAVE IS BOX UPON BOX OF MYSTERIES.
WELL, THE GUY WAS COMPLICATED. YOU ALWAYS KNEW THAT.
I FEEL LIKE I MISSED SOMETHING. MAYBE IF I HAD PAID MORE ATTENTION HE WOULDN'T HAVE -
- THOUGHT HE WAS GOING TO HELL?
MOM SAID HE WANTED TO TELL ME SOMETHING, BUT I WAS IN TOO BIG A HURRY TO LISTEN.
NOW ALL I'VE GOT ARE PILES OF HIS OLD JUNK.
MAYBE HE JUST WANTED TO SAY HE LOVED YOU.
IF THAT WERE TRUE, HIS LAST WORD WOULD HAVE BEEN "COLD"...
..BECAUSE HELL WOULD BE FREEZING OVER.
NASTY BITCH.
?

WHAT ARE YOU LOOKING AT?
ANOTHER OF DAD'S BOXES. IT LOOKS LIKE HIS MILITARY STUFF. PATCHES AND PAPER, PHOTOGRAPHS. GEEZ, HE KEPT IT ALL, HIDDEN AWAY FROM EVERYONE.
COULD BE HE WAS HIDING IT FROM HIMSELF. HE WAS JUST A KID BACK THEN. THE THINGS THAT MEANT SOMETHING WHEN HE WAS YOUNG MIGHT HAVE TAKEN ON A DIFFERENT MEANING BY THE TIME HE GOT OLD.
MY MILITARY MISSAL
KODAK
Your Military Life
TWENTY YEN
ROBBIE
THIS COULD BE A CHANCE TO SEE HIS LIFE THE WAY HE DID, AS A YOUNG MAN, NOT AS YOUR FATHER.
HEY, I GOTTA GET BACK TO MY SHIFT. YOU'RE OKAY, RIGHT?
YEAH, I'M FINE.
OKAY. HANG IN THERE.
SEE YA.

MAYBE ROBBIE WAS RIGHT.
I'D BEEN LOOKING AT MY FATHER'S THINGS FROM THE POINT OF VIEW OF AN OLD GEEZER.
I NEEDED TO SEE THEM THROUGH THE EYES OF A YOUNG MAN JUST A FEW YEARS REMOVED FROM A SHELTERED CATHOLIC ALTAR BOY.
ALTHOUGH STILL, I HAD TO WONDER...
...HAD THAT NAIVE LITTLE ALTAR BOY EVER *REALLY* GONE AWAY, OR DID HE JUST GO INTO HIDING, LIKE THIS BOX OF MEMORIES?

COME TO THINK OF IT, I HAD SEEN THIS PARTICULAR BOX BEFORE.

I REMEMBER DAD HOLDING IT, GAZING SILENTLY AT ITS CONTENTS.

WHATCHA LOOKIN' AT?

SNAP!

NOTHING.

SHOOF!

ARMY STUFF? CAN I SEE?

NO!

SOMEONE WHO DIDN'T LIVE THROUGH IT WOULDN'T UNDERSTAND!

EVEN AS A KID I KNEW THAT WAS B.S. IF WE COULD ONLY UNDERSTAND OUR OWN EXPERIENCES, WHY BOTHER TALKING ABOUT ANYTHING ELSE?
DAD WASN'T PROTECTING ME FROM SOMETHING I WOULDN'T UNDERSTAND. HE WAS SHIELDING HIMSELF FROM SOMETHING *HE* DIDN'T WANT TO FACE.
AND FRANKLY, I'D HAD ENOUGH OF HIS SECRETS.
DUMP!

IT WAS A BIT DAUNTING...

...BUT THE FIRST THING I PULLED FROM THE PILE CAME WITH A SURPRISE.

DAD GRADUATED FROM O'DEA IN JUNE, 1947. I KNEW HE'D BEEN IN THE MARINE CORPS RESERVE BEFORE JOINING THE REGULAR ARMY, BUT I DIDN'T KNOW THAT HE SIGNED UP WHILE STILL A SENIOR IN HIGH SCHOOL.

WAS THIS A LINE DRAWN IN THE SAND, AN ACT OF DEFIANCE TO LET HIS MOTHER KNOW HE WAS *NOT* RESIGNED TO JOINING THE PRIESTHOOD? PERHAPS THE THREAT OF A MILITARY CAREER WAS WHAT IT TOOK TO WIN HER APPROVAL AND ALLOW HIM TO ATTEND BUSINESS CLASSES AT SEATTLE UNIVERSITY.

THE SUMMER AFTER GRADUATING, HE APPARENTLY SPENT TWO WEEKS IN BASIC TRAINING AT CAMP PENDLETON IN SOUTHERN CALIFORNIA.

THAT WOULD HAVE BEEN QUITE AN ADVENTURE FOR A KID STILL FIVE MONTHS SHY OF EIGHTEEN.

HE SENT HOME A TROVE OF POST CARDS, WHICH HE MUST HAVE RETRIEVED AFTER HIS MOTHER PASSED AWAY IN 1972.

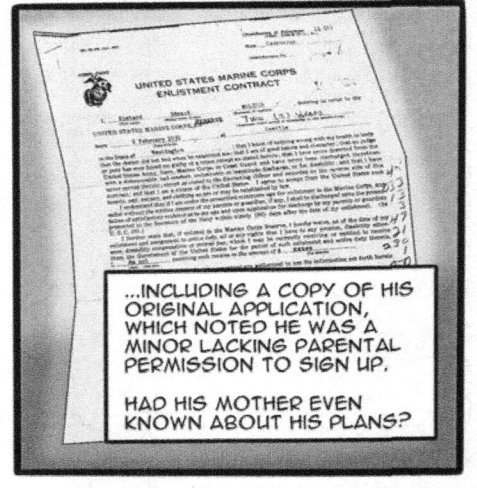

THERE WAS NO TRACE OF ANIMOSITY OR DEFIANCE IN THE CORRESPONDENCE.

IN FACT, SHORTLY AFTER HIS DEPARTURE HE SEEMED TO MAKE AN EFFORT TO CONVINCE HER HE HADN'T FORGOTTEN THE CHURCH.

ALL HIS RECORDS FROM THE USMC WERE THERE IN THE PILE...

...INCLUDING A COPY OF HIS ORIGINAL APPLICATION, WHICH NOTED HE WAS A MINOR LACKING PARENTAL PERMISSION TO SIGN UP.

HAD HIS MOTHER EVEN KNOWN ABOUT HIS PLANS?

OF COURSE.

THE MARKS HE EARNED DURING HIS RESERVE EXPERIENCE WERE PRETTY MUCH AVERAGE EXCEPT FOR TWO CATEGORIES IN WHICH HE EXCELLED: SOBRIETY AND OBEDIENCE.

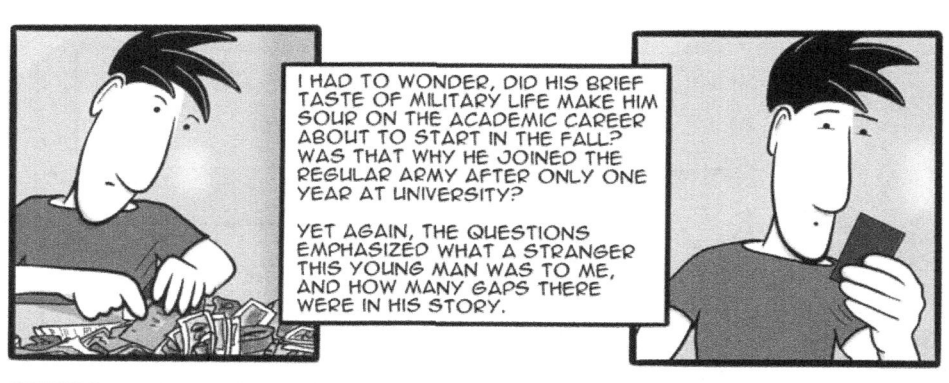

I HAD TO WONDER, DID HIS BRIEF TASTE OF MILITARY LIFE MAKE HIM SOUR ON THE ACADEMIC CAREER ABOUT TO START IN THE FALL? WAS THAT WHY HE JOINED THE REGULAR ARMY AFTER ONLY ONE YEAR AT UNIVERSITY?

YET AGAIN, THE QUESTIONS EMPHASIZED WHAT A STRANGER THIS YOUNG MAN WAS TO ME, AND HOW MANY GAPS THERE WERE IN HIS STORY.

BUT THEN, SOME OF THOSE GAPS WERE ABOUT TO BE FILLED IN.

FLIP! FLIP!

IN A TINY NOTEBOOK FILLED WITH HIS OWN TIGHTLY PRINTED WRITING WAS A COMPLETE RECORD OF ALL THE CAMPS AND BASES TO WHICH HE'D BEEN POSTED, FROM HIS INITIAL ENLISTMENT AND TRAINING TO HIS RETURN FROM OVERSEAS AND FINAL MUSTERING OUT.

TWO ROCK RANCH STN, CAL
2 DEC 49   3 JAN 50

CAMP STONEMAN, CAL.
3 JAN 50   10 JAN 50

USAT DANIEL L. SULTAN
10 JAN 50   25 JAN 50

HQ & HQ CO. (ASAPAC)
TOKYO, JAPAN
25 JAN 50   7 FEB 50

126TH SIG. SV. CO.
KYOTO, JAPAN
7 FEB 50   23 JUL 51

126TH SIG. SV. CO.
CHUNCHON, KOREA
23 JUL 51 - AUG. 51

326TH COMM RECON CO
SEOUL, KOREA
8 AUG 51   13 MAR 52

HQ & HQ CO. (ASAPAC)
TOKYO, JAPAN
13 MAR 52   19 MAR 52

327TH COMM RECON CO
NAHA, OKINAWA
19 MAR 52

INCLUDED IN THE LITTLE BOOK WAS YET ANOTHER SURPRISE: OUT OF THE 3-1/2 YEARS HE SERVED IN THE ARMY, LESS THAN 8 MONTHS WERE ACTUALLY SPENT IN KOREA.

126TH SIG. SV. CO.
CHUNCHON, KOREA
23 JUL 51 - AUG. 51

326TH COMM RECON CO
SEOUL, KOREA
8 AUG 51   13 MAR 52

I THOUGHT IT HAD BEEN FOREVER.

PIECING TOGETHER THE CRAZY QUILT OF MY FATHER'S LIFE, IT HAD BECOME OBVIOUS THERE WERE PIECES MISSING AND PROBABLY LOST FOREVER. BUT SOME NEW SQUARES HAD BEEN ADDED AND FAINT HINTS OF A PATTERN WERE BEGINNING TO EMERGE.

I FOUND IT IMPOSSIBLE TO IGNORE THE OCCASIONAL DARK THREADS WOVEN INTO THE FABRIC, HIDDEN AMONG THE VARYING COLORS AND STITCHED-TOGETHER REMNANTS, BUT UNDENIABLY THERE.

WHEN DID THOSE THREADS FIRST BECOME A PART OF HIS STORY? WHAT WAS THEIR SOURCE AND WHY DID IT HAUNT HIM HIS ENTIRE LIFE?

AND WHY, THE LAST OF MY EVER MORE PRETENTIOUS QUESTIONS ASKED, DID THOSE THREADS SEEM TO WRAP AROUND HIS PSYCHE LIKE A SLOWLY TIGHTENING NOOSE?

LOOKING THROUGH HIS MEMORABILIA REINFORCED MY SUSPICION THAT THE ANSWERS WOULD BE FOUND WITHIN THE SHORT SPAN OF TIME HE SPENT IN KOREA DURING THE WAR.

I HAD TO DISCOVER MORE ABOUT WHAT WENT ON BACK THEN...

...AND LEARN WHAT CAUSED HIM TO BECOME SO AFRAID OF ALL THAT CAME AFTER.

104

4

GOING THROUGH MY FATHER'S LONG-HIDDEN MILITARY STUFF SENT ME ON A JOURNEY BACK IN TIME DETERMINED TO FIND OUT WHY HIS EXPERIENCES DURING THE KOREAN WAR HAD LEFT HIM WITH SUCH DEEPLY HIDDEN MENTAL SCARS.

THE SMALL, HAND WRITTEN NOTEBOOK I'D FOUND OFFERED MORE INFORMATION ABOUT HIS ARMY CAREER THAN I'D EVER SEEN BEFORE.

THIS LITTLE BOOK WOULD BE MY GUIDE AS I CONTINUED TO SEARCH FOR THE YOUNG MAN WHO WOULD BECOME MY DAD.

I'D ALREADY HAD ONE SURPRISE. ALL HIS LIFE HE'D MADE A BIG DEAL ABOUT BEING IN THE MARINES. I'D KNOWN IT WAS ONLY THE MARINE CORPS *RESERVE*, BUT THE ID CARD STASHED WITH HIS OTHER MILITARY MATERIAL REVEALED THAT HE'D BEEN A MEMBER FOR JUST A LITTLE OVER A YEAR. APART FROM A FEW CLASSES IN SEATTLE, HE'D SPENT JUST ONE TWO-WEEK PERIOD IN ABBREVIATED BASIC TRAINING AT CAMP PENDLETON IN SOUTHERN CALIFORNIA.

SO, YEAH, I GUESS HE EARNED THE RIGHT TO PUT A BUMPER STICKER ON EVERY CAR I EVER SAW HIM DRIVE, BUT JEEZ, HE SURE GOT A LOT OF MILEAGE OUT OF THOSE TWO WEEKS.

SEPT 1948

BUT NOW THE STORY REALLY PICKS UP, AS DAD AND THREE OTHER "PHINNEY RIDGE BOYS" CLIMB ABOARD AN ARMY TROOP TRAIN BOUND FOR DISTANT LANDS...

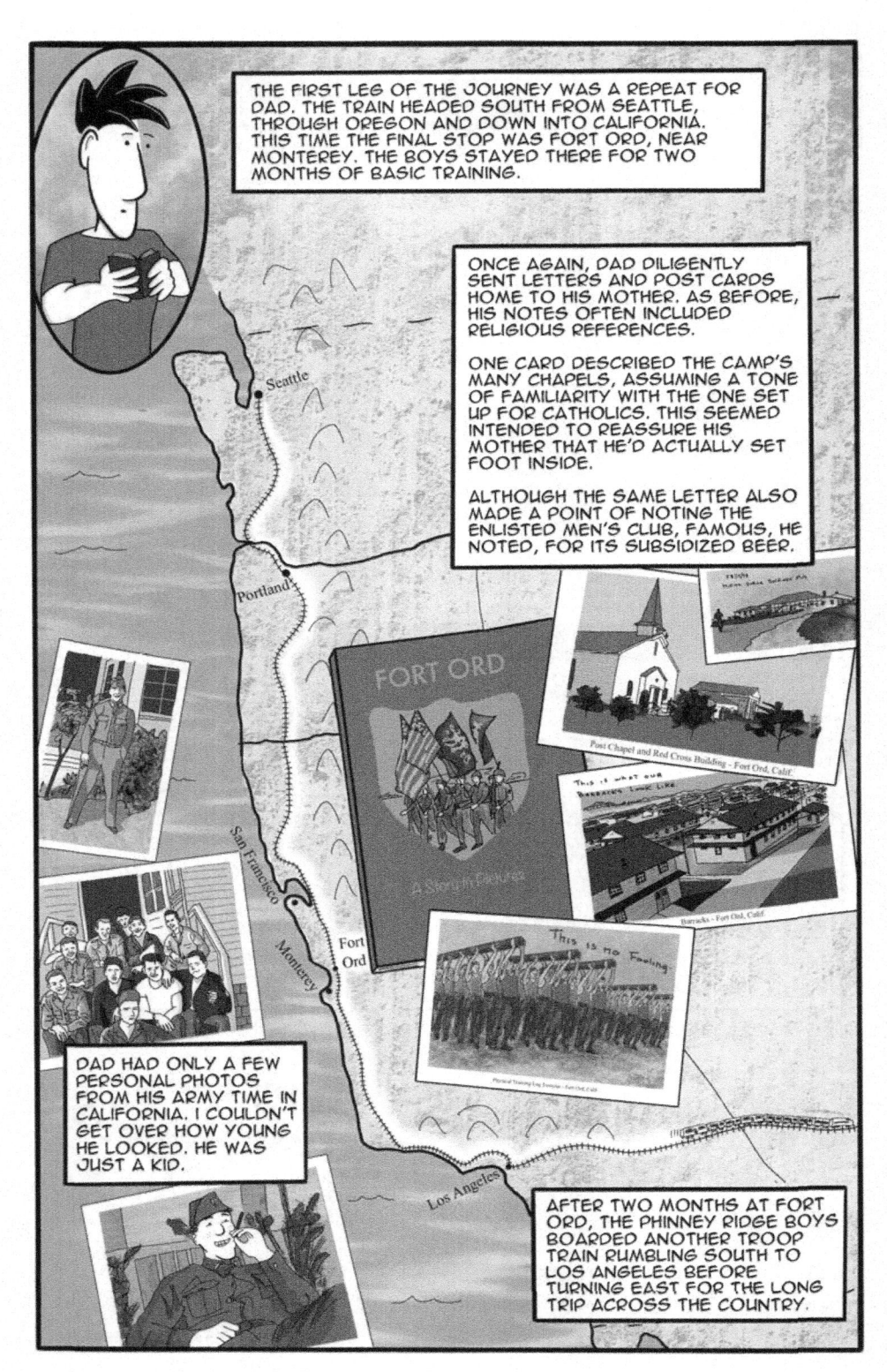

THE FIRST LEG OF THE JOURNEY WAS A REPEAT FOR DAD. THE TRAIN HEADED SOUTH FROM SEATTLE, THROUGH OREGON AND DOWN INTO CALIFORNIA. THIS TIME THE FINAL STOP WAS FORT ORD, NEAR MONTEREY. THE BOYS STAYED THERE FOR TWO MONTHS OF BASIC TRAINING.

ONCE AGAIN, DAD DILIGENTLY SENT LETTERS AND POST CARDS HOME TO HIS MOTHER. AS BEFORE, HIS NOTES OFTEN INCLUDED RELIGIOUS REFERENCES.

ONE CARD DESCRIBED THE CAMP'S MANY CHAPELS, ASSUMING A TONE OF FAMILIARITY WITH THE ONE SET UP FOR CATHOLICS. THIS SEEMED INTENDED TO REASSURE HIS MOTHER THAT HE'D ACTUALLY SET FOOT INSIDE.

ALTHOUGH THE SAME LETTER ALSO MADE A POINT OF NOTING THE ENLISTED MEN'S CLUB, FAMOUS, HE NOTED, FOR ITS SUBSIDIZED BEER.

DAD HAD ONLY A FEW PERSONAL PHOTOS FROM HIS ARMY TIME IN CALIFORNIA. I COULDN'T GET OVER HOW YOUNG HE LOOKED. HE WAS JUST A KID.

AFTER TWO MONTHS AT FORT ORD, THE PHINNEY RIDGE BOYS BOARDED ANOTHER TROOP TRAIN RUMBLING SOUTH TO LOS ANGELES BEFORE TURNING EAST FOR THE LONG TRIP ACROSS THE COUNTRY.

THREE DAYS AND NIGHTS LATER THEY ARRIVED AT THE SIGNAL CORPS TRAINING CENTER AT CAMP GORDON, GEORGIA, WHERE THEY'D REMAIN FOR CLOSE TO A YEAR.

WHEN THEY'D ENLISTED, ALL THE PHINNEY RIDGE BOYS INDICATED A PREFERENCE FOR RADIO INTELLIGENCE WORK WITH THE ARMY SECURITY AGENCY. I SUSPECTED, BUT DIDN'T KNOW FOR SURE, THEY THOUGHT THIS MIGHT KEEP THEM OUT OF THE ACTUAL FIGHTING.

THE ACCOMMODATIONS WEREN'T QUITE AS LUXE AS THEY'D ENJOYED AT FORT ORD, BUT THERE WERE OTHER AMENITIES NEARBY.

PHOTOS FROM THIS TIME DOCUMENT VACATION DAYS IN AUGUSTA, SAVANNAH, TAMPA, AND PARTS IN-BETWEEN. THE BOYS AND THEIR NEW ARMY PALS WERE SEEING PARTS OF THE COUNTRY THEY'D PROBABLY NEVER HEARD OF BEFORE.

DAD STILL KEPT UP WITH LETTERS AND CARDS TO HIS MOTHER. A FAN OF FRANKLIN ROOSEVELT, SHE MUST HAVE BEEN THRILLED WITH THE OFFICIAL PORTRAIT HE SENT FROM FDR'S "LITTLE WHITE HOUSE" IN GEORGIA. ALTHOUGH PERHAPS SHE'D HAVE BEEN HAPPIER IF HE'D SENT A PORTRAIT OF *HIMSELF* IN AN ARMY CHAPLAIN'S UNIFORM.

EVENTUALLY, IN NOVEMBER, 1949, DAD AND THE REST SPENT A COUPLE OF WEEKS AT THE ASA'S HUSH-HUSH OPERATIONS CENTER AT VINT HILL FARMS STATION IN VIRGINIA. THIS IS WHERE HE RECEIVED HIS FINAL TRAINING IN RADIO SIGNAL INTERCEPTION AND HIGH SPEED MORSE CODE.

JUDGING FROM PHOTOS IN HIS COLLECTION, HE ALSO HAD TIME OFF TO EXPLORE WASHINGTON, D.C., AND SEVERAL OLD CIVIL WAR SITES. STUDYING *THAT* WAR WOULD BECOME SOMETHING OF A PASSION IN LATER YEARS...OR AT LEAST THE CLOSEST THING TO A PASSION I EVER SAW IN HIM.

MEANWHILE, 11 THOUSAND MILES AWAY IN KOREA, THE CURRENT WAR RAGED ON. MY KNOWLEDGE OF THIS ERA WAS WOEFULLY INADEQUATE.

"THE FORGOTTEN WAR," AS IT'S BEEN LABELED, NEVER REALLY MONOPOLIZED THE NATION'S ATTENTION, AT LEAST NOT THE WAY THE NEXT ONE IN THE SERIES, VIETNAM, CONSUMED BOTH ITS CHAMPIONS AND OPPONENTS.

FOR MY GENERATION, KOREA SLIPPED THROUGH THE CRACKS. ABSENT ANY INSIGHT FROM MY FATHER, I LEARNED NEXT TO NOTHING ABOUT THE WAR IN 12 YEARS OF PUBLIC SCHOOLING.

LIKE SO MUCH OF THAT ERA, IT HAD ITS ROOTS IN THE AMBITIONS OF THE WWII VICTORS. THE SOVIET UNION WANTED ITS SPHERE OF INFLUENCE TO BE AS WIDE AS POSSIBLE, AS DID THE UNITED STATES AND CHINA.

IN KOREA, THE SOVIETS HAD BEEN RESPONSIBLE FOR REMOVING THE IMPERIAL JAPANESE PRESENCE NORTH OF THE 38TH PARALLEL. THE U.S. TOOK CONTROL OF EVERYTHING SOUTH OF THAT LINE, WHICH, IN 1948, BECAME THE BORDER OF TWO SEPARATE KOREAS, THE REPUBLIC OF KOREA IN THE SOUTH AND THE DEMOCRATIC PEOPLE'S REPUBLIC OF KOREA IN THE NORTH.

IN JUNE OF 1950, NORTHERN FORCES INVADED THE SOUTH. THE UNITED NATIONS AUTHORIZED A MILITARY RESPONSE AND OVER 20 COUNTRIES SENT TROOPS IN WHAT WAS DESCRIBED AS A "POLICE ACTION." THE U.S. CONTRIBUTED BY FAR THE MOST MEN AND RESOURCES – INCLUDING RAPIDLY AGING WWII EQUIPMENT – AND EFFECTIVELY LED THE EFFORT.

THE DPRK ARMY QUICKLY ADVANCED SOUTH, ALMOST TAKING THE ENTIRE PENINSULA, BUT THE U.N. FORCES, LED BY GENERAL DOUGLAS MACARTHUR, STAGED AN AMPHIBIOUS LANDING AT INCHEON, WEST OF THE SOUTH KOREAN CAPITAL OF SEOUL, CUTTING NORTHERN SUPPLY LINES AND FORCING A RAPID RETREAT BACK NORTH.

MACARTHUR PUSHED THE BATTLE PAST THE 38TH PARALLEL TOWARD THE YALU RIVER AND THE BORDER WITH CHINA.

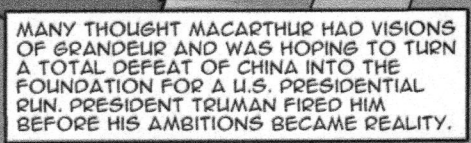

MANY THOUGHT MACARTHUR HAD VISIONS OF GRANDEUR AND WAS HOPING TO TURN A TOTAL DEFEAT OF CHINA INTO THE FOUNDATION FOR A U.S. PRESIDENTIAL RUN. PRESIDENT TRUMAN FIRED HIM BEFORE HIS AMBITIONS BECAME REALITY.

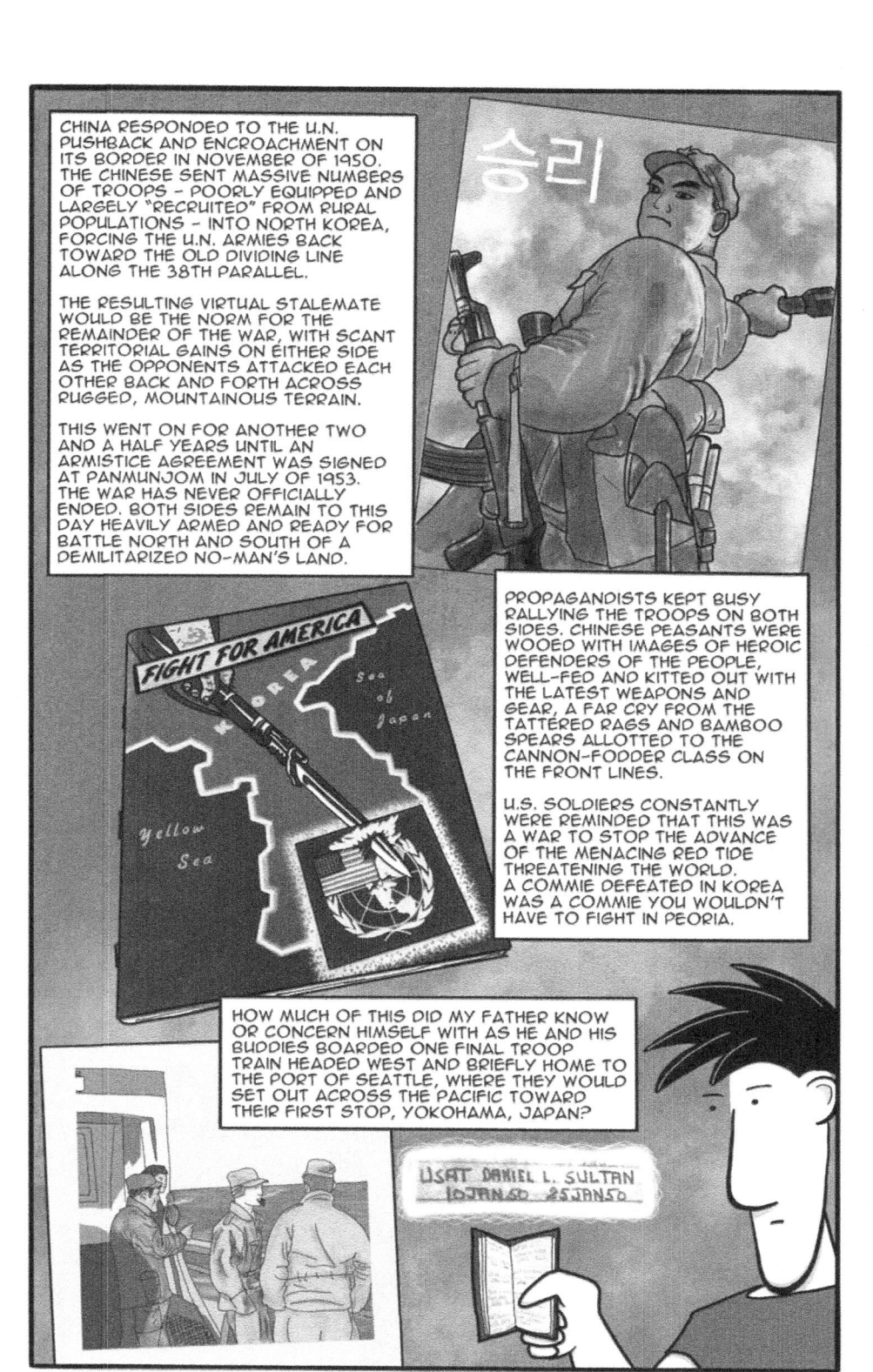

CHINA RESPONDED TO THE U.N. PUSHBACK AND ENCROACHMENT ON ITS BORDER IN NOVEMBER OF 1950. THE CHINESE SENT MASSIVE NUMBERS OF TROOPS - POORLY EQUIPPED AND LARGELY "RECRUITED" FROM RURAL POPULATIONS - INTO NORTH KOREA, FORCING THE U.N. ARMIES BACK TOWARD THE OLD DIVIDING LINE ALONG THE 38TH PARALLEL.

THE RESULTING VIRTUAL STALEMATE WOULD BE THE NORM FOR THE REMAINDER OF THE WAR, WITH SCANT TERRITORIAL GAINS ON EITHER SIDE AS THE OPPONENTS ATTACKED EACH OTHER BACK AND FORTH ACROSS RUGGED, MOUNTAINOUS TERRAIN.

THIS WENT ON FOR ANOTHER TWO AND A HALF YEARS UNTIL AN ARMISTICE AGREEMENT WAS SIGNED AT PANMUNJOM IN JULY OF 1953. THE WAR HAS NEVER OFFICIALLY ENDED. BOTH SIDES REMAIN TO THIS DAY HEAVILY ARMED AND READY FOR BATTLE NORTH AND SOUTH OF A DEMILITARIZED NO-MAN'S LAND.

PROPAGANDISTS KEPT BUSY RALLYING THE TROOPS ON BOTH SIDES. CHINESE PEASANTS WERE WOOED WITH IMAGES OF HEROIC DEFENDERS OF THE PEOPLE, WELL-FED AND KITTED OUT WITH THE LATEST WEAPONS AND GEAR, A FAR CRY FROM THE TATTERED RAGS AND BAMBOO SPEARS ALLOTTED TO THE CANNON-FODDER CLASS ON THE FRONT LINES.

U.S. SOLDIERS CONSTANTLY WERE REMINDED THAT THIS WAS A WAR TO STOP THE ADVANCE OF THE MENACING RED TIDE THREATENING THE WORLD. A COMMIE DEFEATED IN KOREA WAS A COMMIE YOU WOULDN'T HAVE TO FIGHT IN PEORIA.

HOW MUCH OF THIS DID MY FATHER KNOW OR CONCERN HIMSELF WITH AS HE AND HIS BUDDIES BOARDED ONE FINAL TROOP TRAIN HEADED WEST AND BRIEFLY HOME TO THE PORT OF SEATTLE, WHERE THEY WOULD SET OUT ACROSS THE PACIFIC TOWARD THEIR FIRST STOP, YOKOHAMA, JAPAN?

USAT DANIEL L. SULTAN
10JAN50 25JAN50

WHILE DAD WAS ON BOARD THE TROOP SHIP FOR ITS 2-WEEK VOYAGE ACROSS THE PACIFIC, THE U.N. FORCES IN KOREA WERE IN RETREAT AND SEOUL WAS ONCE AGAIN IN THE HANDS OF THE NORTH.

THE DANIEL L. SULTAN ARRIVED IN YOKOHAMA HARBOR ON JANUARY 25, 1950. SOLDIERS WERE DISPATCHED ACCORDING TO THEIR ORDERS. DAD AND MOST OF HIS FRIENDS WENT TO TOKYO FOR A TWO-WEEK STAY BEFORE TRAVELING SOUTH TO THEIR OFFICIAL ASSIGNMENTS AT AN ASA STATION IN KYOTO.

THEY WOULD STAY THERE, 400 MILES FROM THE FIGHTING IN KOREA, FOR OVER A YEAR AND A HALF.

IN A RARE MOMENT OF CANDOR, I REMEMBER HEARING DAD SAY IT WAS THE BEST TIME OF HIS LIFE.

SOUVENIR CARD GIVEN TO TROOPS AS THEY CROSSED THE INTERNATIONAL DATE LINE.

IT DIDN'T LAST, OF COURSE.

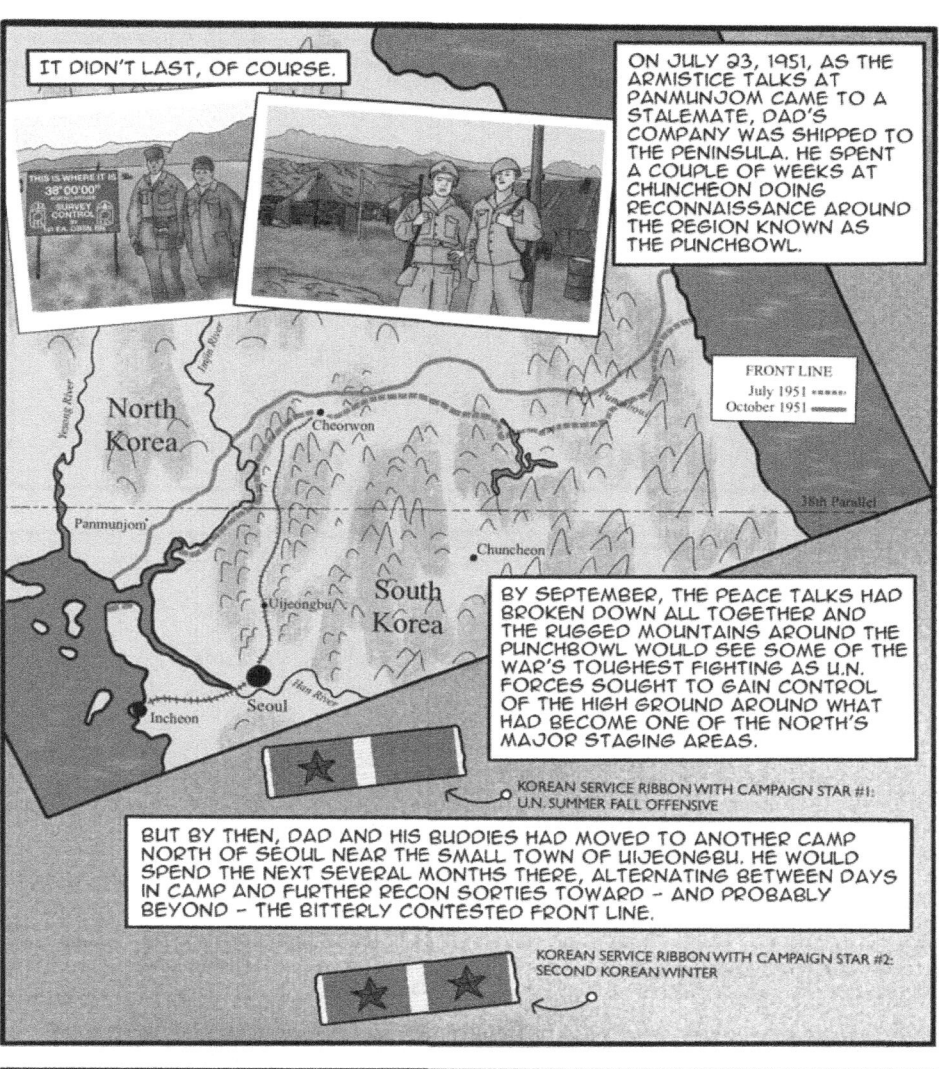

ON JULY 23, 1951, AS THE ARMISTICE TALKS AT PANMUNJOM CAME TO A STALEMATE, DAD'S COMPANY WAS SHIPPED TO THE PENINSULA. HE SPENT A COUPLE OF WEEKS AT CHUNCHEON DOING RECONNAISSANCE AROUND THE REGION KNOWN AS THE PUNCHBOWL.

FRONT LINE
July 1951 ━━━
October 1951 ━━━

BY SEPTEMBER, THE PEACE TALKS HAD BROKEN DOWN ALL TOGETHER AND THE RUGGED MOUNTAINS AROUND THE PUNCHBOWL WOULD SEE SOME OF THE WAR'S TOUGHEST FIGHTING AS U.N. FORCES SOUGHT TO GAIN CONTROL OF THE HIGH GROUND AROUND WHAT HAD BECOME ONE OF THE NORTH'S MAJOR STAGING AREAS.

KOREAN SERVICE RIBBON WITH CAMPAIGN STAR #1: U.N. SUMMER FALL OFFENSIVE

BUT BY THEN, DAD AND HIS BUDDIES HAD MOVED TO ANOTHER CAMP NORTH OF SEOUL NEAR THE SMALL TOWN OF UIJEONGBU. HE WOULD SPEND THE NEXT SEVERAL MONTHS THERE, ALTERNATING BETWEEN DAYS IN CAMP AND FURTHER RECON SORTIES TOWARD – AND PROBABLY BEYOND – THE BITTERLY CONTESTED FRONT LINE.

KOREAN SERVICE RIBBON WITH CAMPAIGN STAR #2: SECOND KOREAN WINTER

AFTER JUST OVER SEVEN MONTHS ON THE PENINSULA, DAD'S FINAL ASSIGNMENT TOOK HIM TO THE ASA'S TORII STATION ON OKINAWA, JAPAN, A LOCATION NEAR A LARGE MILITARY HOSPITAL WHERE MANY SHELL-SHOCKED SOLDIERS RECEIVED WHAT PASSED FOR TREATMENT. PERHAPS TELLINGLY, HE STAYED HERE FOR THREE MONTHS, THE REMAINDER OF HIS ENLISTMENT. MEANWHILE, THE WAR WOULD SLOG ON FOR ANOTHER YEAR.

AND SOMETIME IN ALL OF THIS A TEENAGED BOY BECAME A MAN, A MAN WITH DEEP PERSONAL SCARS THAT AFFECTED HIS RELATIONSHIP WITH HIS MOTHER, HIS CHURCH, HIS FUTURE WIFE... AND THEIR SON.

I STILL DIDN'T KNOW HOW TO CONNECT THE TWO – THE TEENAGER WHO WENT OFF TO WAR AND THE YOUNG MAN WHO CAME HOME AGAIN.

OBVIOUSLY, THE TEENAGER HAD BEEN UNDER PRESSURE, BOTH ECONOMIC AND RELIGIOUS. HIS FATHER'S DEATH FORCED HIM TO WORK LONG HOURS, WHICH TOOK A TOLL ON HIS SCHOOLWORK. WHILE AT THE SAME TIME, HIS MOTHER'S WISH TO SEE HIM ENTER THE PRIESTHOOD SEEMED TO PUSH HIM TOWARD EXTREME ALTERNATIVES THAT DIDN'T NECESSARILY WORK OUT AS PLANNED.

THERE MUST HAVE BEEN PRESSURE FROM OTHER DIRECTIONS, AS WELL. TOO YOUNG TO HAVE BEEN THE HEROES OF WWII, HE AND HIS BUDDIES WERE AN ENTICING TARGET TO THOSE PREPARING FOR THE NEXT CONFLICT.

THE APPARENT INEVITABILITY OF A DRAFT NO DOUBT HAD AN INFLUENCE ON MANY YOUNG MEN, INCLUDING COLLEGE KIDS STRUGGLING WITH THEIR STUDIES.

BUT WITH WHOM DID THE IDEA OF ENLISTMENT ORIGINATE? DID ALL THE PHINNEY RIDGE BOYS THINK IT UP INDEPENDENTLY OR WAS THERE ONE AMONG THEM, PERHAPS MY FATHER HIMSELF, CHAMPIONING THE IDEA?

I WONDERED AGAIN ABOUT DAD'S OLD NEWSPAPER CLIPPING. WAS THE DEFACEMENT OF POOR JACK VALENTINO AN EARLY SIGN OF DISSENT AMONG THE GROUP? DID HE HAVE SECOND THOUGHTS ABOUT THEIR MILITARY ADVENTURE? DID HIS DOUBT EARN THE CENSURE OF THE OTHERS AND THE IGNOMINY OF DAD'S PEN?

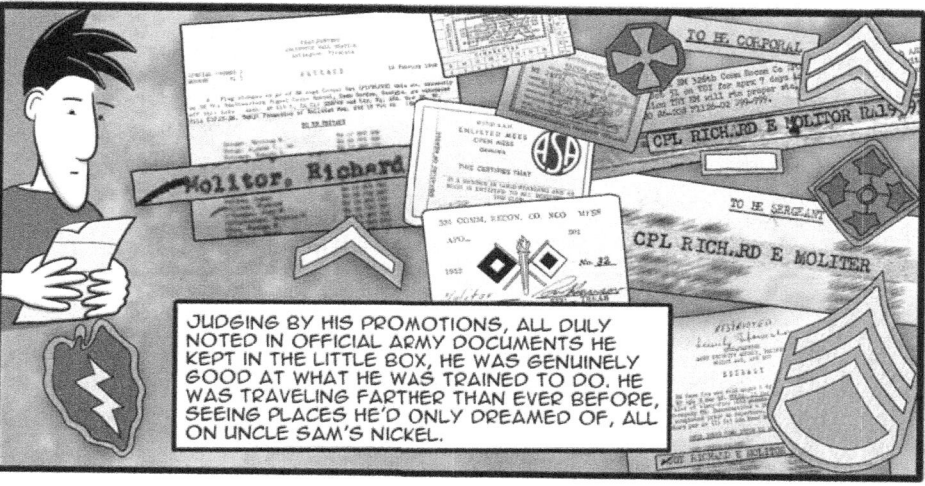

DESPITE HIS COMPLAINTS IN LATER YEARS, I HAVE NO DOUBT DAD REALLY TOOK TO ARMY LIFE. HERE WAS AN ORGANIZATION WHERE PEOPLE HAD ANSWERS. THEY HAD A PLAN, A CLEAR PATH YOU COULD FOLLOW TO... WHERE? IT PROBABLY DIDN'T MATTER. MAYBE IT MEANT ENOUGH TO BE GOING SOMEWHERE, ANYWHERE, OTHER THAN THE PLACES HIS FAMILY, HIS CHURCH, EVEN HIS CLASSMATES WHO HAD PROPHESIED HIS DEAD-END FUTURE WANTED HIM TO GO.

JUDGING BY HIS PROMOTIONS, ALL DULY NOTED IN OFFICIAL ARMY DOCUMENTS HE KEPT IN THE LITTLE BOX, HE WAS GENUINELY GOOD AT WHAT HE WAS TRAINED TO DO. HE WAS TRAVELING FARTHER THAN EVER BEFORE, SEEING PLACES HE'D ONLY DREAMED OF, ALL ON UNCLE SAM'S NICKEL.

MAYBE HE DISCOVERED NEW IDEAS, TOO. ALTHOUGH EVERYTHING NO DOUBT CAME FILTERED THROUGH THE LENS OF ARMY STANDARDS, SURELY HE MUST HAVE WONDERED IF LIFE WASN'T MORE NUANCED THAN HE'D BEEN LED TO BELIEVE.

PERHAPS THAT'S WHERE THE LITTLE BRASS BUDDHA COMES INTO THE STORY. MAYBE HE REALIZED HIS CATHOLIC FAITH WASN'T THE ONLY WAY TO INTERPRET THE BIG WIDE WORLD HE'D BEEN TOSSED INTO.

FOR NOW, THAT WORLD WAS JAPAN, WHERE THE BULK OF HIS OVERSEAS DEPLOYMENT TOOK PLACE.

CAMP STAFFORD WAS THE ARMY SECURITY AGENCY'S BASE IN KYOTO, LOCATED IN THE FUSHIMI WARD AT THE SOUTHEAST EDGE OF THE OLD CITY, AN AREA FAMOUS FOR ITS SPRING WATERS AND THE SAKE DISTILLERIES THAT PUT THEM TO USE. NO DOUBT THE SOLDIERS WERE MORE INTERESTED IN THE SAKE THAN THE SPRINGS.

AS FAR AS MILITARY ASSIGNMENTS WENT, IT SEEMED LIKE A CHOICE GIG.

DAD'S MEMORY STASH INCLUDED PHOTOS OF THE CAMP AND THE MEN OF HIS COMPANY. THERE WERE A DOZEN OR SO ASA GUYS AMONG SEVERAL HUNDRED OTHER SOLDIERS.

THREE OF THE PHINNEY RIDGE BOYS STAYED HERE ALMOST 18 MONTHS.

AFTER ONLY SIX MONTHS, JACK VALENTINO WAS ASSIGNED TO A UNIT IN KOREA. I DIDN'T FIND ANY MORE PICTURES OF HIM IN THE BOX.

THE ASA HAD BEGUN INTERCEPTING NORTH KOREAN RADIO SIGNALS SOON AFTER THE INVASION IN 1950, BUT KOREAN TRANSLATORS WERE IN SHORT SUPPLY SO OFTEN AS NOT THE MESSAGES WOULD SIT AROUND FOR DAYS BEFORE BEING PASSED UP THE CHAIN OF COMMAND.

당신의 어머니는 햄스터 였고 당신의 아버지는 엘더베리 냄새가났습니다

TO PREVENT THAT FROM HAPPENING AGAIN, THE ASA SQUAD AT CAMP STAFFORD INCLUDED TRANSLATORS AND CODE-BREAKERS. THEY WORKED LONGER SHIFTS THAN NORMAL, SITTING AT SHORT WAVE RADIO RECEIVERS FOR 12 HOURS OR MORE AT A STRETCH, SCANNING THE FREQUENCIES FOR HIGH SPEED MESSAGES AMONG DPRK TROOPS ON THE KOREAN PENINSULA, AS WELL AS COMMUNICATION BETWEEN NORTH KOREAN AND CHINESE MILITARY AND DIPLOMATIC MISSIONS.

BUT THE EPHEMERA SPREAD OUT BEFORE ME INCLUDED PHOTOS AND PAPERS THAT SUGGESTED IT WASN'T ALL WORK. JAPAN DURING THE OCCUPATION YEARS OFFERED PLENTY OF ATTRACTIONS. A SHORT DRIVE AWAY WAS LAKE BIWA AND ITS MUCH ADVERTISED SCENERY. DURING THE WINTER, THE MOUNTAINS TO THE NORTH OFFERED SKIING AND TRADITIONAL LODGES. DAD ACTUALLY HAD AN OFFICIAL HUNTING LICENSE, THOUGH EXACTLY WHAT HE HUNTED REMAINED A MYSTERY.

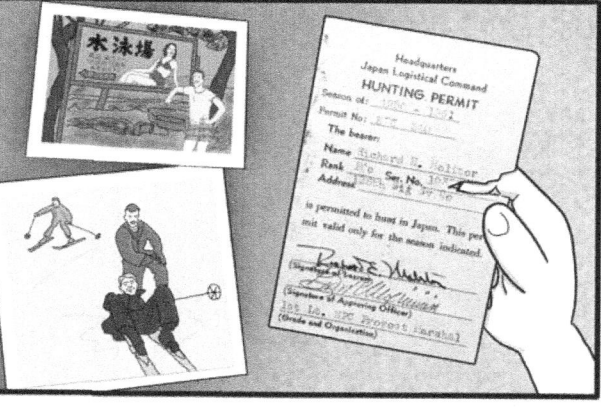

I SUPPOSE SOME GAME WAS EASY ENOUGH TO TRACK DOWN.

A COLLECTION OF BOTTLE LABELS SUGGESTED ONE SPORT OF CHOICE WAS DOWNING BEER IN THE CAMP'S ENLISTED MEN'S CLUB.

AND JUDGING BY THE ASSORTMENT OF MATCHBOOKS AND BUSINESS CARDS HE KEPT, THE U.S. SOLDIERS FOUND PLENTY OF OFF-BASE HANGOUTS, TOO. THE LOCALS MUST HAVE DONE THEIR BEST TO MAKE THEM HAPPY, AS HAPPY G.I.S WERE KNOWN TO LEAVE BEHIND THEM TRAILS OF HARD CURRENCY.

IT WAS EASY TO SEE WHY DAD HAD FOND MEMORIES OF THOSE DAYS.

THE GOOD TIMES MUST HAVE MADE WHATEVER CAME AFTER SEEM THAT MUCH WORSE.

AN ARMY-ISSUED LICENSE ALLOWED DAD TO DRIVE A LIGHT TRANSPORT TRUCK TO PICK UP SUPPLIES FROM LARGER CAMPS NEARBY.

APPARENTLY, THE ASA WAS ALWAYS SHORT OF RADIO COMPONENTS.

DAD HAD BEEN DRIVING, LEGALLY OR NOT, SINCE HIS FATHER DIED. HE ADAPTED TO DRIVING ON THE LEFT AS THEY DO IN JAPAN, ALTHOUGH THE OLD ROADS WERE SO NARROW IT HARDLY MADE A DIFFERENCE.

RATTLE! RATTLE!

EVERY NOW AND THEN HE'D SNAP A PICTURE OF THE LOCALS WITH THE CAMERA HE'D BOUGHT IN TOKYO.

IF THE JAPANESE SHOWED ANY SIGN OF ANTAGONISM, IT DOESN'T APPEAR IN HIS PHOTOS.

MAYBE THIS IS WHEN HE GOT USED TO THE PERKS OF AUTHORITY.

A GREATLY REDACTED U.S. ARMY REPORT FROM SEPT. 1950, RECORDS AN INCIDENT WITH ONE OF THE CAMP'S TRUCKS. IT SEEMS THE DRIVER, ID'D ONLY BY HIS SERIAL NUMBER, WAS RETURNING ALONG ONE OF THE MAIN STREETS OF THE NEIGHBORING MOMOYAMA DISTRICT WHEN...

SKREEEEEKERRAKK!

THE LOCAL CONSTABLE, OFFICER IBUKI, NOTED THE CIRCUMSTANCES AND COMMENDED THE DRIVER FOR HIS QUICK REACTION.

THE WARD CHIEF, MR. TOFUKU, WAS NOT SO GENEROUS.

THE AMERICAN SOLDIER WAS TOLD TO TAKE MR. TOFUKU'S CARD AND CALL HIM IMMEDIATELY IF ANYONE *ELSE* AT CAMP STAFFORD NEEDED REMEDIAL DRIVING LESSONS.

THE CRUMBLY OLD MIMEOGRAPHED ARMY REPORT AND THE CARDS SAVED WITH IT MADE ME SURPRISINGLY HAPPY.

IN 1950, PFC MOLITOR WAS A DECENT GUY.

I'D BE A NITWIT IF I DIDN'T GIVE THE CHURCH SOME CREDIT FOR THAT.

NOT SURPRISINGLY, DAD'S ARMY STUFF INCLUDED SEVERAL PUBLICATIONS TAILORED TO CATHOLIC SOLDIERS.

MY MILITARY MISSAL

A TATTERED AND OBVIOUSLY WELL-USED MISSAL* ADAPTED THE MASS TO WARTIME, SUGGESTING VARIOUS WAYS A SOLDIER COULD REMAIN IN GOOD STANDING WITH GOD ABSENT A REGULAR CHURCH SERVICE.

*THE TEXT AND OTHER INSTRUCTIONS FOR THE CATHOLIC MASS

I KNEW THAT MILITARY CHAPLAINS PLAYED A ROLE IN SPREADING CHRISTIANITY IN SOUTH KOREA...

...NO DOUBT THEY HAD A HAND IN KEEPING THE ALREADY FAITHFUL IN THE FOLD, TOO.

ALTHOUGH I DIDN'T FIND ANY NOTES OR PHOTOS THAT SUGGESTED DAD HAD ROUTINELY BEEN IN CONTACT WITH ONE.

NOT THAT HE HAD MUCH INTERACTION WITH PRIESTS LATER, WHEN I WAS GROWING UP. BY THEN THE WEEKLY TRIPS TO SUNDAY MASS HAD BECOME AN EMPTY RITUAL, SOMETHING YOU DID BECAUSE SOMEONE TOLD YOU TO. AND HONESTLY, THERE DIDN'T SEEM TO BE ANY REWARD FOR THE FAITHFUL.

HOW MANY TIMES HAD HE SAT THROUGH THE WHOLE PERFORMANCE...

...ONLY TO BE LEFT AT THE MERCY OF THE WORLD ONCE IT WAS OVER?

!*#☆!

1964 CHEVY CORVAIR "UNSAFE AT ANY SPEED" ...INCLUDING ZERO

THE COLD WINTERS OF CENTRAL WASHINGTON WERE THE BACKDROP FOR MORE THAN ONE SILENT, BITTER WALK HOME.

THAT WOULD HAVE BEEN ENOUGH TO HARDEN THE HEART OF ANY MAN, ESPECIALLY ONE FACING OTHER, MORE WORLDLY PROBLEMS.

BUT THE WEEKLY MASSES CONTINUED, AT LEAST FOR A LITTLE WHILE.
BORED SILLY, I MADE UP GAMES TO PASS THE TIME. "COUNT THE ASTERISKS IN THE HYMNAL" WAS A FAVORITE.
THE GOAL WAS TO RANDOMLY FLIP TO A PAGE WITH MORE FOOTNOTES THAN THE PREVIOUS ONE.
WE HAVE A WINNAH!
SNATCH!
!!
SLAM!
SHUSH
'HH!
NOT EVERYONE APPRECIATED THE SUBTLE NUANCES OF THE GAME.
I GUESS YOU WERE SUPPOSED TO GO THROUGH THE MOTIONS OF THE MASS IN TORTURED SILENCE.

Panel 1: IN A LAST DITCH EFFORT TO CATHOLOCIZE ME, DAD ENROLLED ME IN ONE OF THE CHURCH'S CCD* KIDDIE CLASSES.

*CONFRATERNITY OF CHRISTIAN DOCTRINE

Panel 2: THEY WERE TAUGHT ONE NIGHT A WEEK BY THE LOCAL "CHURCH LADIES"...

Welcome Little Sinners

BLAH BLAH BLAH.
JESUS!
BLAH BLAH BLAH.

Panel 3: ...WHO DID LITTLE MORE THAN PARROT CHILD FRIENDLY VERSIONS OF VATICAN-APPROVED DOCTRINE.

BLAH BLAH BLAH.
SQUAWK!

Panel 4: THE LESSONS WERE NOT EXACTLY COMPELLING.

BLAH BLAH BLAH

Panel 5: EVENTUALLY, CCD BECAME THE FIRST CLASS I EVER SKIPPED...

Panel 6: ...AND THE ONLY CLASS I EVER FLUNKED.

DAD NEVER TALKED ABOUT IT, BUT HE DIDN'T SEND ME BACK THE NEXT TERM.

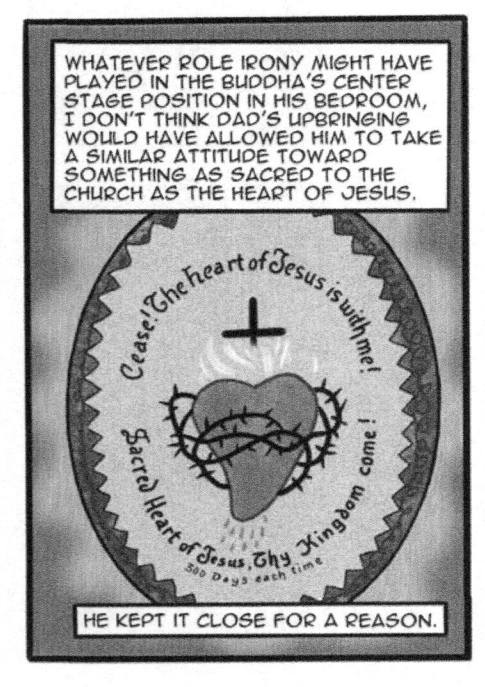

WITHIN A FEW MONTHS, THE WEEKLY SLOGS TO MASS WERE CUT BACK TO EASTER AND CHRISTMAS ONLY. THAT LASTED A COUPLE MORE YEARS, THEN THEY, TOO, FINALLY STOPPED.

I SUSPECT BY THEN THE EMPTINESS OF THE RITUALS WAS JUST TOO APPARENT. ABSENT THE CONSTANT PUSH FROM HIS MOTHER OR THE BROTHERS AT O'DEA, IT SEEMED DAD'S FAITH HAD BECOME DISPOSABLE. THE BOOKS AND TRINKETS HE'D COLLECTED SINCE CHILDHOOD HAD BECOME MERE SOUVENIRS...

...LIKE THE FAT GUY.

A FINE THEORY, EXCEPT...

...IT DIDN'T EXPLAIN THE LITTLE PRAYER BADGE IN HIS POCKET ON THE DAY HE DIED.

WHATEVER ROLE IRONY MIGHT HAVE PLAYED IN THE BUDDHA'S CENTER STAGE POSITION IN HIS BEDROOM, I DON'T THINK DAD'S UPBRINGING WOULD HAVE ALLOWED HIM TO TAKE A SIMILAR ATTITUDE TOWARD SOMETHING AS SACRED TO THE CHURCH AS THE HEART OF JESUS.

Cease! The heart of Jesus is with me!
Sacred Heart of Jesus, Thy Kingdom come!
300 Days each time

HE KEPT IT CLOSE FOR A REASON.

WAS THE SIMPLE INCANTATION ON THAT BADGE MORE IMPORTANT TO HIM THAN ALL THE COMPLEX THEOLOGY HE'D BEEN TAUGHT?

IN SOME WAYS, I THINK DAD'S EVENTUAL TAKE ON RELIGION WAS KIND OF ADMIRABLE.

HE STOPPED TRYING TO PUSH IT ON OTHERS...

...EVEN IF HE NEVER WHOLLY GAVE UP ON IT HIMSELF.

WHICH ONCE AGAIN LED ME BACK TO WHERE I'D STARTED. MAYBE THE RELIGIOUS ANGLE *WASN'T* THE KEY THAT WOULD UNLOCK MY FATHER'S PSYCHE. MAYBE HIS BELIEFS JUST WENT THROUGH THE USUAL FLUCTUATIONS BROUGHT ON BY AGE AND THE CHALLENGES THAT LIFE THROWS AT YOU. HE CERTAINLY HAD MORE THAN HIS SHARE OF THOSE.

BUT I WAS STILL GUESSING. EVEN WHEN THE WORST SHIT WAS SPLATTERING ON THE FAN, DAD, AS USUAL, NEVER TALKED ABOUT IT.

YOU COULD TELL, THOUGH, SOMETIMES, HE WAS HIDING FROM SOMETHING.

MAYBE FROM A LOT OF THINGS.

JUST AFTER I STARTED GRADE SCHOOL, MOM GOT A JOB AS A TEACHER. WE NEEDED THE INCOME AND I THINK SHE WAS JUST BORED WITH BEING A HOUSEWIFE.
DAD TOOK THIS TURN OF EVENTS PERSONALLY, AS IF HE HAD FAILED TO PROVIDE FOR HIS FAMILY.
FINANCIALLY, OF COURSE, HE *HAD*.
PRETTY QUICKLY, MOM BECAME THE PRIMARY BREADWINNER.
WHICH, IN A DIFFERENT ERA, MIGHT HAVE BEEN JUST FINE.
BUT NOT JUST THEN.
...
IN THOSE DAYS...
—
...DINNERS WERE QUIET AFFAIRS.

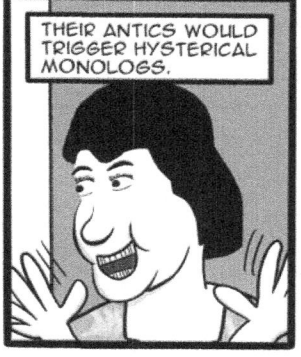

IT HADN'T ALWAYS BEEN THAT WAY.

YEARS EARLIER, I REMEMBER MOM DIFFERENTLY.

SHE LOVED TO LAUGH, A BIG, VOLUMINOUS LAUGH THAT FILLED THE ROOM.

SHE'D TELL STORIES ABOUT THE CRAZY PEOPLE SHE KNEW.

THEIR ANTICS WOULD TRIGGER HYSTERICAL MONOLOGS.

MOM COULD BARELY GET THROUGH THE ANECDOTES, HER LAUGHTER ALONE EVENTUALLY TAKING OVER.

WHICH DIDN'T SIT WELL WITH DAD.

NO ONE CAN HEAR YOUR STORY, SO WHY BOTHER TELLING IT?

CUT CUT

CHEW CHEW

*Fresca is a registered trademark of The Coca-Cola Company

CUT CUT
TIK TIK
TIK TIK
CUT CUT CHEW CHEW
TIK TIK
LIKE MUCH OF EVERYTHING ELSE, DAD KEPT HIS THOUGHTS ABOUT MOM TO HIMSELF, EVEN AFTER THEY WERE NO LONGER HAPPY HUSBAND AND WIFE.
CHEW CHEW
TIK TIK

A CHANCE WRINKLE? OR A DELIBERATELY DOG-EARED PAGE?

FLIP!

ACT of CONTRITION

A prayer to be said daily by the soldier following acceptance of his transgressions.

O MY GOD! I am heartily sorry for having offended Thee, and I detest all my sins, because I dread the loss of heaven and the pains of hell, but most of all I have offended Thee, my God, Who art all good and deserving of all my love. I firmly resolve, with the help of Thy grace, to confess my sins, to do penance, and to amend my life. Amen.

?
Ching booyah shallower
my life. Amen
MARGINAL NOTES IN SOME SPOOKIFIED CODE...
...OR THE KEY TO ALL THE MYSTERIES OF DAD'S UNIVERSE?
THUNK!
WHY WAS I DOING THIS?!

133

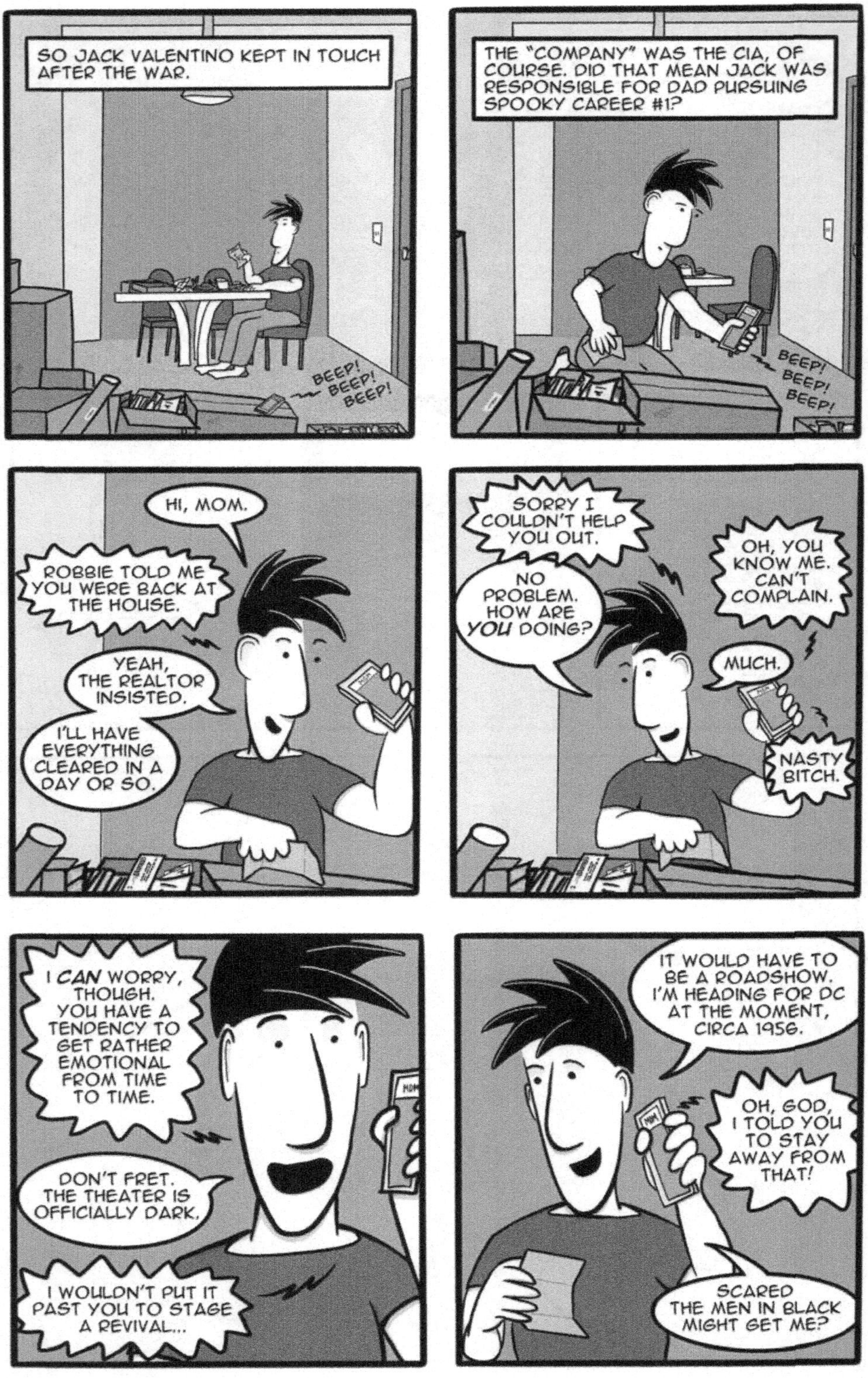
SO JACK VALENTINO KEPT IN TOUCH AFTER THE WAR.
BEEP! BEEP! BEEP!
THE "COMPANY" WAS THE CIA, OF COURSE. DID THAT MEAN JACK WAS RESPONSIBLE FOR DAD PURSUING SPOOKY CAREER #1?
BEEP! BEEP! BEEP!
HI, MOM.
ROBBIE TOLD ME YOU WERE BACK AT THE HOUSE.
YEAH, THE REALTOR INSISTED.
I'LL HAVE EVERYTHING CLEARED IN A DAY OR SO.
SORRY I COULDN'T HELP YOU OUT.
NO PROBLEM. HOW ARE YOU DOING?
OH, YOU KNOW ME. CAN'T COMPLAIN.
MUCH.
NASTY BITCH.
I CAN WORRY, THOUGH. YOU HAVE A TENDENCY TO GET RATHER EMOTIONAL FROM TIME TO TIME.
DON'T FRET. THE THEATER IS OFFICIALLY DARK.
I WOULDN'T PUT IT PAST YOU TO STAGE A REVIVAL...
IT WOULD HAVE TO BE A ROADSHOW. I'M HEADING FOR DC AT THE MOMENT, CIRCA 1956.
OH, GOD, I TOLD YOU TO STAY AWAY FROM THAT!
SCARED THE MEN IN BLACK MIGHT GET ME?

NOT LIKELY. YOU AREN'T A PART OF THEIR STORY. CREDIT YOUR FATHER FOR THAT.
SPEAKING OF DAD, I'M JUST GETTING TO THE PART WHERE HE HOOKS UP WITH SOME SOUTHERN BELLE, THANKS TO JACK'S HEADS-UP ABOUT THE CIA JOB.
JACK?
MOM
VALENTINO. ONE OF THE PHINNEY RIDGE BOYS. I THINK HE'S THE ONE WHO CONVINCED DAD TO JOIN THE SPOOKS.
OH, *THAT* JACK. JACK*ASS.*
YOUR FATHER DIDN'T THINK MUCH OF HIM FOR SOME REASON. HE NEVER TOLD ME WHY.
WELL, HE MUST HAVE LISTENED TO HIM AT LEAST ONCE.
PLEASE! WITH YOUR NUTTY PARENTS, I'M SURPRISED YOU HAVEN'T BEEN COMMITTED ALREADY.
DANNY, I HOPE YOU'RE GETTING WHAT YOU NEED FROM THIS.
ROBBIE SAID IT WAS BETTER THAN YOUR THERAPY.
MOM
LOOK, SWEETIE, ABOUT YOUR DAD AND I...
...YOU KNOW IT WAS A HAPPY STORY BACK THEN. IT REALLY WAS.
YOU'RE NOT SUPPOSED TO KNOW I'M IN THERAPY.
I KNOW, MOM. THINGS HAPPEN.
YES, THEY DO. AND YOU CAN'T ALWAYS EXPLAIN WHY.
BUT I HAVE TO TRY.
I SUPPOSE YOU DO. I WISH I COULD HELP, BUT...
I'M GLAD YOU CALLED. I'LL LET YOU KNOW ABOUT THE HOUSE.
THANKS.

WAIT! BEFORE YOU HANG UP... ONE QUESTION! THAT THING YOU BELIEVED DAD WANTED TO TELL ME...
DID IT BY ANY CHANCE HAVE SOMETHING TO DO WITH THE WAY HE TREATED YOU...BACK WHEN THINGS WEREN'T SO HAPPY?
———.
MOM
MOM?
NO. I'M ALMOST CERTAIN IT DID NOT.
GO HOME AS SOON AS YOU CAN.
OKAY.
BWOOP
MAYBE MOM COULD HAVE SAID MORE, MAYBE SHE COULDN'T. I SUSPECT SHE WAS LONG PAST CARING.
VIET-NAM
WASHINGTON
FE 1 5 PM
1956
Mr. Richard E. Molito
U.S.A.
AND MAYBE I DIDN'T NEED TO SOLVE EVERY MYSTERY.
MAYBE IT WAS ENOUGH JUST TO KNOW A LITTLE BIT MORE.
PAR AVION

INCLUDED IN THE STASH OF LETTERS I'D FOUND WERE FIFTY OR SO FROM MOM, WRITTEN WHILE SHE WAS IN SAIGON AND DAD WAS BACK IN WASHINGTON, DC.

IF I WAS GOING TO MAKE IT THROUGH THEM, A LITTLE FORTIFICATION WAS IN ORDER.

I KNEW THE BASICS OF MOM'S "HAPPY STORY."

IT STARTED WHEN A SOUTHERN BELLE FROM MORRISTOWN TENNESSEE GRADUATED FROM MARY WASHINGTON COLLEGE AT FREDERICKSBURG, VIRGINIA, FIFTY MILES SOUTH OF WASHINGTON.

ANASTASIA PETRO WAS A LANGUAGE MAJOR, FLUENT IN FRENCH AND SPANISH AND A SMATTERING OF RUSSIAN.

SHE WANTED TO JOIN THE U.S. DIPLOMATIC CORPS, IF FOR NO OTHER REASON, TO SEE A BIT OF THE WORLD BEYOND THE SMOKY MOUNTAINS.

PHOOMPH!

TO THE HORROR OF HER GREEK IMMIGRANT FATHER AND HILLBILLY MOTHER, WHOSE TREPIDATION BUT UNCONDITIONAL SUPPORT WAS MENTIONED SEVERAL TIMES IN HER LETTERS, SHE APPLIED FOR A JOB AS A TRANSLATOR/SECRETARY AT THE U.S. EMBASSY IN SAIGON, VIETNAM.

"AU REVOIR, INDOCHINE!"

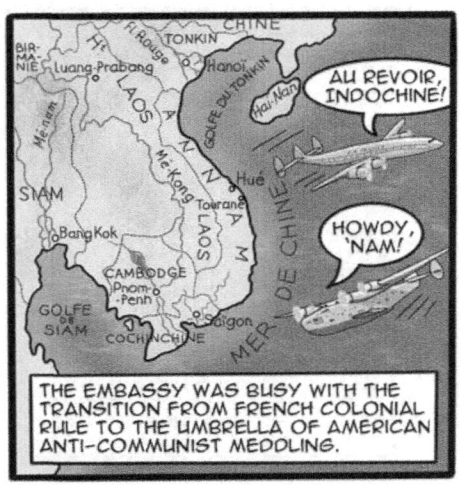

"HOWDY, 'NAM!"

THE EMBASSY WAS BUSY WITH THE TRANSITION FROM FRENCH COLONIAL RULE TO THE UMBRELLA OF AMERICAN ANTI-COMMUNIST MEDDLING.

THAT MEANT THE CIA WAS INVOLVED. SOON, YOUNG ANASTASIA FOUND HERSELF IN AN OFFICE IN DC'S FOGGY BOTTOM DISTRICT, WHERE SHE WAITED FOR AN INTERVIEW NEXT TO ANOTHER RECENT COLLEGE GRADUATE LOOKING FOR SOMETHING TO DO WITH HIS LIFE.

DICK AND ANASTASIA BECAME AN ITEM, EVEN THOUGH FATE WOULD SEPARATE THEM FOR OVER A YEAR SCARCELY FOUR MONTHS LATER.

ANASTASIA HAD GOTTEN THE JOB. AFTER SEVERAL MONTHS OF TRAINING SHE BOARDED THE FIRST OF SEVERAL PLANES THAT WOULD FLY HER ACROSS THE COUNTRY AND OVER THE PACIFIC TO SAIGON.

SHE SPENT THE NEXT 12 MONTHS EMPLOYED AT THE EMBASSY. JUDGING BY HER LETTERS, FROM THE MOMENT OF HER ARRIVAL SHE WAS COUNTING THE DAYS UNTIL SHE COULD LEAVE.

NONETHELESS, SHE DID SATISFY A LITTLE WANDERLUST. VACATION DAYS ALLOWED HER TO TAKE SHORT TRIPS TO HONG KONG, BANGKOK, ANGKOR WAT IN CAMBODIA, AND THE LOCAL BEACH RESORT AT CAP ST. JACQUES.

HER EXPECTATIONS WERE LARGELY OUT OF SYNC WITH THE REALITY OF MID-CENTURY VIETNAM. BASED ON WHAT SHE WROTE TO DAD, SHE WAS AWARE THE AMERICANS AT THE EMBASSY WERE CLUELESS ABOUT THE CULTURES THEY WERE TRYING TO MANIPULATE, BUT I SUSPECT SHE WAS TOO NAIVE TO GUESS THE DEPTHS TO WHICH THEY'D SINK TO CARRY OUT THEIR PLANS.

THE SCALE OF THEIR PERFIDY AND THE MISERY IT CAUSED WENT FAR BEYOND MOM'S GENTEEL SOUTHERN UPBRINGING.

SHE MIGHT HAVE BEEN THE QUINTESSENTIAL INNOCENT ABROAD, PLONKED DOWN IN A HUB OF HIGH STAKES DIPLOMACY AND POLITICAL MANEUVERING BY GLOBAL POWERS WITH LITTLE STAKE IN, OR CARE FOR, THE LOCAL REALITIES.

MIGHT HAVE BEEN, HAD IT NOT BEEN FOR HER "OTHER" EMPLOYER. THE HOME OFFICE EXPECTED DETAILED SUMMARIES OF ALL THE CORRESPONDENCE AND MEETING NOTES SHE TYPED FOR THE EMBASSY BRASS, AS WELL AS REPORTS ON OTHER ACTIVITIES OUTSIDE OF NORMAL DIPLOMATIC DUTIES.

DECADES LATER, SHE EXPRESSED DISGUST WITH THE "DUMB-DUMBS" STIRRING THE MUCK IN VIETNAM, BUT AT THE TIME HER LETTERS HOME CONCENTRATED FOR THE MOST PART ON HER OWN DIGESTIVE TROUBLES, THE OPPRESSIVE HEAT, DIFFICULTIES WITH THE MAID, THE TIRING NECESSITY OF SOCIALIZING WITH VARIOUS DIPLOMATIC AND MILITARY PERSONNEL...

...AND, INTERESTINGLY ENOUGH, BACK AND FORTH DISCUSSIONS WITH DICK MOLITOR REGARDING THE REQUIREMENTS OF AN OFFICIAL CONVERSION TO CATHOLICISM.

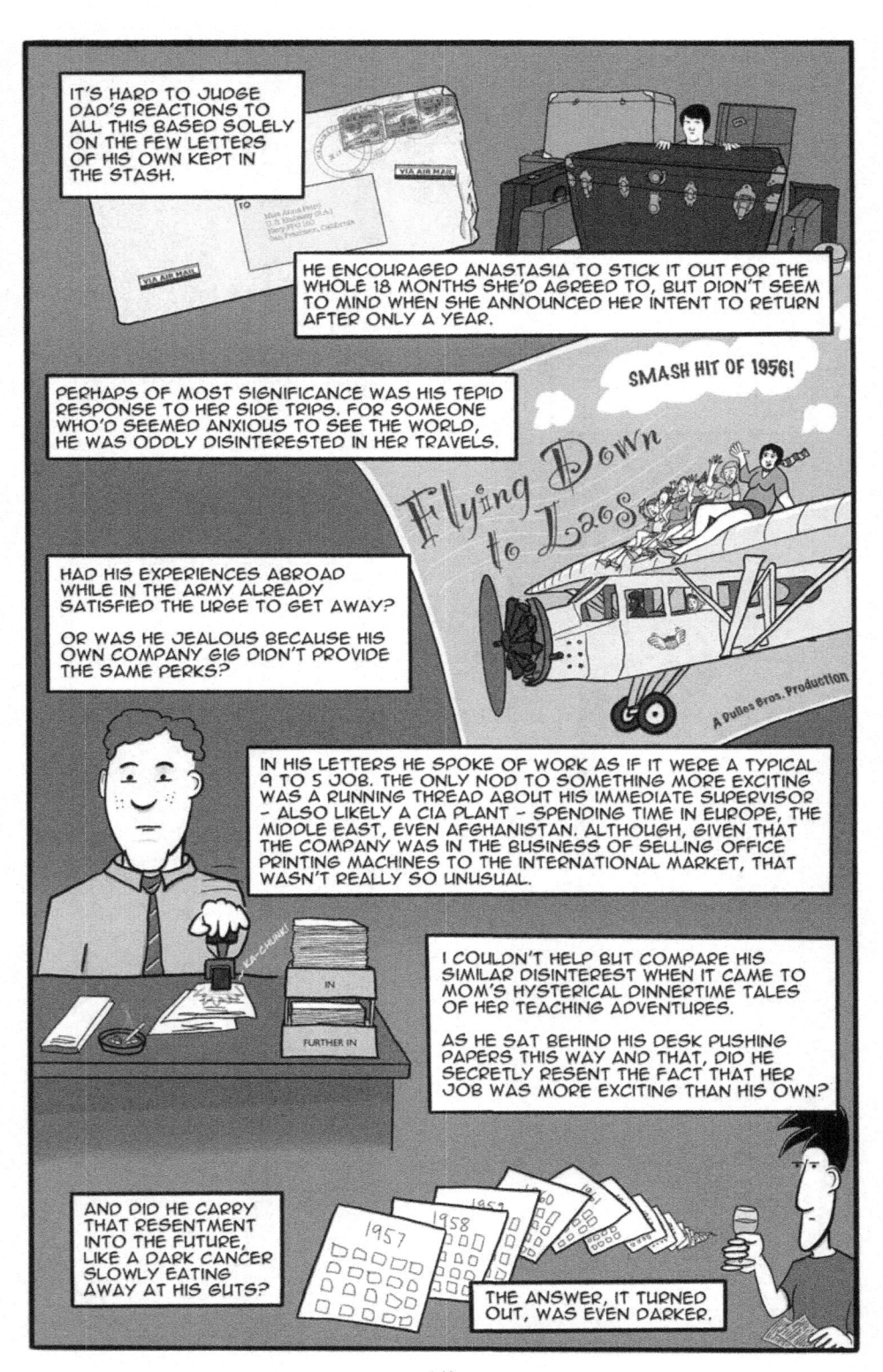

IT'S HARD TO JUDGE DAD'S REACTIONS TO ALL THIS BASED SOLELY ON THE FEW LETTERS OF HIS OWN KEPT IN THE STASH.

HE ENCOURAGED ANASTASIA TO STICK IT OUT FOR THE WHOLE 18 MONTHS SHE'D AGREED TO, BUT DIDN'T SEEM TO MIND WHEN SHE ANNOUNCED HER INTENT TO RETURN AFTER ONLY A YEAR.

PERHAPS OF MOST SIGNIFICANCE WAS HIS TEPID RESPONSE TO HER SIDE TRIPS. FOR SOMEONE WHO'D SEEMED ANXIOUS TO SEE THE WORLD, HE WAS ODDLY DISINTERESTED IN HER TRAVELS.

SMASH HIT OF 1956!
Flying Down to Laos
A Dulles Bros. Production

HAD HIS EXPERIENCES ABROAD WHILE IN THE ARMY ALREADY SATISFIED THE URGE TO GET AWAY?

OR WAS HE JEALOUS BECAUSE HIS OWN COMPANY GIG DIDN'T PROVIDE THE SAME PERKS?

IN HIS LETTERS HE SPOKE OF WORK AS IF IT WERE A TYPICAL 9 TO 5 JOB. THE ONLY NOD TO SOMETHING MORE EXCITING WAS A RUNNING THREAD ABOUT HIS IMMEDIATE SUPERVISOR — ALSO LIKELY A CIA PLANT — SPENDING TIME IN EUROPE, THE MIDDLE EAST, EVEN AFGHANISTAN. ALTHOUGH, GIVEN THAT THE COMPANY WAS IN THE BUSINESS OF SELLING OFFICE PRINTING MACHINES TO THE INTERNATIONAL MARKET, THAT WASN'T REALLY SO UNUSUAL.

I COULDN'T HELP BUT COMPARE HIS SIMILAR DISINTEREST WHEN IT CAME TO MOM'S HYSTERICAL DINNERTIME TALES OF HER TEACHING ADVENTURES.

AS HE SAT BEHIND HIS DESK PUSHING PAPERS THIS WAY AND THAT, DID HE SECRETLY RESENT THE FACT THAT HER JOB WAS MORE EXCITING THAN HIS OWN?

AND DID HE CARRY THAT RESENTMENT INTO THE FUTURE, LIKE A DARK CANCER SLOWLY EATING AWAY AT HIS GUTS?

THE ANSWER, IT TURNED OUT, WAS EVEN DARKER.

5

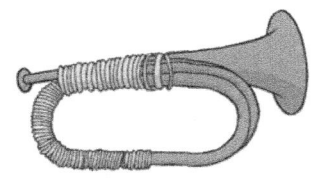

CLEARING OUT MY FATHER'S HOUSE AFTER HE DIED PROVIDED ME WITH A RARE OPPORTUNITY TO EXPLORE HIS PAST, A PAST HE'D NEVER TALKED ABOUT, BUT WHICH CAST A SHADOW OVER HIM FOR THE ENTIRETY OF HIS LIFE.

READING THROUGH A STASH OF LETTERS HE'D KEPT, I PICKED UP HIS STORY IN THE FALL OF 1955. THAT SUMMER HE'D BEEN RECRUITED BY THE CIA AND PLANTED IN AN OFFICE MACHINE MANUFACTURING COMPANY AS THE ASSISTANT TO THE DIRECTOR OF INTERNATIONAL SALES.

FAR FROM THE EXCITING CAREER IN INTELLIGENCE THE CIA RECRUITERS LIKELY SOLD HIM ON, HIS WORK WAS LARGELY A BORING DESK JOB.

TO MAKE MATTERS WORSE, ONCE OR TWICE A WEEK HE'D RECEIVE LETTERS FROM ANASTASIA PETRO, NASCENT GIRLFRIEND AND FUTURE WIFE, WHOSE OWN CIA GIG IN VIETNAM WAS, AT LEAST COMPARED TO HIS, FAIRLY EXCITING.

THE DIFFERENCES IN THEIR EXPERIENCES COULD NOT HAVE BEEN MORE DRAMATIC.

L'Aventure Exotique avec Anastasia Petro de L'Indochine — NOW PLAYING

THE RED TAPE MENACE starring Dick Molitor and a cast of thousands of bureaucrats — HELD OVER

THE 1950s WAS AN ERA OF THE CIA IN ASCENDANCE. IN 1954, THE ORGANIZATION BACKED ITS FIRST FOREIGN COUP, IN GUATAMALA, WHERE IT HELPED REMOVE A DEMOCRATICALLY ELECTED LEADER AND REPLACE HIM WITH AN ANTI-COMMUNIST MILITARY STRONGMAN. IT WOULD BE THE FIRST OF MANY SUCH ACTIONS.

KNOWING IT HAD TO KEEP UP WITH MODERN TECHNOLOGY, THE CIA STARTED DEVISING NEW WAYS OF GATHERING INTEL, WHICH IS WHERE OFFICE MACHINES ENTER THE PICTURE. THE COMPANY DAD WORKED FOR WAS A FIRST STEP. JUST A FEW YEARS LATER, THE IBM CORPORATION WOULD INSTALL CIA CAMERAS IN SELECT MODELS OF ITS COPIERS, WHICH ALLOWED THE MACHINES TO PHOTOGRAPH AND STORE EVERY DOCUMENT THEY REPRODUCED. BUT THAT HIGH TECH GEAR WAS STILL IN THE FUTURE. THE PRINTERS DAD SOLD WERE LESS SOPHISTICATED, BUT THEY WERE BIG AND BULKY, AND IN NEED OF FREQUENT SERVICING BY "EXPERTS" AND SO WERE CONVENIENT PLACES TO STASH RECORDING DEVICES OR SIMPLE CACHES FOR DOCUMENTS AND PHOTOS.

APART FROM OCCASIONALLY ROUTING ORDERED EQUIPMENT THROUGH CIA WAREHOUSES IN VIRGINIA AND PHILADELPHIA WHERE THEIR "EXTRA" FEATURES COULD BE INSTALLED, DAD HAD NOTHING TO DO WITH THE OPERATIONS GOING ON IN THE FIELD...INCLUDING THOSE BEING PLANNED FOR VIETNAM.

HE TRIED OTHER APPROACHES TO FURTHERING HIS NEW CAREER. HE ENROLLED IN NIGHT SCHOOL AT CATHOLIC UNIVERSITY IN DC, AND STUDIED ON HIS OWN IN HOPES OF LANDING A MORE INTERESTING INTERNATIONAL ASSIGNMENT.

"GOOTUN TOK! ICK BIN EIN OWSSENDEENST-MITARRBITER OWS AMERIKA."

HE LASTED ONLY TWO TERMS AT CU.

IN HER LETTERS, ANASTASIA ENCOURAGED HIM, BUT DAD'S RESPONSES MADE IT CLEAR HE WASN'T CUT OUT FOR ANY MORE ACADEMICS. AS LONG AS I KNEW HIM, HE'D HAD A JEALOUS DISDAIN FOR "EGGHEADS" WHO MADE LEARNING A LIFELONG ACTIVITY.

IN THE MID-FIFTIES, WASHINGTON AND THE COUNTRY IN GENERAL WERE HEADED FOR INTERESTING TIMES. THIS PROBABLY DIDN'T SIT WELL WITH MY FATHER IN HIS LITTLE OFFICE ON NEW HAMPSHIRE AVENUE. IF THERE WAS ONE THING I KNEW HE HELD ONTO THROUGHOUT HIS LIFE, IT WAS A PREFERENCE FOR THE STATUS QUO.

THE BUCK DOESN'T STOP HERE

STREETCAR STRIKE
PEACE MARCH for JUSTICE
give us the ballot!

THIS WAS THE BACKDROP FOR MOM'S RETURN FROM SAIGON IN THE SPRING OF 1957.

TALK ABOUT A CHANGE IN THE STATUS QUO... THREE MONTHS LATER, SHE AND DAD WERE MARRIED. DAD'S YOUNGER BROTHER DROVE TO DC FROM SEATTLE, BUT LEFT AGAIN ONE DAY BEFORE THE WEDDING. NO ONE ELSE FROM HIS FAMILY ATTENDED.

THEY HONEYMOONED ON MARYLAND'S EASTERN SHORE. SHORTLY AFTERWARDS, DAD RESIGNED FROM HIS JOB.

Greetings from Ocean City M.D.

I ASSUMED THE TWO OF THEM HAD DISCUSSED THIS BEFORE, BUT I DON'T KNOW FOR SURE HOW INVOLVED MOM HAD BEEN IN THE DECISION-MAKING. LIKELY, NOT VERY MUCH.

IN ANY CASE, ARMED WITH A GUSHING LETTER OF REFERENCE FROM HIS BOSS, HE AND MOM HEADED BACK TO SEATTLE.

THE CYNIC IN ME COULDN'T HELP BUT THINK THE NAIVE ALTAR BOY HAD BEEN CHEWED UP AND SPAT OUT BY MEAN OL' REALITY.

147

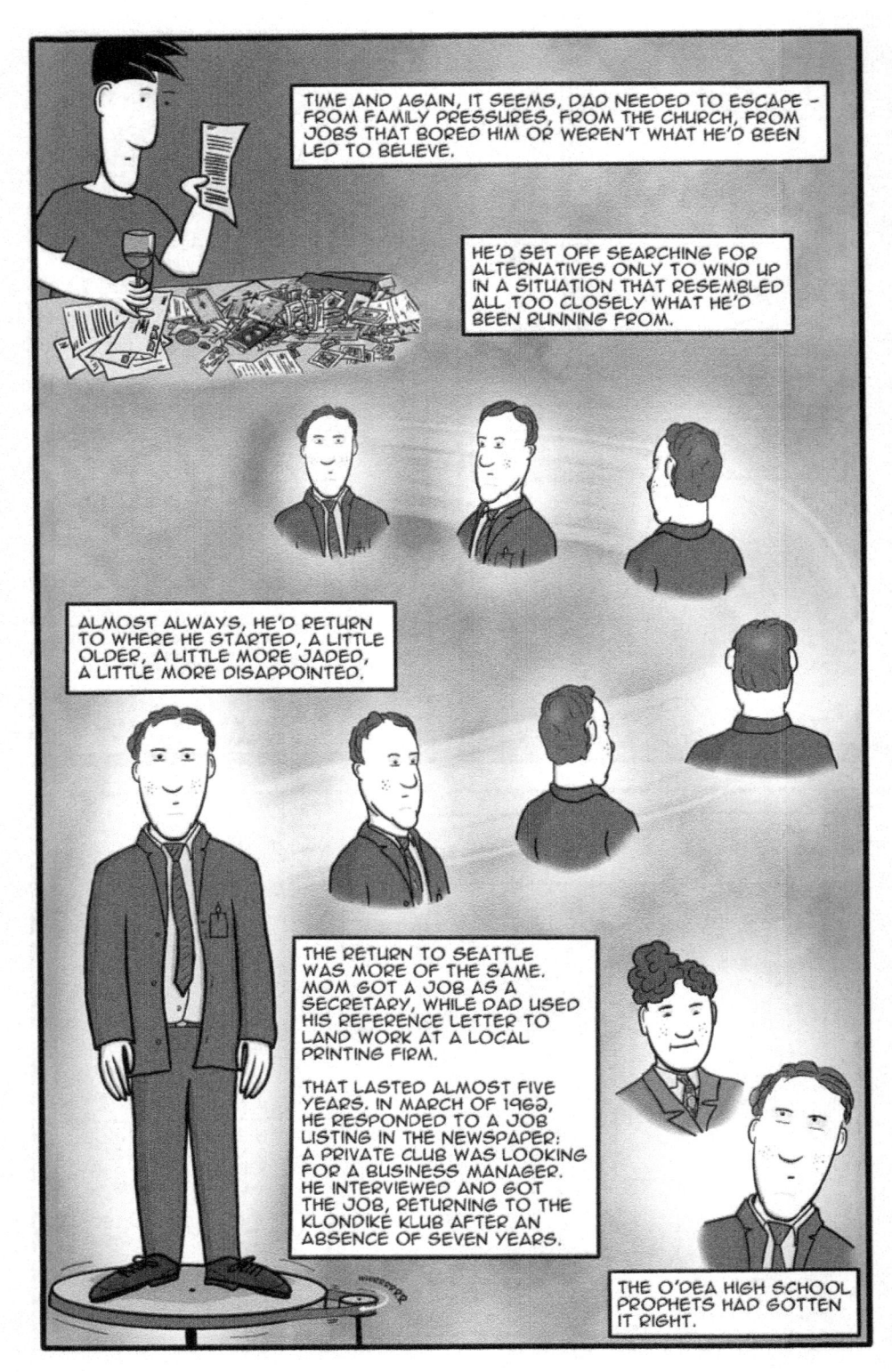

TIME AND AGAIN, IT SEEMS, DAD NEEDED TO ESCAPE — FROM FAMILY PRESSURES, FROM THE CHURCH, FROM JOBS THAT BORED HIM OR WEREN'T WHAT HE'D BEEN LED TO BELIEVE.

HE'D SET OFF SEARCHING FOR ALTERNATIVES ONLY TO WIND UP IN A SITUATION THAT RESEMBLED ALL TOO CLOSELY WHAT HE'D BEEN RUNNING FROM.

ALMOST ALWAYS, HE'D RETURN TO WHERE HE STARTED, A LITTLE OLDER, A LITTLE MORE JADED, A LITTLE MORE DISAPPOINTED.

THE RETURN TO SEATTLE WAS MORE OF THE SAME. MOM GOT A JOB AS A SECRETARY, WHILE DAD USED HIS REFERENCE LETTER TO LAND WORK AT A LOCAL PRINTING FIRM.

THAT LASTED ALMOST FIVE YEARS. IN MARCH OF 1962, HE RESPONDED TO A JOB LISTING IN THE NEWSPAPER: A PRIVATE CLUB WAS LOOKING FOR A BUSINESS MANAGER. HE INTERVIEWED AND GOT THE JOB, RETURNING TO THE KLONDIKE KLUB AFTER AN ABSENCE OF SEVEN YEARS.

THE O'DEA HIGH SCHOOL PROPHETS HAD GOTTEN IT RIGHT.

IT MUST HAVE BEEN STRANGE BEING BACK IN THE OLD CLUB. THINGS PROBABLY HADN'T CHANGED MUCH.
HEY!
FETCH ME A BOTTLE OF THE STRONG STUFF! THERE'S A GOOD BOY!
YES, SIR!
FAT OLD BOOZE HOUND.
HEY!
1962
I KNOW IT'S A WEEK EARLY, BUT I'D LIKE TO GIVE OUR FINANCIAL REPORT TO THE BOARD TOMORROW.
SET IT ON MY DESK BEFORE YOU LEAVE TONIGHT. THERE'S A GOOD MAN.
YES, SIR!
FAT OLD BROWN-NOSER.

SPREAD ACROSS SEVERAL OF THE LETTERS SENT BACK AND FORTH BETWEEN SAIGON AND WASHINGTON, DC, WAS A CURIOUS EXCHANGE REGARDING NIGHTMARES, WHICH HAD BECOME A REGULAR PART OF DAD'S SLEEP. APPARENTLY, THEY WERE OF TWO VARIETIES, SOME NAMELESS HORROR THAT HE NEVER DISCLOSED OR LUCID ENCOUNTERS WITH AN UNKNOWN VISITOR WHO WOULD EITHER EYE HIM SILENTLY OR HARANGUE HIM WITH A BARRAGE OF ANGRY BUT INCOMPREHENSIBLE VITRIOL. THOUGH IT WASN'T INCLUDED IN THE LETTER STASH, IT SEEMS DAD HAD ONCE CONFIDED TO ANASTASIA THAT THE DREAMS WERE RELATED TO SOME TERRIBLE ACT FROM HIS THE PAST, SOMETHING HE'D DONE THAT TRIGGERED SOME SERIOUS CATHOLIC GUILT.

Saturday, Feb. 11

Sure wish you were around to talk to. I am becoming a hermit, slowly but surely. Guess I will have to take to the drink again, at least then I will have company in the form of pink elephants, etc. I still have my nocturnal visitor occasionally, but he has become mute once again and so we just sit and stare at one another.

Oh well, in a few months your family will be visiting you and then you can have someone to talk to instead of your nightly visitor.

Dick also whatever it is that you have been trying to tell me for so long, I want you to tell me. I have pictured everything from murder, rape etc. I can't understand why you tell me you are so horrible. I can't see anything horrible in any aspect of you.

I WONDER IF THIS WAS THE FIRST STATEMENT OF UNCONDITIONAL SUPPORT HE'D HAD SINCE LEAVING THE SAFETY OF HOME?

UNCONDITIONAL AND, AS IT TURNED OUT, IRONICALLY MISGUIDED.

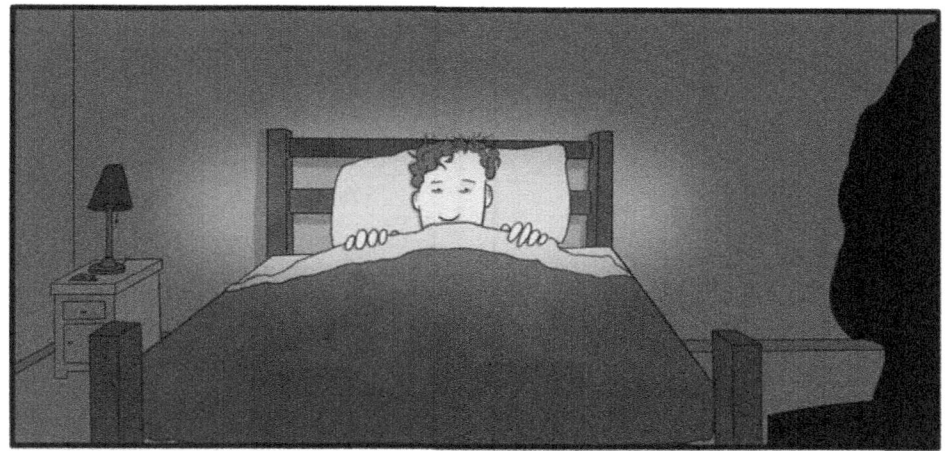

THIS WAS THE FIRST I'D HEARD OF THE NIGHTMARES.

I DON'T KNOW IF THEY EVER STOPPED OR IF THEY CONTINUED THROUGHOUT HIS LIFE.

AND I HAD NO IDEA WHO THE MYSTERIOUS VISITOR MIGHT BE.

WAS IT A SCOLDING PRIEST OR NUN FROM DAD'S SCHOOL DAYS, OR SOMEONE HE'D MET DURING HIS MILITARY SERVICE IN JAPAN OR KOREA? OR WAS IT JUST A FIGMENT OF HIS BORED IMAGINATION?

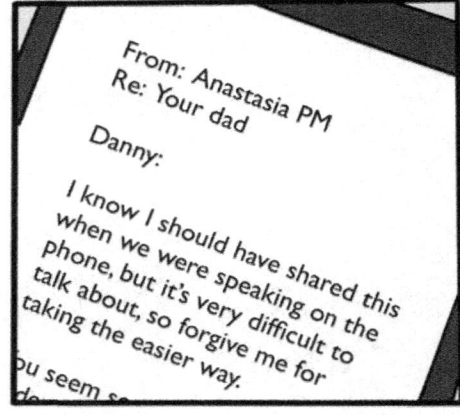

WITH HER USUAL EERILY PERFECT TIMING, MOM WAS ABOUT TO OFFER A TANTALIZING CLUE.

BWOOP!

EMAIL+ FROM MOM
OPEN

BWIP!

From: Anastasia PM
Re: Your dad

Danny:

I know I should have shared this when we were speaking on the phone, but it's very difficult to talk about, so forgive me for taking the easier way.

"YOU SEEM SO INTENT ON UNDERSTANDING YOUR FATHER,

I FIGURED I OWED YOU AT LEAST THIS ONE MORE SMALL PIECE OF THE PUZZLE.

BUT PLEASE, DON'T READ MORE INTO IT THAN IS THERE. DICK HAD SOME DIFFICULT TIMES AND HE NEVER DID KNOW HOW TO ASK FOR HELP. BACK THEN IT WASN'T CONSIDERED PROPER FOR MEN TO ADMIT TO SUCH THINGS. ALL THAT STUPID MACHISMO AND WHATNOT. I GUESS THAT'S WHY YOU AND HE FOUGHT SO MUCH LATER ON. IT'S NOT THAT HE DIDN'T LOVE YOU, DANNY, HE JUST DIDN'T ALWAYS COMPREHEND THE WAY THE WORLD REALLY WORKED.

ANYWAY, WHAT I WANT TO TELL YOU ABOUT HAPPENED RIGHT AFTER WE WERE MARRIED AND HAD JUST MOVED TO SEATTLE..."

"WE'D SETTLED INTO AN APARTMENT ON CAPITOL HILL, JUST A FEW BLOCKS FROM O'DEA HIGH SCHOOL AND ST. JAMES CATHEDRAL."

"IT WASN'T MUCH, BUT WE DIDN'T HAVE A LOT OF MONEY AND WE WERE STILL YOUNG."

"THE FIRST NIGHT AFTER WE MOVED IN, ABOUT AN HOUR AFTER WE'D GONE TO BED, YOUR DAD STARTED MUTTERING IN HIS SLEEP."

"I COULDN'T UNDERSTAND WHAT HE WAS SAYING, BUT IT SOUNDED AS IF HE WERE GETTING ANGRIER AND ANGRIER."

DICK....?

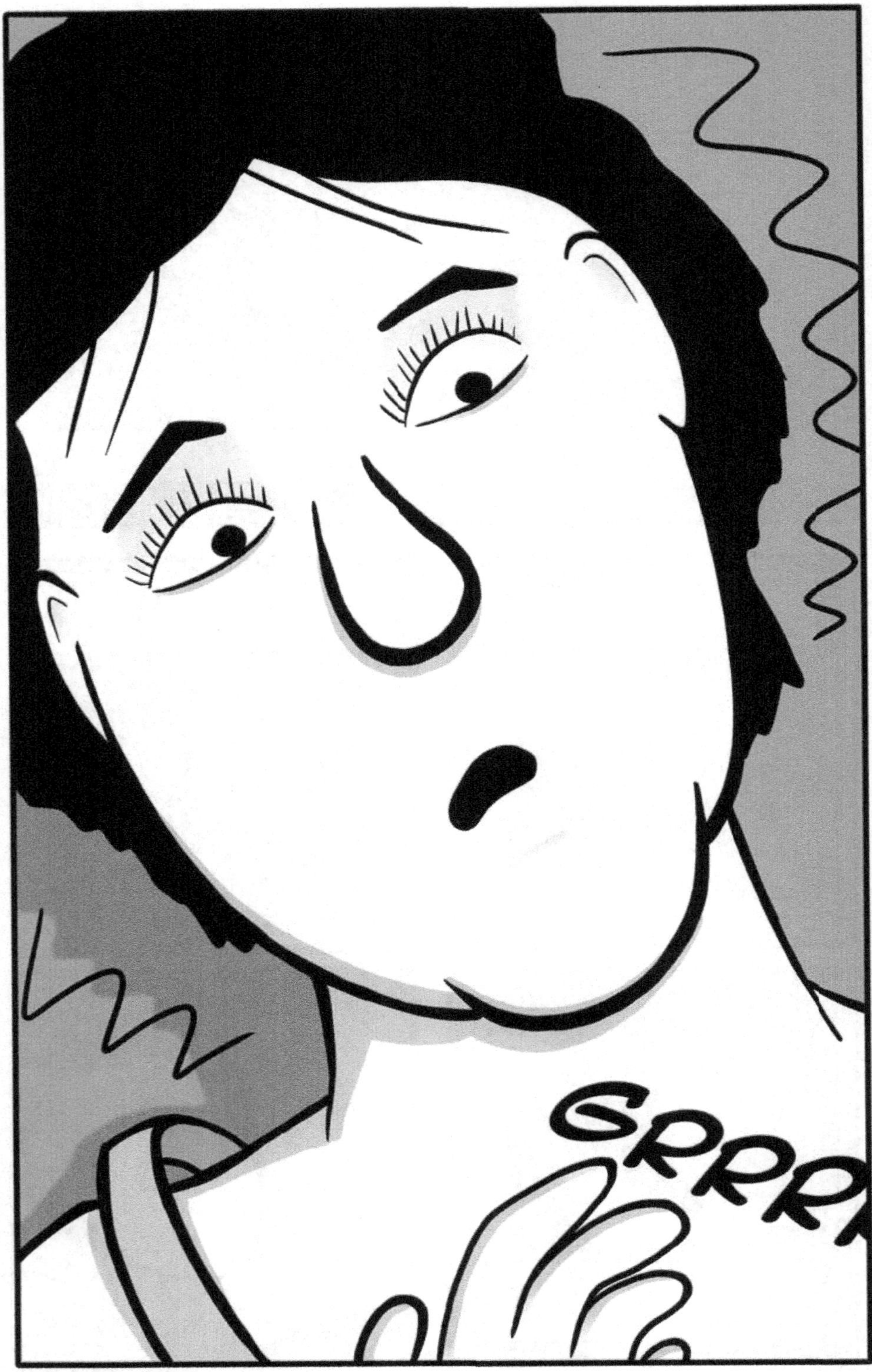
GRRR

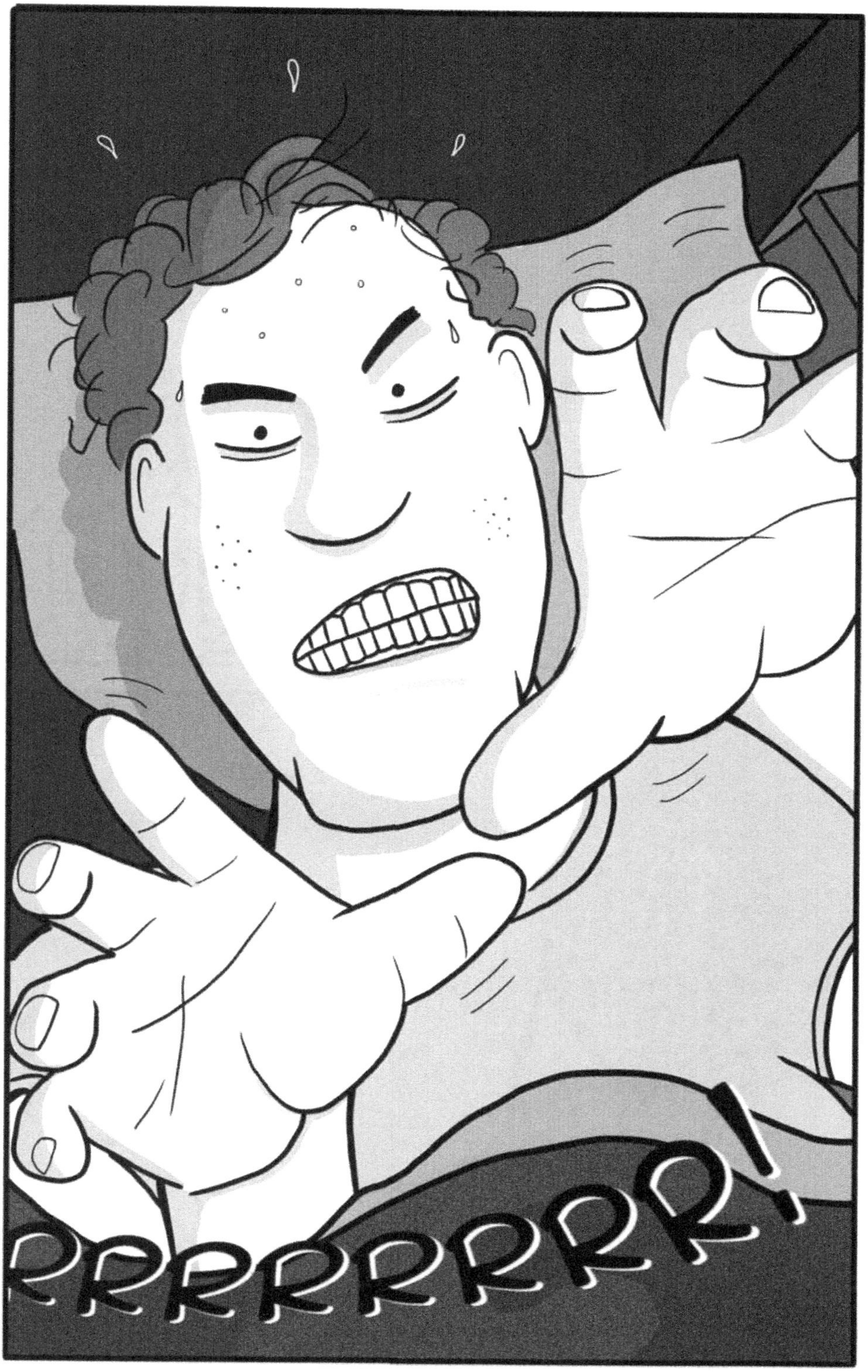
RRRRRRRRR!

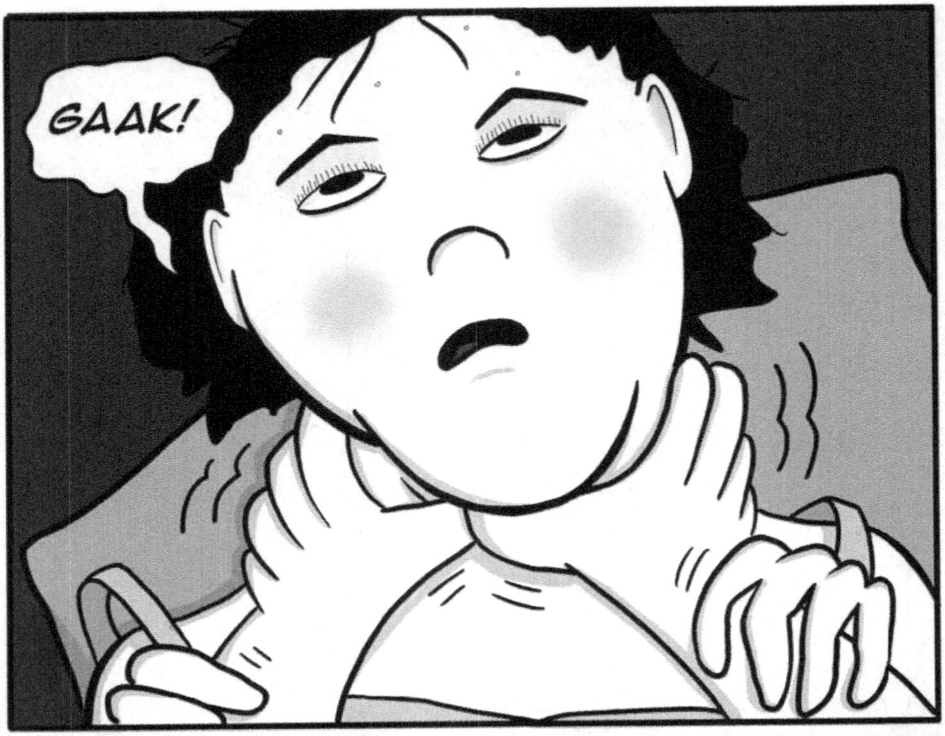
GAAK!

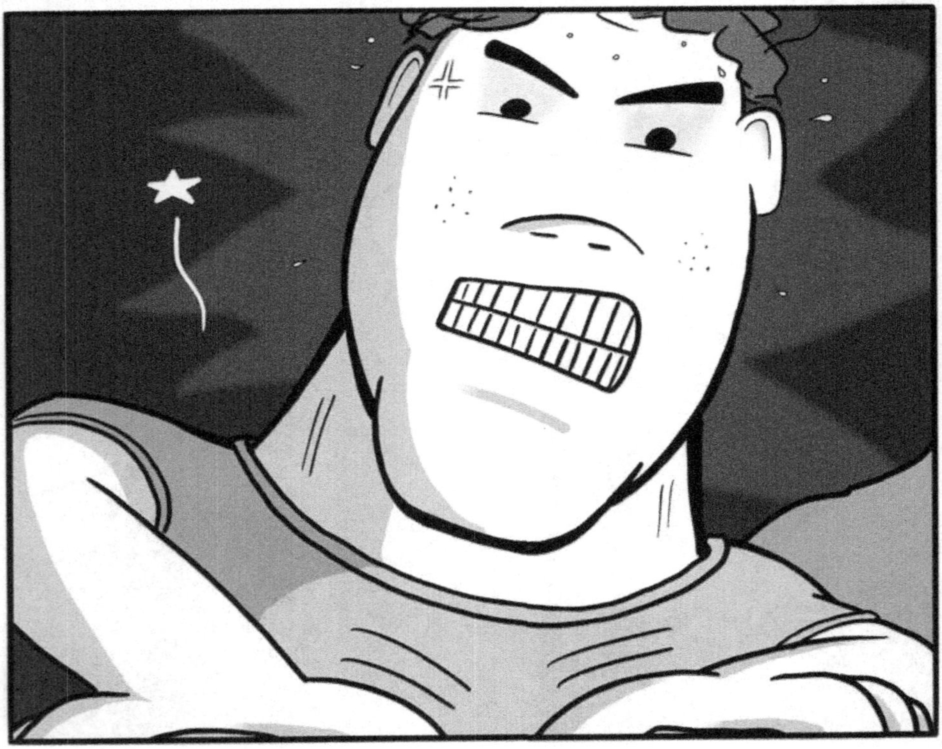

"IT STOPPED AS SUDDENLY AS IT HAD STARTED."

"HE SETTLED BACK ONTO HIS SIDE OF THE BED..."

"...LEAVING ME GASPING FOR BREATH."

"I SPENT THE REST OF THE NIGHT ON THE COUCH. IN THE MORNING, YOUR FATHER COULDN'T REMEMBER WHAT HE'D DONE."

"WHEN I TOLD HIM WHAT HAD HAPPENED, HE STOOD SILENTLY FOR A MOMENT AND THEN VERY QUIETLY SAID, 'I HEARD THE BUGLES.'"

"WE NEVER TALKED ABOUT IT AGAIN, BUT IT WASN'T THE ONLY TIME HE'D HAVE NIGHTMARES. I LEARNED TO PUT A PILLOW BETWEEN US WHENEVER HE STARTED TALKING IN HIS SLEEP."

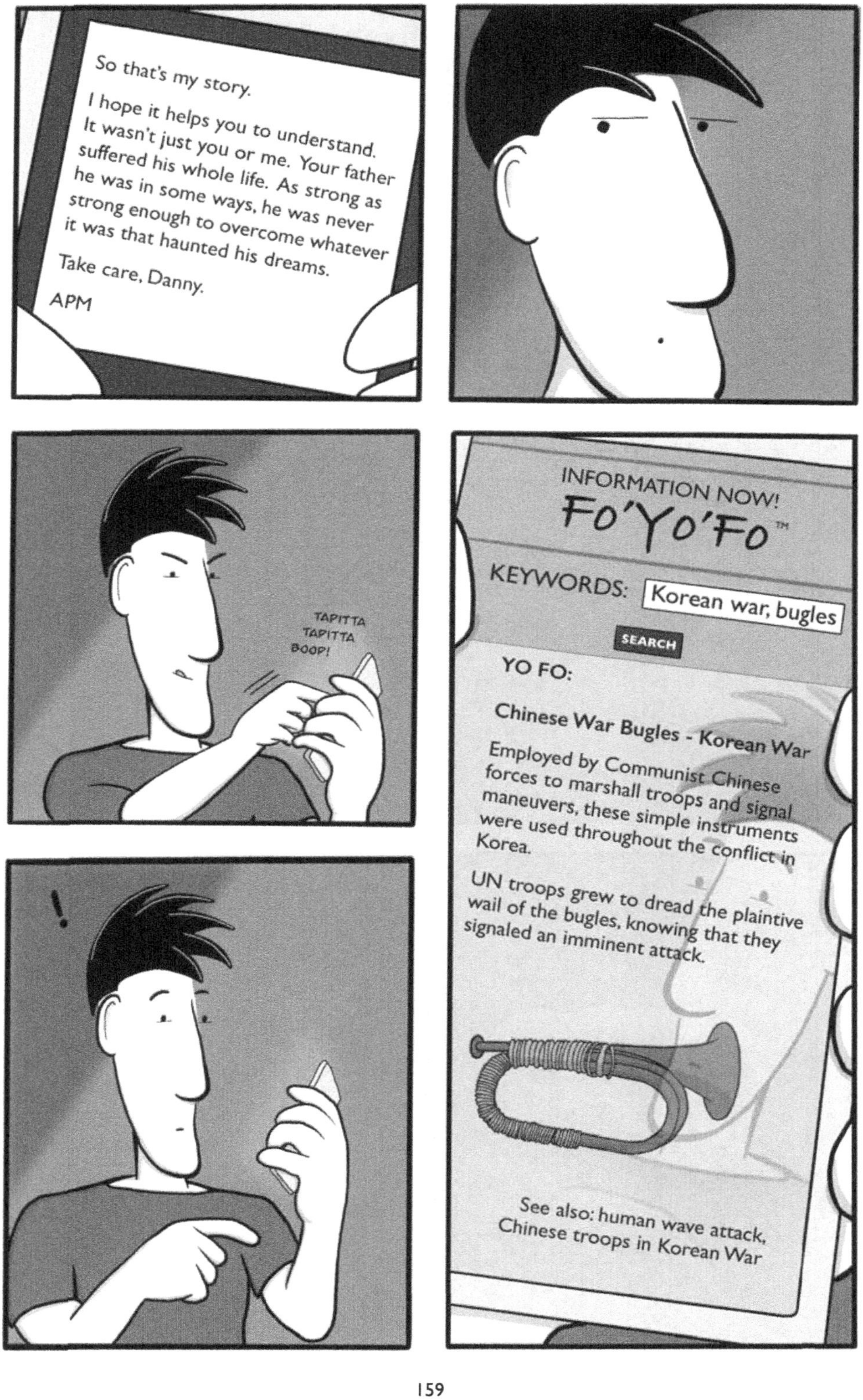
So that's my story.
I hope it helps you to understand. It wasn't just you or me. Your father suffered his whole life. As strong as he was in some ways, he was never strong enough to overcome whatever it was that haunted his dreams.
Take care, Danny.
APM
TAPITTA TAPITTA BOOP!
!
INFORMATION NOW!
FO'YO'FO™
KEYWORDS: Korean war, bugles
SEARCH
YO FO:
Chinese War Bugles - Korean War
Employed by Communist Chinese forces to marshall troops and signal maneuvers, these simple instruments were used throughout the conflict in Korea.
UN troops grew to dread the plaintive wail of the bugles, knowing that they signaled an imminent attack.
See also: human wave attack, Chinese troops in Korean War

"I HEARD THE BUGLES."

WHEN I WAS A KID, THE YAKIMA COUNTY FIRE DEPARTMENT DEPENDED UPON VOLUNTEERS.

IF A BIG FIRE BROKE OUT, A LOUD SIREN MOUNTED ON THE ROOF OF THE LOCAL STATION JUST UP THE HILL FROM OUR HOUSE WOULD SWITCH ON.

YOU COULD HEAR THE EERIE RISE AND FALL OF THE SIREN FOR MILES AROUND, WHICH WAS THE INTENT, I SUPPOSE.

AT NIGHT, IT WAS ESPECIALLY SPOOKY.

WHILE VOLUNTEER FIREMEN RACED TO THE STATION, I WOULD DUCK UNDER MY BLANKETS FEELING SCARED AND LONELY.

IT NEVER DAWNED ON ME THE FIREMEN'S SUMMONS MIGHT TRIGGER THE SAME REACTION IN SOMEONE ELSE, SOMEONE WHO ASSOCIATED ITS DISTANT WAIL WITH ANOTHER SOUND NOT HEARD IN OVER A DECADE.

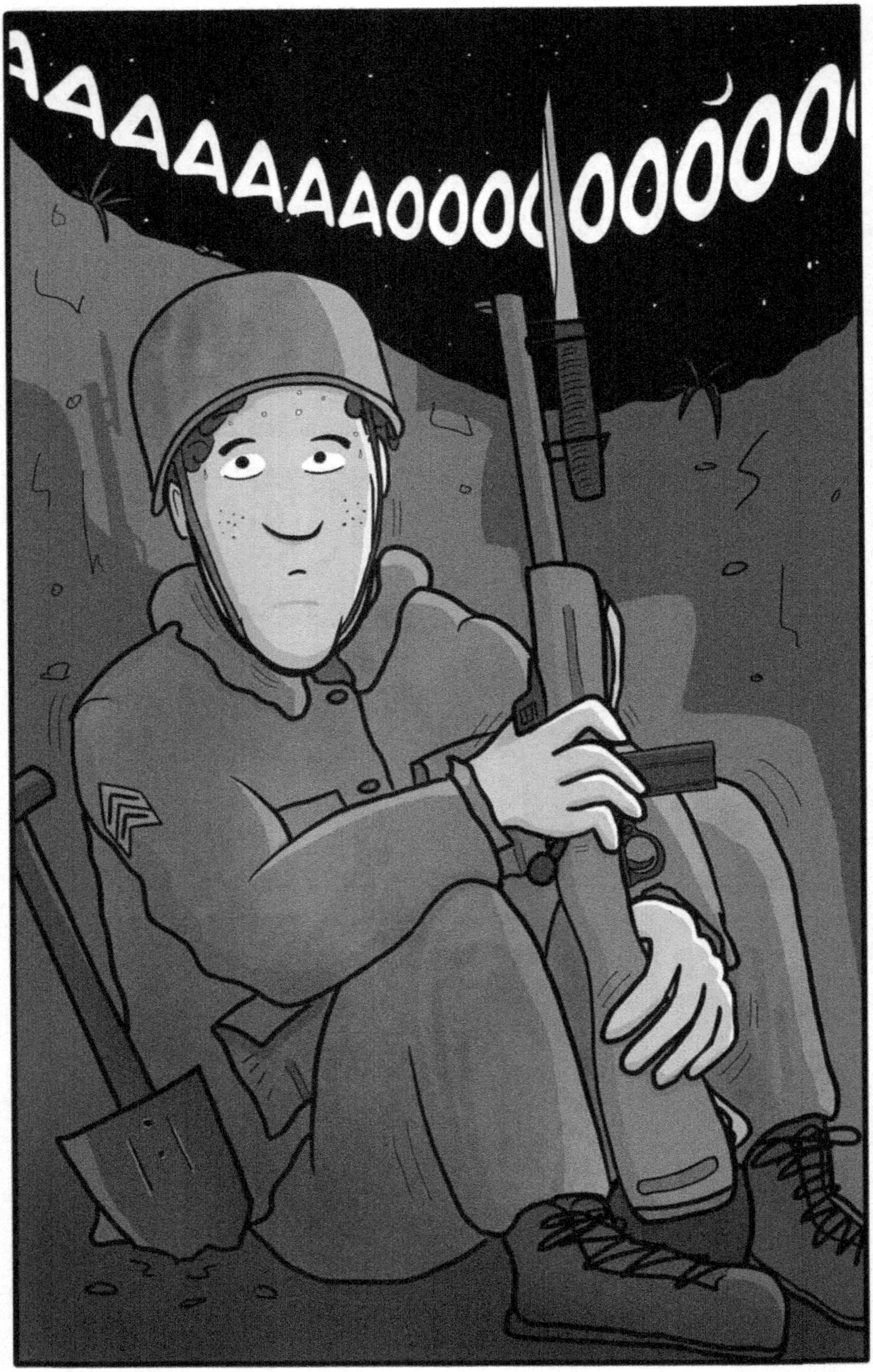
AAAAAAAAOOOOOOOOOO

OOOOOOOOOO

FOR HOW LONG DID THOSE BUGLES BLOW, DAD? DID THEIR DARK SYMPHONY EVER END, AND THE NIGHTMARES THEY SUMMONED CEASE TO HAUNT YOUR DREAMS?

OR HAD YOU LONG SINCE GIVEN UP ON DREAMS?

KLACK!

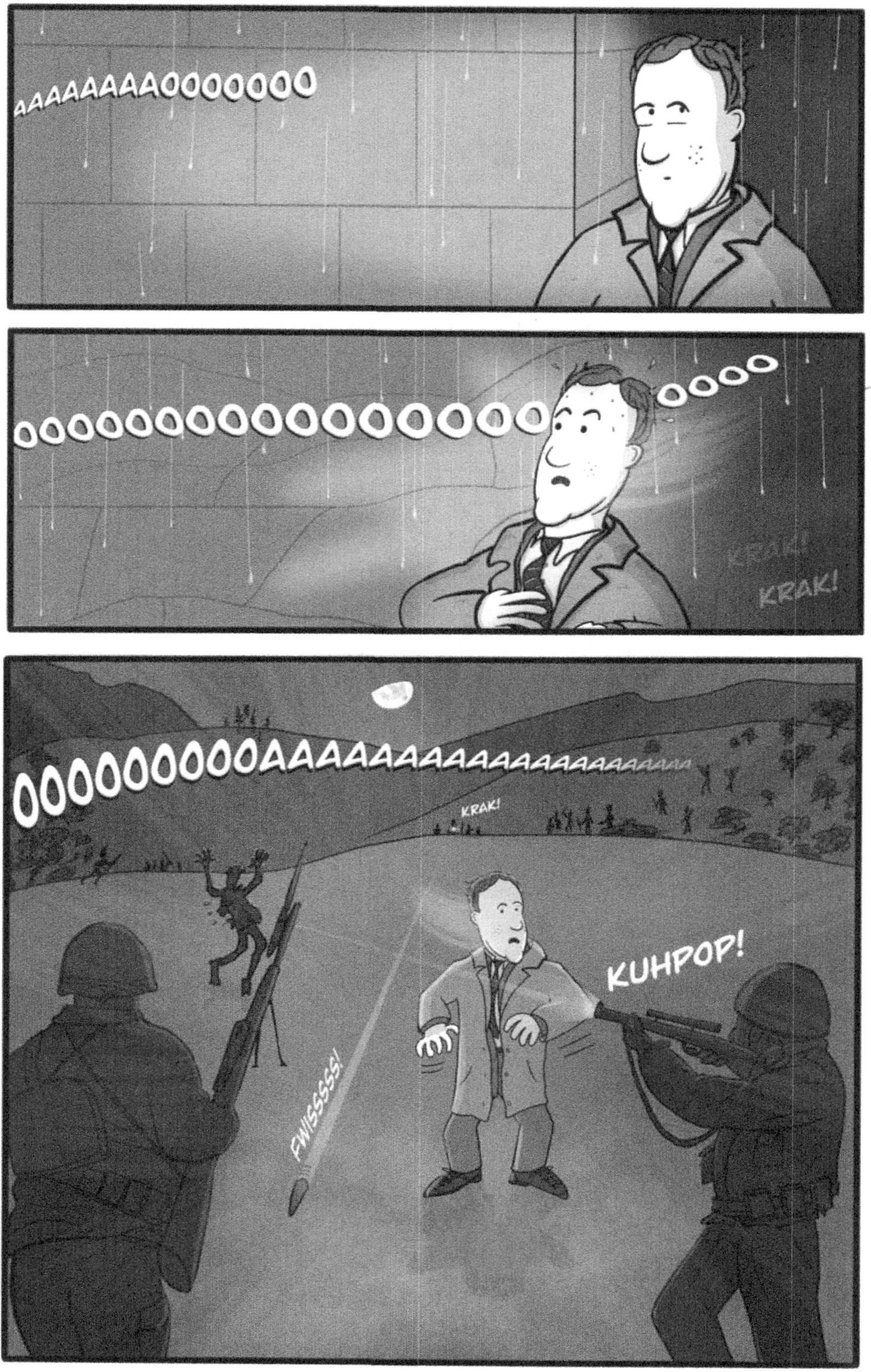

AAAAAAAAOOOOOOO
OOOOOOOOOOOOOOOOOOOOOOOOO
KRAK!
KRAK!
OOOOOOOOOAAAAAAAAAAAAAAAAAAA
KRAK!
KUHPOP!
FWISSSSS!

AAAAAAAAAAAAEEEEE
KUHPOP!
KRAK!
EEEEEEEEEEEEEEEEE
?
EEEEEEEEEEEEEEEEEOOOOOOOOOOO
POLICE 42 SEATTLE
OOOOOOOOOOOEEEEEEE
WHAT I DIDN'T KNOW AT THE TIME, BUT SOON WOULD DISCOVER...
...WAS JUST HOW FREQUENTLY MY FATHER'S PAST BECAME MIXED UP WITH HIS PRESENT.

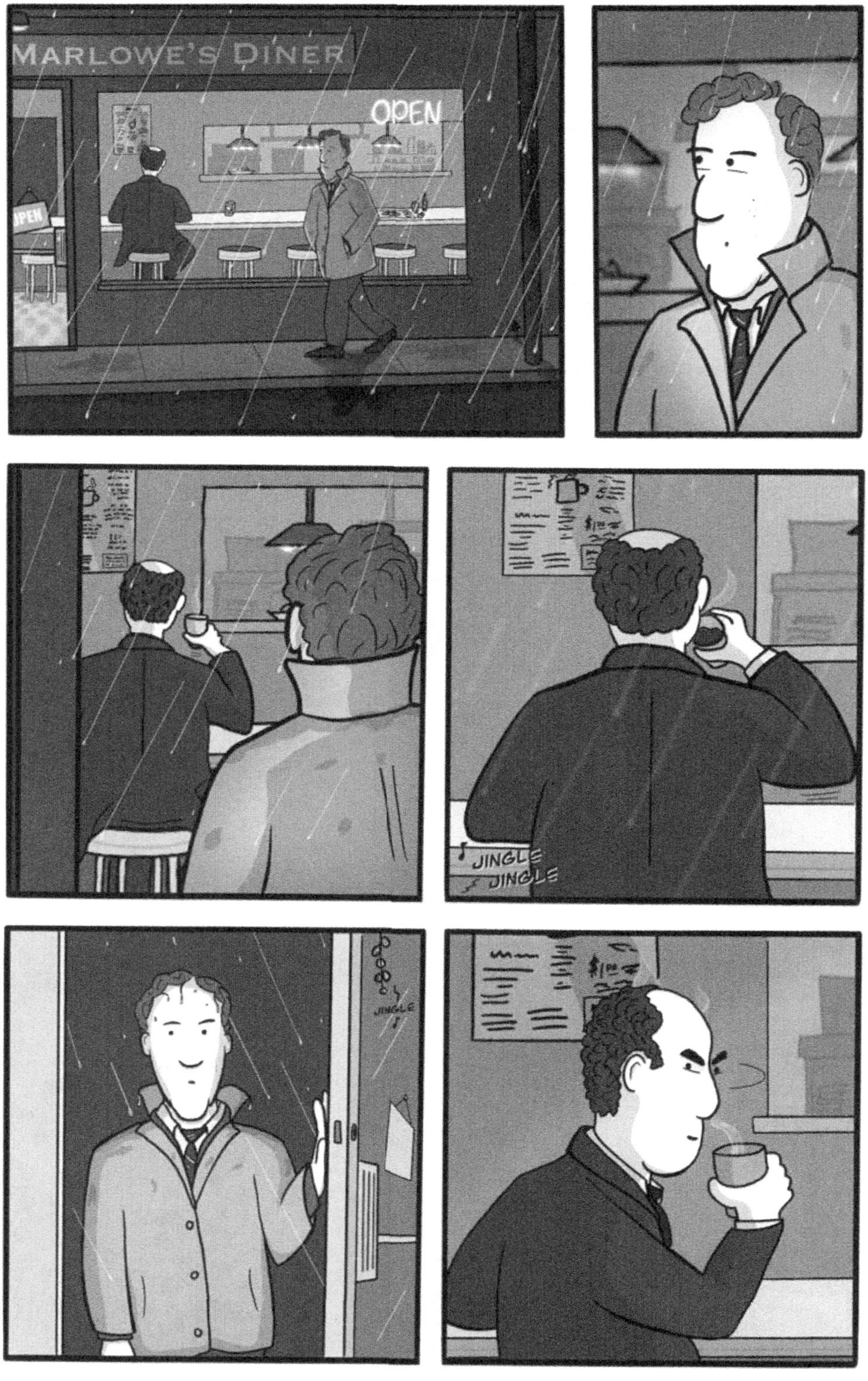
MARLOWE'S DINER
OPEN
OPEN
JINGLE
JINGLE
JINGLE

WELL, LOOKEE HERE!
IF IT ISN'T OLD FAITHFUL HIMSELF!
I KNEW YOU WOULDN'T TURN DOWN A CHANCE TO SEE ONE OF THE OLD GANG!
Breakfast
Lunch
Dinner
AAH! SEATTLE JOE!
AIN'T NO FINER BREW!
SLURRRP!

SO, HOW YA DOIN', ALTAR BOY?
HOW'S THE LIFE OF A GLORIFIED BELLHOP?
BETCHA MISS THE OLD BUSINESS, EH?
NOT IN THE LEAST.
I GAVE THAT UP WHEN I LEFT THE SERVICE.
OF COURSE YOU DID.
IN D.C. YOU WERE JUST SELLING MIMEO MACHINES TO BUDDING CAPITALISTS IN CENTRAL AMERICA AND INDOCHINA!
CUT THE CATHOLIC SCHOOLBOY CRAP!
I GOTTA GREAT OPPORTUNITY FOR YOU!
DOINK! DOINK!

*September, 1960: the "Martin and Mitchell Scandal." Two NSA cryptologists, one from Ellensburg, Washington, defected to the USSR.

LIKE I SAID... RIGHT UP YOUR ALLEY.
THIS REALLY IS GREAT COFFEE! BETTER THAN THAT MUD THE NIPS SERVE BACK IN KYOTO.
SLURP!
IT'S TOO BAD HOW TOUGH IT IS FOR GUYS LIKE YOU.
NOT LIKE IT WAS IN THE SERVICE, EH? NOTHING TO WORRY ABOUT, EVERYTHING TAKEN CARE OF...

I CAN TAKE CARE OF MYSELF!
OF COURSE! YOU CAN TAKE CARE OF YOURSELF, YOUR WIFE...
SPEAKING OF ANA, I HEAR SHE LEFT THE COMPANY TO FOLLOW YOU HOME TO SEATTLE. THAT WAS SWELL OF HER, GIVING UP HER OWN CAREER AS AN INTELLIGENCE AGENT FOR YOURS AS A...UH... WHATEVER IT IS THAT YOU DO.
AND NOW YOU TWO GOT A KID! ANOTHER ALTAR BOY IN THE MAKING, NO DOUBT.
BY THE WAY, WHEN'S THE LAST TIME YOU SAW EITHER OF THEM AWAKE?
SLURRRP!

I HAVE TO GO.
LIFE'S SHORT, DICK! YOU GOTTA DECIDE WHAT'S IMPORTANT!
JINGLE!
THANKS FOR THE ADVICE...
...AGAIN.
ANY TIME. LOOK ME UP WHEN YOU CHANGE YOUR MIND.
WE BOTH KNOW YOU WILL.
JINGLE! JINGLE!
SLAM!
SLURP!

BUS STOP 42
"WHEN'S THE LAST TIME YOU'VE SEEN EITHER OF THEM AWAKE?"
BALLARD
42 NORTH
I'M SURE WHATEVER WEIGHED DOWN ON DAD HADN'T BEEN LIGHTENED ANY BY MY ARRIVAL. WITH HELP FROM MOM'S FATHER, HE'D BOUGHT A SMALL HOUSE JUST A FEW BLOCKS FROM THE OLD NEIGHBORHOOD IN PHINNEY RIDGE. BUT MONEY WAS TIGHT. WITH MOM AT HOME LOOKING AFTER ME, DAD WORKED LONG HOURS TO MAKE ENDS MEET.
I WAS SO YOUNG, I HAVE FEW MEMORIES OF THOSE DAYS.
EXCEPT...

MOM USED TO BRING ME ALONG WHEN SHE WENT SHOPPING AT THE BIG BON MARCHE DEPARTMENT STORE DOWNTOWN.
1962's MOST STYLISH
IS THAT DADDY?
!
NOW THAT WOULD TAKE SOME 'SPLAININ', WOULDN'T IT?
HEH! HEH!

I DON'T RECALL, BUT I'M SURE MY MOTHER MUST HAVE TOLD DAD WHAT HAD HAPPENED.

I CAN ONLY IMAGINE IT ADDED EVEN MORE WEIGHT TO HIS LOAD AND PROBABLY PUSHED HIM TOWARD YET ANOTHER ATTEMPT TO ESCAPE FROM WHAT HIS LIFE HAD BECOME.

SOON WE WERE ON A TRAIN TO YAKIMA, WHERE DAD HAD RENTED US A HOUSE. THAT FIRST WINTER, MOM THOUGHT WE'D MOVED TO SIBERIA.

BUT BY SUMMER THERE WAS SUNSHINE, A YWCA FOR THE WOMENFOLK, AND PUBLIC TENNIS COURTS.

HER OUTGOING NATURE KICKED IN AND MOM QUICKLY MADE FRIENDS, ONCE AGAIN SETTLING IN TO SMALL TOWN LIFE.

MEANWHILE, DAD HAD TAKEN A JOB AS A TRAVELING SALESMAN FOR A PRINTING COMPANY SPECIALIZING IN CALENDARS AND PROMOTIONAL ITEMS. THAT WAS THE OFFICIAL EMPLOYMENT. THERE WAS, OF COURSE, THE *OTHER* BUSINESS.

ONLY NOW WAS I REALIZING HOW MUCH OF HIS LIFE WAS TAKEN UP BY THE SPOOKY STUFF, AND HOW MUCH MORE THERE WAS TO UNCOVER...

6

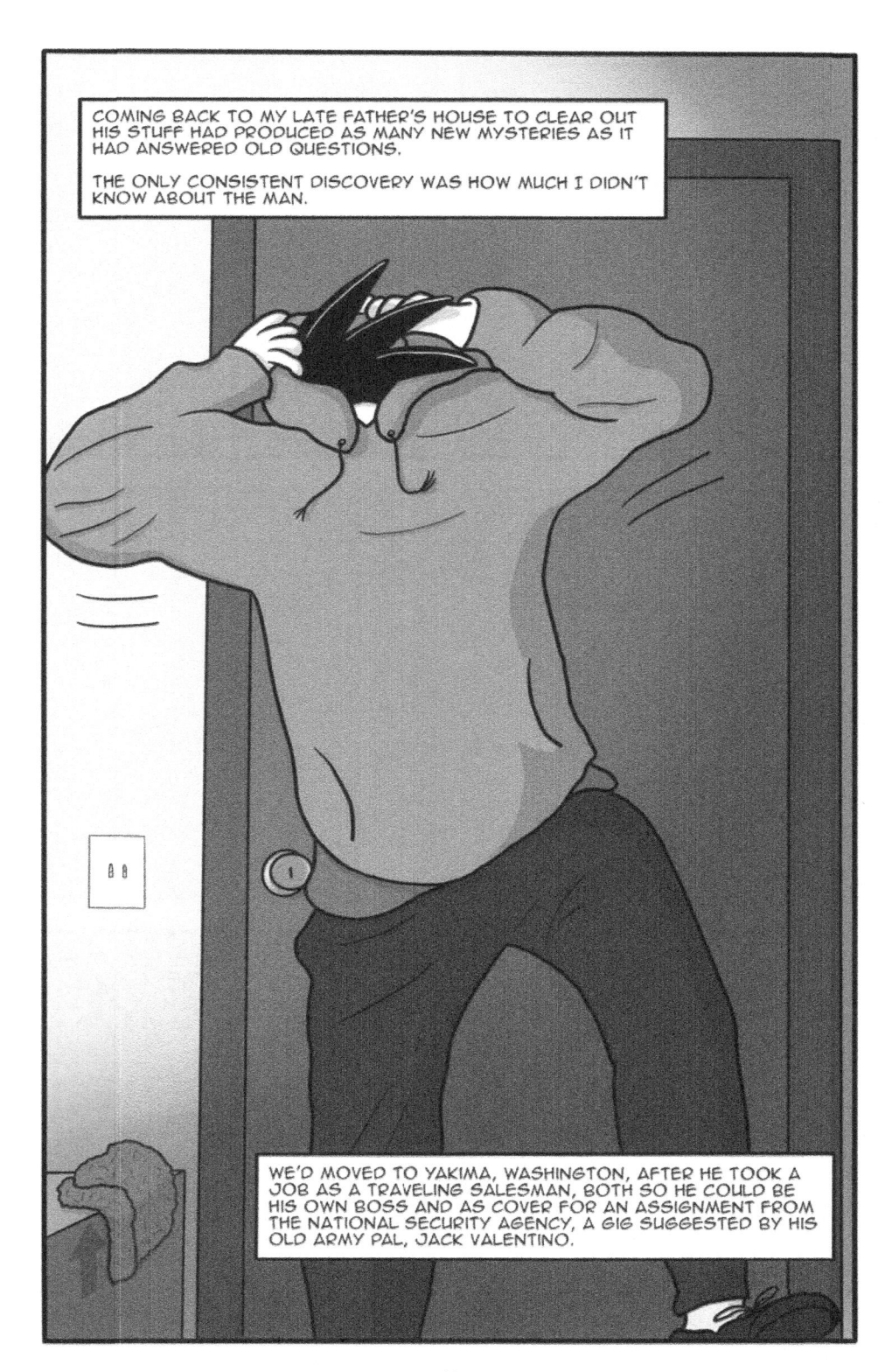

COMING BACK TO MY LATE FATHER'S HOUSE TO CLEAR OUT HIS STUFF HAD PRODUCED AS MANY NEW MYSTERIES AS IT HAD ANSWERED OLD QUESTIONS.

THE ONLY CONSISTENT DISCOVERY WAS HOW MUCH I DIDN'T KNOW ABOUT THE MAN.

WE'D MOVED TO YAKIMA, WASHINGTON, AFTER HE TOOK A JOB AS A TRAVELING SALESMAN, BOTH SO HE COULD BE HIS OWN BOSS AND AS COVER FOR AN ASSIGNMENT FROM THE NATIONAL SECURITY AGENCY, A GIG SUGGESTED BY HIS OLD ARMY PAL, JACK VALENTINO.

SOMETHING HAD GONE DOWN BETWEEN DAD AND "JACK-ASS..."
...BUT STILL I HAD NO CLUE AS TO WHEN OR WHY IT HAPPENED...
...OR WHETHER IT EVEN MATTERED.
SSG
RICHARD MOLITOR
U.S. ARMY
ZZZZZZ
SSG
RICHARD
U.S. ARMY

THE UNIFORM WAS A PALIMPSEST OF DAD'S MILITARY CAREER. EVERY PATCH AND PIN REPRESENTED COUNTLESS PEOPLE, PLACES, AND EVENTS – FOOTPRINTS ON HIS PATH THROUGH MILITARY LIFE.

INSIGNIA OF THE 25TH INFANTRY, ONE OF SEVERAL DIVISIONS DAD BELONGED TO AS THE ARMY WAS ORGANIZED AND REORGANIZED THROUGHOUT THE WAR.

PATCH OF THE RYUKUS ISLANDS COMMAND, WHICH LED ALL UNITS IN THE ARCHIPELAGO THAT INCLUDES OKINAWA

MERITORIOUS UNIT CITATION, AWARDED TO THE ASA COMPANY IN KYOTO WHEN THEIR CODEBREAKERS CRACKED A KEY CHINESE CYPHER. ALL THE SOLDIERS IN THE UNIT GOT TO WEAR THE PATCH.

INSIGNIA OF A STAFF SERGEANT, DAD'S FINAL RANK AFTER SEVERAL UPS AND DOWNS FROM PRIVATE TO CORPORAL AND BACK AGAIN.

"COLLAR BRASS" RECOGIZING THE ASA COMPANY'S PLACE WITHIN THE U.S. ARMY SIGNAL CORPS.

CAMPAIGN RIBBONS AND CITATIONS AWARDED TO SOLDIERS SERVING IN KOREA. THE BRONZE STARS ON THE KOREAN WAR SERVICE RIBBON INDICATED DAD PARTICIPATED IN TWO DIFFERENT MILITARY CAMPAIGNS DURING HIS SEVEN MONTHS ON THE PENINSULA.

REPUBLIC OF KOREA PRESIDENTIAL UNIT CITATION, A RIBBON AWARDED BY THE ROK GOVERNMENT TO BOTH THEIR OWN SOLDIERS AND MEMBERS OF THE U.N. COALITION OF ARMIES.

LAPEL PIN WITH CREST OF THE ARMY SECURITY AGENCY.

BUT WOULD I EVER KNOW WHY THE JOURNEY BEGAN OR WHAT WENT THROUGH THE MIND OF THE TRAVELER AFTER HE'D REACHED THE END OF THE TRAIL?

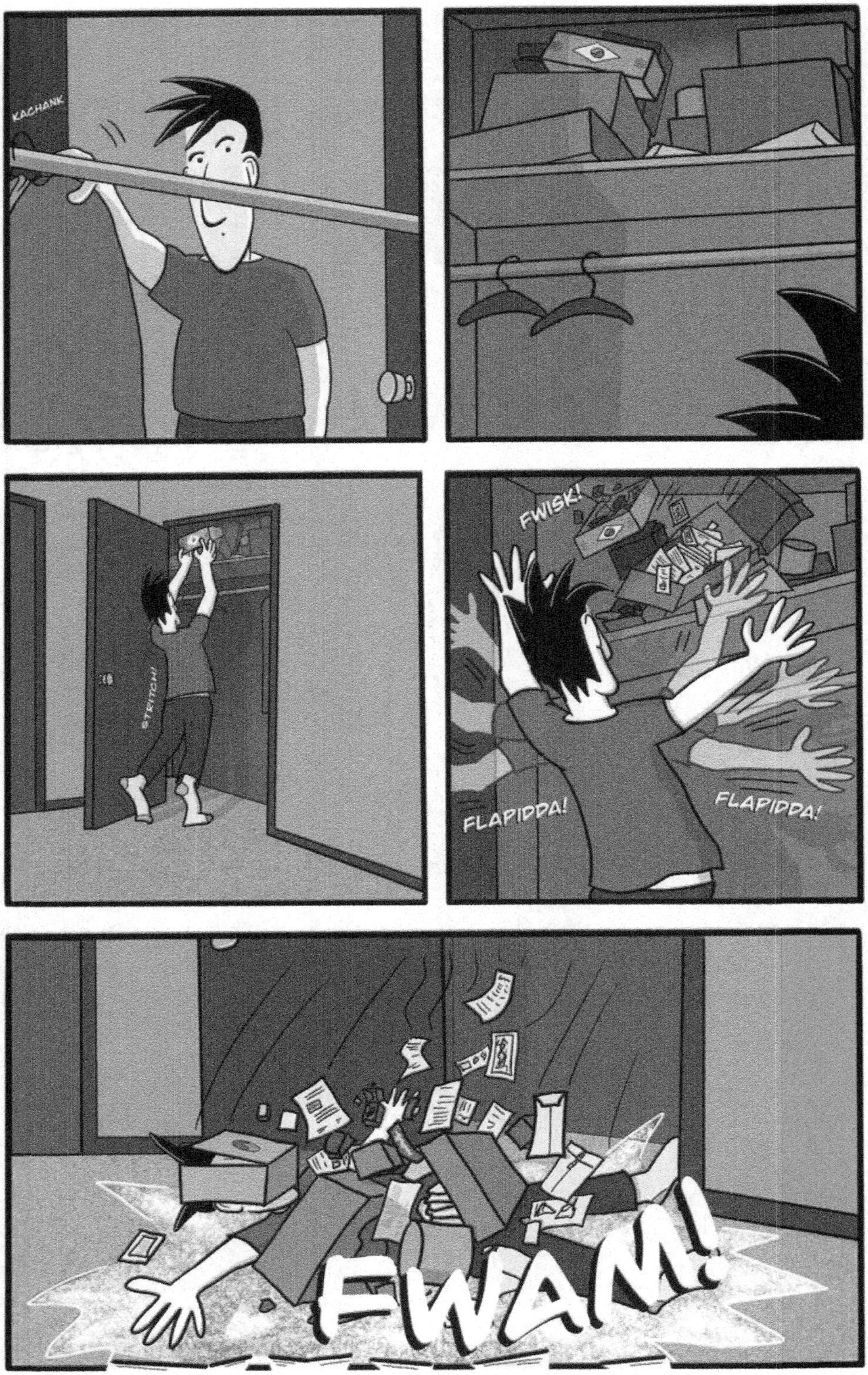
KACHANK
STRITCH!
FWISK!
FLAPIDDA!
FLAPIDDA!
FWAM!

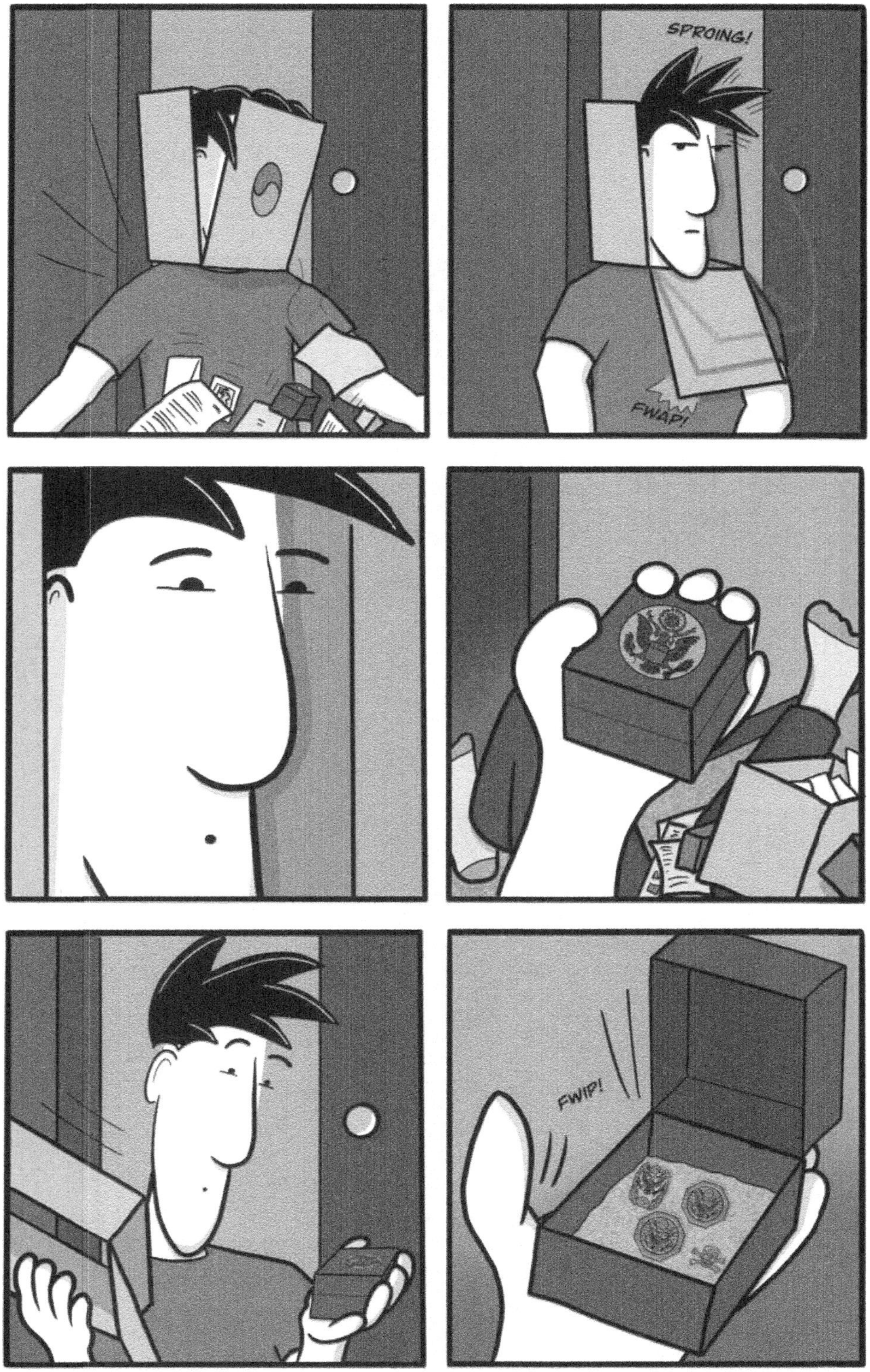
SPROING!
FWAP!
FWIP!

EVERY GLIMPSE INTO MY FATHER'S PAST OFFERED A LITTLE BIT MORE THAN I'D EVER KNOWN AND MORE THAN HE EVER SHARED HIMSELF.

HERE, HIDDEN AWAY IN A TINY BOX, WAS THE SUMMATION OF HIS FINAL YEARS AS A SECRET AGENT MAN.

THESE LITTLE PINS MARKED 15 YEARS OF SERVICE TO AN UNNAMED U.S. GOVERNMENT AGENCY THAT EMPLOYED HIM UNTIL THE DAY HE DIED. HIS BANK RECORDS FROM THAT TIME LIST FREQUENT DEPOSITS FROM THE DEPARTMENT OF LABOR, BUT MOST LIKELY THAT WAS A FRONT FOR THE NSA. APPARENTLY THEY DO THAT SORT OF THING ALL THE TIME.

ACCORDING TO THOSE SAME RECORDS, AFTER LEAVING WASHINGTON, D.C., DAD NEVER AGAIN WORKED FULL TIME FOR ANY GOVERMENT AGENCY. HE CERTAINLY NEVER MADE MUCH MONEY FROM WHATEVER PART TIME ENTERPRISES THE NSA PUT HIM UP TO. IF IT WEREN'T FOR MY MOTHER'S TEACHING SALARY AND PENSION, HE'D HAVE BEEN AS BROKE AS HE EVER WAS.

I COULD LAUD HIM FOR THE WHOLE "PRO PATRIA" THING, BUT I HAD TO WONDER WHAT EXACTLY HE SAW IN THE SPOOKY JOBS, NOT TO MENTION WHAT THE CHIEF SPOOKS SAW IN *HIM*.

A LITTTLE BACKGROUND RESEARCH LED TO ONE POSSIBLE ANSWER...

WHEN ALL THIS WAS GOING ON, OPERATIONS OF THE CIA, NSA, AND HALF A DOZEN OTHER INTELLIGENCE AGENCIES WERE INTERTWINED IN A COMPLEX WEB OF WHO WAS SUPPOSED TO BE DOING WHAT, WHERE, AND WITH WHOM, NONE OF WHICH WAS ENTIRELY SETTLED TO THE LIKING OF THOSE INVOLVED.

TURF WARS WERE COMMON, AND SEVERAL ATTEMPTS WERE MADE TO CLARIFY EACH AGENCY'S ROLE AND SET UP CLEAR GUIDELINES GOVERNING HOW THEY WERE TO WORK TOGETHER OR, AS WAS FREQUENTLY THE CASE, AROUND EACH OTHER.

PRESIDENT LYNDON B. JOHNSON ORDERED A FULL REVIEW, SPECIFICALLY OF SIGNAL INTELLIGENCE OPERATIONS – DAD'S SPECIALTY – IN 1968, AS MANY NEWCOMERS IN THE INTELLIGENCE FIELD WERE BEGINNING TO QUESTION THE USEFULNESS OF THE OLD EQUIPMENT AND TECHNIQUES IN THE NASCENT AGE OF THE COMPUTER.

THIS WASN'T A SIMPLE CASE OF NEW TECHNOLOGIES BEING BETTER THAN OLD. AS WOULD BECOME APPARENT LATER, WHILE THE OLD WAYS WEREN'T ALWAYS EFFECTIVE WHEN DEALING WITH A SUPERPOWER SUCH AS THE SOVIET UNION, THEY STILL WERE NECESSARY WHEN KEEPING TABS ON TARGETS THAT WEREN'T AS SOPHISTICATED. THE TROUBLE WAS, AS EARLY AS THE LATE 1960S, MANY OF THE OLD TECHNIQUES INVOLVING SHORTWAVE RADIO COMMUNICATION WERE BECOMING LOST ARTS. AS THE OLD GUARD RETIRED OR DIED OFF, THE NUMBER OF AGENTS WITH SHORTWAVE EXPERIENCE DECLINED. THIS PROBLEM CONTINUED INTO THE 21ST CENTURY, AND ACTUALLY LED TO THE LAST ASSIGNMENT MY FATHER EVER RECEIVED.

Time Out for Verbosity

SELECTED SPOOKY CONTEXT FOR THE ERA IN QUESTION

1960 – NSA CRYPTOLOGISTS MARTIN & MITCHELL DEFECT TO USSR

1961 – ASA "RADIO RESEARCHER" BECOMES FIRST AMERICAN COMBAT CASUALTY IN VIET NAM.

1962 – CUBAN MISSILE CRISIS

1964 – GULF OF TONKIN INCIDENT

1968 – NORTH KOREA SEIZES U.S. SURVEILLANCE VESSEL CONTAINING TOP SECRET CRYPTO EQUIPMENT

IT HAPPENED ABOUT 10 YEARS BEFORE DAD DIED. THE KINGDOM OF SAUDI ARABIA WANTED TO TRACK HOUTHI TRIBES IN YEMEN, WHICH WERE ALLIED WITH THE KINGDOM'S ARCH ENEMY, IRAN. THE U.S. SAW VALUE IN HELPING THE SAUDIS TO COUNTER IRAN'S GROWING INFLUENCE IN THE REGION.* A PLAN WAS PITCHED TO SEND NSA AGENTS TO SAUDI ARABIA TO TEACH THE LOCALS HOW TO MONITOR HOUTHI RADIO SIGNALS AND TRACK THEIR SOURCES, JUST THE SORT OF THING DAD AND HIS BUDDIES HAD DONE IN JAPAN AND KOREA.

DAD GOT THE CALL, BUT BY THEN HIS HEALTH WASN'T THE GREATEST AND FOR THE FIRST TIME THAT I KNOW OF HE TURNED DOWN THE ASSIGNMENT. ACCORDING TO MOM, WHO KNEW ABOUT THE OFFER AND HELPED TALK DAD OUT OF ACCEPTING IT, HE RETIRED FROM GOVERNMENT WORK SHORTLY THEREAFTER.

RETIRED FROM A JOB THAT DIDN'T EXIST.

*DUE IN NO SMALL PART TO OUR DISASTROUS WAR WITH IRAQ.

THE LAST PIN IN THE BOX WAS THE SOLE RECORD OF THE WORK THAT HAD FIRST DRAWN DAD AWAY FROM SEATTLE AND BACK INTO THE WORLD OF THIRD-TIER SPOOKERY.

NSA COVERT OPS PIN

IT LOOKED LIKE SOMETHING FROM A CRACKER JACK BOX, A SHINY PRIZE TO ENTICE LITTLE BOYS.

WHICH, IN A WAY, I GUESS, IT WAS.

I KNEW A LITTLE SOMETHING ABOUT THIS PARTICULAR SPOOKINESS.

SOME OF DAD'S ROAD TRIPS WERE AN OBVIOUS COVER FOR OTHER ACTIVITIES, THOUGH AT THE TIME THEY WERE EXPLAINED AS THE ODIOUS REQUIREMENTS OF HIS JOB AS A TRAVELING SALESMAN.

EVERY NOW AND THEN HE WOULD TAKE ME ALONG WHILE HE MADE THE ROUNDS OF HIS TERRITORY. USUALLY, IT WAS A DAY OF STOPS AT AN ASSORTMENT OF BANKS AND PRINT SHOPS, BUT ONCE IN A WHILE HE'D GO SOMEPLACE A LITTLE DIFFERENT.

LOOSE TALK is a chain reaction for ESPIONAGE!

THIS WAS STILL THE HEIGHT OF THE COLD WAR. PARANOIA, WHILE NOT AS BAD AS DURING THE McCARTHY ERA, STILL RAN HIGH, ESPECIALLY AROUND ANYTHING HAVING TO DO WITH NUCLEAR WEAPONS, E.G., THE HANFORD RESERVATION, 44 MILES DOWN THE ROAD FROM YAKIMA.

THE ROSENBERG SPY SCANDAL STILL STUNG, EVEN YEARS AFTER THE HUSBAND AND WIFE TEAM HAD BEEN TOASTED IN THE ELECTRIC CHAIR.

LIKEWISE, THE MARTIN & MITCHELL AFFAIR STILL STUCK IN THE CRAW OF THE NSA, AN IRRITANT MADE WORSE AS CERTAIN ELEMENTS WITHIN THE CIA KEPT BRINGING IT UP.

ALL ACROSS THE COUNTRY, THE SPOOK AGENCIES WERE SWEEPING OUT THE CLOSETS.

Man-Wife Spy Team Sentenced To Death

Rosenbergs To Get Chair

Russians Claim U.S. Spy Caught With Secrets

MISSING SECURITY COUPLE GIVEN ASYLUM IN RUSSIA

DAD WAS ONE OF THE JANITORS.

Panel 1: THE STAFF AT HANFORD SEEMED TO KNOW MY FATHER.

Panel 2: AFTER DROPPING ME OFF IN THE PUBLIC EXHIBIT AREA, DAD MET WITH HIS CONTACT, A TALL, THIN MAN IN A GREY SUIT.

Panel 3: THEY WENT OFF SOMEWHERE ELSE WHILE I STAYED AND EXPLORED THE WONDERS OF THE ATOM AGE.

Panel 4:

ATOMIC MARBLE
From the DEPARTMENT of ENERGY'S
HANFORD SITE
Richland, Washington

This glass marble was colored by exposure to gamma radiation from a Cobalt-60 source used for developing the peaceful atom at (DOE'S) Pacific Northwest Laboratory, operated by Battelle. The marble is not radioactive and is perfectly safe to handle.

I STILL HAD THE SOUVENIR BURIED AWAY BACK HOME.

Panel 5: I NEVER KNEW EXACTLY WHAT MY FATHER AND THE MAN IN THE GREY SUIT TALKED ABOUT, BUT IT PROBABLY INVOLVED CHECKING UP ON SUSPECT EMPLOYEES WHOSE POLITICAL VIEWS DID NOT MATCH THE PATRIOTIC IDEALS OF THE NSA.

BETWEEN THE COMMIES, THE HOMOSEXUALS, AND MEMBERS OF THE NASCENT ANTI-NUCLEAR MOVEMENT, THE SPOOKS HAD A MULTITUDE OF CHOICES WHEN IT CAME TO BOGEYMEN.

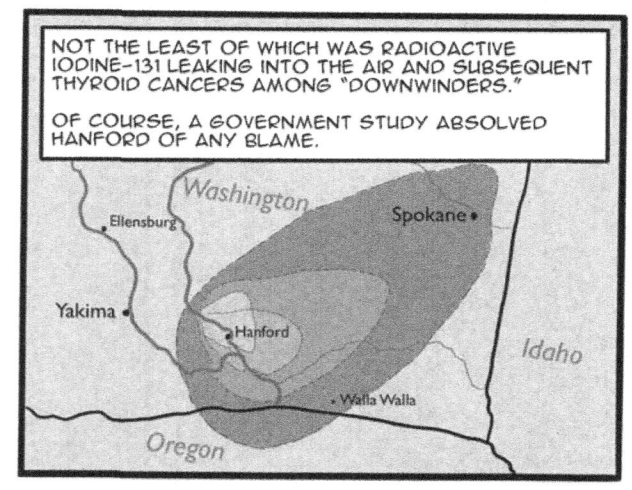

IT'S NOT LIKE THERE WEREN'T MORE OBVIOUS PROBLEMS TO SOLVE AT HANFORD.

CONTAMINATED AREA
GROUND SURFACES CONTAMINATED
STAY ON ROADWAY TO NEXT JUNCTION
RADIOLOGICAL SCIENCE DEPT

NOT THE LEAST OF WHICH WAS RADIOACTIVE IODINE-131 LEAKING INTO THE AIR AND SUBSEQUENT THYROID CANCERS AMONG "DOWNWINDERS."

OF COURSE, A GOVERNMENT STUDY ABSOLVED HANFORD OF ANY BLAME.

FOR DECADES, THE HUGE NUCLEAR WASTE ISSUE WAS IGNORED. TOO BAD IT WASN'T AS SAFE TO HANDLE AS MY ATOMIC MARBLE.

BUT THAT WAS NOTHING TO WORRY ABOUT...

CAUTION
RADIATION AREA and CONTAMINATION AREA

United States Department of Energy
Hanford Site
TUNNEL COLLAPSE

Radioactive Waste from Hanford Oozing Toward the Columbia R.

...COMPARED TO INAPPROPRIATE POLITICS, WHICH APPARENTLY TOPPED THE SPOOKY NO-NO LIST.

THE GREEN PARTY WAS OF PARTICULAR CONCERN. WHEN I WAS IN COLLEGE, THE PROMINENT GERMAN ANTI-NUCLEAR ACTIVIST AND GREENIE, PETRA KELLY, SPOKE ON CAMPUS, PART OF A NATIONWIDE NO NUKE TOUR. I RECALL HER WELL-REASONED TALK INTERRUPTED COUNTLESS TIMES BY FAKE STUDENT "DISRUPTORS" HIRED BY U.S. SPOOKS, WHO HAD BEEN TRAILING HER AROUND THE COUNTRY. EVERY COUPLE OF MINUTES THEY'D POP UP OUT OF THE AUDIENCE LIKE MECHANICAL JACK-IN-THE-BOXES, SPOUTING OBVIOUSLY SCRIPTED NONSENSE ABOUT THE EVIL GREENS AND THEIR ASSAULT ON THE GREAT PAX NUCLEI.

ON A PHONE CALL HOME I RELATED THIS TO DAD, WHOSE ONLY COMMENT WAS A QUESTION: DID I KNOW WHAT THE GREEN PARTY WAS ALL ABOUT? NOT SURPRISINGLY, HE NEVER ANSWERED THE QUESTION HIMSELF. PROBABLY, HIS HANDLERS HAD NEVER TOLD HIM THE ACCEPTABLE ANSWER.

BEYOND THE GENERAL SUBJECT MATTER, I'D NEVER BEEN ABLE TO FIGURE OUT JUST WHAT DAD'S SPOOK ACTIVITIES FROM THIS ERA ENTAILED.

IT WASN'T CLOAK AND DAGGER STUFF, I'M PRETTY SURE OF THAT.

Spy vs. Spy © E.C. Publications

BASED ON HIS ARMY TRAINING, IT MIGHT HAVE INVOLVED SITTING AROUND MONITORING SHORTWAVE RADIO TRAFFIC, CB RADIOS, TAXI DISPATCHERS, EVEN PRIVATE PHONE CONVERSATIONS IN SEARCH OF SOME NUGGET OF USEFUL INFORMATION.

SO WHAT TIME ARE YOU COMING HOME FOR DINNER?

YEARS LATER, SUCH DATA MINING WOULD BE CARRIED OUT ON A GLOBAL SCALE WITH AUTOMATED COMPUTER ALGORITHMS, BUT THIS WAS STILL THE AGE OF ANALOG DINOSAURS.

AND THEN SHEILA SAID TO BETTY, SHE SAID...

"BETTY!" SHE SAID...

THE COVERT OPS PIN IMPLIES THERE MIGHT HAVE BEEN ACTUAL CONTACT WITH "SUBJECTS."

THOUGH EVEN THAT WAS PROBABLY PRETTY MUNDANE.

MAYBE THE PIN *DID* COME FROM A BOX OF CRACKER JACK.

SECRET DECODER RING!

INTERACTION WITH HIS HANDLER MUST HAVE BEEN A THRILL-FEST.
PHHT. NOT MUCH HERE.
BECAUSE THERE'S NOT MUCH TO PUT THERE!
THERE'S ALWAYS SOMETHING.
WHAT DO YOU THINK OF THIS GUY?
I HARDLY KNOW HIM.
I DIDN'T ASK IF YOU WERE DATING! I WANT TO KNOW WHAT YOU *THINK* OF HIM.
COULD HE PASS FOR A COMMIE AGITATOR?
MY WIFE'S WASHING MACHINE AGITATES MORE THAN THIS GUY.
MAYBE HE NEEDS A LITTLE ENCOURAGEMENT.

WE OUGHTA BE ABLE TO COOK SOMETHING UP.
MAYBE GET ONE OF THOSE FAIRIES IN ELLENSBERG TO MEET UP WITH HIM, CONVINCE HIM TO GO HOMO FOR HIPPIES OR WHATNOT.
YEAH, SOMETHING LIKE THAT.
?
YOU GOT A PROBLEM WITH THAT?
JESUS. NO WONDER YOU'RE STUCK IN THIS PODUNK TOWN!
MAYBE IT'S TIME TO HAND THIS OVER TO SOMEONE WITH A LITTLE MORE IMAGINATION.
TAP TAP

HOT BUTTON

KA-CHUCK!

AFTER MOVING TO YAKIMA, DAD WAS HYPERSENSITIVE ON THE SUBJECT OF BIG CITY TYPES, E.G., PRETTY MUCH EVERYONE, VERSUS THE RUBES OF CENTRAL WASHINGTON, E.G., US.

WHENEVER POSSIBLE, HE MADE A POINT OF BELITTLING AND RIDICULING CITY FOLK. THEY DROVE LIKE CRAZY PEOPLE. THEIR WEATHER WAS AWFUL. THEY LIVED AMONG TOO MANY "JIGABOOS." ANYTHING TO JUSTIFY HIS DECISION TO MOVE AWAY.

YAKIMA WAS SAFE. IT NEVER CHANGED. IT SEEMED PERPETUALLY TEN OR FIFTEEN YEARS BEHIND EVERYWHERE ELSE. NOTHING MUCH EVER HAPPENED THERE. IN SHORT, YOU DIDN'T **NEED** AN IMAGINATION TO LIVE IN YAKIMA

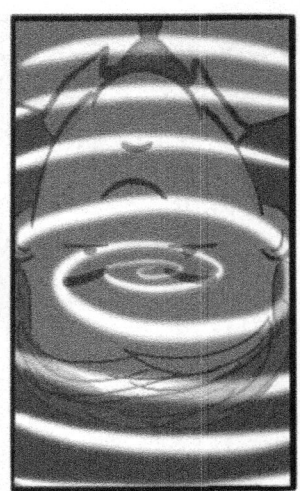

"SOMEONE WITH A LITTLE IMAGINATION."

FAMILY LEGEND HAS IT THAT DAD'S BAPTISM WAS HANDLED BY A DEVOUT, IF BUTTER-FINGERED, NEIGHBOR.

1930 FEB

JUST AS THINGS WERE ABOUT TO GET GOING, SO THE STORY GOES, BABY DICK SLIPPED FROM HER HANDS AND FELL HEAD-FIRST TO THE STONE FLOOR.

	APPARENTLY, THE POOR WOMAN WAS CONVINCED SHE'D DONE THE BOY IRREPARABLE HARM.
	IN LATER YEARS, WHENEVER SHE SAW HIM SHE WOULD START TO CRY AND APOLOGIZE PROFUSELY.
BONK!	MY FATHER THOUGHT THIS INCIDENT MIGHT EXPLAIN THE DIFFICULTY HE HAD GRASPING ABSTRACT CONCEPTS AND HIGH LEVEL MATHEMATICS. HE WAS, HE FELT, UNIMAGINATIVE THROUGH NO FAULT OF HIS OWN.

ALL THROUGH THOSE YEARS, FROM THE TIME I WAS IN MIDDLE SCHOOL THROUGH HIGH SCHOOL, THINGS WEREN'T RIGHT FOR DAD. I CAN SEE THAT NOW, BUT ONLY BECAUSE THE YEARS HAVE BROUGHT A HINT OF CLARITY TO WHAT REMAINED BURIED FOR SO LONG.

THERE WASN'T ANY SCREAMING IN THE NIGHT, OR STRANGLING, OR NATURALLY ANY TALK OF WHAT WAS WRONG, BUT HE SEEMED TO SLIDE DEEPER AND DEEPER INTO SOME HAZY CLOUD OF...WHAT? APATHY? ACCEPTANCE? INEVITABILITY? IT WAS AS IF HE'D STOPPED TRYING TOO HARD AT ANYTHING BECAUSE HE KNEW IT WASN'T GOING TO WORK OUT; HIS FATE WAS SET.

I WONDER IF THAT'S WHY HE KEPT UP THE LOW-GRADE SPOOK WORK, EVEN AFTER HIS SALES BUSINESS PRETTY MUCH DRIED UP? IT WAS CLEAR, REQUIRED NO DEEP THOUGHT OF HIS OWN, AND MUST HAVE PROVIDED THE COMFORT OF SOMEONE ELSE CALLING THE SHOTS.

AND BECAUSE IT WAS "SECRET," NO ONE COULD PUBLICALLY CRITICIZE OR LOOK DOWN ON IT.

EVENTUALLY, AFTER I'D GONE OFF TO COLLEGE AND MOM HAD LONG SINCE MOVED ON INTO HER OWN SUCCESSFUL CAREER AS A TEACHER AND UNION BIGWIG, WHAT WAS LEFT FOR DAD BUT OLD MEMORIES SHUT AWAY IN BOXES AND SHOVED INTO CLOSETS?

WHO THE HELL KNEW?

AND NOW, WHO THE HELL CARED...

...EXCEPT THE ONES WHO WERE THERE?

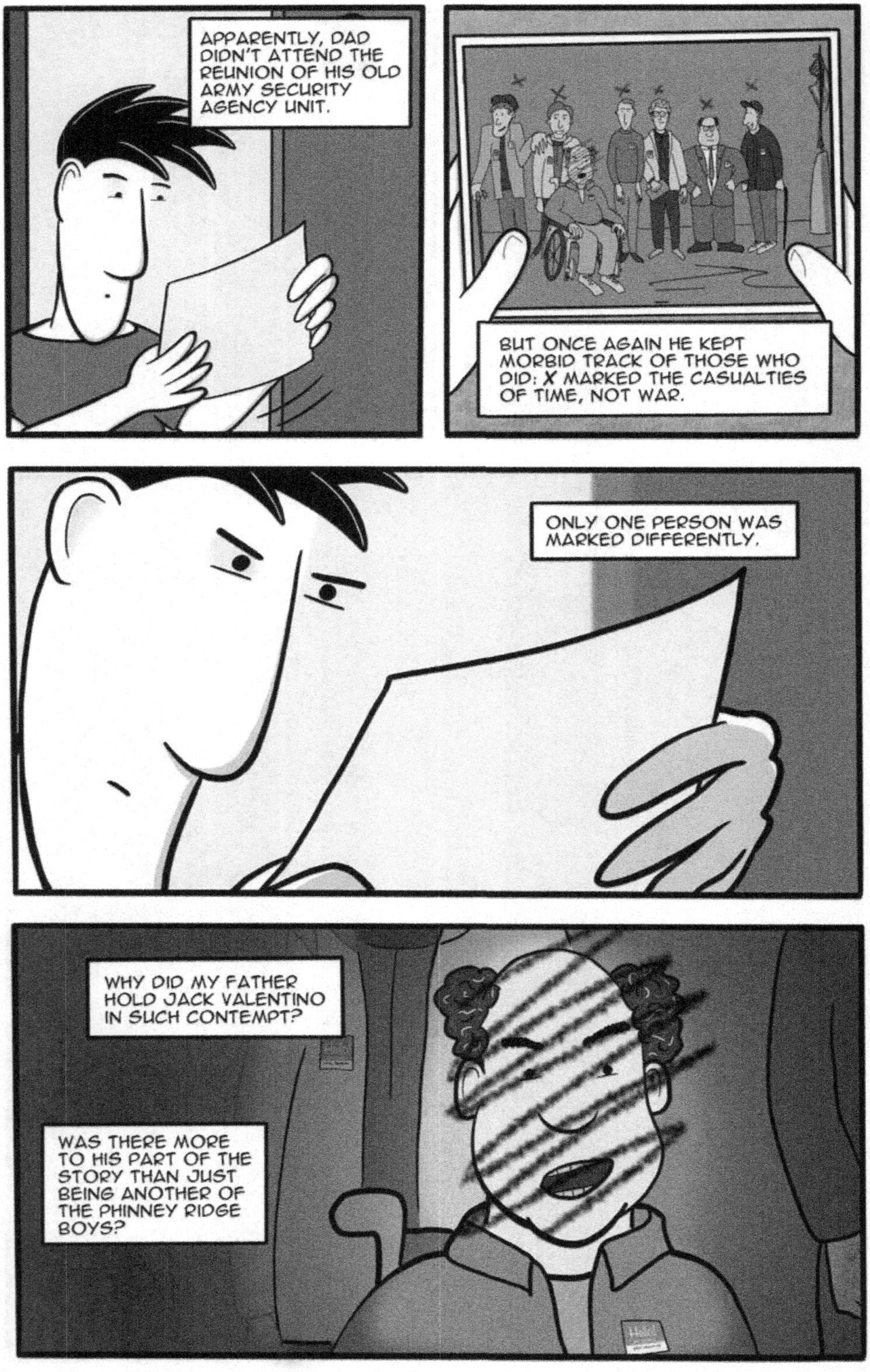
APPARENTLY, DAD DIDN'T ATTEND THE REUNION OF HIS OLD ARMY SECURITY AGENCY UNIT.
BUT ONCE AGAIN HE KEPT MORBID TRACK OF THOSE WHO DID: X MARKED THE CASUALTIES OF TIME, NOT WAR.
ONLY ONE PERSON WAS MARKED DIFFERENTLY.
WHY DID MY FATHER HOLD JACK VALENTINO IN SUCH CONTEMPT?
WAS THERE MORE TO HIS PART OF THE STORY THAN JUST BEING ANOTHER OF THE PHINNEY RIDGE BOYS?

WOULD JACK'S PHOTOS PROVIDE AN ANSWER?

THEY SEEMED TO BE CANDID SNAPSHOTS OF ACTIVITY FAR FROM CAMP, PERHAPS ON ONE OF THE ROUTINE SORTIES THE ASA UNIT CONDUCTED.

WITH MORE X'D OUT FACES...

...AND ONE RATHER ODD INSCRIPTION, APPARENTLY FROM THE MAN HIMSELF.

Remember, Altar Boy! An eye for an eye A tooth for a tooth Ex 21:24

THE PHOTOS APPEARED TO BE TAKEN DURING LATE SUMMER OR EARLY AUTUMN, WHICH WOULD SET THE DATE AROUND AUGUST OF 1951.

ACCORDING TO DAD'S LITTLE RECORD BOOK, THAT WOULD PUT HIM AT CHUNCHEON, ABOUT 40 MILES NORTHEAST OF SEOUL.

IT WAS HERE THAT HIS ASA UNIT DID RECON FOR THE BLOODY BATTLES SOON TO START AROUND THE PUNCHBOWL.

WHEN VIEWED IN SEQUENCE, THE PICTURES TOLD A STORY THAT, LIKE MANY MILITARY TALES, STARTED WITH THE MUNDANE AND QUICKLY ESCALATED INTO THE HORRIFIC.

SOMETHING HAPPENED DURING THE BRIEF MOMENT BETWEEN TWO SNAPS OF THE CAMERA'S SHUTTER. SOMETHING UNEXPECTED, BUT SURELY NOT UNIMAGINABLE.

PERHAPS IT WAS SOMETHING THAT JUST FOR A SECOND OR TWO THE MEN HAD SUCCEEDED IN PUSHING FROM THEIR THOUGHTS...

SHUFFLE SHUFFLE

...BUT NOT SO FAR IT COULD HIDE FROM THE UNBLINKING EYE OF THE CAMERA.

WAS THE DEAD SOLDIER A FRIEND? HAD DAD KNOWN HIM LONG?

DID IT MATTER?
FOR GOD'S SAKE, HE HAD HIS BRAINS SHOT OUT RIGHT IN FRONT OF EVERYONE, INCLUDING WHOEVER WAS BUSY SNAPPING PICTURES! HOW COULD ANYONE **NOT** BE AFFECTED?
I FOUND MYSELF MORE ANGERED THAN REPULSED BY THE PHOTOS.
WHY WOULD ANYONE GIVE SUCH IMAGES TO AN OLD SOLDIER, ONE WHO WAS THERE, WHO SURELY COULD NOT HAVE FORGOTTEN THE BLOODY INCIDENT?

IS THIS WHAT TRIGGERED DAD'S EFFORTS TO SCRATCH JACK VALENTINO OUT OF THE RECORD, TO FOREVER BLOT HIS FACE FROM MEMORY?
MORE IMPORTANTLY AND FINALLY, IS THIS WHAT HAUNTED DAD ALL THOSE YEARS, MADE HIM AFRAID OF THE CARTOONISH CATHOLIC FATE AWAITING HIM IN THE AFTERLIFE?
BUT HOW COULD IT BE? THE MAN'S DEATH COULDN'T POSSIBLY BE BLAMED ON MY FATHER. IT WAS NO ONE'S FAULT, JUST ONE OF THOSE TERRIBLE THINGS THAT HAPPENED IN COMBAT, A BOX CHECKED OFF THE LIST OF WARTIME HELLISHNESS.

FWAP!

INSIDE THE CAREFULLY WRAPPED BUNDLE WERE THREE OBJECTS, OBVIOUSLY CHINESE IN ORIGIN, AND AT LEAST SEVERAL DECADES OLD.

A SMALL MEDALLION MADE OF LEAD PLATED WITH BRASS DEPICTED THE BUDDHIST BODHISATTVA, MANJUSHRI, SAID TO BE A GUIDE TOWARD WISDOM AND ENLIGHTENMENT.

THE BACK HAD BEEN INCISED WITH AN INSCRIPTION, BUT IT WAS LARGELY WORN AWAY, AS IF ERASED BY FIDGETING FINGERS NERVOUSLY RUBBING AWAY THE ONCE SHINY METAL.

A TINY COMPASS LABELED WITH CHINESE CHARACTERS WAS SMALLER THAN A DIME AND MADE OF TIN SO THIN IT SEEMED MORE A CHILD'S TOY THAN A USEFUL NAVIGATIONAL AID.

I HOPED THE USER HAD GOOD EYESIGHT, AS THE MINISCULE NEEDLE WAS ALL BUT IMPOSSIBLE TO SEE. PERHAPS IT WAS MORE A PSYCHOLOGICAL BOOSTER THAN A WAYFINDING INSTRUMENT.

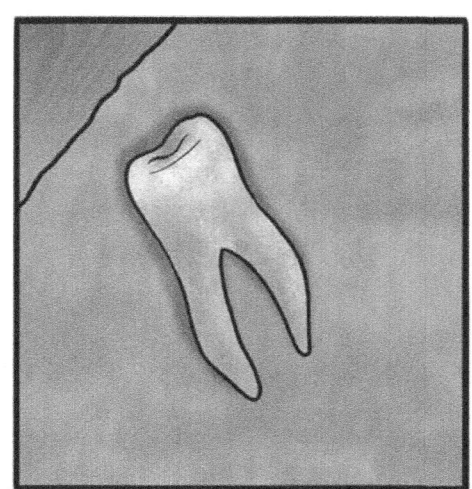

AND THERE WAS A FRAGILE WOODEN TAG, DRILLED WITH A HOLE FOR A MISSING STRING, BUT NOW BROKEN. CRUDELY SCORCHED INTO THE WOOD WERE FOUR CHINESE CHARACTERS.

NUDGE NUDGE

AN EYE FOR AN EYE

A TOOTH FOR A TOOTH

INSTANT MEMORIES
MADE WITH REAL VAGUE RECOLLECTIONS
INSTANT MEMORY #1
MY TOOF ITH LOOTH BUT IT WONE COME OUTH.
WHICH ONE?
THIF ON RI HE-
!
GRAB!
YOINK!
SPLUT!
PROBLEM SOLVED.

INSTANT MEMORY #2
YI YI YI YIII!
SCALP!
WHY WOULD THEY DO THAT?
A SOUVENIR. IT PROVES YOU KILLED ONE OF THE ENEMY.

程立杰

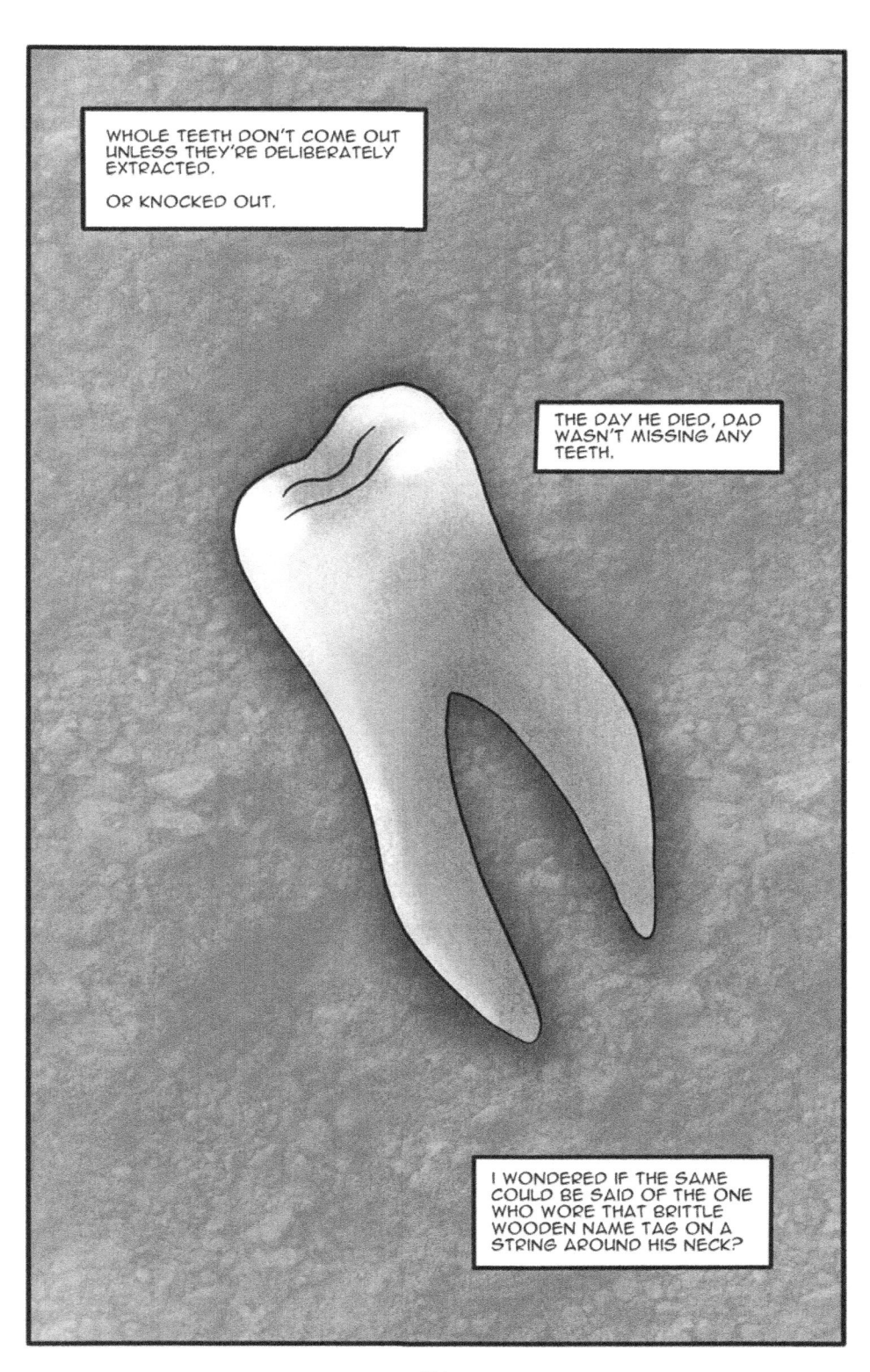

WHOLE TEETH DON'T COME OUT UNLESS THEY'RE DELIBERATELY EXTRACTED.

OR KNOCKED OUT.

THE DAY HE DIED, DAD WASN'T MISSING ANY TEETH.

I WONDERED IF THE SAME COULD BE SAID OF THE ONE WHO WORE THAT BRITTLE WOODEN NAME TAG ON A STRING AROUND HIS NECK?

SO... THERE IT WAS.

ALL THE MYSTERY, THE TUCKED-AWAY ANGER AND RESENTMENT.

THE FEAR.

ARMY SERIAL NUMBER RA 19335569 WAS A YOUNG AND WILLING ENLISTEE IN THE U.S. ARMY. HIS REASONS FOR SIGNING UP PROBABLY HAD LITTLE TO DO WITH FIGHTING COMMUNISM OR RESCUING KOREA FROM MAO'S MINIONS. NONETHELESS, HE WAS THERE BY CHOICE AND HE'D DONE WHAT SOLDIERS IN WAR DO.

I COULDN'T READ THE CHINESE WRITING SCORCHED INTO THE FOREIGN SOLDIER'S TAG. MOST LIKELY HE WAS A CONSCRIPT FROM A RURAL VILLAGE, ORDERED TO CHOOSE BETWEEN THE ARMY AND STARVATION, AND PROBABLY GIVEN MINIMAL TRAINING OR EQUIPMENT.

WHAT, IF ANYTHING, COULD THESE TWO HAVE HAD IN COMMON? WERE THEY THE SAME AGE? DID THEY SHARE ANY COMMON INTERESTS BESIDES THE DESIRE TO SURVIVE?

IN A DIFFERENT TIME AND PLACE, MIGHT THEY HAVE BEEN FRIENDS?

OR HAD IT ALWAYS BEEN THEIR FATE TO REMAIN STRANGERS, BOUND ONLY BY A SINGULAR DEATH AND A LIFETIME OF GUILTY REGRET?

7

SO MY FATHER KEPT SOUVENIRS FROM THE WAR.

DIDN'T EVERY SOLDIER? BATTLEFIELDS AREN'T SOME KIDDIE ATTRACTION IN AN AMUSEMENT PARK. PEOPLE GET KILLED. PEOPLE KILL. MOST OF THEM EVENTUALLY FIND THEIR WAY BACK INTO THE NORMALCY OF EVERYDAY LIFE.

DAD WASN'T THE ONLY ONE WITH BAGGAGE, BUT BACK THEN THE POWERS THAT BE WEREN'T TOO CONCERNED WITH WHAT A SOLDIER MIGHT BRING HOME TUCKED AWAY IN THE SHADOWY CORNERS OF HIS HEAD. HE SPENT HIS LAST THREE MONTHS OF SERVICE ON OKINAWA, CLOSE TO THE HOSPITAL WHERE WHAT LITTLE TREATMENT FOR "SHELL SHOCK" OR "BATTLE FATIGUE" EXISTED PROBABLY AMOUNTED TO A FEW HOURS OF COUNSELING MIXED IN WITH HIS REGULAR ASA SIGINTEL DUTIES.

WHEN HIS TIME WAS UP, HE BOARDED A TROOP SHIP AND SAILED HOME. CASE CLOSED.

WAS ANY OF THIS RESPONSIBLE FOR WHY, LATER ON, HE COULD BE KIND OF A JERK, OR WHY HE KEPT SO MUCH INSIDE HIMSELF, BUILDING WALLS TO KEEP ME AND EVEN MY MOTHER FROM GETTING TOO CLOSE?

OR WAS ALL OF THIS ANGST IN *MY* HEAD? WAS I OBSESSING OVER A PRODUCT OF MY OWN IMAGINATION?

MAYBE DAD WASN'T WRACKED WITH GUILT AND PRAYING FOR FORGIVENESS. MAYBE HE WAS JUST AN ORDINARY MAN CONTINUALLY DISAPPOINTED BY A LIFE THAT DIDN'T GO AS HE'D BEEN LED TO BELIEVE IT MIGHT.

AND MAYBE EVEN *THAT* WAS BULLSHIT. PERHAPS MY FATHER WAS JUST A CRANKY OLD GUY, TIRED, READY TO GO, SICK OF THE WHOLE THING.

SLAM!

SOME PLACES LOOK THEIR BEST WHEN VIEWED FROM A DISTANCE. I GUESS SOME LIVES ARE LIKE THAT, TOO. IT'S JUST HARDER TO GET FAR ENOUGH AWAY TO SEE THEM FROM THE RIGHT PERSPECTIVE.
BEEP BOOP BEEP
BOOP BOOP BEEP
BEEP BEEP BOOP BEEP
DOODLE DEEDLE...
DOODLE DEEDLE...
HEY.
HOWDY. I'M LEAVING NOW, BUT I'M MAKING A SLIGHT DETOUR.

YOU'RE GOING TO SEATTLE?
JUST FOR A DAY OR TWO.
YOU'RE A FOOL FOR PUNISHMENT, AREN'T YOU?
I MARRIED YOU, DIDN'T I?
BEST DECISION *YOU* EVER MADE.
NASTY BITCH.
DO ME A FAVOR?
WHAT?
FIND A WAY TO CUT YOUR DAD SOME SLACK, OKAY?
OKAY.

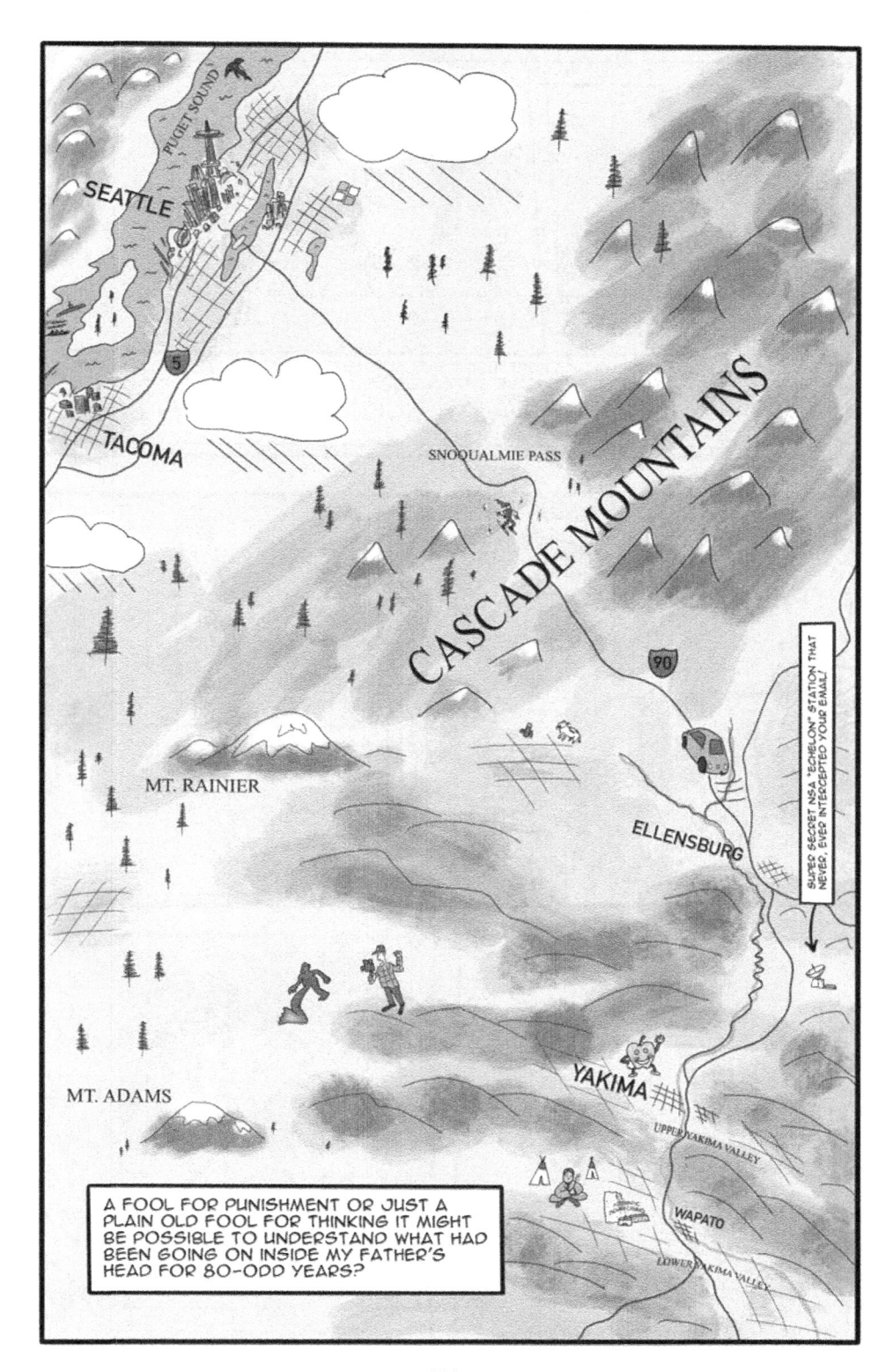

SUPER SECRET NSA "ECHELON" STATION THAT NEVER, EVER INTERCEPTED YOUR EMAIL!

A FOOL FOR PUNISHMENT OR JUST A PLAIN OLD FOOL FOR THINKING IT MIGHT BE POSSIBLE TO UNDERSTAND WHAT HAD BEEN GOING ON INSIDE MY FATHER'S HEAD FOR 80-ODD YEARS?

WHEN I WAS A KID, IT TOOK THREE HOURS TO DRIVE TO SEATTLE. IT SEEMED LIKE FOREVER. NOW THE SUBURBS HAVE SPREAD HALFWAY UP THE MOUNTAINS THAT DIVIDE THE STATE BETWEEN SOGGY EAST AND ARID WEST. THESE DAYS, THE DISTANCE BETWEEN SEATTLE AND YAKIMA IS MORE POLITICAL AND SOCIAL THAN GEOGRAPHICAL.

VREEEE! VREEEE! VREEEE!

BACK THEN, OUR ARRIVAL IN THE CITY WAS AUGURED BY EERIE SOUND EFFECTS. THE OLD MOTORS THAT DROVE THE WINDSHIELD WIPERS INTERFERED WITH THE CAR RADIO, ADDING EVEN MORE STRANGENESS TO THE UNFAMILIAR VOICES OF THE ANNOUNCERS.

DRIVING IN SEATTLE WAS LIKE EXPLORING AN ALIEN WORLD. EVERY STREET BEGAN OR ENDED ON A HILL.

AND "LIQUID SUNSHINE" FELL FROM THE SKY.

TODAY, SEATTLE IS ONE BIG TRAFFIC JAM MADE WORSE BY PEOPLE WHO DRINK TOO MUCH COFFEE AND NEVER STOP FOR YELLOW LIGHTS.

WILL GLARE FOR CAFFEINE

ITS OBNOXIOUS PANHANDLERS HAVE THE MOST AGGRESSIVE FACIAL HAIR IN THE COUNTRY.

BUT, DESPITE ITS CRUMBLING, MOSS-COVERED INFRASTRUCTURE AND OVER-ABUNDANCE OF PALE HIPSTERS AND PROFESSIONAL ANARCHISTS, IT'S A BEAUTIFUL AND ENERGETIC PLACE.

I NEVER FORGAVE MY PARENTS FOR MOVING AWAY.

I WASN'T SURE WHAT I EXPECTED TO FIND HERE.
O'DEA HIGH SCHOOL
PERHAPS IT WAS A DISTRACTION WHILE I STEELED MYSELF FOR THE REAL GOAL OF THE SEATTLE DETOUR...
...OR MAYBE IT WAS JUST CURIOSITY.
I'D GROWN UP WITH AN INNATE DISTRUST OF AUTHORITY BASED SOLELY ON RANK OR POSITION.
AND I REALLY DIDN'T LIKE IT WHEN SOMEONE CLAIMED A MONOPOLY ON "THE TRUTH."
I COULDN'T FATHOM WHAT IT MUST HAVE BEEN LIKE TO BE SCHOOLED LIKE THAT, ESPECIALLY IN MY FATHER'S TIME WHEN THE BLACK AND WHITE WORD WAS HANDED OUT LIKE CRACKERS ON A SHINY GOLD PLATE.

NO WONDER DAD AND I BUTTED HEADS. HOW COULD WE NOT? HE WAS RAISED TO RECEIVE ANSWERS. I GREW UP ASKING QUESTIONS.
YOU WARM ENOUGH?
HOT!
SCHLUMPF!
IT WAS THE !%#%#@!! HEATER!
NOT THE !%@*#%!! FIRES OF HELL!

ONCE I GOT PAST MY OWN PREJUDICES, I HAD TO ADMIT THERE WAS NOTHING ALL THAT DIFFERENT ABOUT THE STUDENTS ENTERING O'DEA HIGH SCHOOL. APART FROM APPEARING A LITTLE MORE CLEAN-CUT THAN MOST, THEY WERE JUST A BUNCH OF KIDS LIKE ANY OTHER.

THE OFFICE WAS STAFFED BY A PAIR OF CHEERFUL MIDDLE-AGED WOMEN.

"WE LOVE IT WHEN ALUMNI CHILDREN COME TO VISIT!"

"BASED ON HIS TRANSCRIPT, YOUR FATHER OBVIOUSLY WAS VERY DEDICATED TO THE CHURCH."

THAT WAS A POLITE WAY OF SAYING HE WASN'T VERY DEDICATED TO MUCH ELSE.

ON THEIR DIGITIZED RECORDS I SAW THE SAME MEDIOCRE REPORT CARDS MY GRANDPARENTS SAW WHEN YOUNG DICK DUTIFULLY BROUGHT THEM HOME FOR SIGNATURES.

"DID STUDENTS BACK THEN INTERACT MUCH WITH KIDS FROM OTHER SCHOOLS?"

"SURE! O'DEA BOYS COME FROM ALL OVER THE CITY. MANY OF THEIR FRIENDS GO TO NEIGHBORHOOD PUBLIC SCHOOLS."

"OF COURSE, AT O'DEA THEY'RE BROUGHT UP TO RESPECT A HIGHER AUTHORITY THAN OTHER STUDENTS. THAT'S WHAT SETS THEM APART."

IT WILL TAKE JUST A SEC TO PRINT YOUR FATHER'S RECORDS.
BROTHER BRIMSTONE, WE CALL HIM. HE WAS AROUND WHEN YOUR DAD WAS A STUDENT.
THEY SAY IF HE COULDN'T CONVINCE YOU THAT YOU WERE GOING TO HELL, IT'S POSSIBLE YOU WERE ALREADY THERE.
IS IT OKAY IF I POKE AROUND A BIT?
OF COURSE! YOU DON'T LOOK LIKE A PERV.
THANKS. I THINK I HIDE IT WELL.
?

THE MOST IMPORTANT OF GOD'S COMMANDMENTS DO NOT TELL US WHAT TO DO. THEY TELL US WHAT NOT TO DO! THOU SHALT NOT! THOU SHALT NOT! WHEN IN DOUBT, THOU SHALT NOT!
WHY SUBJECT YOUR SOUL TO THE ETERNAL TORMENTS OF HELL WHEN GOD'S WORD IS SO CLEAR?
THOU SHALT NOT!

DO YOU STEAL FROM YOUR MOTHER'S LARDER OR LOOK ENVIOUSLY UPON YOUR BROTHER'S POSSESSIONS? THOU SHALT NOT!
DO YOU LEER AT WOMEN IN AN UNGODLY, UNHEALTHY FASHION? THOU SHALT NOT!
DO YOU INFLICT BODILY HARM UPON OR TAKE THE LIFE OF ANOTHER OF GOD'S CHILDREN?
DO YOU DEBASE THE HOLY TEMPLE OF YOUR BODY WITH THE DEVIL'S BREW... ALCOHOL?
IF YOU CANNOT ANSWER, NO, BOYS AND BROTHERS IN CHRIST, THE BIBLE DOES NOT MINCE WORDS ABOUT YOUR FATE!
THOU SHALT NOT! OR YOU WILL BE CAST AMONG THE DAMNED AND BURN FOR ALL TIME IN THE HOT FIRES OF HELL!

PEOPLE ARE PRETTY GOOD AT FINDING WAYS AROUND RULES.
SOMEWHERE ALONG HIS JOURNEY, DAD MUST HAVE LEARNED ABOUT MORAL LOOPHOLES.
I REMEMBER ONCE, THE TOPIC OF KILLING CAME UP. DAD WAS UNEXPECTEDLY QUICK TO POINT OUT THE EXCEPTIONS TO THE BIBLICAL COMMANDMENT.
IT'S A SIN EXCEPT IN TIME OF WAR. ANYTHING GOES THEN.
AFTER FINDING HIS "SOUVENIRS" FROM KOREA, I COULD SEE WHY HE NEEDED TO BELIEVE THAT IDEOLOGICAL SHELL GAME.
AND YET, IN THE END, HE DIDN'T SEEM THAT CONVINCED.
IN MEMORIAM
O'DEA STUDENTS WHO GAVE THEIR LIVES IN TIME OF WAR
1936
1945
1965
1942
1966
1943
1967
1944
1968

Albert Hall
1967
1951
Martin Shrepp
Caleb Joat
1952
ys Sail for Kore
Frank Duquesne
5,000 soldiers departing for
Army transport ship
SOMEONE YOUR FATHER KNEW?
YEAH. THEY WERE BUDDIES.
I DIDN'T KNOW HE WAS A FELLOW O'DEA STUDENT.
THE BROTHERS ALWAYS MAKE SURE TO HONOR THE NAMES OF BOYS KILLED IN ACTION.
HOW DO THE BROTHERS RECONCILE WAR WITH GOD'S COMMANDMENT NOT TO KILL?
CATHOLIC DOCTRINE HAS IT THAT WAR IS SOMETIMES NECESSARY, EVEN COMMANDED BY GOD, IN ORDER TO DEFEAT EVIL.
IT'S HARD TO FIGHT A WAR WITHOUT PEOPLE GETTING HURT OR KILLED, SO I GUESS IN GOD'S EYES IT'S SOMETIMES OKAY. I SUPPOSE EVERY SOLDIER MUST CHOOSE FOR THEMSELVES WHAT TO DO. GOD WILL BE THERE, WHETHER OR NOT THEY CHOOSE WISELY.
TIME OF WAR
I THINK THAT'S WHAT DAD WAS AFRAID OF.

IN TIME OF WAR
1965
1952
I GATHER YOUR FATHER DIDN'T PASS HIS FAITH ON TO YOU?
WELL, HE TRIED. HE GETS POINTS FOR THAT, RIGHT?
THE FACT THAT YOU'VE TAKEN AN INTEREST IN HIS PAST TELLS ME HE RAISED A FINE YOUNG MAN.
I FOUND MYSELF GENUINELY LIKING DAD'S OLD SCHOOL.
PERHAPS MY PREJUDICES ABOUT CATHOLIC EDUCATION WERE WEIGHTED TOO HEAVILY BY MY OWN LONG-AGO EXPERIENCES.
OR BY A MISUNDERSTANDING ABOUT HOW MUCH OF IT DAD REALLY HELD ONTO.

CATHOLIC DIOCESE OF SEATTLE

HEAVY CHURCH DOORS...TRYING TO KEEP THE HEATHENS OUT OR THE CHRISTIANS IN?

KRRREEEEEEEEEE

FLIP! FLOOP!

Magnificat

FIVE STARS! WE HAVE A WINNAH!

THEY CALL IT "RECONCILIATION" NOW, NOT CONFESSION. I GUESS IT NEEDED A MORE POSITIVE SPIN TO APPEAL TO THE MODERN AGE OF BLAMELESS ENTITLEMENT.

RECONCILIATION
MON - 10-12
WED - 10-12
THU - 10-12
SAT - 8-11 2-4

RECONCILIACIÓN
LUNES - 10-12
MIÉ - 10-12
JUEVES - 10-12
SAB - 8-11 2-4

I DON'T REMEMBER SEEING DAD EVER GO TO CONFESSION. DID HE, WHEN HE WAS YOUNGER?

BEING SUCH A STAUNCH CATHOLIC, HIS MOTHER MUST HAVE SENT HIM.

BEFORE HE DIED, I ALWAYS THOUGHT HIS DEVOTION WAS ROTE BEHAVIOR DRUMMED INTO HIM BY NUNS AND PRIESTS. I PICTURED HIM WONDERING WHY I DIDN'T JUST GO THROUGH THE MOTIONS, TOO.

ONCE HE REALIZED I DIDN'T BELIEVE, HE NEVER PUT UP A SERIOUS FIGHT TO CHANGE MY MIND.

HE JUST...GAVE UP.

IS THAT THE KEY TO MY DISCOMFORT?

DID I ROB MY FATHER OF THE CONTRITION THAT WOULD HAVE ASSUAGED HIS OWN GUILT?

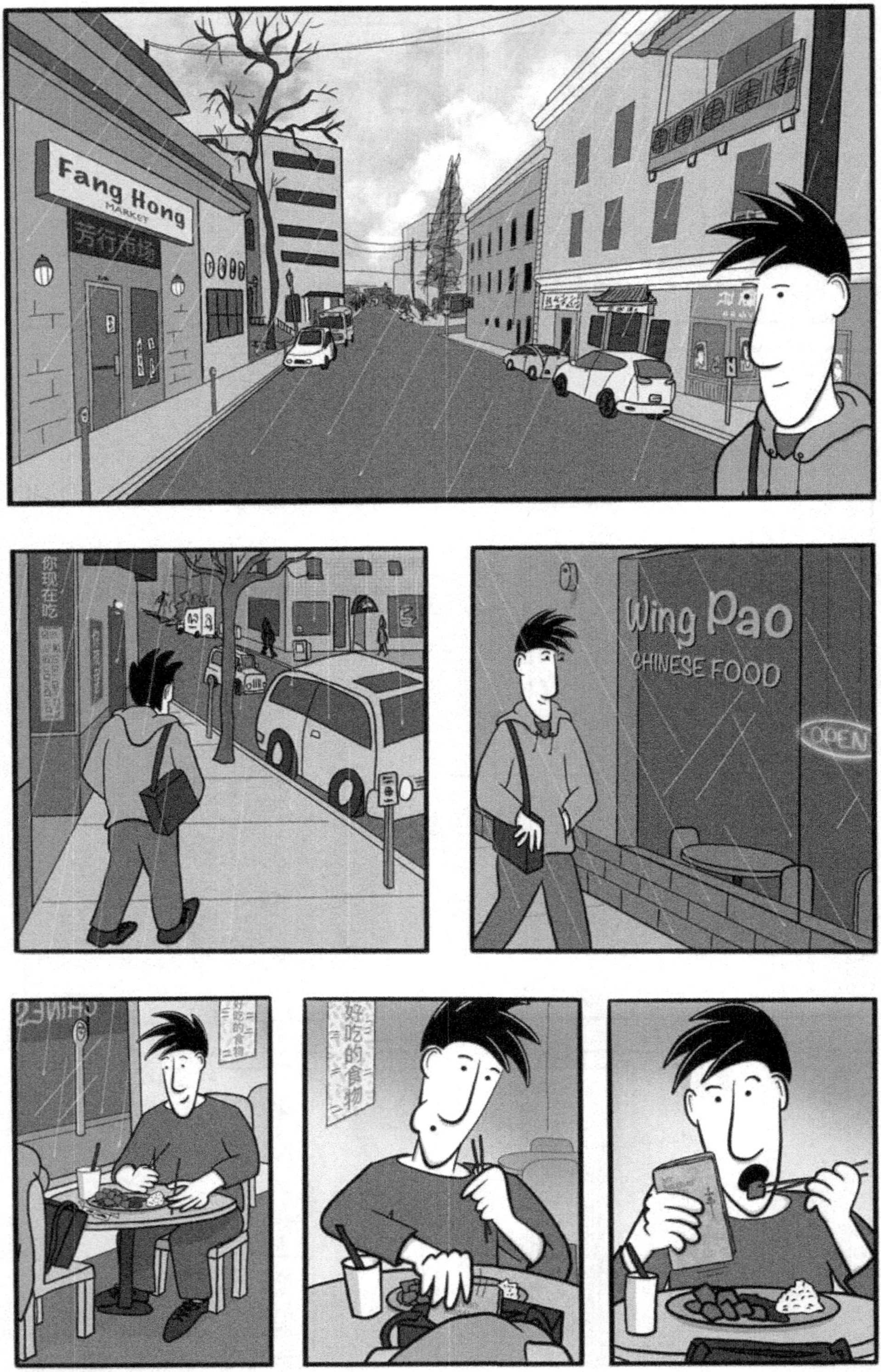
Fang Hong
MARKET
芳行市场
你现在吃
Wing Pao
CHINESE FOOD
OPEN
好吃的食物

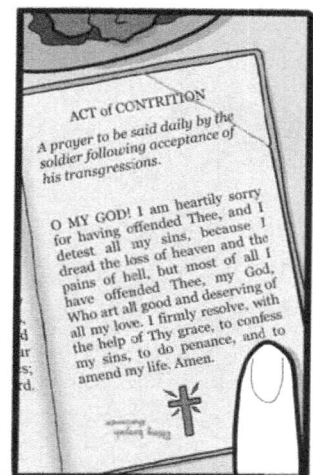

ACT of CONTRITION

A prayer to be said daily by the soldier following acceptance of his transgressions.

O MY GOD! I am heartily sorry for having offended Thee, and I detest all my sins, because I dread the loss of heaven and the pains of hell, but most of all I have offended Thee, my God, Who art all good and deserving of all my love. I firmly resolve, with the help of Thy grace, to confess my sins, to do penance, and to amend my life. Amen.

CHING BOOYAH SHALLOWER...

WHY THE FUCK WOULD I WANT TO KILL YOU?

OR ARE YOU SAYING MY FOOD IS BAD?
NO! IT'S DELICIOUS! I JUST... THAT IS... MY DAD, HE... UM...WROTE SOMETHING IN THIS PRAYER BOOK...
I SHOWED THE COOK THE ARMY MISSAL AND THE MYSTERIOUS NOTE WRITTEN ON THE PAGE WITH THE PRAYER FOR CONTRITION.
I TOLD HIM ABOUT DAD AND HOW I'D BEEN DEALING WITH ALL HIS STUFF, INCLUDING THE BAGGAGE HE'D CARRIED HOME FROM THE KOREAN WAR.
THE YOUNG MAN WASN'T IMPRESSED.
YOUR FATHER COULDN'T SPELL FOR SHIT.
TAP! TAP!
BUT HE WAS TRYING TO WRITE PEASANT MANDARIN:
QING BUYAO SHA WO.
IT MEANS, "PLEASE DON'T KILL ME."

AND THAT CONFIRMED IT. A PROVERBIAL NAIL IN AN ALL-TOO LITERAL COFFIN.
SO, HE WAS SOME KIND OF PSYCHO KILLER?
NOT EXACTLY.
I MEAN, NO, DEFINITELY NOT, BUT...
HANG ON A SEC.
BY ANY CHANCE...
SCRIBBLE SCRIBBLE
程立杰
...CAN YOU READ THIS?

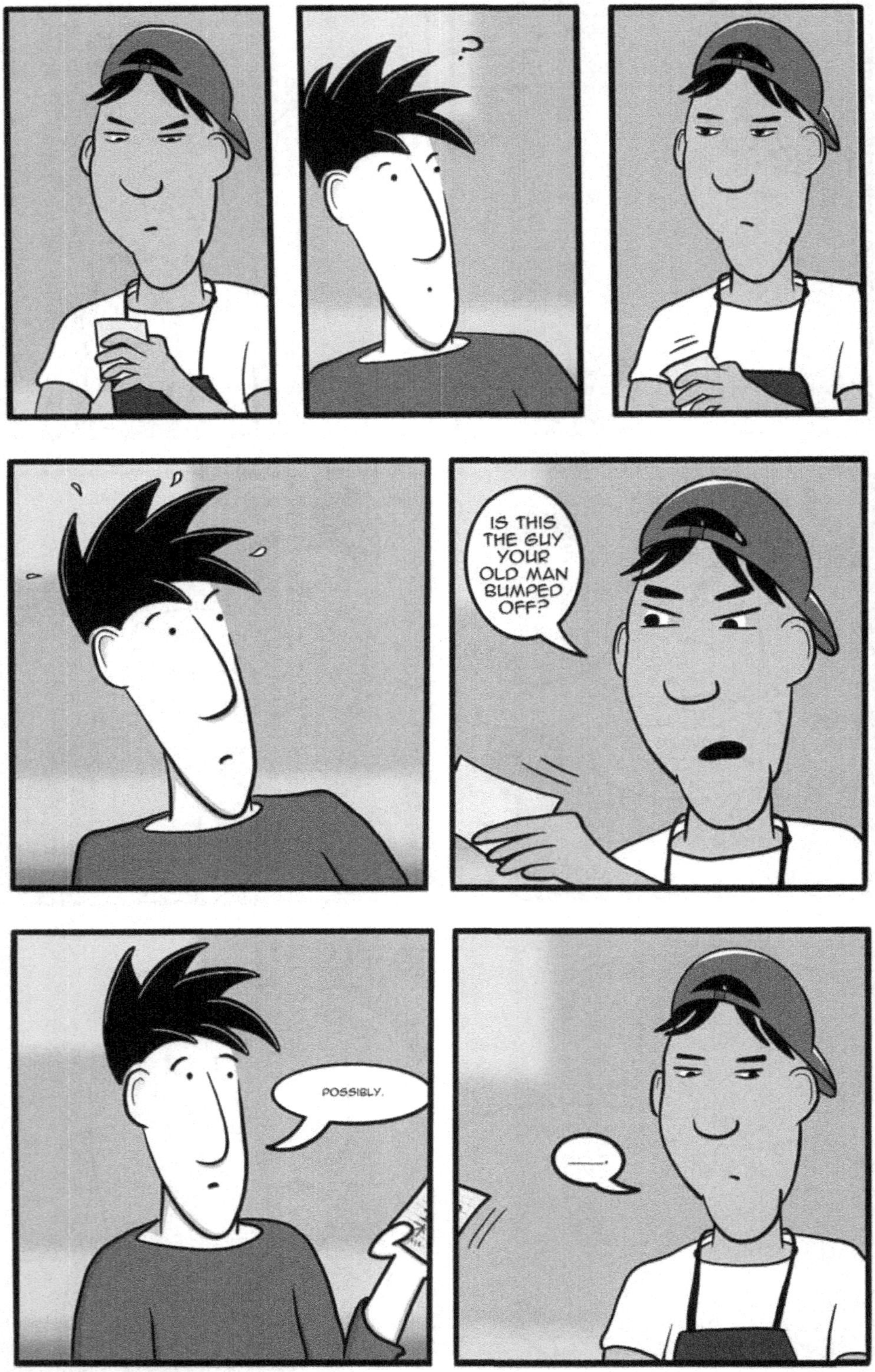
?
IS THIS THE GUY YOUR OLD MAN BUMPED OFF?
POSSIBLY.
......?

BEING FROM THE COUNTRY, HE WOULDN'T HAVE MEANT MUCH TO THE REDS.
THE POOR GUY PROBABLY WAS LEFT TO ROT WHERE HE FELL.
THEY SHOULD HAVE SENT HIM HOME FOR PROPER BURIAL NEAR HIS ANCESTORS.
HIS NAME WAS CHENG LI JIE.
SAY IT WITH RESPECT. YOU'RE PROBABLY THE ONLY ONE WHO KNOWS HE EVEN EXISTED.
CHENG LI JIE...
...THE MAN MY FATHER KILLED.

HISTORICAL SUPPOSITION WESTERN EDITION
19 JUNE 48
YOUNG RICHARD...
I WAS TOLD YOU'D BEEN SPOTTED BACK AT O'DEA.
I THOUGHT THE UNIVERSITY HAD ITS OWN CHAPEL. NOT THAT OUR GRADUATES AREN'T WELCOMED HOME AT ANYTIME.
PERHAPS YOU'RE HERE SEEKING GUIDANCE.
I'VE HEARD OF YOUR DECISION TO JOIN THE MILITARY.
A CHOICE SUCH AS THAT IS NOT WITHOUT CONSEQUENCES.
GUILT
YOUR MOTHER IS DISAPPOINTED, I'M SURE.

YOU AREN'T THE FIRST BOY TO CHOOSE THIS PATH. SEVERAL OF YOUR FORMER CLASSMATES ARE ENLISTING, TOO.
I GATHER IT'S ALL THE RAGE NOW.
JUST BE CERTAIN IT'S *YOUR* DECISION, NOT THE POISONOUS FRUIT OF SOMEONE ELSE'S DESIRE.
TAKE THIS AND KEEP IT WITH YOU ALWAYS.
REGARDLESS OF WHAT LIES AHEAD, NEVER NEGLECT YOUR PENANCE.
AND TRY NOT TO ADD EVEN MORE TO YOUR BURDEN.

HISTORICAL SUPPOSITION, EASTERN EDITION

WAIPO HERE. SHE SEE GRANDSON BEFORE HE GO AWAY.

NOT GOOD, GO FIGHT IN FOREIGN COUNTRY.
MAYBE GRANDSON NOT COME BACK LONG TIME. WAIPO NOT SEE BEFORE SHE DIE.
MAYBE GRANDSON DIE IN FOREIGN WAR. WAIPO STILL NOT SEE AGAIN.
ALWAYS SADNESS. ENDING CERTAIN FOR ALL.
MANJUSHRI MAKE ENDING COMPLETE. NO MORE BEGINNINGS. NO MORE SADNESS.
MANJUSHRI GUIDE GRANDSON, TOO, SHOULD ENDING COME.
I COULD MAKE UP STORIES ALL DAY. MAYBE THEY'D BE CLOSE TO THE TRUTH, MAYBE THEY WOULDN'T. AFTER SO MANY DECADES, DID IT MATTER?

Wing Pa
CHINESE FOO
THIS WASN'T JUST MY FATHER'S STORY ANYMORE. A MAN NAMED CHENG LI JIE HAD APPEARED – AND DISAPPEARED – THREE QUARTERS OF A CENTURY AGO TO PLAY WHAT I WAS CONVINCED WAS A KEY ROLE IN THE WHOLE MELODRAMATIC PRODUCTION.
WAS HE A YOUNG MAN AT THE TIME, THE SAME AS MY FATHER? OR PERHAPS OLDER, IN WHICH CASE DID SOMEONE CALL HIM HUSBAND OR DAD? WERE THERE PEOPLE SOMEWHERE IN CHINA WHO STILL MOURNED HIS DEATH OR WONDERED WHAT HAD HAPPENED TO HIM ALL THOSE YEARS AGO?
OR, AS THE COOK SAID, WAS HE JUST ANOTHER FORGOTTEN SOUL WHOSE PRESENCE ON EARTH SCARCELY CAUSED A RIPPLE?
IF HIS BODY HAD BEEN LEFT UNBURIED IN A STRANGE LAND, DID HIS RESTLESS GHOST WANDER AIMLESSLY IN SEARCH OF HOME? PERHAPS MY DAD *WAS* HAUNTED, NOT BY HIS CONSCIENCE, BUT BY THE TIRED SPIRIT OF A LONG GONE CHINESE CONSCRIPT.
GAAAAHHH

STOMP! STOMP!

REGARDLESS OF HOW THE STORY UNFOLDED...

...

THONK!

...THERE HAD TO BE A BETTER ENDING.

VISITING DAD'S OLD SCHOOL AND ENCOUNTERING PHANTOMS IN THE STREET WEREN'T THE PRIMARY GOALS OF MY DETOUR TO SEATTLE.

I DON'T KNOW WHY, BUT I WASN'T LOOKING FORWARD TO THE NEXT STOP — AND MY REAL REASON FOR COMING HERE.

IN FACT, I DREADED WHAT HAD TO COME NEXT, A MEETING WITH THE ONE MAN WHO FINALLY MIGHT HAVE THE ANSWERS I WAS LOOKING FOR.

WHY? HADN'T THIS EXERCISE IN DRAMA QUEENERY GONE ON LONG ENOUGH? SURELY IT WAS BETTER TO LEARN THE TRUTH, EVEN IF THAT TRUTH TURNED OUT TO BE UTTERLY MUNDANE.

IT WAS TIME TO ADD "THE END" TO THIS PRODUCTION, TIME TO MEET THE LAST SURVIVING PHINNEY RIDGE BOY, THE MAN MY FATHER HAD SYSTEMATICALLY TRIED TO ERASE FROM HIS MEMORIES.

I HAD TO TALK WITH JACK VALENTINO.

8

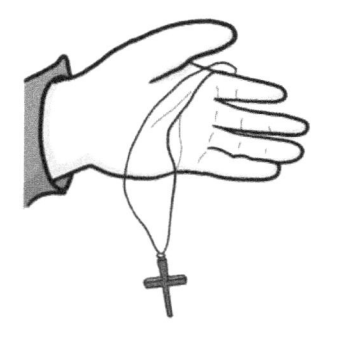

MY FATHER'S STORY BEGAN IN SEATTLE AND SEATTLE WAS WHERE I'D COME TO FINISH THE WHOLE SORDID SAGA.
ONLY ONE OF DAD'S OLD ARMY BUDDIES STILL LIVED HERE. I FOUND HIM LISTED AS A RESIDENT IN A POSH NURSING HOME IN THE CITY'S QUEEN ANNE NEIGHBORHOOD, ABOUT AS FAR AS YOU COULD GET FROM DAD'S COMFORT ZONE OF LOWER MIDDLE CLASS PHINNEY RIDGE OR... *SHUDDER!*... YAKIMA, THE PODUNK TOWN WHERE HE'D DRAGGED US ALL AND WHERE HE LIVED OUT THE MAJORITY OF HIS LIFE.
ASA KOREA
CONTACT LIST
om Burnett
187 Columbia Ave
Jerome, ID 92876
Jack Valentino
Sun Terrace Leisur
Suite 11A
4409 Prince Olaf Drive
Seattle, WA 97954
FOR SOME REASON, I DREADED MEETING JACK VALENTINO, THE LAST SURVIVOR OF THE PHINNEY RIDGE BOYS. MAYBE IT WAS THE WAY DAD TRIED TO DELETE HIM FROM THE HISTORICAL RECORD, INKING HIM OUT OF PHOTOS AND NEWSPAPER CLIPPINGS, OR MAYBE I'D SIMPLY COME THIS FAR ONLY TO REALIZE WHAT JACK MIGHT TELL ME WAS NOT SOMETHING I REALLY WANTED TO HEAR.
SOMETIMES, YOU HAVE TO TURN THE PAGE JUST SO YOU CAN SAY YOU'VE FINISHED THE DAMN BOOK.
SUN TERRACE LEISURE LIVING, HOW MAY I HELP YOU?
CAFÉ
MECCA
BAR
YEAH, I'M CALLING ABOUT VISITING A RESIDENT, JACK VALENTINO?
MR. VALENTINO CAN TAKE VISITORS UNTIL 7 PM. SHALL I TELL HIM YOU'RE COMING?
PLEASE DO.

Sun Terrace
SOMEONE HAD DONE VERY WELL FOR HIMSELF.

MR. VALENTINO IS CURRENTLY RESTRICTED TO HIS BED, BUT HE SAID HE'S MORE THAN HAPPY TO SEE YOU.
SUITE 11A IN THE PALATINE WING.

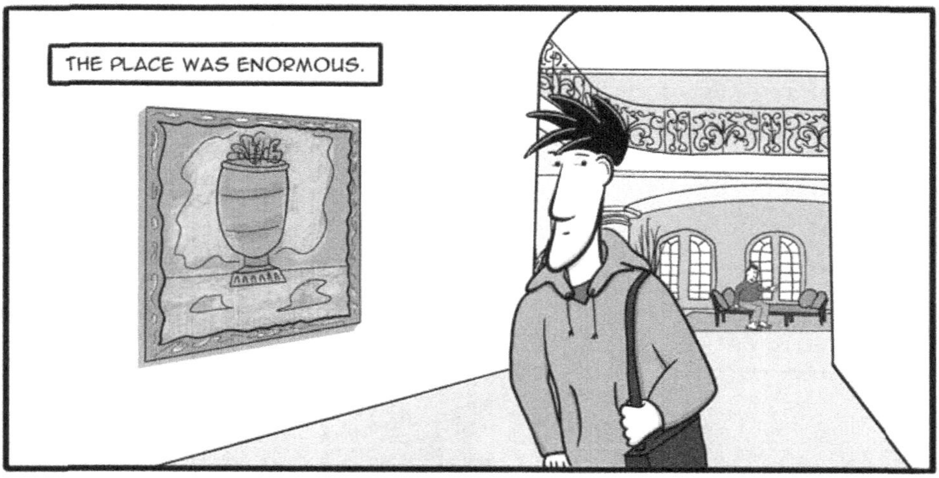
THE PLACE WAS ENORMOUS.

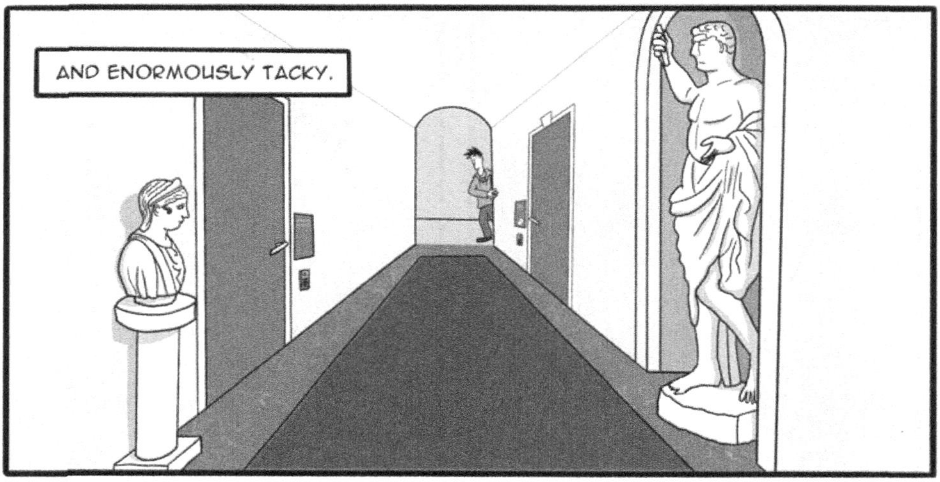
AND ENORMOUSLY TACKY.

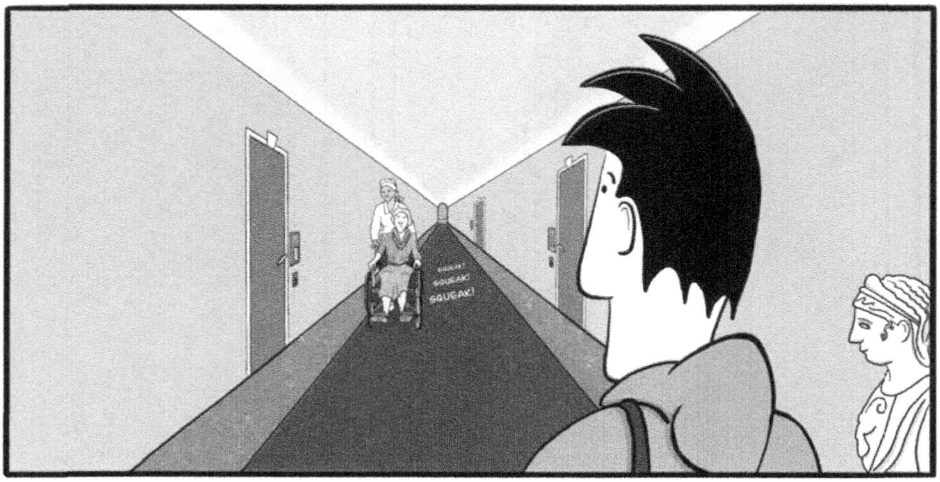
SQUEAK!
SQUEAK!

THE PRIM NURSES' UNIFORMS WOULD HAVE FIT RIGHT IN ON THE SET OF A 1940S HOLLYWOOD POTBOILER.
WHILE THE RESIDENTS HAD MORE OF A FELLINI VIBE.
SQUEAK!
SQUEAK!
WINK! WINK!
KISS! KISS!
TWIDDLE! TWIDDLE!
SQUEAK!
SQUEAK!
SQUEAK!
SQUEAK!
Palatine
SUITES 1-10
SUITES 11-20

SUITE 11A
Mr. Jack Valentino
SUITE 11A
Mr. Jack Valentino
C'MON IN, KID! THE DOOR'S OPEN!

COME CLOSER. DYING AIN'T CONTAGIOUS!
DON'T WORRY, I'M NOT A CORPSE YET.
I DON'T STINK TOO BAD.

MR. VALENTINO? MY NAME'S –
– MOLITOR. YEAH, YEAH, I KNOW.
I DON'T SHELL OUT THE BUCKS FOR THIS PLACE FOR NOTHING.
SKWEEZE!
YOU GOT YOUR POP'S LOOK OF WIDE-EYED INNOCENCE.
IT FIGURES HE'D GO AND SPAWN A PANSY.

NO OFFENSE, KID. I'M TOO OLD TO PRETEND I'M NOT A JACKASS.
I WAS **NOT** GOING TO LET THIS GUY GET TO ME.
NO OFFENSE TAKEN. I WORK IN SHOW BIZ. I'M USED TO JACKASSES.
HEH HEH!
I LIKE YOU. YOU'RE OKAY.
SORRY ABOUT YOUR OLD MAN, BY THE WAY. I SAW THE OBIT.
JACK VALENTINO DIDN'T EXACTLY EXUDE TRUSTWORTHINESS. I NEEDED TO LISTEN TO HIM, BUT I DIDN'T FEEL LIKE ***TELLING*** HIM MUCH.
THANKS. I'M JUST NOW GETTING EVERYTHING SQUARED AWAY.
AND YOU HAD TO COME SEE OL' VALENTINO TO SORT IT ALL OUT, EH?
SOMETHING LIKE THAT.

PULL UP A CHAIR! AS LUCK WOULD HAVE IT, MY APPOINTMENT BOOK IS WIDE OPEN.
SO LONG AS THE DOPE KEEPS FLOWING, I'M A JOLLY GOOD TALKER.
NO PAIN AND NO GAIN!
JUST A WELL-LUBRICATED SLIDE INTO OBLIVION.
VALENTINO HAD NO TROUBLE RECOLLECTING THE PAST, NOR WAS HE RELUCTANT TO TALK ABOUT IT.
TO HEAR HIM TELL IT, HE WAS PRETTY MUCH THE UNDISPUTED CENTER OF THE UNIVERSE, SMARTER, CRAFTIER, AND MORE CHARISMATIC THAN ANYONE AROUND, ESPECIALLY THE OTHER PHINNEY RIDGE BOYS.
BOBBY GAVE IT UP A FEW YEARS BACK.
FRANK, OF COURSE, NEVER MADE IT HOME FROM KOREA.
NO SURPRISE I OUTLIVED 'EM ALL.

YOU AND DAD KNEW EACH OTHER BEFORE ENLISTING, RIGHT?
SURE, I WAS PALS WITH ALL THE GUYS, EVEN THE ALTAR BOYS WHO SKIPPED THE NEIGHBORHOOD SCHOOL FOR O'DEA!
I'M THE REASON ALL OF 'EM HAD IT SO GOOD DURING THE WAR.
WELL, EXCEPT FOR FRANK.
HEY, EVERYONE DID BETTER.
IF IT HADN'T BEEN FOR ME, THEY'D ALL BE OVER THERE FERTILIZING THE DIRT!
"I CONVINCED 'EM TO SIGN UP BEFORE TRUMAN'S DRAFT GOT STARTED. ENLISTING EARLY GOT US A BETTER DEAL. THAT'S HOW WE ALL GOT IN THE ASA, WHICH LEMME TELL YA, WAS A SWEET ASSIGNMENT."
U.S. ARMY ENLISTMENT CENTE
SEE! EXOTIC KOREA!
VISIT JAPAN

SO THAT CLARIFIED ONE PART OF THE STORY.
EVENTUALLY, DAD MUST HAVE COME TO A DIFFERENT OPINION ABOUT JACK'S GUIDANCE.
DID THIS GUY KNOW ONE OF HIS "PALS" TRIED TO SCRATCH HIM OUT OF MEMORY?
NOT THAT IT WOULD CHANGE HIS OPINION OF HIMSELF.
TRUMAN, THE LITTLE BASTARD, LATER EXTENDED THE LENGTH OF ENLISTMENT.
THAT WAS RIGHT BEFORE DICK AND THE OTHERS GOT SENT TO THE PENINSULA.
I'D SHIPPED OUT SIX MONTHS BEFORE.
HECK, THOSE GUYS SAW LESS THAN A YEAR OF THE REAL STUFF.
PRETTY SLICK, IF YOU ASK ME.
THAT WASN'T THE LAST SWEET DEAL I GOT YOUR POPS.
YOU CONVINCED HIM TO MOVE TO YAKIMA FOR THE HANFORD NSA GIG.

WELL, AREN'T YOU THE SMART ONE.
MUST HAVE GOT SOME BRAINS FROM YOUR MOTHER.
SHAME ABOUT HER. SHE MARRIED THE WRONG GUY. THEY WERE BETTER OFF APART.
BUT ANYWAY...YEAH, I GOT HIM THAT JOB. I'D STAYED WITH ARMY INTELLIGENCE AFTER DICK BAILED.
THAT LED TO POSITIONS WITH VARIOUS OTHER AGENCIES.
HANFORD WAS AN EASY ASSIGNMENT, JUST DIGGING UP DIRT ON A BUNCH OF COMMIES TRYING TO MESS WITH THE PROGRAM.
EVEN YOUR POP COULDN'T SCREW IT UP.
DIGGING UP DIRT?
IT AIN'T ALL JAMES BOND HEROICS, KID. THERE'S LOTS OF GRUNT WORK BEHIND EVERY OPERATION.
DICK WAS A USEFUL GRUNT IN A WORLD FULL OF MOSTLY USELESS GRUNTS.
I LIKE TO THINK HE WAS MAKING A DIFFERENCE.

MMPHH!
MWAHHH HA HA HA HAAAAAA!
HACK! KOFF!
HUFF! HEH HEH! MAYBE THE APPLE DIDN'T FALL FAR FROM THE TREE AFTER ALL. LEMME GUESS, DICK FILLED YOU UP WITH ALL THAT CATHOLIC CRAP!
I'M NOT RELIGIOUS.
DEFINITELY NOT CATHOLIC.
GOOD! THAT B.S. NEVER GOT ANYBODY ANYWHERE!
WHAT YOU "BELIEVE" HAS PRECIOUS LITTLE TO DO WITH WHAT GOES DOWN IN THE REAL WORLD.
AT LEAST WE AGREED ON SOMETHING.

"LISTEN, KID, YOUR DAD AND ME, AND ALL THE ASA BOYS, WE HAD IT GREAT!"

"KYOTO STATION WAS A BARREL OF FUN!"

"WE WERE YOUNG MEN WITH PRIVILEGE! THE U.S. ARMY IN OCCUPIED JAPAN!"

VALENTINO'S WORDS ADDED THE MUCH-NEEDED PERSPECTIVE OF SOMEONE WHO WAS THERE TO THE PHOTOS AMONG DAD'S STUFF.

"IMPERIAL JAPAN WAS BEATEN, BUT THE COMMON FOLK LIKED THE CHANGES WE WERE BRINGING. THE EMPEROR HAD PUT 'EM THROUGH HELL AND THEY HAD SQUAT TO SHOW FOR IT."
AND THE GUYS IN CHARGE KNEW THAT UNCLE SAM WOULD TURN A DEAF EAR WHEN THE KOREANS STARTED TALKING ABOUT ALL THE NASTY STUFF THE JAPS DID TO 'EM DURING THEIR OWN OCCUPATION AND THE WAR WITH CHINA.
SO EVERYONE WAS HAPPY!
"YOUR POP, BEING A NAIVE KID STILL WET BEHIND THE EARS AND AWAY FROM MAMA FOR THE FIRST TIME, TOOK FULL ADVANTAGE OF THE SITUATION."
ウェルカムサービスマン
"HE HAD A GOOD TIME JUST LIKE ALL THE REST OF US."

"THERE WAS ONLY SO MUCH THE ASA COULD DO IN JAPAN, BUT WE WORKED LONG HOURS AND NABBED EVERYTHING THE REDS BROADCAST."
"THE EGGHEADS IN THE UNIT EVEN CRACKED THE CHINK CODES, SO WE KNEW ALL THEIR PLANS."
BUT SOMETIMES WE HAD TROUBLE GETTING THE INTEL TO OUR OWN BRASS.
GOOD MEN DIED NEEDLESSLY 'CAUSE THE REAR ECHELON CLOWNS DIDN'T KNOW THE VALUE OF WHAT WE WERE GIVING 'EM.
BUT THAT'S ANOTHER STORY.
押聖
"ANYWAY, WE DID OUR JOBS AND WE HAD FUN. THE LOCALS PROVIDED BOOZE AND FOOD, AND DAMES FOR THOSE WHO WERE SO INCLINED."
"THE GUYS WHO RAN THE PLACES WHERE WE'D HANG OUT WERE A SLICK BUNCH OF ENTREPRENEURS."
私たちはあなたのお金を喜んで受け取ります
WERCOME TO HAPPY ESTABRISHMENT DEDICATION TO MAKE YOU WONDELFUR TIME IN JAPAN, PREASE.

I'D ALREADY SEEN DAD'S COLLECTION OF JAPANESE BEER BOTTLE LABELS, SO I KNEW VALENTINO WASN'T STRETCHING THE TRUTH TOO MUCH.

© Asahi Group Holdings, Ltd.; Kirin Brewery; Sapporo Breweries, Ltd.; Nippon Beer Co, Ltd.

IT MUST HAVE BEEN LIKE LIVING ON ANOTHER PLANET.

YEAH, THE PLANET OF NON-CHRISTIANS. TALK ABOUT PARADISE!

BUT DON'T PAINT TOO ROSY A PICTURE. THERE WAS STILL A WAR GOING ON.

"SOME OF THE GUYS YOU'D BE DRINKING WITH ONE DAY WOULD GET SENT TO THE PENINSULA THE NEXT.

AND SOMETIMES THEY DIDN'T COME BACK."

"THAT KEPT YOUR POP AND THE OTHER ALTAR BOYS ON THEIR KNEES COME SUNDAY."
"OF COURSE, I WAS ALWAYS HAVING TO CHEER UP THE CHRISTIANS AFTER THE CHAPLAIN HAD BEEN AT 'EM."
"GLOOMIEST DAMN RELIGION THERE IS."
GLUK!
LIKE I TOLD 'EM...
BOYS, YOU GOTTA LIVE WHILE YOU GOT THE CHANCE!

AIN'T THAT RIGHT, WILMA?
THAT LIGHT! BOYS RIVE NOW! DLINK BEEL!
YOU HEARD THE RADY, DLINK!
CRINK!
ウェルカムサービスマン
KANPAI!
BOTTOM UP!

IF YOU ASK ME, SOME OF THE GOD SQUAD WERE THE BIGGEST PLAYERS IN UNIFORM.
THE ARMY DIDN'T CARE, SO LONG AS THEY PUT IN THEIR SHIFTS.
I'M SURE YOU'LL BE HAPPY TO LEARN I DON'T INCLUDE YOUR POP IN THAT GROUP.
THAT'S NICE TO KNOW... I GUESS.
DON'T GET ME WRONG. DICK WAS NO SQUARE.
HE WAS A STRAIGHT-UP GUY, EVEN IF HE DID TAKE THAT J. CHRIST STUFF A LITTLE TOO FAR.
HOW FAR WAS THAT?
I TELL YA, KID, IN WAR IT'S ALL ABOUT LUCK. YOU CAN PRAY TO A MAGIC JELLY BEAN AND IT WILL DO AS MUCH FOR YOU AS ANY GOD.

"THERE WAS ONE TIME UP AT CHUNCHEON, WHERE WE FIRST MET UP AGAIN ON THE PENINSULA..."

"CHUNCHEON IS WHERE THE HAN MERGES WITH THE SOYANG RIVER. IT WAS A MAJOR TRANSPORTATION HUB FOR POINTS NORTH AROUND THE PUNCHBOWL AND OTHER PLACES YOU MIGHT HAVE HEARD ABOUT."

WE'D BEEN THERE ABOUT A WEEK. THERE WAS A LOT GOING ON ALL AROUND.

YOU KNOW ABOUT THE BUGLES?

YEAH.

CREEPIEST DAMN THINGS YOU EVER HEARD.

NO ONE WHO HEARD THOSE BUGLES EVER FORGOT 'EM.

"AROUND MIDNIGHT, THAT'S WHEN THEY'D START, WAY UP IN THE HILLS. YOU COULD NEVER TELL EXACTLY WHERE, BUT YOU KNEW IT WAS A SIGN THE REDS WERE LAUNCHING AN ATTACK. 'HUMAN WAVES' THEY CALLED 'EM."
THAT'S RICH! THERE WASN'T AN OUNCE OF HUMANITY IN THE WHOLE SORDID MESS.
"THE CHINESE DIDN'T HAVE ENOUGH GUNS, SO HALF THEIR INFANTRY WERE ARMED WITH BAMBOO STICKS. THE POOR DUMBASSES WERE BRAINWASHED INTO THINKING THEIR SACRIFICE WOULD DEFEAT THE EVIL CAPITALISTS FROM OVERSEAS. THE MACHINE GUNS MOWED 'EM DOWN LIKE SO MUCH GRASS, BUT THERE WERE JUST SO DAMN MANY OF 'EM!"
"EVENTUALLY WE'D HEAR THE POP OF SMALL ARMS FIRE AND KNOW THE BLOODY TIDE WOULD BE FLOODING OVER OUR GUYS."
"DAMN SHITTY FEELING, KNOWING THAT SOLDIERS WERE FIGHTING AND DYING UP THERE AND THERE WAS NOTHING YOU COULD DO ABOUT IT."
MIND YOU, WE SAW OUR OWN FAIR SHARE OF BUSINESS.
IN WAR, THERE'S ALWAYS PLENTY OF SHIT TO SPREAD AROUND.

BUT SOLDIERS HAVE A JOB TO DO AND WE DID IT.
TROUBLE WAS, WE WERE SITTING DUCKS OUT IN THE OPEN WHERE OUR GEAR WOULD WORK.
THE DAYTIME WAS OUR ENEMY.
"THIS ONE DAY, WE'D JUST SET UP OUR ANTENNAS AND WERE STRINGING WIRE TO THE GENERATOR WHEN THE REDS STARTED POPPING AT US FROM A RIDGE ABOUT HALF A MILE AWAY."
FLASH!
WHUMP!
INCOMING!
FOOM!
"IT USUALLY TOOK A COUPLE OF ROUNDS BEFORE THEY'D GET THEIR TARGETING RIGHT. THAT GAVE US TIME TO TAKE COVER AND CALL IN AIR SUPPORT TO TAKE 'EM OUT."
HIT THE DIRT, NOW! COVER YOUR ASS AND KEEP IT COVERED!

THE CHRISTERS ALL HAD THEIR LITTLE MEDALS AND GEWGAWS.
THESE WERE SUPPOSED TO SEE 'EM THROUGH ANYTHING.
"I TOLD 'EM THE M-1 RIFLE WAS A BETTER TALISMAN."
BESIDES, THEIR LUCKY CHARMS PUT OTHERS AT RISK.
"SEE, THE CHINKS COULDN'T GET A BEAD ON US IF EVERYONE STAYED DOWN. THE WANNABE SAINTS HAD TROUBLE REMEMBERING THAT."
WHUMP!
KAPOW!
KAPOW!
FOOM!
"LADY LUCK DOESN'T CARE ONE WAY OR THE OTHER WHAT SORT OF TRINKET THE GUY IN THE NEXT FOXHOLE HAS DANGLING FROM HIS NECK. ONCE SHE'S GOT YOU IN HER SIGHTS, THAT'S THAT."

"I'M SURE THEIR RELIGION GAVE THEM COMFORT, AND THERE'S NOTHING WRONG WITH THAT..."
SKREEEEEEEEEEEEE...
PAF!
"...UNTIL YOU START THINKING *YOUR* MUMBO-JUMBO IS GONNA MAKE *OTHERS* IMMUNE FROM DYING!"
FOOM!!
FLOP!
——!
TWITCH! TWITCH!
THAT WAS THE FIRST TIME WE LOST GUYS FROM OUR SQUAD.
IT WASN'T THE LAST.

"AS RANKING OFFICER, IT WAS MY JOB TO KEEP THE CASUALTIES TO A MINIMUM, AND IF THAT MEANT DOING A LESS-THAN-KOSHER JOB OF BURYING WHAT WAS LEFT OF A GUY WHO'S ALREADY DEAD IN ORDER TO KEEP OTHERS ALIVE, THAT'S THE WAY IT WENT DOWN."
"AFTER THE ARMISTICE, A SPECIAL UNIT TRIED TO RECOVER AS MANY OF THE DEAD AS THEY COULD, BUT THEY NEVER GOT 'EM ALL. HELL, THEY'RE STILL DIGGING 'EM UP, 70 YEARS LATER."
ENOUGH WITH THE HOLY-MOLY SHIT!
GET YOUR PACKS ON YOUR BACKS AND YOUR REARS IN GEAR.
SAVE IT FOR THE POPE. WE'RE MOVING OUT!

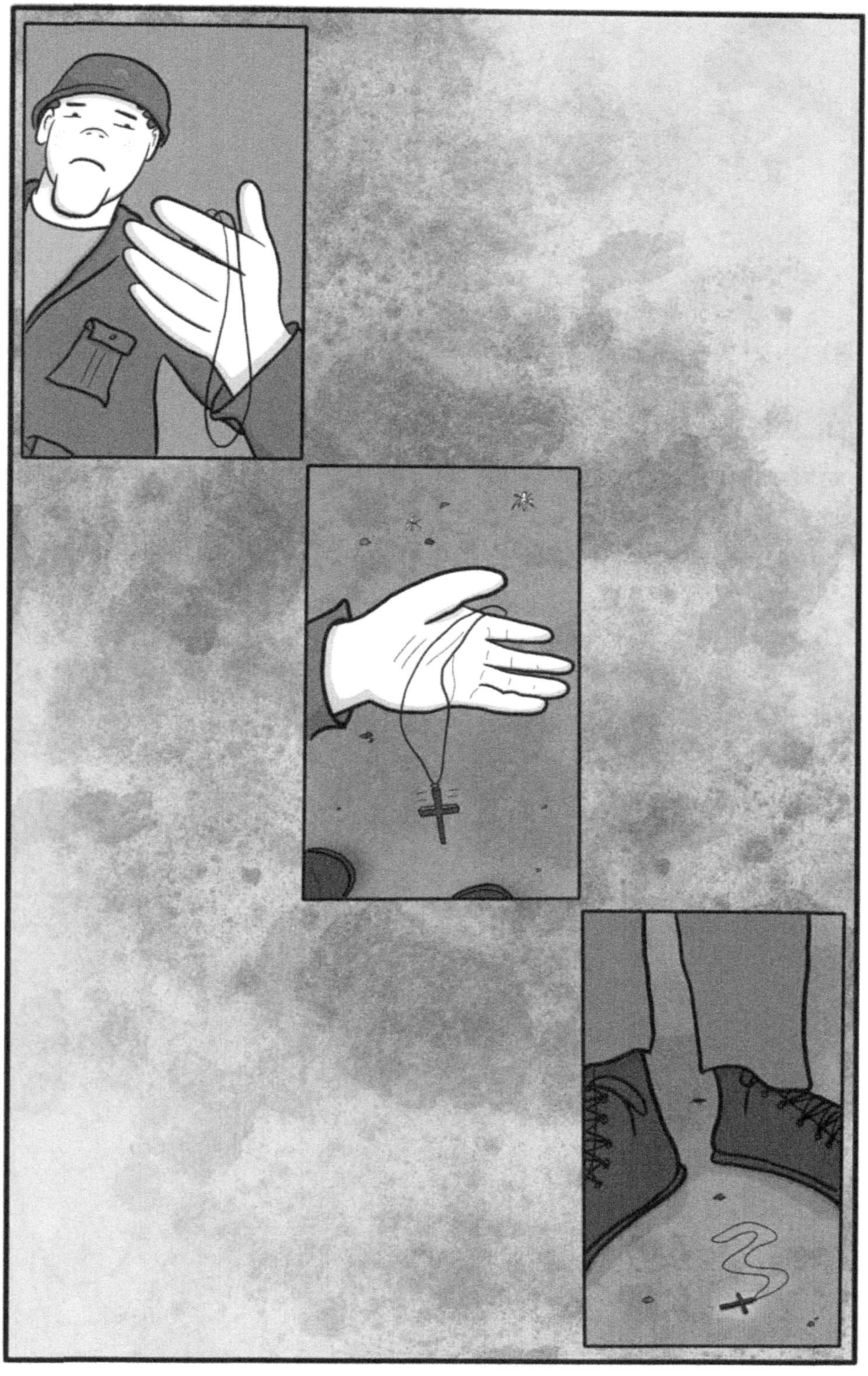

S'MATTER? LEGS NOT WORKING?
I SAID, MOVE IT, #!%*@%!!
WE'RE GOING! CHRIST, SHOW SOME RESPECT!
I'LL SHOW SOME RESPECT, CORPORAL, WHEN I'M BACK HOME SLURPING DOWN A BOWL OF IVAR'S CLAM CHOWDER!
CLICK!
TRY IT, ALTAR BOY...
...AND YOU'LL NEED A GUARDIAN ANGEL TO FLY YOU BACK TO CAMP.

HMMPH.
PUT A GUN IN SOMEONE'S HANDS AND YOU NEVER REALLY KNOW WHAT THEY'RE GOING TO DO.
SOME GET HEROIC. OTHERS JUST GET STUPID.
EITHER WAY, PEOPLE GET HURT...AND NOT ALWAYS THE ONES YOU EXPECT.
KOREA WASN'T THE FIRST PLACE WHERE SOMEONE GOT TAKEN OUT BY FRIENDLY FIRE.
FRIENDLY FIRE... YOU MEAN WHEN YOU ACCIDENTALLY SHOOT ONE OF YOUR OWN?
ACCIDENTALLY... YEAH, SURE.
TOWARDS THE END, ONE OF THE BIG SHOTS IN OUR COMPANY TOOK A BULLET RIGHT BETWEEN THE EYES.
THAT WAS WHERE IT CAME OUT. IT HAD ENTERED FROM THE *BACK* OF HIS SKULL.
SOMETIMES, EVEN GOOD SOLDIERS GET PUSHED OVER THE LINE. IN THOSE CASES, RESPECT FOR AUTHORITY DOESN'T MEAN SQUAT.

SCUTTLEBUTT AMONG THE RANKS HAD ONE OF OUR ASA GUYS DOING IT...
...THOUGH NOBODY EVER FESSED UP.
AND THE BRASS WISELY LET IT BE.
DO YOU THINK MY DAD -
NO. I DO NOT.
MIND YOU, NOT BECAUSE OF SOME FINELY TUNED MORAL COMPASS INSIDE HIS SWEET LITTLE HEAD...
...BUT BECAUSE NOBODY TOLD HIM TO DO IT.

SEE, AS UPRIGHT A GUY AS YOUR POP WAS, HE WAS NOT ONE TO TAKE THE INITIATIVE ON HIS OWN.
"THAT MADE HIM A GOOD SOLDIER. IN THE ARMY, IF YOU STICK WITH DOING AS YOU'RE TOLD, CHANCES ARE YOU'LL GET BY OKAY."
"BUT CIVILIAN LIFE IS A WHOLE OTHER BALLGAME, ISN'T IT? THERE'S NOBODY HIGHER UP MAKING ALL YOUR DECISIONS FOR YOU. YOU'VE GOT TO FIGURE THINGS OUT FOR YOURSELF."
"AND THINGS CHANGE REALLY FAST OUT IN THE REAL WORLD. IF YOU CAN'T CHANGE EVEN FASTER, YOU MIGHT AS WELL CALL IT QUITS."
I DON'T THINK DICK LIKED IT WHEN THINGS CHANGED.
NONE OF THE ALTAR BOYS DID.
CHANGE IS HARD TO RECONCILE WITH THE IMMUTABLE TRUTH THE CHURCH HAS BEEN TELLING YOU FOR A COUPLE THOUSAND YEARS.

I COULDN'T DENY VALENTINO'S WORDS. THERE'S NO QUESTION DAD DIDN'T REACT WELL TO SHIFTS IN THE STATUS QUO, ESPECIALLY WHEN HIS OWN EVOLVING CIRCUMSTANCES FORCED *HIM* TO CHANGE.

THAT'S WHY HE LEFT THE BOOMING SEATTLE OF THE POST WWII YEARS AND MOVED TO A SMALL TOWN PERMANENTLY STUCK IN ITS OWN TIME CAPSULE. THAT'S ALSO WHY HE COULDN'T DEAL TOO WELL WITH HIS LITTLE BOY GROWING UP, OR A WIFE WHO WANTED MORE THAN A CLEAN HOUSE AND A HUSBAND PARKED IN FRONT OF A COLOR TV.

BUT JACK VALENTINO HAD GROSSLY SIMPLIFIED DAD'S POINT OF VIEW. THE CAREER SPOOK HAD SETTLED A LITTLE TOO QUICKLY ON THE RELIGIOUS ANGLE, FALLING PREY TO THE SAME OVERSIMPLIFICATION THAT LED TO DAD'S FRUSTRATION WITH AN INCREASINGLY COMPLICATED WORLD.

IT'S TRUE, DAD WAS OKAY WITH BEING TOLD WHAT TO DO, BUT ONLY WHEN THE ONE DOING THE TELLING WASN'T MADE OF FLESH AND BLOOD. HE WAS SKEPTICAL OF ANYONE IN A POSITION OF POWER, YET RELIED ON ABSTRACT AUTHORITIES FOR ALMOST EVERY BRICK IN HIS MORAL FOUNDATION. BE IT TIMELESS CHURCH DOGMA, THE HALF-REMEMBERED PRONOUNCEMENTS OF HIS MOTHER AND FATHER OR THE DUTIFULLY REDACTED ASSESSMENTS OF FACELESS HIGHER-UPS IN THE ARMY, THE CIA OR NSA, WORDS FROM ON HIGH DICTATED THE WAY THINGS WERE, THE WAY THINGS ARE, AND THE WAY THEY OUGHT TO BE, NO QUESTIONING ALLOWED.

VALENTINO GOT ONE THING RIGHT: ALL TOO OFTEN DAD *DID* SEEM TO JUST CALL IT QUITS RATHER THAN MODIFY HIS WAY OF THINKING. ESPECIALLY AFTER THE DISAPPOINTING WAY I TURNED OUT, I THINK HE GAVE UP CARING ABOUT ANYTHING THAT CHALLENGED HIS VIEW — INFORMED BY THOSE INVISIBLE ABSOLUTES — OF HOW THINGS WERE SUPPOSED TO BE.

THERE WAS, OF COURSE, ONE FINAL SUBJECT I NEEDED TO BROACH WITH THE LAST OF THE PHINNEY RIDGE BOYS. KNOWING THE CIRCUMSTANCES THAT BROUGHT TOGETHER THE YOUNG SOLDIER FROM AMERICA AND A CHINESE PEASANT NAMED CHENG LI JIE WOULD, I WAS CONVINCED, HELP ME TO FINALLY UNDERSTAND MY FATHER'S BEHAVIOR AND, PERHAPS...

...EVEN REVEAL *WHY* HE BEHAVED THAT WAY.

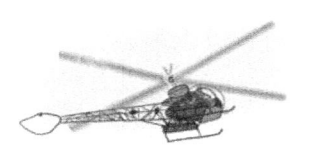

THUP!
THUP!
THUP!
THUP!

9

Jack Valentino had talked the other three Phinney Ridge boys into enlisting in the army before they could be vacuumed up by the Korean War draft. They trained together at Army Security Agency facilities in the United States before shipping out to Japan in January, 1950. Dad once described the 18 months that followed as the best time of his life.

Eventually, the good times ended and the group of young men were dispatched to the Korean peninsula, where the war suddenly became very real, and very deadly. One of the Phinney Ridge boys would not come back. Another, my father, came back psychologically damaged by what he'd seen and done. He never spoke about it, allowing the pain to fester and infect his family, his work, and the rest of his life.

It was only now, after his death, that I'd begun to piece together the story.

HMMPH.

IT DOESN'T MATTER WHAT SAINTS OR GODS YOU'VE GOT LOOKING OUT FOR YOU...

WAR IS A LOTTERY. SOMEONE HANDS YOU A TICKET AND YOU TAKE YOUR CHANCES.

IS THAT A REGRET?
NO.
AT THE ASA REUNION A FEW YEARS BACK, YOU HAD SOME PHOTOS.
YOU WANTED DAD TO SEE THEM.
YEAH, I DID.

I'D HEARD THROUGH THE GRAPEVINE THAT HE WAS HAVING TROUBLE.
THAT'S WHAT'S WRONG WITH THAT RELIGIOUS SHIT!
IT TAKES THE SIMPLE FACTS OF LIFE AND LOADS 'EM UP WITH A TON OF CRAP! AND WHY? SO YOU'LL BE WEIGHTED DOWN WITH GUILT THAT - SURPRISE! - ONLY THE CHURCH CAN ABSOLVE!
WHAT WE HAD TO DO IN KOREA WAS *WAR*, PLAIN AND SIMPLE.
THERE AREN'T ANY GOOD GUYS IN WAR.
THE ONES YOU SHOOT AT ARE THE ONES SHOOTING AT YOU.
I GOT THE IMPRESSION THE PHOTOS WERE TAKEN AS YOUR SQUAD CAME UNDER ATTACK.
YOUR DAMN RIGHT! THAT WAS MY POINT!
THEY KILLED US, WE KILLED THEM! AN EYE FOR AN EYE, IF YOU WANT TO GET ALL BIBLICAL ABOUT IT!

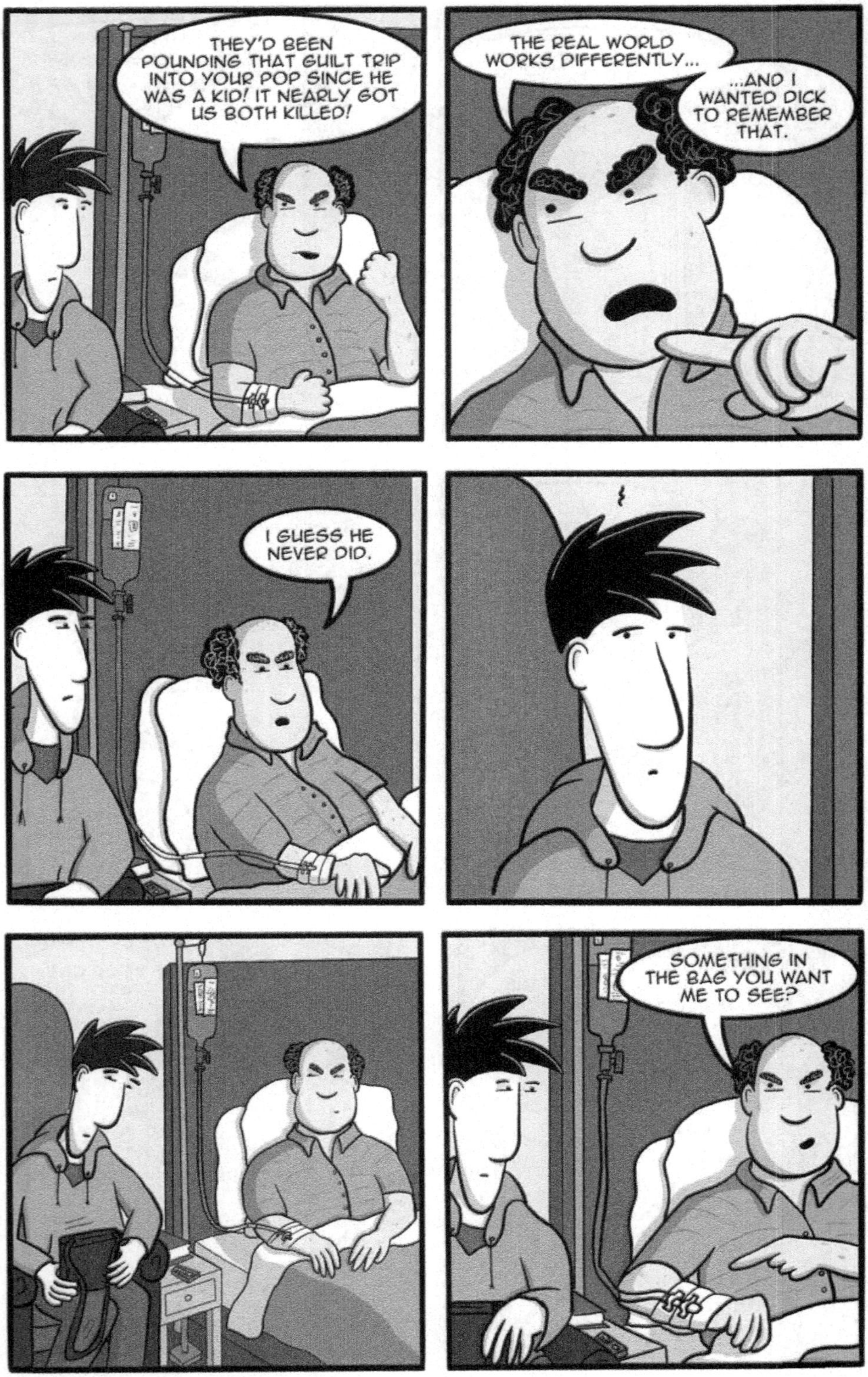
THEY'D BEEN POUNDING THAT GUILT TRIP INTO YOUR POP SINCE HE WAS A KID! IT NEARLY GOT US BOTH KILLED!
THE REAL WORLD WORKS DIFFERENTLY...
...AND I WANTED DICK TO REMEMBER THAT.
I GUESS HE NEVER DID.
SOMETHING IN THE BAG YOU WANT ME TO SEE?

GO ON! SHOW ME! I'M THE SOLE SURVIVING PHINNEY RIDGE BOY!
IF YOU'VE GOT QUESTIONS, I'M YOUR LAST CHANCE AT GETTING ANSWERS!
ZZZZZZIP!
?
WHAT'S THAT?
WHATCHA GOT THERE?
程立杰

JESUS! ALL THESE YEARS...
HE COULDN'T JUST LET IT GO.
THERE WAS MORE...
YEAH, I KNOW. I REMEMBER!
WHY DID HE HAVE THIS STUFF?
WHAT HAPPENED?
SHIT HAPPENED! LIKE IT ALWAYS DOES!

TELL ME ABOUT IT.
PROBABLY BEST THAT PARTICULAR STORY STAYS WITH ME.
I WANT TO HEAR IT.
NO YOU DON'T!
HACK!
KOFF! KOFF! KOFF!
LISTEN KID, TRY TO UNDERSTAND. LIKE I SAID, WAR IS WAR.
IT WAS NO BIG DEAL.
IT WAS A BIG DEAL... TO MY FATHER.
I NEED TO KNOW WHAT HE DID.
WHAT A GOOD SOLDIER ALWAYS DOES!
WHAT HE'S TOLD TO DO!

HMMPH.

IT WAS THE WINTER OF '52. WE WERE ABOUT 30 MILES FROM OUR CAMP AT UIJEONGBU, NORTH OF SEOUL.

HALF A DOZEN OF US WERE HEADING OUT TO A FORWARD LISTENING POST WE'D SET UP BEFORE.

"NEGOTIATORS FROM BOTH SIDES WERE IN PANMUNJOM, TALKING TRUCE. IN THE MEANTIME, THE REDS WERE TRYING TO GRAB AS MUCH TERRITORY AS THEY COULD GET. THE 'KUMSONG BULGE' WAS SOME CHOICE REAL ESTATE THEY WERE AFTER. IT WAS OUR JOB TO FIGURE OUT WHAT THEY WERE UP TO SO THE TACTICAL UNITS COULD STOP 'EM. WE WEREN'T SUCCESSFUL, AS IT TURNED OUT, BUT THAT'S GETTING AHEAD OF THINGS."

"WE WERE ONE, MAYBE TWO MILES BEHIND THE LINE. PRETTY ROUTINE."

"EXCEPT WE GOT A LITTLE TOO CLOSE TO A COMMIE PATROL."

"WE HAD TO LAY LOW UNTIL THEY PASSED AND AIR COMMAND COULD SEND A CHOPPER TO PICK US UP."

IT WAS STANDARD PROCEDURE FOR THE REDS TO SEND ONE OR TWO MEN TO CHECK OUT THEIR FLANKS.
YOUR BUDDY THERE MUST HAVE DRAWN A SHORT STRAW.
WE MET HIM AS WE WERE STRATEGICALLY EXTRICATING OURSELVES FROM THE AREA.
THOSE POOR S.O.B.S WERE DELIBERATE TARGETS, SENT OUT TO DRAW FIRE FROM ANY ENEMY TROOPS THAT MIGHT BE AROUND.
ONE SHOT AND THEY'D KNOW WHERE WE WERE. THEN ALL HELL WOULD RAIN DOWN.
THE CHINESE 82MM MORTAR WAS A DAMN FINE WEAPON.
"SO IT CAME DOWN TO A SIMPLE CHOICE: ALL OF US... OR ONE UNLUCKY CHINK."
"LIKE I SAID, WAR IS A LOTTERY WITH VERY FEW WINNERS..."
"...AND A WHOLE LOT OF LOSERS."

"I'D RADIOED BASE FOR AN AIRLIFT, BUT IT WOULD TAKE A WHILE FOR 'EM TO GET TO US. MEANTIME, WE COULDN'T AFFORD TO GET INTO A FIREFIGHT WITH THE REDS, WHICH WOULD HAPPEN IF THIS BASTARD GOT BACK TO HIS PLATOON."
OR IF THEY HEARD SO MUCH AS A POP FROM ONE OF OUR WEAPONS.
YOU'RE SMART ENOUGH TO KNOW WHERE THIS IS GOING.
QING BUYAO SHA WO.

HAVEN'T HEARD THAT IN A LONG TIME.
I'M SURPRISED HE SHARED IT WITH YOU.
HE DIDN'T.
BUT YOU WILL.
HMMPH. HEH HEH. SURE.
I'LL TELL YOU ALL ABOUT WHAT YOUR POP DID TO THAT POOR CHINAMAN.
請不要殺我
"LIKE I SAID, WE HAD A PROBLEM, AND THE DUMB S.O.B. MADE IT WORSE BY MAKING NOISE."
"A LOT OF NOISE."
WE GOTTA SHUT HIM UP...FAST. MOLITOR! DEAL WITH IT!
!
FOLLOW YOUR ORDERS, SOLDIER!

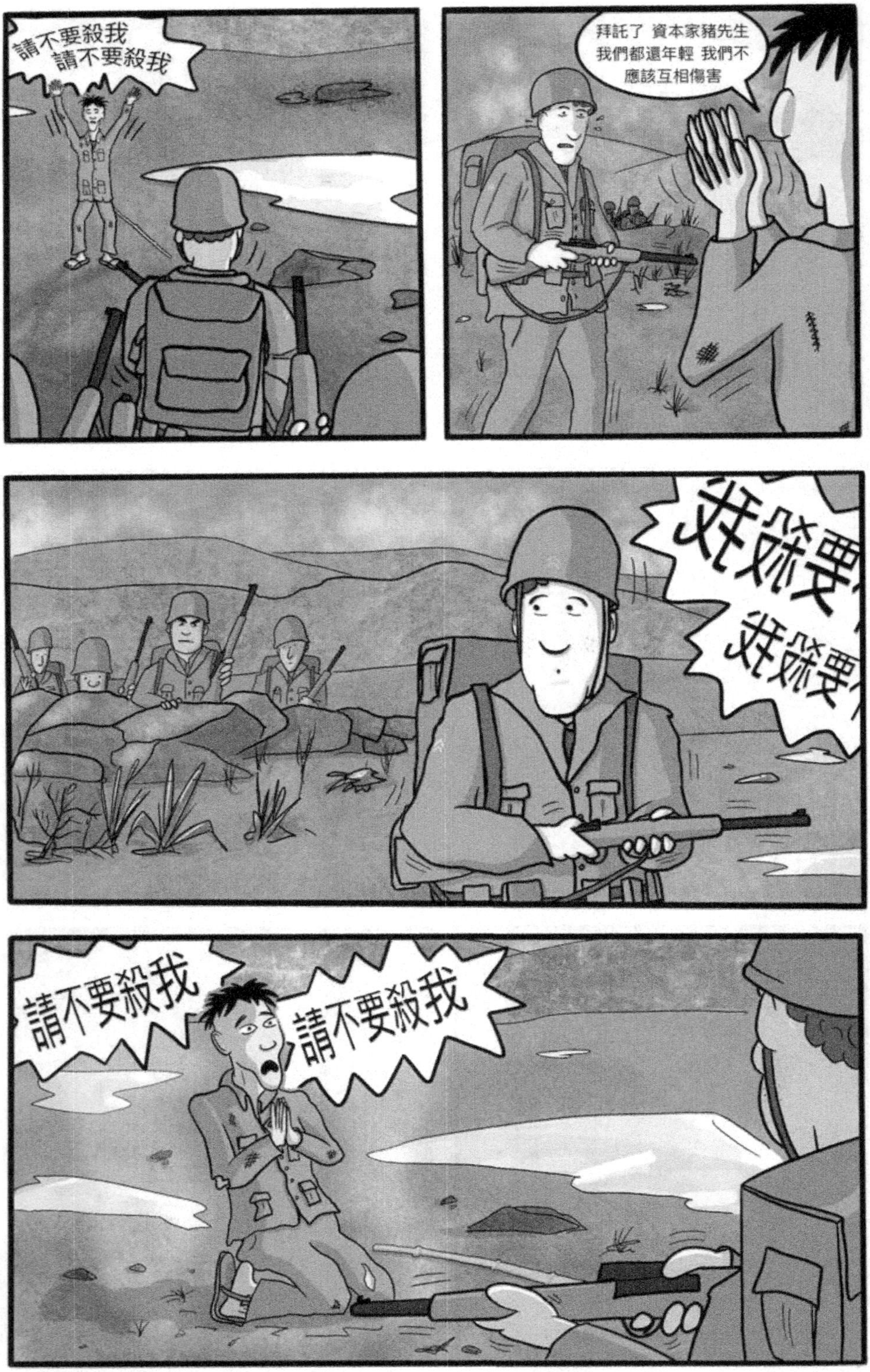
請不要殺我
請不要殺我
拜託了 資本家豬先生
我們都還年輕 我們不
應該互相傷害
請不要殺我
請不要殺我

THOU SHALT NOT!!
請不要殺我
GOD DAMMIT ALTAR BOY! SHUT HIM UP!
請不要殺我
請不要殺我
#!*%@!! !&#@%#!!!
YOU WANT TO GET THE WHOLE #%*!! SQUAD KILLED?
請不要殺我
請不要殺我
請不要殺我
#!*%@!!

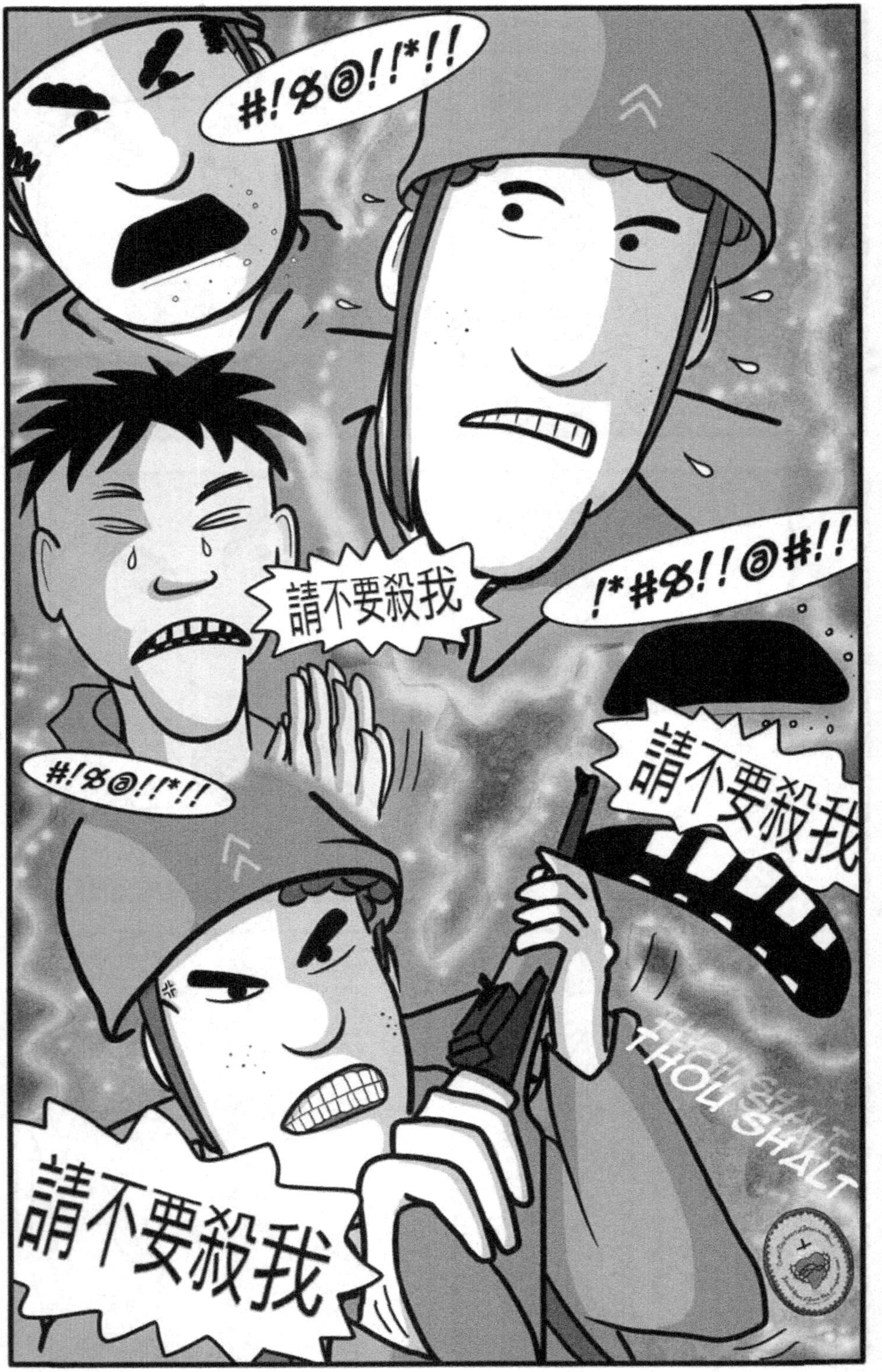
#!%@!!*!!
請不要殺我
!*#%!!@#!!
請不要殺我
#!%@!!*!!
請不要殺我
THOU SHALT

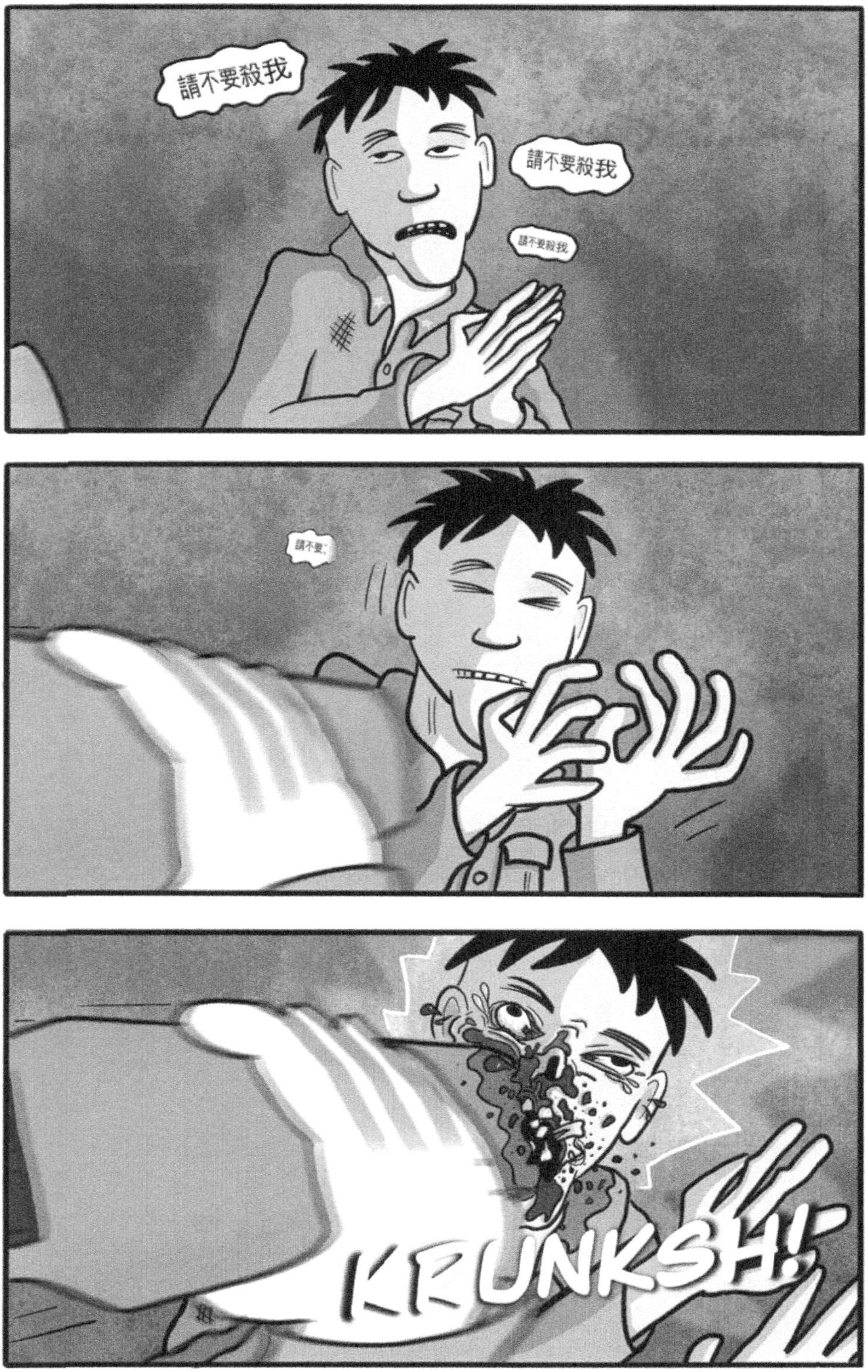
請不要殺我
請不要殺我
請不要殺我
請不要
KRUNKSH!

SLUMP!

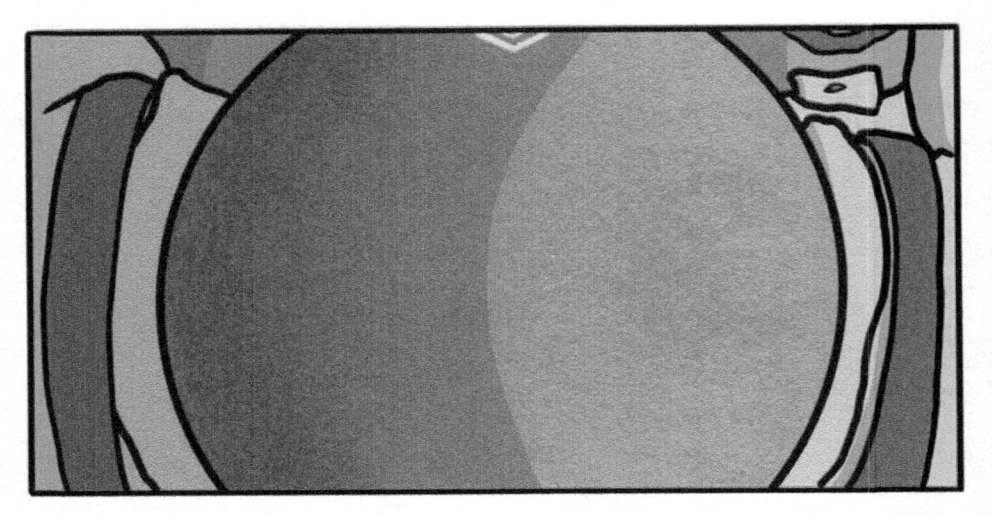

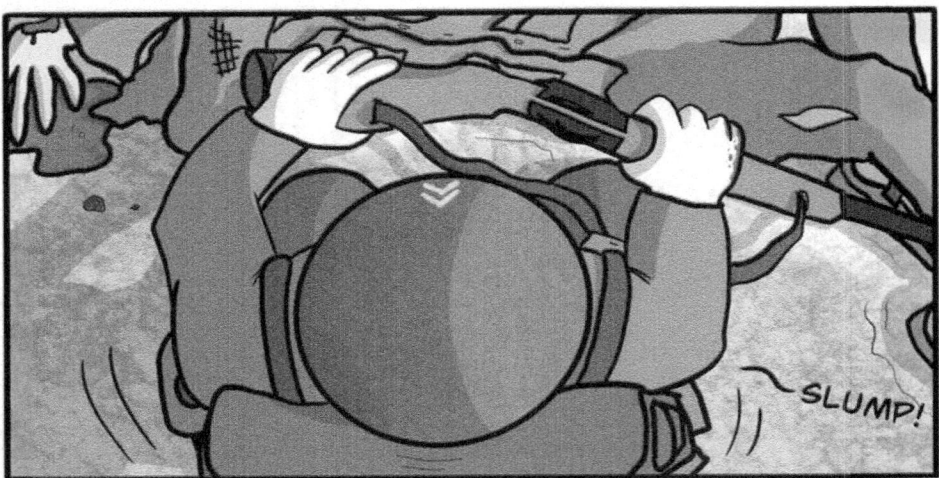

THUP! THUP! THUP! THUP!
THUP! THUP! THUP! THUP!
CHOPPERS!
GET READY TO LAY DOWN COVER FIRE! LOOK ALIVE OR YOU'LL ALL BE LOOKING MIGHTY DEAD!
THUP! THUP! THUP! THUP!

LET'S SEE WHAT WE GOT HERE.
SNAP!
RIFLE! RIFLE!
YANK! SPLUT!
HERE YOU GO!
WIPE! WIPE!
KEEPSAKES FOR THE GRANDKIDS.

PRETTY SLIM PICKINGS. CHEAP COMMIES!
MAKES YOU APPRECIATE GOOD OL' UNCLE SAM, EH?
THUP! THUP! THUP!
THUP! THUP! THUP! THUP! THUP!
HUH! WHO'D HAVE THOUGHT THEY'D GET HERE SO FAST?
PROBABLY DIDN'T NEED TO DROP THAT GUY, AFTER ALL.
THUP! THUP!
PLONK!
THUP! THUP! THUP!

THUP! THUP!
THUP! THUP!
THUP! THUP!
THUP! THUP! THUP!
THUP!
THUP! THUP! THUP!
THUP!
THUP
GAK!

THUP! THUP! THUP! THUP!
WEEEEEEEEOOOOOOOOOOOOOOOOOOOOOOOO!
殺死骯髒的洋基隊
THUP! THUP! THUP!
THUP! THUP! THUP!
ONE IN THE BALL, TWO ON THE SKIDS! MOVE IT!
THUP! THUP! THUP! THUP!
WEEEEEEEOOOOOOOOO
!#*#@!&!!

THUP! THUP! THUP!
KNOCK IT OFF, LOVEBIRDS, AND GET THE HELL ON BOARD!
THUP! THUP! THUP! THUP!
THUP! THUP! THUP! THUP!
OOOOOOOOEEEEEEEEEEEEEEE
KAPOW!
KAPOW!

THUP! THUP! THUP!
KPOP! KPOP! KPOP!
BLOW THIS OUT YOUR HORN, YOU COMMIE SON OF A BITCH!

THUP! THUP! THUP! THUP!
HACK!
KOFF!

THUP! THUP! THUP! THUP!
KPOP! KPOP!
HRRRUMPH!

WHEEZE!
OOOOOOOOOOOO
!*#%@!!
OOOOOOEEEEEEEEEEE
THUP! THUP! THUP! THUP!
GET YOUR ASS ON THAT WHIRLYBIRD, SOLDIER.
OOOOOOOOOOOOOOOO
EEEEEEEEEEEEEEEEEE
KAPOW!
THUP! THUP!
OOOOOOOOOOEEEEEEEE
KAPOW!
KAPOW!

THUP! THUP! THUP! THUP!
MOVE IT! #!$*^@!!
THUP! THUP! THUP! THUP!
THUP! THUP! THUP! THUP! THUP! THUP! THUP! THUP!

ON THE SKIDS AND STRAP IN! WE'RE TAKIN' OFF!
THUP! THUP!
THUP! THUP!

THUP! THUP! THUP! THUP!
KAPOW!
KAPOW!

KAPOW!
THUP!
THUP!
THUP!
THUP!
KAPOW!
KAPOW!
THUP! THUP!
KAPOW!
KAPOW!
THUP! THUP!
FWISS!
FWISS!
KAPOW!
THUP!
THUP!
THUP!
THUP!

THUP! THUP! THUP! THUP!

請不要殺我

THUP! THUP! THUP!

請不要殺我

THUP! THUP!

請不要殺我

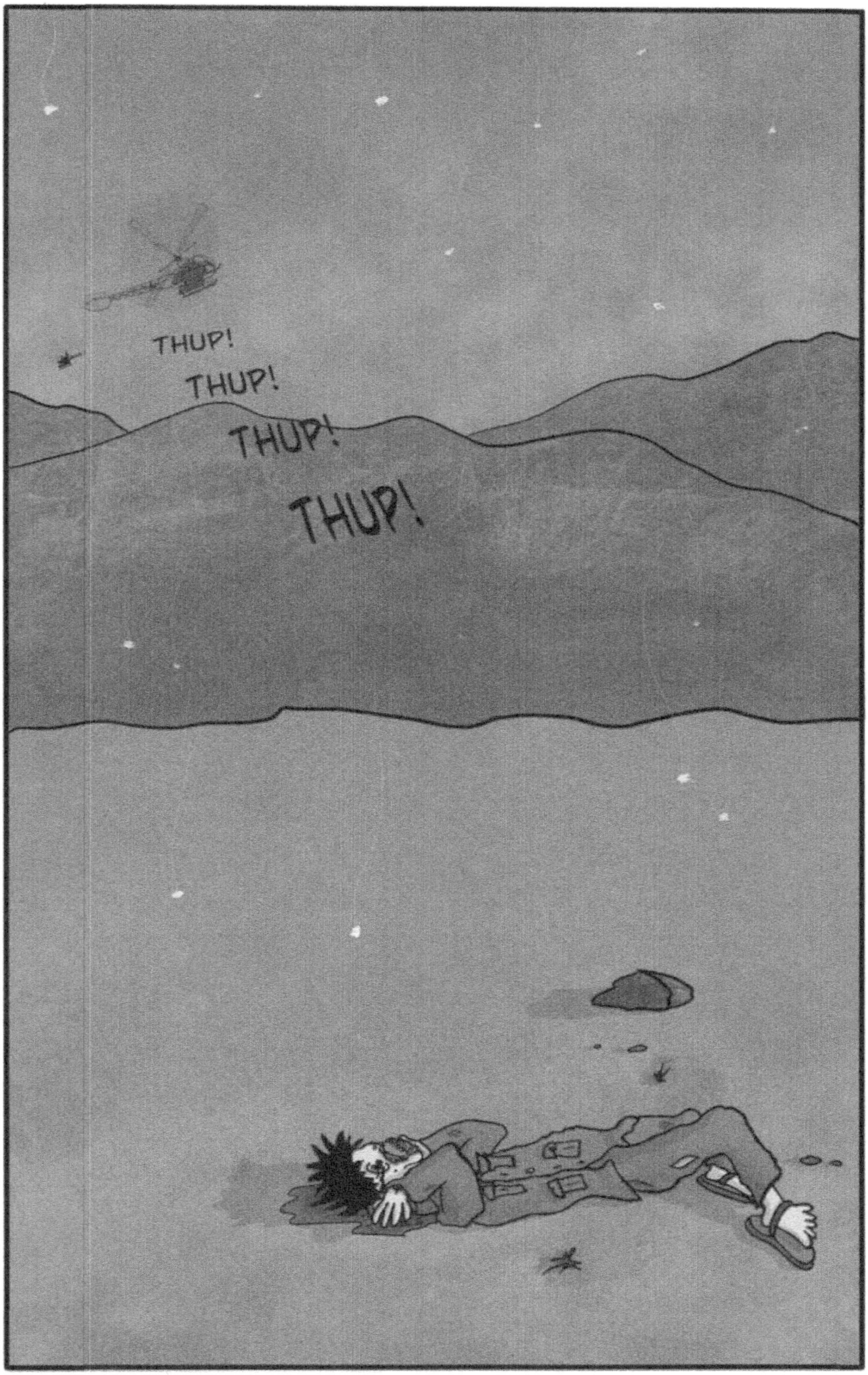
THUP!
THUP!
THUP!
THUP!

THAT WAS A LONG RIDE BACK TO CAMP.
YOUR POP WAS PRETTY MESSED UP AFTERWARDS.
I PUT IN A REQUEST FOR THE SQUAD TO GET SOME TIME OFF IN SEOUL, BUT THE BRASS TOOK IT ONE STEP FURTHER.
BOBBY, DICK, AND I GOT REASSIGNED TO THE 327TH RECON HEADQUARTERS ON OKINAWA. THAT WAS IN MARCH OF 1952.
COINCIDENTALLY, THAT'S WHERE THE ARMY'S ONLY PSYCH HOSPITAL WAS LOCATED. I THINK THE BIG SHOTS WERE LOOKING TO AVOID ANY BAD PRESS ABOUT SOLDIERS COMING HOME ALL LOONEY TUNES.
ALL OF US GOT OUR HEADS EXAMINED, BUT THEY WERE CHECKING OUT YOUR POP FOR A COUPLE OF WEEKS.
HE DIDN'T TALK MUCH ABOUT WHAT WENT DOWN THEN.
"I DON'T THINK HE WAS IN SUCH GREAT SHAPE."
"AND THE QUACKS IN UNIFORM WERE NO HELP."

BACK THEN, THE ARMY DIDN'T KNOW WHAT TO DO WITH GUYS LIKE DICK. THERE WASN'T ANY PTSD OR WHATEVER YOU WANT TO CALL IT.
YOU WERE EXPECTED TO MAN UP AND DEAL WITH ISSUES THE OLD FASHIONED WAY, BURYING THEM DEEP ENOUGH SO THEY COULDN'T GET OUT.
IT WAS A DIFFERENT AGE, WHEN EVERYONE WASN'T SUCH A PANSY.
NOT THAT THERE'S ANYTHING WRONG WITH THAT.
HEH!
"ANYWAY, AFTER A MONTH OR SO, I GOT SENT BACK TO THE PENINSULA. BOBBY STAYED A WHILE LONGER, THEN ENDED UP IN KYOTO AGAIN."
"YOUR POP STAYED ON OKINAWA FOR THE DURATION, OFFICIALLY ASSIGNED TO THE RADIO INTERCEPT GROUP THERE, BUT WE KNEW THAT WAS JUST A COVER FOR MORE PSYCH EVALUATION AT "CAMP MERCY," AS THEY CALLED IT. EVENTUALLY HE SHIPPED BACK TO THE STATES AND MUSTERED OUT IN JULY OF '52."

"I DON'T IMAGINE THE HEADSHRINKERS EVER "CURED" HIM. KNOWING YOUR POP, HE PROBABLY NEVER REALLY OPENED UP TO WHAT WAS GOING ON INSIDE HIS SKULL.

"I'M SURE HIS CATHOLIC BUDDIES IN BLACK BACK HOME WERE NO GREAT HELP EITHER. BIG SURPRISE!"

APRIL 1952

MAYBE VALENTINO WAS RIGHT, BUT I SUSPECT MY FATHER STILL HAD MORE FAITH IN THE CATHOLIC CHURCH THAN HE'D EVER GRANT TO ANY PSYCHOLOGIST, WHOSE PRACTICES PROBABLY WERE VIEWED ON A PAR WITH VOODOO OR, HEAVEN FORBID, PROTESTANTISM.

THAT HE DID INDEED SEEK GUIDANCE FROM THE CHURCH WAS MADE OBVIOUS BY HIS TRANSCRIPT FROM SEATTLE UNIVERSITY, LOADED WITH THEOLOGY AND RELIGION JUST MONTHS AFTER HIS RETURN FROM KOREA.

HE WAS ONLY 22 YEARS OLD. THE GUILT OVER WHAT HE'D HAD TO DO AS A SOLDIER MUST HAVE WEIGHED HEAVILY ON HIS CONSCIENCE, EVEN AS IT SANK DEEPER AND DEEPER INTO HIS ADULT PSYCHE.

I WISH I'D KNOWN. I WISH HE COULD HAVE OPENED UP TO ME OR ANYONE. NOW, SO MANY YEARS LATER, I WISH THERE WERE SOMETHING I COULD DO.

10

THE MYSTERY OF WHAT HAPPENED TO MY FATHER IN KOREA - AN EVENT THAT HAUNTED HIM FOR THE REST OF HIS LIFE - WAS FINALLY RESOLVED BY HIS CHILDHOOD CHUM AND FELLOW VETERAN, JACK VALENTINO.
HE DID WHAT A GOOD SOLDIER ALWAYS DOES!
請不要殺我
BUT WERE HIS NIGHTMARES DRIVEN BY GUILT AND REMORSE?
OR THE BELIEF THAT HE'D BETRAYED THE TRUST OF ALL THOSE WHO'D MENTORED HIM INTO ADULTHOOD?
MAKE SURE IT'S *YOUR* DECISION!
MAYBE IT WAS GENUINE FEAR BORN OF A SIMPLISTIC UNDERSTANDING OF CATHOLIC DOCTRINE.
OR, PERHAPS, IT WAS SOMETHING ELSE ENTIRELY.

I'D COME TO KNOW MY FATHER'S LIFE WAS MORE COMPLICATED THAN I HAD BELIEVED. WHATEVER ISSUES OR PROBLEMS HE HAD COULDN'T BE PINNED ON ANY ONE CAUSE.

IN HIS HEART, I THINK HE REMAINED THAT INNOCENT LITTLE ALTAR BOY, MAYBE NO LONGER EMBRACING ENTIRELY THE RELIGIOUS FAITH THE ROLE REQUIRED, BUT CLINGING TO THE WORLD VIEW IT ONCE REPRESENTED.

NOT THE STRICT AND RIGID CODES ENFORCED WITH YARDSTICKS AND RAPPED KNUCKLES...

...BUT THE BELIEF THAT ALL THE RITUALS AND RITES, THE TRADITIONS AND TRAPPINGS, ADDED UP TO SOMETHING ON WHICH HE COULD ACTUALLY BUILD HIS LIFE.

SOMETHING THAT WOULDN'T LET HIM DOWN, WOULDN'T CHANGE OR DISAPPOINT.

SOMETHING THAT WOULDN'T GO AWAY.

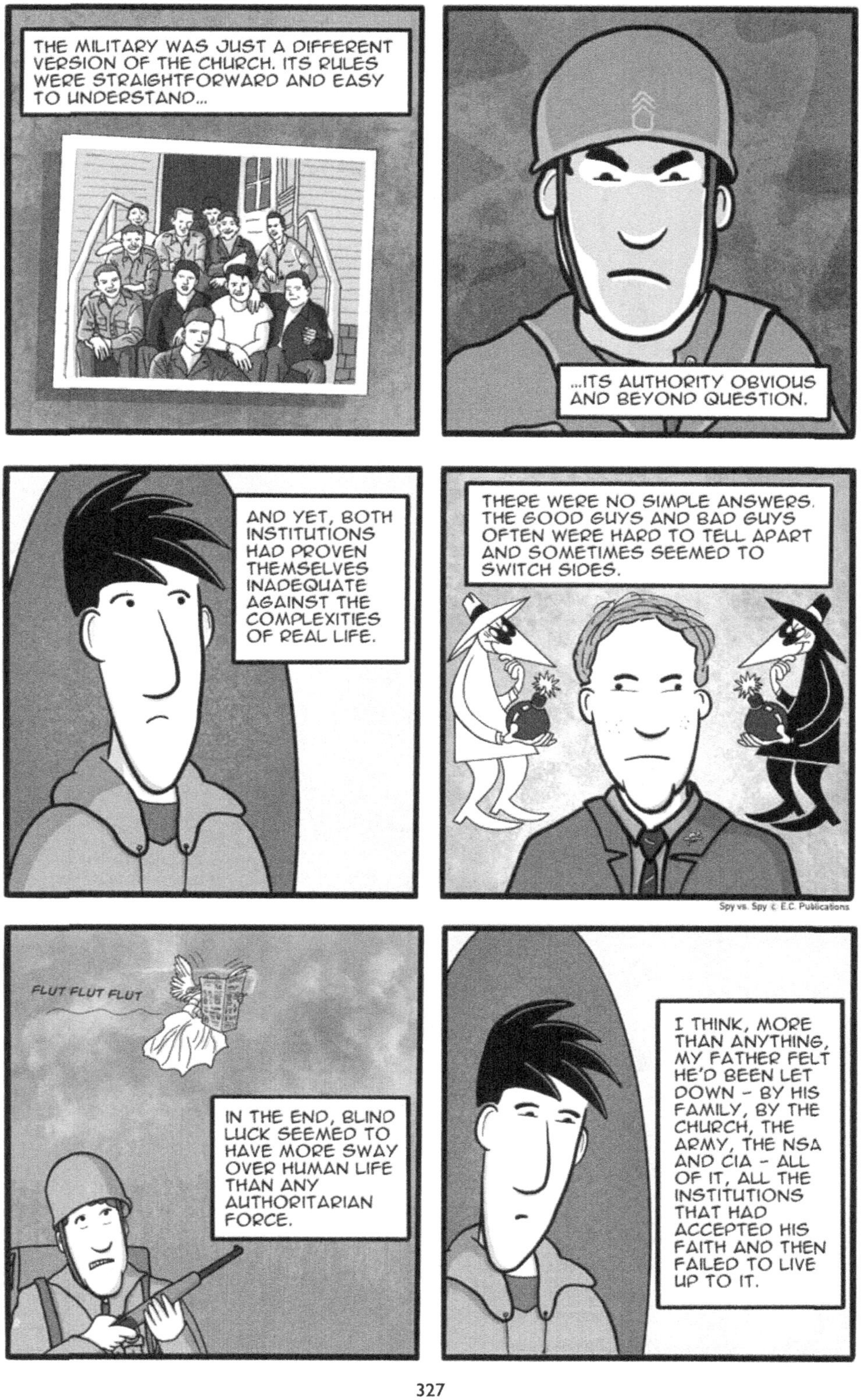

Spy vs. Spy © E.C. Publications

I SUPPOSE I'D HAVE TO INCLUDE MYSELF ON THAT LIST, TOO.
AND NOW COMES THE BAWLING AND WEEPY, FEELING SORRY ROUTINE.
AIN'T LIFE TRAGIC. BOO HOO.

DID YOU EVER HAVE TO KILL A MAN FACE TO FACE DURING THE WAR?
SO WHAT IF I DID? I WOULDN'T OBSESS ABOUT IT FOR 70 YEARS LIKE SOME CATHOLIC SCHOOLBOY SWEATING IN THE CONFESSION BOOTH!
IS THAT A YES...
...OR A NO?
I DON'T SUPPOSE I DID. THAT'S A PERK OF RANK. YOU GET TO TELL OTHERS WHAT TO DO.
SO (YAWN!) IT'S BEEN NICE CHATTING, KID, BUT I THINK I'M GONNA TAKE A LITTLE NAP NOW.

GLAD TO BE OF SERVICE. DON'T TAKE IT PERSONALLY IF I DON'T SEE YOU TO THE DOOR.

Sun Terrace Leisure Living
Exp. 12-12-2
MORPHINE SULFATE
5 mg / mL / hr
WARNING DO NOT LOWER DOSAGE WITHOUT MD APPROVAL

SKREEEEE...
...KLIK-KLATCH!

BEEP!
BEEP!
BEEP!
BEEP!
BEEP!

SEVENTY YEARS AGO, AN 18-YEAR-YOUNG MAN BOARDED A TROOP SHIP IN THE PORT OF SEATTLE AND SAILED ACROSS THE PACIFIC OCEAN TO JOIN A WAR.

TWO AND A HALF YEARS LATER, ANOTHER SHIP, THE U.S.S. GENERAL J. C. BRECKINRIDGE, SAILED BACK ACROSS THE PACIFIC, CRUISING THROUGH THE GOLDEN GATE AND INTO SAN FRANCISCO BAY ON JULY 5TH, 1952.

A DRAMATIC ENTRANCE ON ANY OCCASION, I COULD ONLY IMAGINE WHAT IT WAS LIKE FOR 5000 SOLDIERS RETURNING HOME FROM WAR.

I WONDER HOW MANY OF THOSE MEN WISHED THERE COULD BE MORE ON BOARD TO SHARE IN THAT MOMENT...?

...OR HAD FLEETING GLIMPSES OF OTHERS WHO MADE THE CROSSING WITH THEM, NOT BECAUSE THEY WERE HEADED HOME, BUT BECAUSE THEY HAD NOWHERE ELSE TO GO EXCEPT INTO MEMORIES AND DREAMS ON DARK, LONELY NIGHTS?

ONE MORE THING TO DO...
CLACK. SHUFFLE. CLICK CLICK.
?
CLACK. SHUFFLE. CLICK CLICK.
CLACK. SHUFFLE. CLICK CLICK.
CLACK.
SHUFFLE.

PLEASE...
HAVE A SEAT.
SOMETHING YOU'D LIKE TO SAY?
OH! RIGHT...
BLESS ME, FATHER, IT'S BEEN 47 YEARS SINCE MY LAST - AND ONLY - CONFESSION.
JEEZ, ARE WE GONNA BE HERE ALL NIGHT?
BETTER LATE THAN NEVER, I GUESS.
YEAH, ABOUT THAT. TELL ME...
...IS IT POSSIBLE TO CONFESS FOR SOMEONE ELSE?

CONFESSION IS ABOUT RECONCILING YOURSELF WITH GOD.
IT'S A PERSONAL CONVERSATION BETWEEN YOU AND THE LORD. I'M AFRAID SURROGATES WON'T DO.
IS THIS SOMEONE ELSE A PERSON OF FAITH?
IS THERE A REASON THEY CANNOT COME TO CONFESS THEMSELVES?
YEAH, THERE'S A PRETTY GOOD REASON.
I SEE.
PERHAPS YOU COULD SUGGEST A PRAYER FOR THEM, INSTEAD.
FLIP FLIP!

ACT of CONTRITION
A prayer to be said daily by the soldier following acceptance of his transgressions.
MY GOD! I am heartily sorry
WOULD THIS DO?
SILENCE
YES, I THINK THAT WOULD BE APPROPRIATE.
IF IT IS OFFERED WITH SINCERITY.

I DIDN'T KNOW — NEVER COULD KNOW — HOW SINCERE HE WAS WHEN MY FATHER READ AND REREAD THE PRAYER IN HIS DOG-EARED MISSAL, BUT I WAS CERTAIN I KNEW THE REASON *WHY* HE'D MARKED THAT PAGE...

...AND WHY HE WROTE THE CRYPTIC PHRASE BELOW, AS IF THE SOUNDS OF THE CHINESE WORDS HADN'T ALREADY BEEN ETCHED INTO HIS BRAIN.

BUT JUST THEN, I REALIZED SOMETHING ELSE: THAT CHEAP BRASS BUDDHA DAD BROUGHT HOME AND ULTIMATELY DISPLAYED ON HIS DRESSER...PERHAPS IT WASN'T MEANT AS A CHALLENGE TO HIS CATHOLIC UPBRINGING OR THE JEALOUS GOD HE'D BEEN TAUGHT TO WORSHIP.

RATHER, IT HAD BEEN A BETTER-LATE-THAN-NEVER ACKNOWLEDGEMENT THAT *HIS* GOD AND *HIS* RELIGION WERE JUST ONE PAIR IN A GLOBAL ASSEMBLY OF COUNTLESS OTHERS, AND THAT SOMEONE ELSE, SOMEONE HE'D ONLY BRIEFLY ENCOUNTERED ONE HORRIBLE DAY NORTH OF UIJEONGBU, KOREA, HAD SOUGHT SOLACE AND COMFORT IN A DIFFERENT DIVINITY, ONE WHO, PERHAPS AS WELL...

...HAD LET HIM DOWN AND DISAPPOINTED HIM, JUST AS THE CATHOLIC GOD AND A LONG LINE OF MORE EARTHLY AUTHORITIES HAD DONE TO DAD.

THANKS, FATHER. I GUESS I'LL SEE YOU IN ANOTHER FORTY YEARS.
SIGH.
CAN WE TRY FOR THIRTY? I'M NOT A YOUNG MAN.
KRRREEEEEEEEEEE

SHANGHAI
NINE MONTHS LATER
BUSINESS CONTINUED TO BRING ME TO CHINA. THINGS WERE GOING WELL. PROJECTS WERE MOVING FORWARD WITH ONLY THE USUAL BUMPS AND DETOURS.
The ubiquitous spittoon
I WAS GLAD TO BE FOCUSED ONCE AGAIN ON THE FUTURE RATHER THAN THE PAST.
AND YET, SOMETHING KEPT TUGGING ON MY BRAIN, PULLING ME BACK.
HOTEL
帝國主義豬旅館
ONE LAST ISSUE THAT NEEDED TO BE RESOLVED.

赢了肥锄 取出
SKRITCH!
AND SO, ONCE MORE, I DECIDED TO RETURN TO MY FATHER'S PAST.
THIS TIME, I HAD A SPECIFIC GOAL IN MIND.
A CODA, IF YOU WILL. A FINAL CHAPTER TO THIS WHOLE SAGA.

MY FATHER CAME HOME FROM KOREA A DAMAGED YOUNG MAN.

IF HE'D EVER GOTTEN HELP, FROM THE ARMY OR THE CHURCH OR ANYONE, IT DIDN'T WORK.

NOW THAT HE WAS GONE AND I'D LEARNED AS MUCH AS I EVER WOULD ABOUT WHAT HAD HAPPENED BACK IN THE WINTER OF 1952...

...IT WAS TIME TO BURY IT ONCE AND FOR ALL.

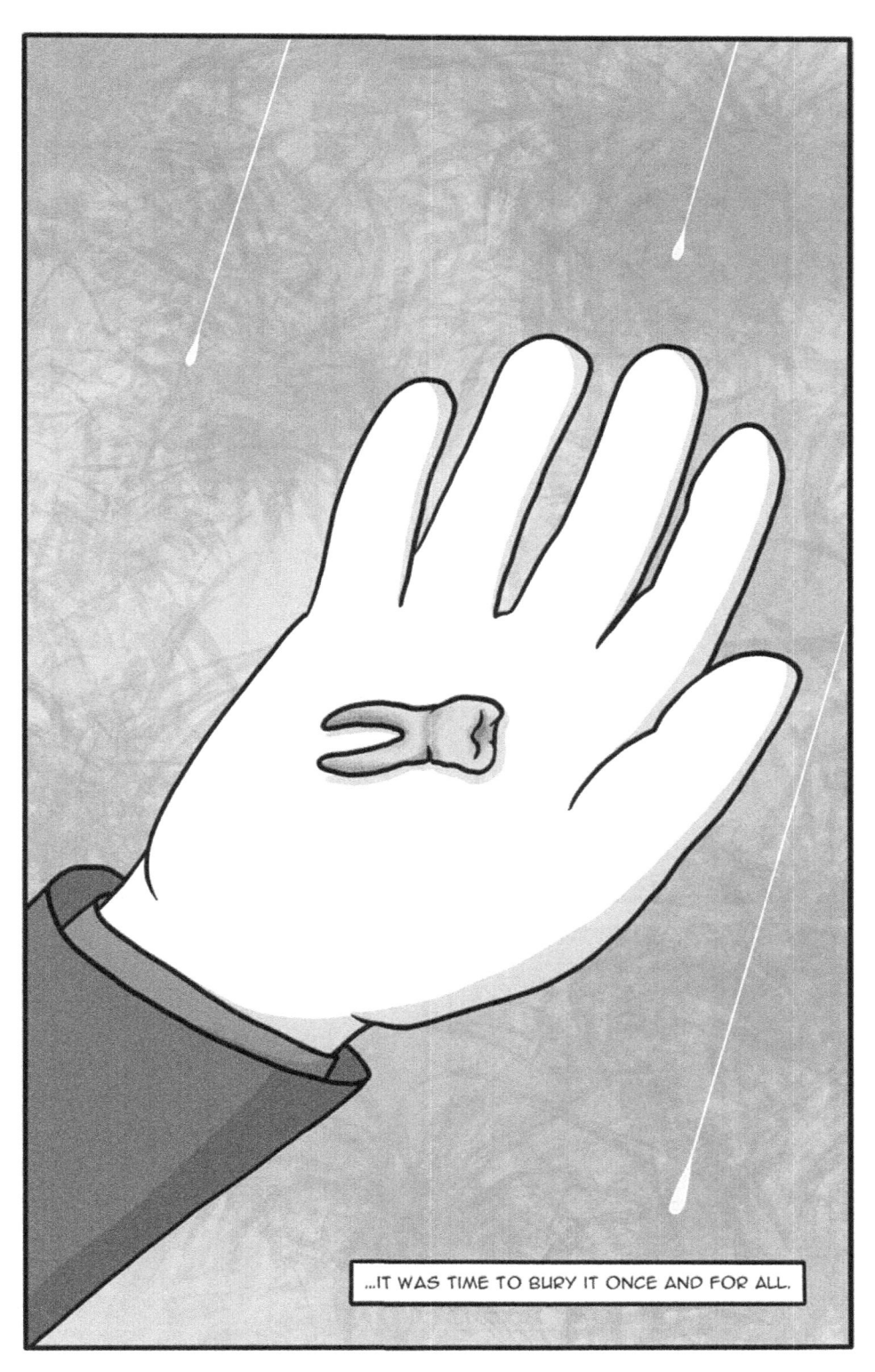

IT WOULD FOREVER BE A MYSTERY WHERE EXACTLY IN CHINA CHENG LI JIE HAD LIVED BEFORE HE'D BEEN SENT TO KOREA.
BUT THIS QUIET LITTLE GARDEN IN SHANGAI SEEMED LIKE A PLEASANT ENOUGH SPOT FOR A HOMECOMING OF SORTS.
DIG DIG
BETTER, AT LEAST, THAN A CARDBOARD BOX CLOSETED AWAY IN YAKIMA, WASHINGTON.
SCOOP!

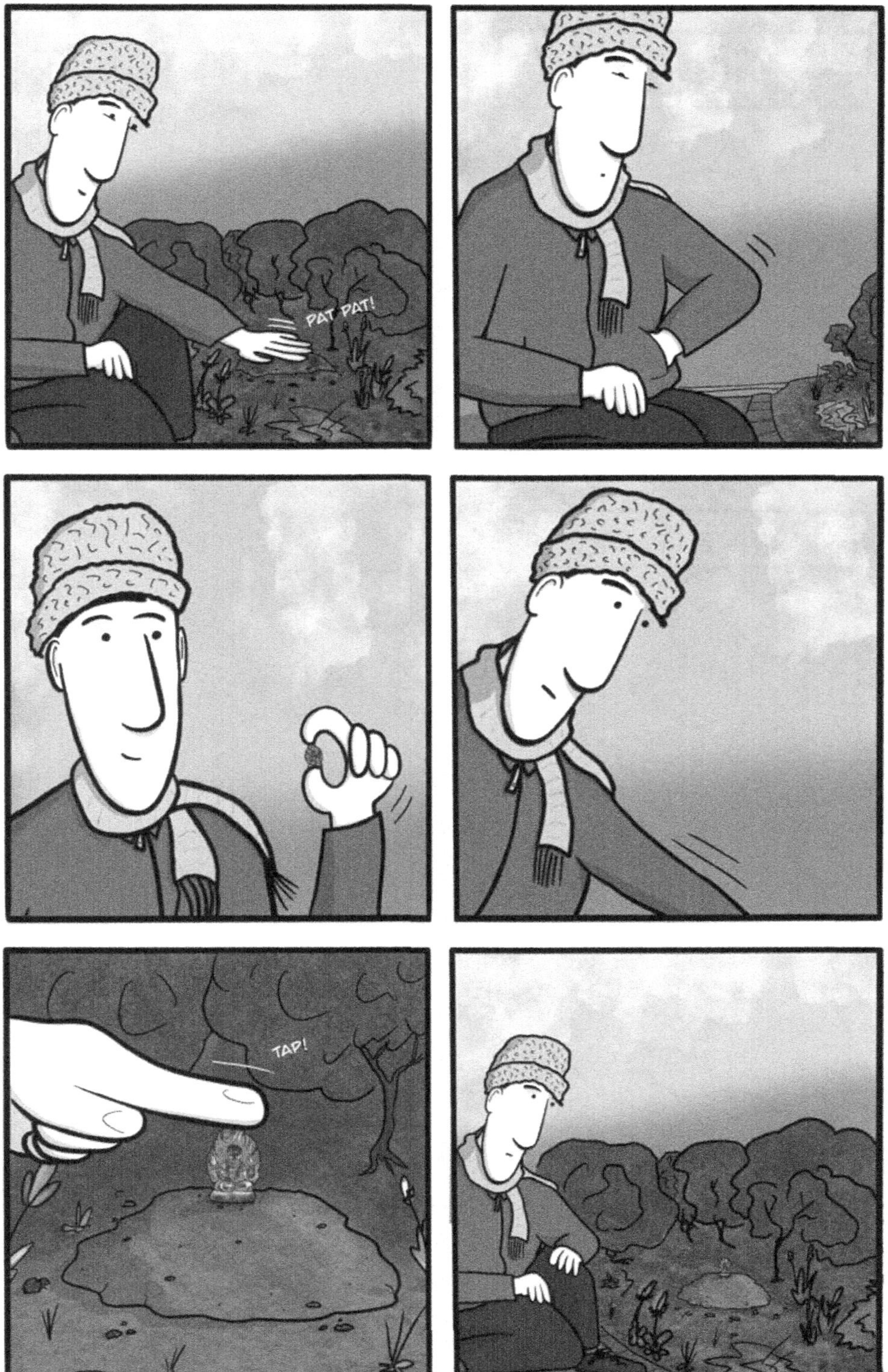
PAT PAT!
TAP!

JACK VALENTINO SAID THERE ARE VERY FEW WINNERS IN WAR AND A WHOLE LOT OF LOSERS.
I WOULD MODIFY THAT SLIGHTLY. THERE ARE *NO* WINNERS IN WAR, ONLY LOSERS.
WE OWE IT TO THEM, AND TO OURSELVES, TO REMEMBER.
SOMEDAY, THOSE MEMORIES WILL BE ALL THAT'S LEFT.

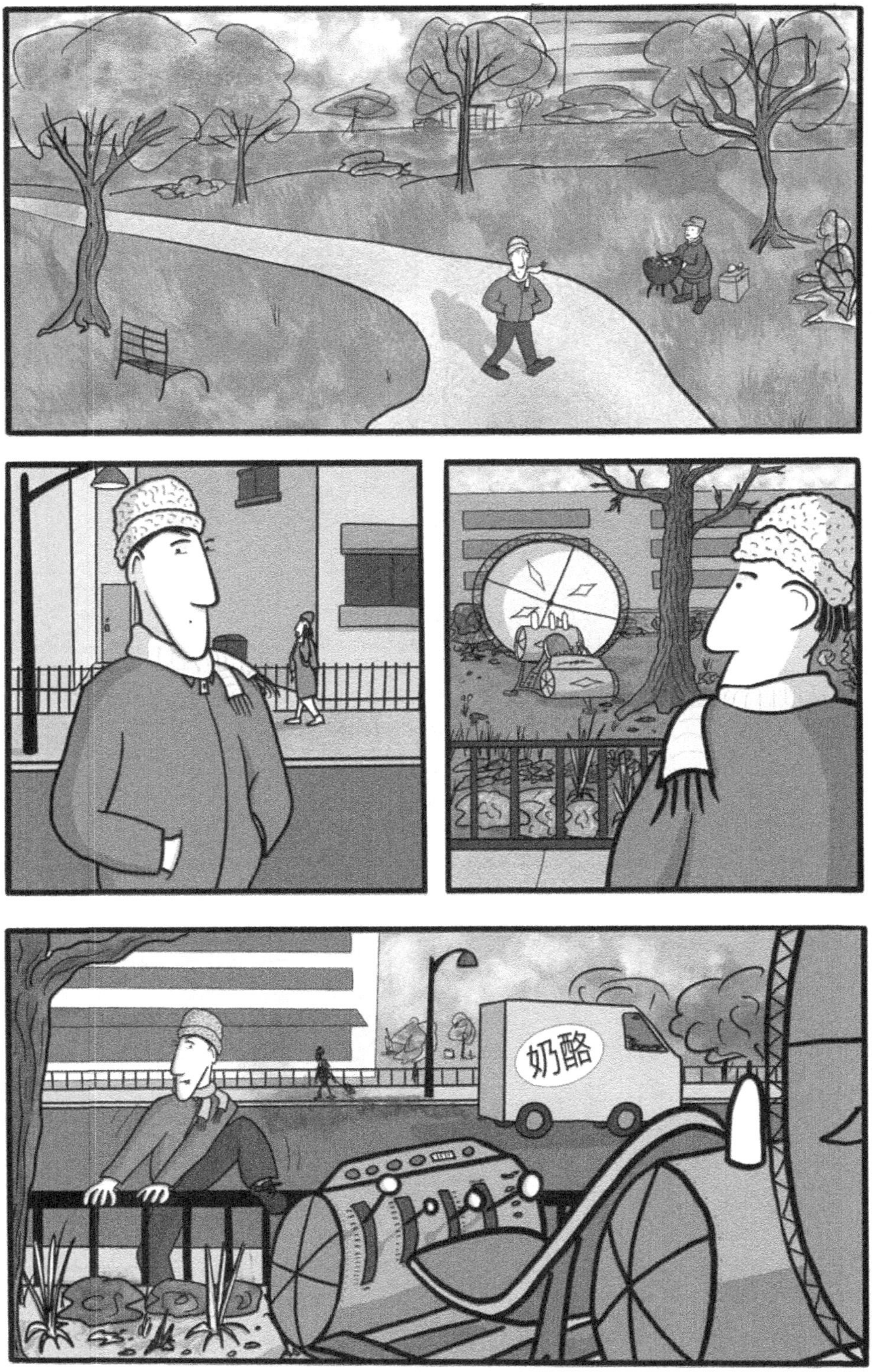
奶酪

CLICK!
FORWARD
BEEP!
BEEP!
BWOOP!
BACKWARD
FORWARD
SHUNK!
BACKWARD

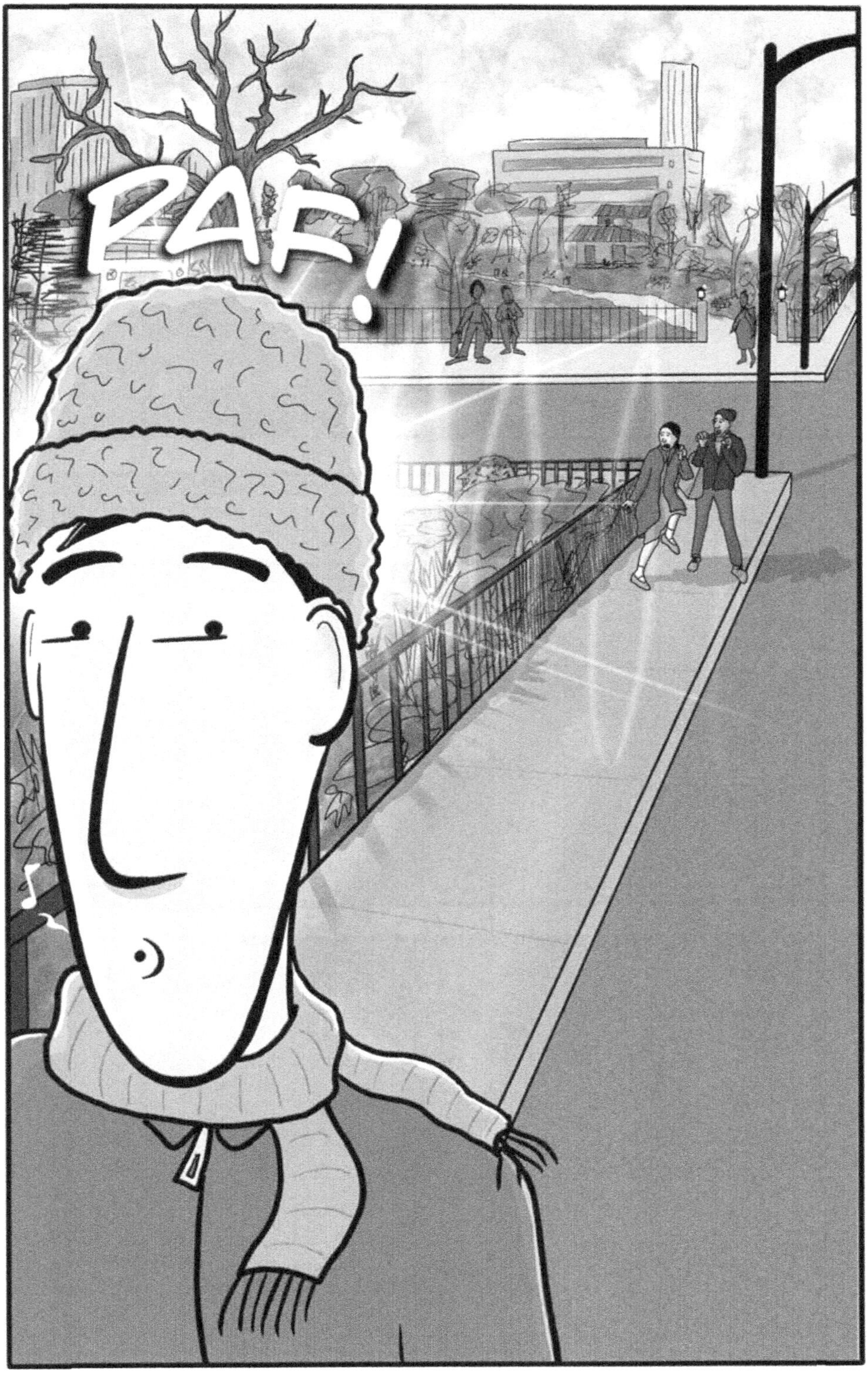
PAF!

WHAT BOMBS AND BLOOD CANNOT BRING ABOUT, TIME AND YOUTH WILL PROVIDE.
— GRAFFITO IN SEOUL

你今天吃奶酪了吗?

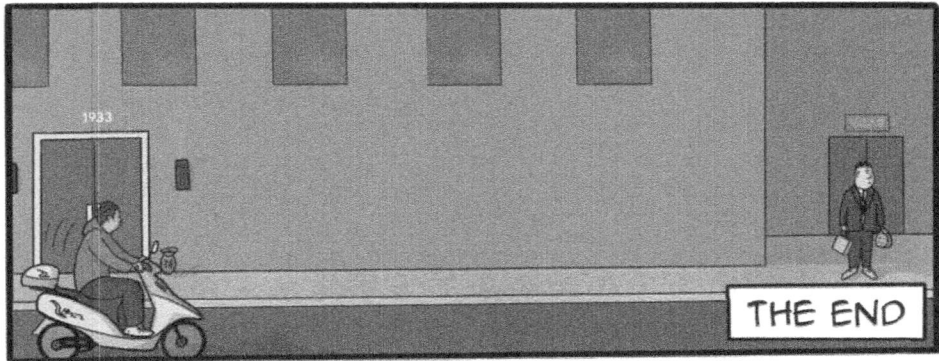

THE END

AUTHOR'S AFTERWORD

As admitted on the cover, this story is "mostly true."

In September, 1948, my father, Dick Molitor, and his friends enlisted in the United States Army. After training with the Army Security Agency in radio intercept and high-speed Morse code, they shipped out across the Pacific to Japan, where they spent a year and a half in Kyoto before deploying to Korea on July 23, 1951. Eight months later, in the summer of 1952, Dad returned to the U.S. and promptly resumed his college education, courtesy the G.I. Bill.

In the months and years that followed, he'd wake up with some frequency in the middle of the night, screaming at the top of his lungs. His mother, then a 60-year-old widow, found this behavior somewhat unnerving. It was she who likely pushed him back into Catholic studies, although by then she was resigned to the fact he would never become a priest; that role would be filled by one of her grandsons, one of my many cousins on the Molitor side of the family.

I had little contact with that extended family because, also true, after graduating from Seattle University, spending a little time in Washington, D.C., as a CIA plant in an office machine company, meeting and falling for a southern belle who would become my mother, marrying same, and moving back to Seattle where I was born, my father really did pack us off to Yakima, then the apple capital of the nation but soon to exchange that title for the less appealing methamphetamine transit hub of the Pacific Northwest. It was also – in my opinion throughout most of my stay there – an all-purpose redneck hellhole. (Others have different opinions on this. They are free to write their own books.)

All of that is true, as is the fact that something happened to Dad in Korea, some event he refused to talk about, but which had a profound effect on our lives. And that is where the story diverges from reality. Not in the "Dad was messed up" part, but in the "affected lives" business. Unlike the narrator of this book, I am not an only child. Two brothers preceded me into the world, both of whom have a multitude of their own stories about our father. I know this, because I borrowed some of them. The youthful memories presented in the previous pages are largely my own, but a few were appropriated from my brothers, Richard, Jr., and Peter, and blended into one narrative. Nothing personal guys, it was just easier that way. If I were a better artist and storyteller, maybe I could have fit you in. Alas...

My mother, Anastasia Petro, also saw her role redefined somewhat to keep this book more personal. Truth be told, she never actually left Dick as implied in these pages, although one cross-country drive with Peter and I in the summer of 1976 almost achieved that goal. Had my oldest brother also been on the trip, I might be narrating this with an East Tennessee accent.

Mom and Dad's relationship is otherwise portrayed accurately, from my own perspective, of course. I give the same excuse for any changes: a more talented artist might have been able to give Anastasia the larger role she deserved. But...

So what about Mr. Cheng? Sadly, he was all-too-real, though once again I made a few dramatic assumptions about him for the simple reason that I had nothing else to go on. Dad never mentioned him, never talked about how they met nor how they parted ways.

Cheng Li Jie (the name is ficticious) *was* killed by Sergeant Dick Molitor, most likely where and how I depicted the event in this book. Based on original U.S. Army records and other items Dad kept hidden (from himself?) until the day he died, as well as a few photographs and the entries in his little notebook, and then my own research into various campaigns of the war and a handful of trips to Korea to track down the actual locations, I can say with confidence, "this is what happened." One or two details might be fuzzy, but generally speaking, Mr. Cheng met his demise because a U.S. soldier was ordered to bring it about.

What followed immediately thereafter is a fiction I admit to adding, not for the sake of melodrama, but for my own need to believe my dad would never of his own accord collect such "souvenirs." *SOMEONE* did, because stored in the same old antique cigar box as the rest of Dad's war stuff were the wooden name tag, the Manjushri medallion, the compass, and...the tooth.

I have a vague memory of seeing the tooth when I was a very small boy. The same memory is linked to the "bayonet" vignette recorded in one of this book's early palimpsests. Details were never forthcoming. I only learned the meaning of the writing on the name tag when a student in one of the English classes I teach, an old Chinese woman, read the characters and pronounced them for me. I'm willing to bet that was the first time that Cheng Li Jie's name had been uttered aloud in nearly 70 years.

Although I still have the other remnants of Mr. Cheng's estate, his tooth really was repatriated while I was on a business trip to China. I'm sure his original home wasn't in Shanghai, but it was as close as I was likely to come to wherever it might have been.

I'll mention one more bit of fiction, this time a deliberate edit. I left out of the epilog the part where I broke down and lost it following the tooth burial. Although I can honestly say I am proud of my father's record in the Army, and the few friends I've made while working on projects in Korea have more than once thanked *ME* for Dad's service to their country, I will never fully be able to get over the terrible consequences of his choices. He might have been the one who killed Cheng Li Jie, but Cheng's death destroyed *HIM* and subsequently left scars on many others.

No one wins in war. No one.

If only they'd stop trying.

Daniel Molitor
Pasadena, California

THIS BOOK IS DEDICATED TO MY FATHER,
RICHARD "DICK" MOLITOR
AND TO A MAN I NEVER MET,
"CHENG LI JIE"

IT IS ALSO DEDICATED TO MY MOTHER,
ANASTASIA PETRO MOLITOR
AND MY TWO BROTHERS,
RICHARD MOLITOR, JR., AND *PETER MOLITOR*
ALL OF WHOM PLAYED A MUCH LARGER ROLE
IN THE STORY THAN HAS BEEN PRESENTED.